THE
BIG KILLING

THE

ANNETTE

BIG

MEYERS

KILLING

BANTAM BOOKS
NEW YORK · TORONTO · LONDON · SYDNEY · AUCKLAND

THE BIG KILLING

A Bantam Book / July 1989

Library of Congress Cataloging-in-Publication Data

Meyers, Annette.
  The big killing / Annette Meyers.
     p.   cm.
  ISBN 0-553-05324-8
  I. Title.
  PS3563.E889B54   1989
  813'.54—dc 19   89–339
                                        CIP

Published simultaneously in the United States and Canada

Bantam Books are published by Bantam Books, a division of Bantam Doubleday Dell Publishing Group, Inc. Its trademark, consisting of the words "Bantam Books" and the portrayal of a rooster, is Registered in U.S. Patent and Trademark Office and in other countries. Marca Registrada. Bantam Books, 666 Fifth Avenue, New York, New York 10103.

PRINTED IN THE UNITED STATES OF AMERICA

DH   0 9 8 7 6 5 4 3 2 1

FOR MARTY

The author wishes to acknowledge the support and assistance of Rita Bernhardt, Dolores Bullard, Merle Gordon, Elizabeth Goren, Fred Klein, Marcia Lesser, John Oakes, Linda Ray, Philip Rinaldi, Bruce Stark, Chris Tomasino and the incomparable Kate Miciak, editor of editors.

Who gets the buck? Everything else is just a lot of conversation.

Attributed to
Abraham Pomerantz, Esquire
Wall Street Attorney

It's about money, it's always about money.

Xenia Smith, Partner
Smith & Wetzon
Executive Search Specialists

He was running for his life. Sweat rolled off his hairline into the red and white sweatband. His shirt was soaked, and he could no longer feel his legs below his knees. His lungs felt about to burst, and he knew they were gaining on him because he could hear the shouting. He put on a last burst of adrenaline, pressed forward, pumping, pumping, and crossed the finish line to an exuberant cheer and an uneven round of applause, more shouting and squealing from the girls, and a decent amount of skin contact with the scantily clad club cheerleaders awaiting Caravanserie members at the finish line.

It was the "Run for Your Life Sweeps," the ten-miler that was run every year for the benefit of the Cardiopulmonary Care Unit at York Hospital. All the health clubs in the City competed.

He placed his fore, middle, and ring fingers on the underside of his wrist and counted. Perfect. He took a big swallow from the proffered water jug and worked his knees slowly up and down. Then he pulled off the soaking wet Caravanserie Club T-shirt and poured the rest of the water in the jug over his head. He stood for a moment shaking out his legs. He was in great shape and knew it. He'd never felt better. He flexed his biceps, admiring the taut swell of his muscles. Perfect control. That was what he wanted, what he had.

He took his pulse again. Great recovery. Already back to seventy-four. He lay on the grass, knees bent, hands clasped behind his neck. He closed his eyes. Feeling good . . . great.

The soft terry of a towel fell across his knees. He opened his eyes and saw a pair of sleek, golden legs in Fila jogging shoes. Long, lean, bare legs. He put the towel over his head and rubbed the sweat out of his hair. Then he draped it around his neck and lazily let his eyes follow the legs upward.

Goddam, today was his lucky day. Here was this sexy blonde in tight, white running shorts and a Shearson sweatshirt coming on with him.

"Shearson, huh?" he said, standing, shaking out his legs.

"Late of Shearson," the blonde said, tossing her long, glossy hair. "I start at Donahue's on Monday."

"Well, waddaya know," Barry said, arching his back, pulling the ends of her red towel across his neck. He was on a roll. "Funny coincidence," he said, bunching up the towel and rubbing his chest suggestively. "That's where I am. Barry Stark." He held out his hand.

"I know," she said, in a flat Connecticut accent. She ran a small pink tongue around small pink lips. "Amanda Guilford." She took his hand.

Strong, athletic handshake. Green eyes. Jesus. "You'll love it at Jake's," Barry told her. "I guarantee it."

"I'm a little nervous about it." She smiled with even white teeth, seeming not at all nervous.

He rubbed his chest again with the towel and handed it back to her. "Don't worry about a thing, babe. Your friend Barry will show you the ropes."

They smiled at each other.

"Well, if it isn't the Barry Stark we all know and love!" Georgie Travers said, loudly, breaking the moment.

Then the other club members who were there began to close in on him. He had, after all, won the race. Amanda Guilford receded into the background and Barry stood, bare-chested, the dark hair on his chest still glistening with sweat and water, accepting the adulation that was his due.

2

"My name is Leslie Wetzon," Wetzon began in her soft, agreeable voice, "and my firm is Smith and Wetzon," she continued, firmer now and subtly more decisive. "We are an executive search firm, Lon, and we work in the brokerage industry."

"Yeah, so you're a headhunter," Lon Campbell said. Campbell was a confidential referral from Eddie Barnes, a broker Wetzon had placed a year earlier. "Well, I'm really pissed off with the Dayne . . . you like that, huh? You got me at just the right time. . . ."

"I love it," Wetzon said. "Why are you pissed off with Dayne Becker?"

"Because they promised anyone who did over a quarter of a mil in the first year a Toyota, and all kinds of extras to go along with—"

"And—"

"And there were three of us and they just *forgot* about it."

"Dayne is not known for generosity."

"I know, I know. . . . They're out-and-out cheap."

Wetzon could almost feel Campbell's discontent through the telephone wire. Good. He was halfway in her pocket. "The firms take the brokers who start with them for granted," she said sympathetically. "They bring people in from other firms who are doing less than you are and give them big up-front deals, an office, a sales assistant. For example, do you have your own sales assistant?" *Go for it,* she thought.

"Not yet, but they promised me . . . I'm supposed to get one . . . I've been using someone, actually . . . we have a thing going—"

"Oh, you believe in living dangerously."

"Yeah, why not—what do I care about whether I get ahead in the company? I'm building my own business. . . . Yeah, we look at each other sometimes, and I see that twinkle in her eye, and we get out of here for a little while. It's really a great thing . . . I don't know why I'm telling you this . . . I don't know you . . . but I do know you, don't I? We just never met."

"But we should, you know. If I can ever get you out of the office at a decent time, I'll buy you a drink."

"I have an appointment that'll get me out of the office early one day next week—"

"Okay, when shall I call you to set it up?"

"Call me Monday."

"Great. Talk to you Monday."

"Take care of yourself, Wetzon, y'hear?"

"Goodbye." She replaced the phone, smiling, and made a note on her calendar. Once they met face to face, the relationship was made. Chances were that if Campbell moved, he'd let her represent him.

She recorded her conversation on a suspect sheet. One day soon they would put everything on computer. In the meantime she and Smith worked from 8½-by-11 profile forms, which search professionals dubbed "suspect sheets."

What she and Smith did was mysterious, in the best sense of the word, and therefore it was glamorous. They saw themselves as detectives, searching out the best candidates for the positions their clients had to fill. The Street called them, and those like them, headhunters, and they didn't really mind. Away from the Street, recruiting professionals were recruiting professionals, and *headhunter* was a derogatory term. But the Street admired toughness and even admired piracy. Anyone who could "get away with it" was respected.

And the clients were not ordinary businesspeople, they were the movers and the shakers of the all-powerful financial community. The Street, with a capital S.

While Smith and Wetzon were not truly insiders, they were not outsiders either. Thus, they were in a perfect position to see every problem objectively and give the client an overview.

They were an odd couple. Smith had come out of personnel, and Wetzon had come out of show business. That together their names were memorably similar to the gunsmiths served only to amuse them, but they used it to enhance their singularity. They were women in a man's world.

They worked out of a small office that had been a one-bedroom apartment in a converted brownstone, just off Second Avenue and Forty-ninth Street. It was ground-floor space, the doors opening onto a lovely garden just now starting to bloom with forsythia. A red brick walkway bordered plantings of tulips, daffodils, and irises.

"Bring those things out here in the back," a voice called. The door opened and Smith emerged, a tall, broad-shouldered young woman in her thirties, leading two overall-clad deliverymen, who carried cast iron garden chairs, white and Victorian, with floral motifs. They set them down on the brick patio, which ran about four feet from the rear of the building, and left Smith to fuss with the direction of the chairs. Moments later they returned with a round table and two more chairs. Smith reached into her suit pocket and gave each of the men, who were waiting expectantly, five dollars. Then she stood surveying the patio, hands on hips, very pleased with herself.

"Well, what do you think?" she demanded of Wetzon, who appeared in the open doorway.

"I love them," Wetzon said, coming out on the patio. Wetzon still moved like the dancer she had been. She turned one of the chairs, adjusting a point of view. "They're perfect."

"Do you think we need anything more?"

"Not just yet. Let's wait and see," Wetzon said, stroking the iron filigree. "Maybe a bench later, but this is a good start."

"We can have our lunches out here pretty soon," Smith said happily, "and get our tans going."

Smith always talked in terms of *our*, when she meant *me*. In the summer she tanned as dark as a gypsy. With her short, thick, dark hair and olive skin tone, she was a natural summer person. Wetzon was pale and blonde, her thin, fine hair still worn in a dancer's knot on top of her head. She kept a hat on when out in the sun.

But she sat in the sun with Smith because that's where they got their best ideas. Last summer they had used old lawn chairs that Wetzon, an avid scrounger, had found at the Irvington Thrift Shop, but they'd just completed a glorious business year, their best year yet, so they had decided to splurge on the white Victorian garden pieces that Wetzon had spotted in a shop on Atlantic Avenue in Brooklyn.

"Smith—" Harold came to the door. His eyes behind horn-rimmed glasses lit up. "Wow."

"Yes," Smith said smugly. "It does look great. You wanted me?"

"Oh, I almost forgot. Frank Farnham is on the phone for you."

Harold Alpert was their assistant. While still in college he had come to work for them as a summer intern, and now that he had graduated, he was eager to become a real headhunter.

They had found Harold through an accident of timing. Smith had been working with a husband and wife team from Dean Witter. She had successfully arranged for them to make a move to Bear, Stearns, but the deal, as lush as it was, did not include their summer employee, a college student, for whom they felt responsible. The problem, as small as it was, seemed to be taking on more importance than it was worth because the Bear simply refused to accept Harold as a summer intern, and everyone was getting sensitive about it. So Smith suggested that she and Wetzon could probably use an assistant, and Harold had come to them for the rest of that summer, during which he grew a mustache and beard to make himself look more mature. That was two summers ago, and now he was a full-time employee.

He had been planning on going to graduate school for an MBA, but now he wasn't sure, and in the meantime he had a good job, which is more than a great many of his classmates from Colgate had.

The stock market crash in October of 1987, otherwise known as Black

Monday, when the market plummeted over five hundred points, had actually enhanced their business. Retail account executives—stockbrokers—who generated good commissions, were in tremendous demand. The brokerage firms were falling all over themselves offering special deals to these individuals. And Smith and Wetzon were delighted to be of service. Therefore, they had agreed that Harold would eventually become an associate, and soon they would start him on telephone interviews, but first they had to hire another assistant to take his place. He kept saying, "Now, Smith? Now, Wetzon? I think I'm ready now. When can I start doing interviews?"

He was too hot—too hungry—for them to keep him waiting much longer. Tomorrow they would begin interviewing the first candidates for his old job.

When Wetzon came back into the room after a last and satisfying survey of the garden, Smith was on the phone with Frank Farnham, the manager at Boyd & Boyd, who still owed them the fee on Roger Compari. They were paid, as were all headhunters in their specialty, a percentage of the broker's gross production; that is, his annual gross commissions on sales of stocks, bonds, and products. Nearly four months before, they had placed Roger Compari at Boyd & Boyd, and every month they had sent their bill, and every month there was a new excuse as to why it had not been paid.

Smith, whose back was to Wetzon, turned in her chair and pointed to the phone, then to her head, making a circle with her hand. Wetzon rolled her eyes and held up her middle finger. Smith put her hand over the mouthpiece and laughed.

The phone rang. And rang again. Where had Harold disappeared to? Wetzon reached for the phone.

"Smith and Wetzon," she said crisply.

"Oh, good, it's you." Wetzon recognized Barry Stark's voice immediately although she could hardly hear him. It had a nasal quality, as if he had a sinus condition, which he probably did—who in New York City didn't?—but it was out of character for him to speak so softly.

Wetzon had known Barry Stark for three years. First at Merrill, now at Jake Donahue's.

"I like your style," he'd told her after she had cold called him that first time. "You're really good. You listen. You can call me anytime." His voice had practically roared at her across the telephone lines.

She had never gotten him to interview, and probably never would, but he was a good source of information. Because he seemed to know everyone, he was able to provide Wetzon, whom he considered a friend, and she was—as much as people were able to have friends in the industry—with lists of names and directories of every broker in each office of each firm he had a contact in, with a description of each individual down to what kind of business he did and how much he earned. One thing you had to say for Barry, he missed nothing. She hadn't spoken to him in months, not since Christmas, when she'd called to wish him happy holidays, and he'd been too busy to talk.

"I have to see you, it's urgent," he was saying now. He sounded tense.

"Are you all right?" Wetzon asked. Smith frequently scolded her for being too kindhearted and a pushover for all these sleazebags with problems, who used Wetzon to vent whatever was bugging them at any time, but Barry wasn't as bad as Smith thought he was.

"Why do you let yourself be used?" Smith was always asking. "That's what they're doing, you know. They're getting off on you. And Barry Stark is just another cokehead."

"Oh, I know what he's doing," Wetzon would respond, "and I don't think he's a cokehead. He's too into the body beautiful. But if someone needs help, how can I say no? It's just not in me."

And she couldn't, which is why she did some quick schedule juggling now in her head. "Hold on a minute, Barry, let me see what I can do. What time do you want to meet? Would five be all right?"

"Five would be great. It'll take me about a half-hour to get uptown. Where do you want to meet?"

"The Four Seasons," Wetzon said. "Go in on the Fifty-second Street entrance between Park and Lexington, go up the stairs on the left. Remember, when you get to the top of the stairs, on your right is the bar and on your left are some chairs. I'll be there."

"Okay," Barry said, "I remember. Where we met before." His voice was still strange, almost a whisper.

"Are you all right, Barry?"

"Something's happened," he said. "They're—I'll tell you later—" He hung up.

Wetzon sighed, replacing the receiver. Poor Barry must have run into a compliance problem. He just had to cut corners, couldn't follow the rules. He'd made a lot of money very quickly, and he was probably still under thirty. He always seemed to live life on the brink, craving action all the time; it was like a drug, and he saw himself as a wheeler-dealer who could make his own deals. Even the Crash hadn't toned him down.

But Wetzon, from her vantage point, saw that Barry was on an ego trip. He'd make mistakes, and one day he'd make a bad one and blow himself and his clients out. He had *self-destruct* written all over him.

Three years ago, when she'd first met him, he had bounded up the stairs of the Four Seasons like a jock, almost larger than life, late. Very tall, over six feet, dark brown curly hair in ringlets almost to his shoulders, cleft chin. He looked like a Greek god in a gray pinstriped suit.

"So talk to me, Wetzon," he'd boomed. "What've you got?"

She smiled, remembering how people had stared.

Smith banged down the phone.

"More excuses?" Wetzon asked.

"The check is in the mail," Smith said, turning, smiling crookedly. "I think Frank has a problem. Booze or drugs. I don't know which, but he has these deep depressions and then these highs. Sometimes he doesn't even make sense." She shook her head. It was a fact of life that drugs were rampant on the Street.

"Listen," Wetzon said. "Last time I talked with Roger, he said things were not going smoothly there, that Frank had promised him his own sales assistant, and a cold caller, and none of that has been forthcoming, plus they're so disorganized about everything, he can't seem to break through. He doesn't even know whom he's supposed to deal with on any level. What do we do if he doesn't stay and they still haven't paid us?"

"We sue them," Smith said, grinning.

"Oh, not again," Wetzon groaned.

They had been fabulously lucky with their lawsuits, and the settlements always included legal fees, but Smith had this penchant for suing, which made Wetzon extremely uncomfortable. Smith was a superb negotiator, and they had always won. They had been so successful that their clients now paid them on time, and those who were sued for nonpayment were not kept on as clients. The only trouble was that lawsuits drag on forever, and Leon and Smith seemed to enjoy the legal skirmishes so much. But Leon, their lawyer, always got paid, one way or the other, so why wouldn't he enjoy it? If they had to sue Boyd & Boyd and Frank Farnham for the money, it might take a year. Their fee was twenty thousand dollars, and they'd probably have to settle for less.

"What time is our first interview tomorrow?" Smith asked Harold, who shuffled in, slurping a Chipwich.

"Mmmph, nine o'clock," he mumbled, "with a Bailey Balaban, who just graduated from Boston University." Chipwich debris clung to his beard.

"Any brokers this afternoon?" Smith asked Wetzon.

"Yes, Barry Stark."

Smith grumbled loudly. "Not again."

"I couldn't say no to him, Smith," Wetzon said. "He really sounded terrible."

"Did he cheat a little old lady out of her life savings again, or maybe they finally got him for dealing drugs. Wetzon, why do you—"

"I know, I know . . . why do I let myself be used," Wetzon finished. "I know. I can't help it. I was going to take a dance class, so I'm not canceling something important, and what if he's really in trouble this time?"

"What if he is? What the hell can you do for him?"

"And Barry didn't cheat the old lady," Wetzon added. "His friend, Georgie Travers, did."

"Humpf," Smith said. "No difference. They're all alike."

3

Twenty minutes later, Wetzon pulled the heavy oak door to her office closed behind her, listening for the click of the lock. She walked up the four brick steps to the sidewalk, a small, slim woman with a graceful dancer's walk. Her ash-blond hair was still up in a smooth knot on top of her head. All of which, with her sharp chin and nose and long, slim neck, might have made the overall impression she gave a cold one, but it wasn't. She had sparkling gray eyes and a wide smile, full of good humor. With her dark gray double-breasted suit she wore a bright red silk blouse and a flowing cashmere scarf of a lighter gray. The effect was smart without being ostentatious. She carried a small black envelope handbag. She had left her briefcase in the office, deciding that this meeting with Barry was hardly a business one.

It was one of those borderline late March days, not yet fully spring and no longer winter. She walked past the two brownstones on Forty-ninth Street between Second and Third, hoping to catch a glimpse of Hepburn, who lived in one, or, second best, Steve Sondheim, who lived in the other. She was always a fan, had never outgrown it. She had known Sondheim a long time ago when she had danced in a revival of *West Side Story,* but he probably would not remember her. Hepburn she had never met.

She turned right on Third Avenue and walked up to Fifty-second Street, turned left, and crossed the street. It was hard to spot the Four Seasons, even when you knew it was there, because the only marking was a flat, unobtrusive brown awning. It always made her think of the story of the restaurant so "in" that it did not publish its phone number.

Smith and Wetzon were regulars. They had put their company together over drinks at the Four Seasons, and now they met there for anniversary dinners, client lunches, and drinks with candidates.

"Hi, Ms. Wetzon," the young man at the coat check said when he saw her. "How are you today?"

"Great, J.P.," Wetzon said. "As you can see, no coat, and I'm always great when spring is here."

She looked at her watch and veered left for the ladies' room. She had time to stop and check her makeup.

A tiny middle-aged woman was perched on the sofa, feet barely touching the floor, going through what looked like an ancient address book; the only other occupant was in front of the row of dressing tables with their theatrical bulb mirrors, doing an extensive eye makeup. The blonde doing her eyes looked at Wetzon in the mirror, automatically sized her up, and then ignored her. The middle-aged woman wore a business suit and had the obligatory brief-case next to her on the sofa. She did not look up, and Wetzon sat down at one of the dressing tables and eyed herself in the mirror.

She took a Kleenex from the box on the wall and blotted any imagined dust from her smooth skin. In the next room a toilet flushed, a door opened and closed, hands were washed, and probably some of the offered skin creams or lotions were accepted. Coins rang on the plate, and a tall, attractive woman appeared. The very high heels she wore added to her height, and her shoulder-length hair was burnished copper, distinctive and unusual. She wore a black hat with a wide, rolled brim and large dark glasses. Her clothing was loose and silky, and she had a dark mink coat over her shoulders. She quickly checked her full-length image in the mirror by the door and left in a flurry of lily-of-the-valley scent. Dior's, perhaps. The woman on the sofa softly cleared her throat. Her eyes met Wetzon's in Wetzon's mirror. Sisters. They both thought: *This gal does not work for a living, at least not our kind of work.* They smiled at each other.

Wetzon touched up her lipstick lightly and stood. It was about five, and Barry Stark was either there already or would arrive any minute. She brushed the shoulders and arms of her suit jacket, pulled her hose up from her ankles, glanced at her image in the long mirror, and headed for the stairs to meet Barry.

On the wall outside the ladies' room was a large color photograph of trees in spring, and upstairs on her left, as she came to the top of the stairs, were the potted trees, also springlike, showing buds. The young men and women who worked in the restaurant were all in their spring uniforms: pale salmon jackets with brown pants. They looked fresh and bright. At her left, three chairs were arranged under the potted trees. Barry was not there.

To her right, beyond the stairs, was the large bar, a square with rounded edges, jammed with people as it usually was at this time of day. And noisy. Everyone was trying to let everyone else know what a lot of fun he was having. She caught a fleeting glimpse of the woman with the dark glasses and the bright hair in animated conversation with a large man at one of the side tables near the bar.

Turning back toward the chairs, she walked smack into Leon Ostrow, their attorney.

"Well, for heaven's sake, Wetzon," Leon said, shading his eyes with his hand, looking down at her. His glasses were, as always, on the tip of his nose, giving him an absentminded, professorial air.

"Leon, what a surprise," Wetzon said. "How are you?"

"Fine, fine," Leon said heartily, pushing his glasses up higher on his nose.

"What are you doing here?" He moved slightly to her left, standing between her and the bar area.

"Meeting a broker, of course. And you?"

"A client, of course. I would have you join us while you're waiting, but . . ." He glanced furtively over her shoulder at the bar.

"No, thanks anyway," she said. "My appointment will be here any minute. I was about to sit down over there." She pointed to the chairs under the potted trees.

Placing his hand on her shoulder a little more firmly than necessary, Leon steered her to the chairs.

"We have to have dinner one of these days soon," he said benignly and ambled away toward the bar, a very tall, awkwardly thin man with a slight stoop.

Wetzon shrugged. Always a little weird, Leon was, but a good lawyer.

Leon Ostrow had been Smith and Wetzon's first step to their own business. He had drawn up their partnership agreement and arranged for their incorporation. They had each known him through another source and trusted him implicitly. Leon was primarily an attorney who handled small businesses, corporations and partnerships, and real estate cases, and when Wetzon and Smith had listed all the people they knew who were lawyers, his name had appeared on both lists. He donated legal services to artists and artistic causes, and Wetzon had met him when she was involved with a group trying to save two Broadway theaters from destruction. Smith had met him when she worked as head of personnel for the Gordonflow Corporation. She had consulted him when her building was going co-op.

Wetzon looked across to the bar area hoping to catch sight of his client, or clients, but it had gotten very crowded.

The heavily made-up blonde glided up the stairs, looking for someone. She turned toward the bar and was greeted by a great whoop from two of the conservatively suited habitants. She smiled, posed a moment, and then walked a slightly swaybacked walk toward them.

Wetzon viewed the Grill Room in front of her: large comfortable chairs, fine leather, or perhaps top-quality Naugahyde, on metal bases. Spacious chairs for spacious bottoms, she thought. At this hour the tables were not accounted for, but at lunch, all the most successful men of New York had their appointed places here.

Martin, the very English maître d' of the Grill Room, had just come on, and he was bustling around, a dapper standout in his black bow tie. He spotted her, as he spotted everyone, and waved.

Barry suddenly materialized, rapidly mounting the stairs on her left. He looked half-crazed, even frightened, she thought with dismay, and he was disheveled—for him. She perceived this only because she knew him. Anyone else who saw him would see a handsome young man in dark glasses, above average in height, wearing a beautifully cut dark blue pinstripe suit, white shirt with French cuffs, and a dark blue and red rep tie. A young man in a hurry. He was carrying a large attaché case. He did not take off his dark glasses, and as he neared her, Wetzon saw the reddish bruise on his jaw and the cut lip.

"I know I'm late," he said in an oddly normal voice, not his usual booming decibels, his head turning from side to side, not really looking at her, surveying the room, the bar area. "I left the office early, but I had to—they're watching me." He was breathing hard and his curly hair fell over his forehead. He shook her hand energetically and winced. She looked down at his hand. His knuckles were raw and red.

"You look terrible," Wetzon said.

"I know," he said unhappily. "All I wanted to do was to get my life together and now I'm in over my head."

With alacrity, Martin arrived at their side. "The balcony?" the maître d' asked, knowing Wetzon preferred this area for its privacy.

"Yes," Barry said, before Wetzon had a chance to answer.

The Grill Room was really three separate areas. The bar area itself was cut off from the main Grill Room by large smoky Lucite panels. These "shields" were not more than five feet high, just enough to cut off the bar and its noisy sportmakers from the more conservative crowd who preferred the main Grill Room.

At the back of the Grill Room was a wall of rosewood paneling, and on either side, a staircase of a dozen or so steps leading up to an open balcony with two long rows of tables overlooking the main room. The balcony had the best view of the entire area. From this location you could see anyone coming or going.

Barry put his hand on her elbow as they climbed the stairs, an odd, almost quaint thing for him to do. The last man who had done that was a very courtly, older Broadway producer who had taken Wetzon to dinner several times and had wanted to make an arrangement with her. She smiled at the memory.

They sat at one of these tables, Martin pulling out the chairs for them.

"The usual?" Martin asked Wetzon, smiling at her with his eyes.

"Yes," she said.

"What can I get for you?" he asked Barry.

"A Bloody Mary," Barry said, with a short laugh.

Martin left them and with dispatch, a salmon-jacketed young man brought a small plate of salted nuts.

Barry was always hyper, but Wetzon had never seen him so agitated. His hands were shaking as he reached for the nuts. And he was continually scanning the floor below, checking everyone who came or left the Grill Room. He winced when the salt of the nuts touched his cut lip.

"What's with the shades?" she asked lightly.

"I had to see you," Barry said, ignoring her question. "I need a favor." He lifted the dark glasses and then lowered them quickly, giving her a fast look at a very bruised eye. She flinched.

"Okay, I'm here. What's the problem?"

"It's a long story." He sighed, brushing his hair back nervously. "Oh, God, look at my hands," he said. "I worked it all out—I had it *made*." He sounded almost boastful. He banged the table with his fist, his voice rising defiantly. "I don't know how he got on to me—"

"Barry," Wetzon said, trying to soothe, "just tell me what—"

"Oh, shit," Barry said, losing his bravura, holding his head in his hands. "You know, Jake runs pretty much on I.P.O.s," he said.

"I know, but that's what you wanted, isn't it?"

"Yeah, I wanted to learn that end of the business, because I figured that's where the big money was to be made over the next few years."

Barry always had a new theory about where and how to make the big money. First it was in the over-the-counter market, then takeover stocks, the success of which was often dependent on insider information. Now, it was I.P.O.s, Initial Public Offerings—new issues—which is what he had at Jake Donahue's.

"I really thought I had it made this time." His laugh was bitter. "In this business you can never know too much, but for once, I think I do. . . ."

"Barry, will you tell me what this is all about?"

"I'm dead," he said. "I—"

Their drinks arrived on a small brown tray with a salmon-colored napkin placed under each drink. Without waiting for the salmon jacket to leave, Barry took a great gulp of his drink.

"Do you know what repos are?"

"Something to do with government securities, but I'm not sure," Wetzon replied. His agitation was making her uneasy.

"Well, they're repurchase agreements. We, and other houses like us, sell governments to banks, municipalities, and private customers and then we agree to buy them back later at a profit for the bank or city—it's called repurchase—or, we reverse that and buy their government securities when they need to raise cash, and they can repurchase them from us at some designated time in the future. You get it?"

"In other words, the firm sells government securities to someone and then buys them back at a higher price on a date both parties agree to in advance."

"Yeah, somewhere between thirty and two hundred seventy days after. The difference in the price is how the customer gets his piece of the profits. And a reverse repo is when we buy the security from the client and agree to sell it back to him later." He scooped up a fistful of nuts from the small dish and pushed them compulsively into his mouth.

"Okay."

"Look, you know me. I never hold it against a guy if he can make money,"

Barry said. "It's that I'm curious. I'd like a piece of it if I can get it." He almost smiled. "I listen. I stay late. I poke around. I want to know what's going on. That's the way I learn."

"I didn't know Jake was into governments—seems tame for him. So what did you find out, Barry?"

"Jake's into anything and everything that makes money. That's why I went there in the first place. But something's going on that's not kosher. I got evidence. I got to cover myself, don't I? No one's going to protect me."

"Evidence of what? Protect you from what?"

"Listen, about six months ago . . . shit, forget it. . . . I need you to do something for me, Wetzon. It's my insurance. It's a cover-up . . . the Feds . . ."

A salmon jacket came close with a large tray of hors d'oeuvres. It was Wetzon's favorite, steak tartare on small pieces of dark bread. Barry took two pieces, then Wetzon took a piece and another napkin. When she turned back to Barry, his face was pasty. Fear spread from the cleft in his chin across his clenching lower jaw. Over the white collar of his shirt the tendons in his neck swelled and tightened. His head began jerking spastically, up and down.

"What's the matter, Barry?" Wetzon was suddenly concerned that he might pass out. "Barry?" She looked over the balcony where Barry was staring but she saw nothing unusual. No one was on the stairs, no one was looking up at them.

"I have to make a phone call." Barry rose abruptly, jarring the table, spilling what was left of his Bloody Mary. The red liquid swelled on the shiny walnut tabletop. "I'm sorry—I'll be right back." He moved away in high gear.

Wetzon was left speechless with the red-stained table and the rest of her Perrier, which had not spilled. Still holding the uneaten piece of steak tartare, she watched Barry rush headlong down the stairs, half-expecting him to fall. Then he stopped, glanced toward the bar, looked back up at her, and sped on until she could no longer see him.

Martin checked her from the floor, a question in his eyes. She shook her head and mouthed, "It's all right."

4

Wetzon polished off what was left of the spicy tartare and stretched her legs under the table. Her right foot thumped against something solid. Easing her chair back, she ducked her head to find the source. It was Barry's big attaché case.

"Now we know he'll be back," she murmured, wondering what kind of trouble he was in. She had never seen him so unsure.

Again she recalled her first meeting with Barry, at the Four Seasons. He had been so full of his own success.

"After all," she had said, beginning her approach, "not every firm is right for every broker. It's very much a chemistry thing between you and the firm, between you and your manager. A lot depends on the kind of business you do, whether it's diverse, full product, or just stocks and bonds. Are you heavy into bonds? Or private placements?"

"Naa," he had said. "Mostly stocks now. Stocks and options."

"So you wouldn't need a firm that was special in limited partnerships or bonds?"

"Listen," he said, drumming his fingers impatiently on the table. "You're a nice lady, that's why I'm sitting here talking to you, but when I move, the only chemistry I'm interested in is the big green, get what I mean?"

"Even if it's with a weak firm?"

"Who cares about the firm? What do I care? I'll get the money up front, then if anything happens, I have the money."

"But what about your clients?"

"They'll come with me wherever I go because they know I make money for them, and if they don't want to come, who needs them. I got them easy enough, I can get others. The bottom line for me is the money."

"What kind of money are you talking about?" Wetzon asked, her voice cool, her gray eyes narrowing.

"Forty, fifty percent up front. I got the offer already."

She drew in her breath, felt a flush clear up to her hairline. "That's hard to believe. It's the highest deal I've heard."

"Do you know any other kind of business where a poor kid from the Bronx can clean up legally?"

"That's more than any of our clients are prepared to offer. In fact, that deal is so good, what are you waiting for? Why haven't you taken it?"

"I'm waiting to build more—when my gross hits four hundred fifty thou, for my trailing twelve, I'm taking off. Then it's bye-bye Mother. I want a check in my pocket for two and a quarter."

Wetzon nodded. The up-front deals were based on a broker's trailing twelve months' gross production. And in this bull market, each month Barry stayed where he was brought him closer to his goal. "How were you introduced to this company?"

"They called me. I have connections." He took a small, flat, foreign-looking box from his inside pocket, removed a brown cigarillo, and replaced the box. "Listen, I'll tell you the company, but you have to promise me you won't spill it. I know the guy who runs the company. Real smart guy. Did all right for himself. No one can get around Jake. He's the best. I can make a lot of money there, besides the up front. It's the way they handle the new issues. I'll make the big killing and retire. I'm not going to do this the rest of my life."

"That's some connection," she said. Wetzon knew without asking that Barry was talking about the financial wunderkind Jake Donahue, who had parlayed a fortunate marriage and a smart plunge into the lower echelon under-writing business into a fortune.

"But look," Barry went on magnanimously, "you really are a nice lady, and you've listened to me bitch and moan for months and you haven't pushed me or hustled me. I appreciate that. So if you can come up with something else that's in the ballpark, I'll listen. What do I have to lose?"

"Jake Donahue." She wrapped her napkin around the swizzle stick, be-mused. "I'm surprised. Donahue's a single-play shop, isn't it? They just do new issues. Their new issues."

"Yeah, and I'll be able to get my hands on as many shares as I want—ten thou, fifty thou even—not like at Merrill, where there are too many mouths to feed and you have to kiss ass to get anything. And at Jake's we can mark them up before we sell them."

"But won't you be taking yourself out of the mainstream? What if the new-issues market dries up? It's done that before, and meanwhile your clients are buying their Big Board, bonds, and mutual funds elsewhere—"

"Right now, new issues are where the big dollars are, and that's for me. But Jake's expanding, getting into other things, and I'll be part of it. I'll be there."

"Barry," she had said, unwrapping the swizzle stick, "I'd love to work with you. You're really good, but how could I tell you not to take a deal like that? You'd be crazy not to. Maybe down the road someday we will work together."

"Listen, Wetzon, maybe I can do something for you." He had leaned back in the big leather chair, lighting the thin cigarillo, confidently eyeing her over a thin curl of smoke. "On the day I leave Merrill, I'll send you the directory of the brokers in my office, and I'll mark them off as to what they do and what each guy's button is. How's that?''

Remembering it, Wetzon laughed out loud. That other Barry, so arrogant, so very sure of himself, was very different from the agitated young man who'd left her ten minutes ago. What had happened to change him?

She reached into her purse and took our her Filofax schedule book, opening it but not really looking at the week's appointments. She was tired and longed to be home in a hot bath.

The small beads that made up the curtains on the tall windows moved, swayed, shimmered, as if they were silk draperies. All in all, it was a miraculous place. At once elegant, intelligent, and supremely masculine. Like a hunting lodge without the old evidence of the hunter—and the hunted. And she knew the game of the hunter was played very well here.

She sipped her Perrier from the long-stemmed wineglass, swooshing the ice shards. Then she poured the remainder of the bottle into the glass, giving the slice of lime a stab with the tip of her swizzle stick. She blotted the spilled Bloody Mary with the napkins. She studied the salted nuts, what was left of them.

The balcony was filling up now. Martin was expertly supervising the joining of two tables near her, and a group of Japanese businessmen with two token Caucasians were seated. Laughter gusted up from the bar.

"Can we get you anything else, Ms. Wetzon?" the waiter asked.

"No, thank you," she said, beginning to feel fidgety. Damn Barry! Did he think he could keep her sitting here forever?

People climbed the steps continuously now, some pausing at the maître d' station to check in for the dining room, others standing at the Grill Room entrance, waiting to be seated. She looked at her watch. No Barry, and it was getting late. He'd been gone over half an hour. What could be keeping him? He was so crazy. He'd probably come back his old self, as if nothing were wrong. *I'll bet he does. Okay, if he does, we treat ourselves to tekamaki for dinner.* She gave him another ten minutes.

She sighed, looked around for the waiter, and signaled with her fingertip for the check. What a waste of time this was.

People continued to come and go.

She offered her American Express Gold Card and signed the back of the bill. And waited for the waiter to return.

Stretching both legs purposefully under the table, she surrounded Barry's attaché case and pulled it toward her. The credit card material arrived on a plate with a pen for her to sign, which she did, adding the tip and total, then automatically pulling off the back copy and the two carbons. She tore them into bits, deposited them in the ashtray, and rose, reaching down for the case.

She carried the attaché naturally, as she usually carried her own, but it was a heavy one. Full of gold bricks, no doubt. It was inconceivable that Barry was still on the phone and just as inconceivable that he had left without his case, without saying anything to her, after all those dramatics about how he needed her.

She went down the stairs, moving left as two couples came up. The phone booths were across the lobby in a rather private cubbyhole. There were two enclosed mahogany booths, very solid and conservative, on the far wall, and a marble ledge with phone books beneath on the near wall.

And there was Barry huddled on the telephone, still talking. His back was toward her. She felt a surge of anger. These guys were all selfish, all they thought about was themselves. What did it matter that she was sitting up there waiting for him? Her time wasn't as valuable as his. Smith was right about them. Thoughtless, thoughtless, thoughtless.

She was burning. She dropped his attaché case and flexed her hand, then tapped on the glass of the closed door and forced a smile, so that when he turned around he would not see how angry she was. He didn't even bother to look up. This was really ridiculous.

"Barry," she said, tapping more sharply.

This was too much. She pushed the door open slightly, and finally he turned toward her. Only, as he moved, he slumped oddly, and slid down in the booth, which was too narrow to hold his bulk, forcing the door open.

She stepped back involuntarily, gasping, as Barry Stark slumped sideways to the floor. She tripped over the attaché case in her frightened effort to get out of the way, and it slammed to the floor on its side with a loud smack. Barry's head came to rest at her feet, the dark glasses grotesquely half-off.

Frozen, she watched the trickle of blood threading from the side of his mouth. *Get a grip on yourself,* she thought. *He's passed out or had an attack of some sort.* She stooped, touching his shoulder. "Barry . . ." she said. And then she saw his eyes, the bruised one closed, the other staring up at her vacantly. His face was strangely twisted, the lower jaw contorted in a spasm of fear or agony.

As she stared, she saw the small handle of the knife, almost obscured by blood, that protruded from his chest. She had never seen death by violence before, but she knew. Barry was dead.

5

"Oh, my God, my God," Wetzon murmured, backing away. Her foot nudged the attaché case, and without thinking, she picked it up. There was a lot of blood, on Barry, on the floor.

A few feet to the right of the phone cubby was the checkroom. It was deserted because the day had been so warm. She edged out of the cubby and walked as calmly as she could to the checkroom.

"J.P.," she said to the young man behind the counter. Her face felt stiff. "Someone's been hurt in the phone booth. Get Martin quickly, please."

Martin, with the assurance under duress which was part of what made him such a good maître d', took charge immediately. J.P. was dispatched upstairs on an errand which Wetzon was unable to hear because Martin's voice began to recede into the babble of people coming and going. At first, Wetzon had felt very levelheaded, but now came the realization of the magnitude of what had just happened. Everything began to sound as if it were coming from the end of a long tunnel. Seemingly forgotten, she sank gratefully into one of the Barcelona chairs that graced the lobby area.

It was hard to believe that a very much alive Barry Stark had been with her less than an hour ago, full of his craziness and yet real, a flesh-and-blood—blood—a flesh-and-blood, breathing Barry, almost desperate to tell her his story. His story.

Her eyes rested blindly on the attaché case, which was in the middle of the lobby between her and the entrance to the phone cubby, where Martin now stood with his back to her.

A security guard of some sort appeared out of nowhere, very official-looking, very burly, closely cut dark hair, pitted skin, and thick features. Irish, muscles bursting in a dark blue suit. He and Martin spoke briefly, and then Martin picked up the attaché case and came toward her. He held out his hand to her, sympathy and concern on his face, and helped her to her feet. Tucking her arm under his, he walked her the few steps to the staircase and up, and soon she was sitting at a corner table on the balcony over the crowded Grill Room. Someone, she didn't notice who, put a drink in front of her. She didn't look up.

"Leslie, my dear . . ." It was Martin, speaking very gently. "Drink some of this. It will help. I promise." She looked at him, questioning. "It's all right, it's vodka." As always, he knew precisely the right thing to do. "We've closed the restaurant, and we're going to make an announcement about an accident," he continued. "And I'm afraid we're going to have to keep everyone here until the police arrive."

As if on cue, Tom Margittai, co-owner with Paul Kovi of the Four Seasons, was speaking, asking for quiet. The crowd at first paid no attention, but at that moment several blue uniforms appeared on the stairs, followed by a few men in nondescript clothing.

"Ladies and gentlemen," Margittai repeated, "I'm afraid we're going to have to ask you to stay where you are. There's been an accident downstairs, and the police will want to ask you some questions. We are very sorry for the inconvenience this may cause you, and we will pick up the checks on all outstanding bills, and the bar will be open for all soft drinks until you are able to leave."

Cries of "What happened?" And "I'm late for . . ." "I must make a phone call . . ." "What about Lucy, she's meeting me here . . ."

The protests rose to a crescendo. People stood up at their tables, perhaps thinking to leave anyway. The waiters all ranged close to the captain's stand, watching for a signal from Martin.

"Ladies and gentlemen," a dark, stocky man in a rumpled suit spoke just loud enough to be heard over the hubbub. "We have no intention of keeping you later than we absolutely have to, so please give us your cooperation."

Wetzon noticed two uniformed policemen guarding the entrance to the corridor to the Pool Room, the more elegant dining area.

"Everyone, please be seated," Mr. Margittai said. He spoke quietly to the man in the rumpled suit, then added, "Our waiters will be available to you for soft drinks and hors d'oeuvres."

"My name is Sergeant Silvestri, and I'm with the Seventeenth Precinct," the man in the rumpled suit said, stepping forward. "My men are going to take your names and addresses and will want to see some identification. If these check out, we won't be keeping you, but we may want to get back in touch with you again. We'll try to make this as easy as possible," he finished, looking around at the uneasy crowd.

"What happened?" a woman cried. "Aren't you even going to tell us what this is about?" Voices rose again, becoming increasingly irritated as more detectives, in their casual mix of street clothes, fanned out in the Grill Room and bar area. They were glaring among the expensively dressed regulars.

"There's been a murder," Silvestri said, and again protests threatened to drown out his voice. He was leaning on the captain's stand, and he waited patiently, his eyes skimming over the tables, until the noise subsided.

A murder, Wetzon thought. Barry had become "a murder." And she had been angry because he had left her and not come back. He was self-involved and maybe not a good broker, and probably he wasn't very honest, unquestionably sold people things they didn't need, and he may even have been a drug dealer as Smith said, but he didn't deserve to die, and not like that. Her hands trembled. She clutched the edge of the table to calm herself, her fingers white against the polished dark wood. Then, seeing the drink, which she had forgotten, she took a hearty swallow from the small shot glass. Stolichnaya. *Bless you, Martin.* She felt a shock of burning warmth and then she relaxed, closed her eyes, and waited. They would get to her eventually, but she knew instinctively she would be here for a while. She opened her eyes again. On the chair beside her was the attaché case. Barry's attaché case. She tried to remember what Barry had said. It was as if she were drugged. She couldn't think clearly.

She watched the detectives work through the bar crowd, and soon the area was empty and quiet. The hum of voices softened from the Grill Room, and two detectives came up to the balcony, but not to Wetzon. Her lids grew heavy. She was having trouble staying awake. Her head slipped down and she caught herself, snapping it back.

A man came and sat in the chair across the table from her. She stared at him. It was the detective who had just introduced himself as Sergeant Silvestri. She took another swallow of her drink.

"You doing all right, Ms. Wetzon?" he asked politely. She nodded. He had a nice face, dark hair, thinning at the top of a high forehead. "Now then, I want you to think carefully and tell me everything that happened here. You found the body?"

"I found him, " she said, moving her lips, but her voice wasn't working. No sound came out. She began to shiver.

Silvestri put his thick hand over hers and said, "All right now. Take deep breaths," in a calm, authoritative tone. There was something reassuring about him, and Wetzon started breathing again, deeply, as a dancer breathes. The shaking began to subside. There were fine dark hairs on the back of his hand.

Silvestri withdrew his hand from hers and took something out of his inner coat pocket. It was a black leather billfold. He took some identification cards from the billfold, and she saw it was Barry's billfold because there were his securities registration, a driver's license, and some credit cards—a Visa and a MasterCard, American Express, and others. Silvestri placed them on the table in front of him and appeared to study them.

"He called me this afternoon," Wetzon said. "It was urgent, he said, and he had to see me. Some problem he was having, I think, in the office or . . ." Her voice trailed off as she looked across at Silvestri.

He was looking back at her, surprise on his face. "Let me understand this," he said slowly. "You *knew* him? You knew Barry Stark?"

"Yes," she said. "Of course. I thought you understood that. I've known Barry for at least three years."

Silvestri settled back. "Okay, Ms. Leslie Wetzon." His tone of voice changed perceptibly; his manner was less friendly. "Tell me about Barry Stark," he said.

Wetzon's eyes burned, as if her mascara had run. She blinked rapidly. "I'm sorry," she said, hands on either side of her head. "This is such a mess. I don't know where to begin."

"All right, take your time," Silvestri said patiently. He took a small notebook from his inside pocket and waited expectantly. "Who was Barry Stark?"

Who was Barry Stark, indeed, she thought, closing her eyes. Was, past tense. Barry Stark was over. No more Barry Stark. She fought to control a giggle that rose in her throat. She opened her eyes and stared at the impassive detective, embarrassed and confused.

"No, this will not do," she said. "Barry Stark . . . Barry Stark was a stockbroker. With Jacob Donahue and Company."

"Jacob Donahue and Company?" Silvestri wrote in his notebook. "I never heard of it."

"It's a small brokerage firm, downtown, on Hanover Square."

"You mean, like Merrill Lynch, only small?"

"No, not at all." She shook her head vehemently and her hair in its once neat knot loosened precariously. "The major brokerage firms, the wire houses like Paine Webber, Dean Witter, Merrill Lynch, Shearson, and Pru-Bache are all full-service firms with branches all over the country, the world."

"Wire houses?"

Wetzon pinned her hair firmly back in place. "In the old days when a firm had many branches, business was conducted through the main office from the branches by wire. Hence the name 'wire house.' It doesn't apply anymore because everything everywhere is computerized, but the designation of wire house has come to mean the major firms." She patted her hair, satisfied that it was as good a job as she could do under the circumstances.

Silvestri nodded. "Go on," he said. "Tell me about . . ." He looked at his notebook. "Jacob Donahue and Company."

"It's a small, new-issues house with about seventy-five brokers and no branches anywhere else," she said. "Jake Donahue likes to have complete control. I don't think he could handle a branch system. It would dilute his command power."

"You know him?"

"Not personally. But everybody knows Jake. He's colorful. He gets inter-viewed in magazines like *Manhattan, Inc.* and *Forbes,* and he gets quoted all the time." She frowned. "You know, I probably wouldn't recognize him if I saw him. He's big, though, physically. Kind of fleshy."

Silvestri's eyes followed her hands, and she suddenly realized that she was talking with her hands, describing Jake Donahue's supposed physique by hand motions. It was something she always did unconsciously. Chagrined, she dropped them back to her lap.

"Anyway," she said, looking down at her hands, commanding them to stay still, "he says he likes to work with his brokers personally. He hand-picks them, gives them good deals, a fifty percent payout—"

Silvestri stopped her with his eyes. There was an odd magnetism about him that she had not felt when she first saw him. Or perhaps, tired and confused, she was simply drawn to an orderliness that he conveyed.

"Most brokers average a thirty-five percent payout on gross commissions," she said, answering his unspoken question. "Jake pays his brokers fifty per-cent, but they have to sell what he tells them to, to earn that commission. He demands loyalty and total commitment to his way of doing business. It's unique. But it's not for everyone. And Jake can be a dangerous enemy."

Silvestri made another note, but there seemed to be no connection between when he jotted a note and what she was saying.

A blue uniform came to the table. "Sergeant, the M.E. is here. And the Lieutenant's on his way." Silvestri looked up, shrugged his shoulders unapolo-getically. "I'll be right back," he said.

She did not respond, knowing there was nothing to say. The ball was in his court.

What was M.E.? she thought. Her mind wasn't working. *Come on, Wetzon,* she scolded herself, *shape up, get it together.* Silvestri would be back, and she didn't want to seem like a dummy or, God help her, an H.W.—hysterical woman.

M.E. had to be medical examiner. Of course. Good girl. But just the same, she felt dazed and fuzzy-minded. She knew she was going through some sort of shock reaction. She felt frozen in time until Silvestri's voice brought her back.

"He was still warm. Figure dead less than an hour," she heard him say to one of the other detectives, a tall, round-shouldered man with deep pouches under his eyes. Silvestri sat down opposite her again. "I'd really like to get a complete statement from you as soon as possible, Ms. Wetzon."

"Still warm," he'd said. He was talking about Barry as if he were a thing.

She heard someone groan and realized with a start that it was she. Silves-tri's eyes turned soft and personal, as if he really saw her, her . . . Leslie Wetzon . . . not a witness. He had blue-green eyes and dark lashes, she noticed. Turquoise eyes. Funny. She was sure they hadn't been that color earlier. It was as if he didn't allow color to come into his eyes when he was being professional.

"Silvestri, a moment please." A man in his late fifties, incongruously dressed in evening clothes, motioned to Silvestri from the top of the stairs in the Grill Room.

Silvestri's eyes turned dark. "Sorry," he mumbled, moving away again.

The man in the evening clothes spoke tersely to Silvestri, a hand on his shoulder. Silvestri listened, nodding. The older man went back down the stairs to the lobby, and Silvestri talked to one of the uniforms and then headed back to Wetzon on the balcony.

"They're taking the body away now," he said. "Do you know any next of kin? There was nothing in the wallet."

It was still hard to believe. Like an expressionistic dream. Dark shadows, distorted figures. Sharp, violent colors.

She shook her head. "I didn't know him all that well. This is only the third time I met him." What *had* she known about his personal life? She had only known him professionally. She thought for a minute. "He once said he'd grown up in the Bronx. . . ." What had he said . . . *where can a poor kid from the Bronx make all this money . . . and legitimately . . . except as a stockbroker.* Something like that.

Silvestri's attention strayed over the balcony railing to the Grill Room floor. He stood. Another detective was motioning to him from below. "The Lieutenant's here," the detective called.

"Excuse me," Silvestri said. "Do you need anything? I may be a while—"

Wetzon shook her head, abstracted, not even seeing him go. She was remembering the second time she had met Barry Stark . . . at Jake Donahue's office.

Donahue & Co. was located downtown in Hanover Square, one of those little, unlikely oases in the Wall Street area. The offices looked down on a tiny park, a rectangle of grass and benches and pigeons, a multitude of pigeons. It was a mecca at lunchtime in good weather. Brokers and operations people, sales help and traders, ate lunch on the benches and exchanged information. The hottest tip, gossip about other brokers, inside information about a particular firm or stock. Every day was market day. Drugs were bought and sold openly amid food vendors who also crowded the small space. One could indulge in Chinese, Mexican, Indian, Greek, Italian, Spanish, or good old American hot dogs, all purchased from pushcarts crowding into the area around noon every weekday.

The Hanover Square building was a renovated modern version of old splendor. Columns painted to look like marble, trompe l'oeil vaulted ceilings.

Donahue & Co. took a whole floor. The elevator doors opened right into a reception area. Wetzon had gotten off the elevator and looked around the drab, almost unfurnished room. A bench with brown Naugahyde cushions and three metal and plastic chairs, artlessly arranged. The floors were covered with indoor-outdoor carpeting. The color was an ugly pale mustard. In these buildings the leases generally called for some floor covering, and this was probably as cheap as Donahue could get. A scarred black metal reception desk stood on the far side of the small space to the left of the elevators; a sign on the wall over the desk read JACOB DONAHUE & CO., INC. A modern phone system stood on the desk, blinking and burping, but no one sat there.

Wetzon had stood for a while, then looked back at the bench. Perhaps she should sit and wait. She was a little early. There were some magazines, *Barron's, Forbes,* and *Business Week,* on a square glass-topped table with a chrome base. On top of the table with the magazines was a hideous pink marble ashtray of formidable size. The ashtray was brimming with butts, and the harsh odor of cigarettes hung in the air. It was the end of another long day on Wall Street.

She didn't sit down. She had the distinct feeling that dirt and ashes would rub off on her.

Next to the reception desk was a door that presumably led to the boardroom and the rest of the offices. It didn't look much different from garment-center offices, but why should it? Wasn't that the business that Jake Donahue had come out of?

She was thinking about what she'd read regarding Jake Donahue and his origins when the elevator doors opened and a young woman got off. She was wearing tight jeans and stiletto-heeled sandals. Smoke trailed from the cigarette in her fingers. She had dozens of little gold chains of varying lengths around her neck, and the rest of her was barely concealed in a tight red T-shirt with the words BROKERS DO IT ON THE FLOOR printed on it in big black letters. Her hair was a shaggy mane, streaked blonde on blonde, and she carried a paper bag, food or sodas or cigarettes.

"Hi," the blonde said amiably. "Can I help you? I guess Jackie took a break." Jackie was obviously the missing receptionist.

Wetzon looked at her and felt uncomfortably overdressed.

"Yes," Wetzon said. "I'm here to see Barry Stark."

"Sure, he's got the office on the right, straight back. Just come through here."

She threw open the door, releasing such a blast of noise that Wetzon involuntarily took a step backward, assailed by a cacophony of voices, raised and subdued, blaring phones, newsprinters and teletype machines, squawk boxes droning information about particular stocks. She stepped into the room, and the young woman bumped the door shut behind her with the seat of her jeans.

"Straight back there." The blonde pointed past a dense clutter of desks. It seemed for all the world like one of those thirties prison movies with the long rows of dining-hall tables and row upon row of men crowded together, all moving in different directions. But this was the Wall Street version, so there was a sprinkling of women, and the table contained Quotron machines and black looseleaf "books," which were the brokers' customer records. Everyone was pitching product, and the noise was deafening. Here, in the case of Jake Donahue, the product was their new issues. Donahue was bringing companies public at an almost alarming rate, and there was so much demand for these new issues that Donahue & Co. didn't have to syndicate any shares to the other houses. They kept it all in house, divided it among their special customers, and the broker's share of fifty percent on gross commissions was an exceptionally attractive hiring tool. In addition, Wetzon knew, Donahue had been writing big checks for up-front money deals to get the best, the hottest salespeople on Wall Street.

Cardboard coffee containers, crumpled paper bags, half-eaten danishes, probably left over from breakfast, sandwiches, soda cans, and Chinese food containers lay amid the chaos on the desks. The air was a thick cloud of cigarette smoke, and the smell in the room was a stale stew of sweat, perfume, cigarettes, fried rice, and, "Greed," she said, "don't forget the common denominator." She had spoken out loud, but in the din, no one could hear her.

So this was what Barry had left Merrill for. This and over two hundred thousand dollars.

The brokers were dressed in everything from jeans and T-shirts to suits similar to hers, but these were definitely in the minority. She could not differentiate among the women, some of whom were brokers and some sales assistants. Looking around, Wetzon decided that those who looked like expensive call girls must be the brokers. Their on-phone and off-phone attitudes conveyed an electric sense of power. The average age in the room couldn't have been more than twenty-five. And a quick count told her there were over seventy people jammed into this small area.

Wetzon had to admit there was something exciting about it, as sleazy as it appeared, the excitement of making money.

Brokers with phones crooked between ear and shoulder were writing up ticket after ticket as she passed by, and they contacted one another by shouting back and forth.

"Ten thou, sure, yeah, more play."

"Listen, I'll try to get more for you, but I can't promise. Everyone wants in."

"Up two points today. More tomorrow. Yeah. Well, you could sell five, take profits, and ride the rest out."

"We're all going to get rich on this one!"

Wetzon knew that five did not mean five shares and probably not even five hundred shares. The big players were attracted to the new-issues market. They might have a regular account with Merrill Lynch or Shearson for the CMA or FMA—the cash-management accounts—but for the excitement of the ride, they came to Donahue's.

Barry's office did not have a door, but it was an office with a window, and just as cluttered with papers, books, and discarded food containers as the boardroom she had just left. Barry was in shirtsleeves, smoking a cigar, his jacket on the back of his chair, his feet up on his desk. Behind him, the grimy window looked out on yet another grimy window. Obviously his production didn't warrant a scenic view of Hanover Square. This was still Wall Street, and the old Wall Street area was a warren of narrow streets and tall, old buildings wearing the dirt of generations. Firms like Jacob Donahue left the brick-and-mortar grandeur and stylish interiors to the major houses. It all boiled down to dollars and cents, or better, dollars and sense. Keep overhead down, impress people with the money you make for them, and they won't care if you're working from a phone booth on the corner of Forty-second and Broadway. The net-net was that it worked.

Barry waved at her with his cigar hand when he saw her in the doorway, motioning toward the chair. Or at least what was probably a chair. You could hardly see it under the stack of newspapers and stock prospectuses. She waved back at him but remained standing.

"Yes, babes, I promise you," Barry was saying expansively, "this one will go through the roof. Wait till you hear this. . . ." He lowered his voice. "They have this new process, a thermometer that's attached to a home computer, that will tell you everything from your cholesterol to whether you're pregnant." He stopped and laughed wickedly. "Really, darling? I had no idea." He made mocking movements with his head, acting out for Wetzon. "You're kidding. I certainly couldn't tell from your voice. Well, that's not old, come on now. How old would you be if you didn't know how old you was, that's what old Satchel Paige used to say." He listened and laughed again. "Well, of course I know who Satchel Paige was."

He was making sweeping motions with his hand, so Wetzon finally picked up the litter from the chair and put it on the floor. When she straightened up, he was smirking at her, and she realized she had bent over without thinking, like a dancer, from the hip instead of with bent knees.

Ah, well, he was so obvious. She sat. The only reason she was here was to see the place and take Barry out for a drink to thank him for the list of Merrill brokers he had sent her.

"So, sweetheart, why not take ten thou then?" he was saying. "The downside risk is only slight. It'll open at five and I guarantee you'll double your money." His other phone rang. "Stay with me, sweetheart." He tucked the receiver into his shoulder and picked up the other phone. "Stark." He frowned. "Only two thou. I've got someone who'll take ten. Don't think too long." He hung up that phone and spoke again into the first. "So what do you say, darling?"

Wetzon was fascinated by him. He was really good, really persuasive. Either he didn't know, which is unlikely, or, more likely, he didn't care that it was illegal to promise people they'd make money in that way.

He'd gotten his order and hung up the phone. "Beautiful, bee-u-tee-ful," he crowed. "I—"

A noise like a police siren drowned out his self-satisfied voice. Wetzon jumped, startled. "What was that?"

"It's the close. Jerry Walsh does it every day at four. Just part of the action around here."

"Was the market hot today? Everybody in the boardroom seems really energized."

"The truth is," Barry replied, sitting up, feet back on the floor, rolling down his shirtsleeves, "we don't give a shit, excuse me, about the Dow, and the Big Board, or the other exchanges. We only care about the OTC market and specifically our stocks. That's what I like about this place. We concentrate. We specialize. It's where the big bucks are. This is where you make the big killing."

A skinny kid with acne scars stuck his head in the open doorway. "Any more orders for me, champ?"

"Yeah, hold on there, let me write up old lady Zimmerman's order." Barry scribbled something quickly and added the last sheet, thrusting the pile at the order clerk. "Here you are, my son," he said grandly, waving the thick stack of orders. "And these are only from the last hour."

"Bless you, father," the clerk said, grabbing the orders and departing.

From the boardroom came a blast of rock music and singing. When Barry and Wetzon came out of Barry's office, everyone was boogying in the narrow aisles.

"Man, do I need that drink," Barry said.

Over the squawk box Jake Donahue's voice, raspy and deep: "A record day, boys and girls, so everyone gets five hundred extra bonus just for today's work, and for the sales assistants, fifty." There was a great shout. "Keep it up."

Barry quirked an eyebrow at Wetzon. "Not bad, huh? A far cry from Mother Merrill, who never even gave me a pat on the head when I opened more accounts than any rookie except Georgie in the Metro area."

"Generous of Jake to share that way," Wetzon agreed.

"He can afford to be," Barry said without gratitude. "We make a lot of money for that guy. Where would he be without us? At least he knows that."

As they worked their way through the frenzied boardroom, they passed the sexy little sales assistant in the tight jeans who had directed Wetzon earlier. She was jiggling to the music, her hair flying, bosom bouncing. Barry slid his hand down her compact backside, and she grinned at him.

"She's a cute kid," Wetzon said, trailing after Barry. "I guess she's got a fun job working for all of you crazy brokers—"

"Who, Margie?" Barry said over his shoulder. "You gotta be kidding. Margie isn't a sales assistant, she's a broker."

In spite of herself, Wetzon had been taken by surprise. "I can't believe it."

"Yeah, she's one of the biggest producers in the office. Last week she grossed over fifty thou, which means she kept about twenty-five for herself."

"I think I'm in the wrong business," Wetzon had said, stunned.

"Tell me about yourself," Silvestri said gruffly.

Wetzon, startled out of her reverie, shivered. He was back where he had been, opposite her, his notebook out again. She wondered how long he had been there, watching her.

"What do you want to know, specifically?" she asked, confused. She was very tired.

"Who are you?" He had a nice smile and nice white teeth. *He doesn't smoke,* she thought. *How nice, he doesn't smoke.*

"I'm Leslie Wetzon, I'm thirty-five, I grew up in South Jersey on a farm and came to New York to be a dancer." She was looking at turquoise eyes again.

"And now?"

"I do executive search," she said.

He looked puzzled. "What does that mean?"

"I'm a headhunter." She reached into her purse and handed him her card.

"A headhunter," he said, studying her card, then slipping it into his notebook.

"A headhunter. I work in the financial community, with a partner. We talk to stockbrokers and managers and persuade them to look at better situations with other firms. You might call me a matchmaker. . . ."

"And who pays you? The stockbroker?" The eyes went flat again.

"No, the firms that hire them, our clients, when we make the introduction."

"Quite a long way from dancing. Are you good at it?"

"Dancing or headhunting?" she asked, feeling a small stir of attraction, a tiny swirl of excitement she hadn't felt in a long time. How curious. He was such an unlikely prospect. Prospect. God, even her language at rest was the language of her business.

"Both," he said with a quirky smile. Flash of turquoise.

"Yes . . . to both," she said seriously, feeling drained.

"You were telling me that you had met Barry Stark only three times," Silvestri said, making a note in his notebook.

"Yes . . . counting today. The first time was also here at the Four Seasons."

"Do you normally interview people at a place like this?"

"It has a cachet about it. Wealth. Power. Brokers are attracted to that. Someone who might not want to meet in a business office will come to the Four Seasons, and a personal meeting is very important—" She stopped. She had been about to say that she "owned" the broker after a personal meeting, but it didn't sound right, and it wasn't necessarily true. "A personal meeting," she said, "cements the relationship. I'd been talking to Barry on the phone for months—"

"How did you get to him in the first place?"

Wetzon pursed her lips, closing her eyes in thought. How had she gotten to Barry Stark in the first place? Ah, yes. "Georgie Travers gave me his name. His friend, Georgie, who worked with him at Merrill—"

"Georgie Travers? T-R-A-V-E-R-S?" Silvestri made another note.

"But Georgie is not at Merrill anymore. He owns the Caravanserie. You know, the disco with the health club attached."

Silvestri nodded. "What is Georgie Travers like?"

"I don't know him at all. Just a couple of conversations on the phone. He had a terrible reputation—unauthorized trading, churning, burning people out on options . . . there were rumors about drugs. I think Merrill finally fired him, or he quit before charges could be filed. I don't remember exactly, and I never met Georgie. But I think he and Barry were close friends."

"You've never been to the Caravanserie?" Silvestri asked, dubious, writing in his notebook.

"No," Wetzon said, feeling defensive, but unable to think why. "Have you?"

The tall, baggy-eyed detective returned. "Excuse me—"

"Metzger?" Silvestri stood up but didn't leave the table. They spoke in low voices. The sounds came to her floating through that long tunnel again. Very far away, growing farther.

9

The Caravanserie.

She had taken Barry to Harry's after meeting him at Jake Donahue's that day. Harry's was one of the favored watering places for stockbrokers in the Wall Street area. Everyone was pitching something, mostly himself, and everyone was celebrating his successful day or someone else's disaster. It was a time for self-aggrandizement. And the numbers that were spoken of often came out of the air or someone's very fertile imagination.

Wetzon had always been amazed by the frenzied, almost hysterical voices and actions of all of these men, because there was definitely an abundance of men. It was as if the lunatics had been released from the asylum. So different from actors and dancers after performances. Actors and dancers, her people, preferred to cool out. The performance was a catharsis of a sort. Dancers did what they loved after a performance—they went dancing.

For the stockbrokers and traders who came to Harry's, Harry's was the catharsis.

"Hey, Barry, how's it going, man?"

Coming from bright light into the dimness, Wetzon had to blink several times to focus.

"Hey, buddy," Barry had said, "long time no see. How's it going at Witter? You're still there, aren't you?" This last was said deprecatingly. "Buddy" was a short, very well-dressed young man with a deep wave in his light brown hair. It looked to Wetzon like a wave that had been made by a perm or a hair clip, helped along with setting lotion. A dip of hair fell across an unlined forehead.

"Great, great. I'm having my biggest month. And I like Witter. It's a great firm, and they've been good to me."

"Sure. Sure. I bet."

"What're you pushing?"

"Who's your friend?"

"Sorry, this is Wetzon, of Smith and Wetzon." Barry laughed loudly. "This animal is Scott Fineberg."

Wetzon shook hands with Fineberg, not letting on that they had been talking for the past six months. On the telephone—they had never met. They had, in fact, been talking more seriously lately because Scott was ready to leave Dean Witter. He had made some record sales, upped his gross production 100 percent, but the firm still saw fit to treat him as if he weren't there. He had to share a sales assistant with eight other brokers, so if he stepped out to the men's room or to lunch with a client, or, heaven help him, he had a doctor's or dentist's appointment, chances were better than good that his phone would go unanswered.

They had finally given him his own office, but it was a converted storage room, a small space hole without a window, and the trip to Paris which he should have received for the record-breaking numbers he had done in the past year had not been forthcoming. Since only two brokers in the Atlantic Region had qualified for the trip, management decided to reconsider awarding the trip this year. They were actually hedging with him, having offered him San Francisco instead.

It was always amazing to Wetzon how foolish the firms were and how cheap. They would rather risk losing a broker than give him sales help so he could make more money for them. And the much-deserved pat on the back—in Scott's case, the trip to Paris—they were being niggardly about.

"Nice to meet you, Wetzon," Scott Fineberg said, without a flicker of recognition.

He was talking seriously to Oppenheimer and Paine Webber, introductions having been set up by Wetzon.

"So what're you selling, baby?" Barry asked impatiently. "What're you drinking, Wetzon?"

"Heineken."

"Two Heinekens over here," Barry shouted over the clamor. The bar crowd was now three deep, and people were still pushing into Harry's behind them.

"I did sixty thou last month in this new government security fund we have."

"Jesus, sixty thou, that's great!" Barry clapped Scott Fineberg on the back, then took the beers, passed over heads to them. "See you." He turned abruptly and moved away from Fineberg; Wetzon followed, making eye contact with Fineberg briefly, nodding.

"What a lying fucker," Barry said. "Excuse the language, but that's what he is. He's not doing anywhere near those numbers. I know him. He couldn't possibly be doing it."

"Why do you say that?"

"Because he's a dumb mother who's connected, and they just feed him business."

"Really?"

"Sure, hey, everyone knows it. Believe me, take my word for it."

"Hey, man, good to see you. Some day, huh?"

"How do you like Jake's, Stark?" a whiskey-thick voice asked. The dense cigarette smoke and the muted lighting of the bar area made it difficult to see people until you walked into them, which was easy to do anyway since there were so many people milling around. You had to shout to be heard by the person standing at your shoulder. Wetzon wondered how the waiters could keep track of who ordered what, and how they were paying. At that point a waiter in a white apron held out a bill to the narrow bit of space between her and Barry.

Barry ignored the check and bent to talk to the short, unattractive woman who had asked the question about Jake's. Wetzon looked at the waiter holding out the bill and took it. "Thank you very much," she said.

"Not at all," he mouthed, bowing slightly and disappearing into the smoke.

"It's great, Mildred, you oughta try it someday." Barry's laugh was snide.

"Is he still pulling that pyramid scam?" Mildred asked, equally snide. Her face was more than homely, it was downright ugly. Leathery skin, splotchy, a small mustache on her wrinkled upper lip, under a very large hook of a nose. Even in the faint light, her eyes glinted with malevolence. "You'd better watch your step, Mr. Smart Ass." She reached up and poked Barry's chest with a bony finger.

"Now, Mildred," Barry said smoothly, looking down at her, "you wouldn't want my friend here to think you were threatening me, would you?" Menace tinged his formerly genial voice. "And get your fucking finger out of my chest."

"I'm not threatening you, you little shit, I'm warning you. Cover your ass or Jake will chop you up in little pieces and flush you down the toilet." She blew cigarette smoke in his face and moved away.

Wetzon saw Barry's fist clench in the darkness. He made a move after Mildred, and then stopped and shrugged.

"God, who is that horror?" Wetzon asked, a hand on his arm. She could feel the tension through his coat sleeve.

"Mildred Gleason. Jake Donahue's ex."

So that was Mildred Gleason. One of Wall Street's famous first ladies, Wetzon thought, and wouldn't you know she'd be a gross woman who looked and talked like a man.

"Boy, does she hate him," Wetzon noted.

"She has a right to, I guess." Barry scowled. "She got him started. He used her money, then dumped her. He started as a broker at her father's firm, married the boss's daughter, took over the firm when the old man died, and changed the name to his. She gets pissed off when she even hears he's hiring good people and making big money, making any money."

"But she has her own firm now, doesn't she?"

"Yeah, but I hear she's not making money hand over fist like Jake's doing. Jake's raking it in. And she doesn't get quoted all the time." He laughed. "She can't help being so mean, but I understand her. So I can say we're friends of a sort. She's just a little hard to take sometimes." He was calming down.

"What pyramid scam is she talking about?"

"When some clients are put in a stock when it opens and others are put in when it's run up, so the clients who get in at the bottom make the money and those who go in at the top make less—"

"Or nothing."

"Or lose. But it all works out, believe me, because you give everybody a chance at one point or another to come in at the bottom, all except the creeps."

"What constitutes a creep?"

"Someone who complains all the time that you're not making enough money for him. Stuff like that."

"I see."

"It's fair," Barry said. She looked at him doubtfully. "Well, it's as fair a shot as you're going to get in the new-issues market anywhere."

"Even at Jake Donahue's?"

"Yeah." He was only half-listening now. Barry, the social animal, was checking everyone out, his eyes darting everywhere with a kind of nervous intensity. They'd finished their beers, and Barry had stopped to talk with another broker to give him a tip on a new issue. Wetzon found a waiter and paid for the drinks.

"Come on," Barry said, "I'll give you a ride uptown. Where're you going?" He hailed a cab right outside Harry's with a piercing whistle.

"West Eighty-sixth Street."

"Good, then you can drop me." He held the door for her, his assumption being that she would have taken a cab to get uptown anyway. But she would not have. She would have gone down into the pit of the IRT and subwayed home. A cab ride cost upward of twenty dollars, and Wetzon worked too hard for her money to throw it away on a cab ride on a nice day.

"Where to?" the driver asked, bored. A pair of dice dangled from his rear view mirror and a small statue of the Virgin Mary sat on top of the dashboard. The radio played hard rock.

"Sixty-fifth and York." Barry turned to Wetzon. "I'm going to the Caravanserie. Great place. You been there yet?"

"Not yet. I know your friend, Georgie Travers, owns it."

"Yeah, I'm the charter member. Got the first card ever issued."

"What exactly do you get for membership, besides a card?"

"The health club, the racquet ball and squash courts, the pool, and let us not forget the disco. The disco is the best."

"You're going to work out now?"

"Not yet. Georgie uses the disco for networking sessions before disco hours. He has them once a month, from six to seven-thirty. I'm going to one right now. You want to come with me? It's not your crowd tonight, it's the entertainment industry, you know, show business."

She smiled at him. "You're right, not my crowd. What does Georgie charge for this?"

"Six bucks, with an invitation. I've made more contacts there than any-where else, all business of course. You interested?"

"I can't tonight—"

"I'll get you on the list." Barry spoke with a kind of self-important generos-ity. "A lot of brokers go there. I've opened a lot of big accounts through these sessions."

They were on First Avenue. Barry leaned forward. "You can drop me at Sixty-fifth Street and take the little lady . . . where did you say?"

"Eighty-sixth and Columbus."

"Yeah," Barry said vaguely. He did not offer to pay the fare. "See ya." He'd gotten out of the cab without looking back.

And Wetzon had not seen him again until today.

She put her hand over her eyes. She was having a hard time keeping them open. She could feel her head drooping. She put her head on her arms on the table. She felt a hand on her shoulder, a warm hand through her suit jacket.

"I'm sorry," Silvestri said gently. His breath brushed her ear. "Why don't I get one of my men to take you home, and I'll talk with you in the morning."

She forced her eyes open and tried to smile at him. "Yes. No," she said. "I'm sorry. I can't seem to get myself together."

"What's your address?" He waved an arm and a young boy in a uniform came to the table. "This is Officer Lyons. Jimmy, I want you to take Ms. Wetzon home." He took some keys from his inside pocket and handed them to Lyons. "You know which is mine?" Lyons nodded. "I'd like to talk with you first thing in the morning, Ms. Wetzon . . . if you don't mind. Can you come to the precinct about ten o'clock?"

She nodded as he handed her his card, which, preoccupied, she placed in the pocket of her suit. She didn't want to go home yet. She wanted to see Smith, had to talk to Smith about what happened. "If you don't mind," she said, "I'd like to go to my friend's apartment instead."

"Okay, Jimmy will take you there. Just write down that address and phone number for me, and yours at home, too," Silvestri said, "in case I have to reach you before tomorrow." He handed her his small notebook and stood up to talk to the baby faced Lyons and Metzger of the eye pouches.

Wetzon looked at the page in his notebook. His handwriting was atrocious, like chicken scratches. Carefully, she printed her address and phone number on the page and then Smith's address and number. She felt as rumpled as they all looked. And tired. Her face was clammy. She stood up clutching her handbag, legs unsteady, and pushed the chair back. Yellow dots danced on her eyes. Shouldn't have had the vodka on an empty stomach. She put her fingers on the edge of the table and took a deep breath. She smoothed her skirt and straight-ened the jacket of her suit. It was warm, very warm, uncomfortably warm.

Then she saw the attaché case. *Oh, lord,* she thought. "Sergeant Silvestri," she said, but he was already a distance from her and didn't hear her call. Noise came from every section of the restaurant. There were blue uniforms every-where and a lot of people who looked like detectives. There were still some customers being interviewed on the balcony and in the Grill Room.

"It's okay, miss," Jimmy Lyons said, taking her arm. He didn't look old enough to shave, let alone be a policeman. She thought about telling him so, but her voice faltered. "Here, let me take your case for you." Lyons picked up the attaché case and she found herself propelled down the stairs from the bal-cony, across the floor of the Grill Room, stared at by men from another world who didn't seem to fit into the elegance of the space, past employees of the Four Seasons, still serving food and drink. She thought she caught a glimpse of Martin, but the pressure on her arm was solid and supportive, and Jimmy was keeping her moving.

They were coming down the stairs now, to the lobby, where, try as she might to look away, her eyes went straight toward the phone area, which, oddly, was almost deserted. She couldn't help wondering what would happen to Barry's body. Who would notify his family? Did he have any family? Everyone had some sort of family. They were going out the door and onto the street now. A rush of cool air. It was dark. She'd lost track of the time. A flash went off, blinding her. She ducked her head and put her hand over her eyes.

"What's your name?" someone demanded roughly, pulling at her arm. "Did you do it?"

"Get back, get back!" There were more uniforms. Wetzon felt dizzy, blinded by the flash, confused by the crowd. She faltered, then felt herself lifted by strong arms. She was in the back of a car. She was sitting on something lumpy. She raised herself slightly and reached underneath and pulled out a leather mitt. A baseball mitt. She put it aside; everything took so much effort.

"There, miss," Jimmy said. "You'll be all right now. I'll get you out of here." He closed the door and she sank back in the seat. If this was Silvestri's car, it was a mess. In the dim light from the street, she saw beside her, under the mitt, what looked like a bundle of laundry. On the floor near her feet were a pair of very dirty torn sneakers and two baseball bats. She leaned forward to see what was going on outside. A face pressed against the window. People were staring. Some carried cameras. The street seethed with police activity. There were barricades, blinking lights, shouts.

Jimmy got into the car. "I'll have you up to Seventy-eighth Street in no time," he said cheerfully. "Just sit back so you don't get hurt."

She sank back next to the bundle of laundry. Right now she felt like a bag of dirty laundry, too, and her longing for a hot bath intensified.

Traffic on Third Avenue was heavy, but Lyons drove quickly, as if he was in a hurry to get back to the action. She peered into the darkness, trying to see where they were, looking for a familiar store front. There was so much con-struction going on now on Third Avenue; a giant crane seemed perched on almost every corner.

Barry. What had he gotten himself into? She wished she could stop thinking about it.

Then Jimmy Lyons pulled up in front of Smith's building.

"I'm all right, really," Wetzon said to the young policeman as he helped her out of the car. He was very conspicuous in his uniform and she felt mildly embarrassed, as if she had done something wrong. It was the "what would people think" syndrome. "Bourgeois nonsense," her friend Carlos called it.

"I'll see you upstairs," Jimmy Lyons said.

"No, no, it's really all right," she assured him. "Tony is here, and he'll take care of me." Smith's doorman was coming toward her with a big welcoming smile and a greedy curiosity in his eyes.

"Okay, miss." Jimmy seemed pleased to be rid of her, chafing to get back to the excitement at the Four Seasons.

"Hello, Ms. Wetzon," Tony was saying. "She got in about an hour ago." He was hovering obsequiously.

"Thanks, Tony," she said. "What time is it anyway?"

"Almost nine o'clock. Are you okay?"

"Yes, I'm fine." Her voice seemed to belong to someone else.

They were in the lobby when Jimmy Lyons was suddenly back beside her, very big and very blue. In the bright light of the lobby she noticed that he had a skimpy blond mustache. Why hadn't she noticed it before? "I almost forgot your case," he said, putting it on the floor beside her. He beamed at her. The elevator door slid open.

"Here, I'll take that for you," Tony said, putting the attaché case into the elevator.

"Wait," Wetzon said, hand extended toward Jimmy. "Wait . . . this . . ."

"It's okay, miss," Jimmy said modestly, assuming he was being thanked.

Tony held the elevator door, blocking her from Lyons. A blowsy woman with a beribboned French poodle came sailing through the lobby, staring at Jimmy, staring at Wetzon, disapproving her way past the group and into the elevator. Now she said, indignantly, "You are holding us up, if you please." She was wearing a mink coat, yards of mink. The poodle sniffed haughtily. Its toenails were painted red.

Wetzon—nervous, upset, tired—giggled. Tony let the door go. "Tell Sergeant Silvestri . . ." Wetzon called, and the door closed.

"There's no accounting anymore." The disapproving woman spoke to her dog. "You'd better press your floor," she said to Wetzon, "or you'll come up to the penthouse with us." Meaning, *and I don't want you near my penthouse.* The poodle sneered, showing teeth.

Wetzon pressed 5, and when they came to a stop, she started off.

"You're forgetting your attaché case," the woman said disdainfully.

I'm always forgetting my case, Wetzon thought with a surge of irritation. *Maybe because it isn't my goddam case.* She reached down and yanked the case out of the elevator and lugged it down the hall to 5G, Smith's apartment. How stupidly heavy the damn thing was. Sighing, she pressed the doorbell.

The peephole clicked. She stuck out her tongue. In seconds the locks were flipped and the door opened.

"Hey, Ma," Mark yelled. "It's okay. I told you she was okay. Wetzon's here." Tony obviously had not announced her. So much for these fancy East Side buildings.

10

So Smith had been expecting her. How could she have known?

"Mom said you'd be here tonight," Mark said proudly. "Isn't she wonderful?"

"It can't have . . . it's too soon . . . did it come over the news already?" Wetzon stammered, struggling to understand. "Did anyone call and tell her?"

"No one told me anything," Smith replied, a disembodied voice coming from somewhere within the apartment. "I read it in the cards. I knew something evil had happened and you were involved. The cards never lie." She stood dramatically in the arched doorway to the living room. She wore a full robe, an "at home" of vivid reds and blacks, from Marimekko, and the towel turban around her head meant she had washed her hair, but it made her look like an exotic fortune-teller. She had been reading her Tarot cards again.

Smith swept Wetzon into her arms and gave her an Obsession-scented hug. Then she pulled back. "You look terrible," she said. "Tell me. Tell me everything. I'm so happy you're all right. You kept coming up in danger with death around you."

"I was," Wetzon said. "And I've got to lie down right now before I fall down." She felt limp, light-headed. She had not eaten anything since lunch, except for the small hors d'oeuvres at the Four Seasons.

She staggered, leaning on Smith, into Smith's bedroom, kicked off her shoes, and fell on the bed, which in typical Smith fashion was still unmade from the morning and had the accumulated disarray of several days on it. Wetzon found herself resting amid the clothes Smith had worn, the papers she'd been reading, books, a hairbrush thick with hair, blankets and bedclothes, candy wrappers, and a hair dryer.

Normally Wetzon was put off by the chaos of Smith's home base, but now it was welcome. She was just too tired to care. Probably somewhere on the bed were those damn cards, but let Smith worry about them. She lay back and closed her eyes, then opened them, startled. Looking up at the ceiling, she saw herself looking back. Smith had mirrored the ceiling over her bed.

"Hey, Smith," she began.

Smith had the grace to blush. "Mark, honey," she said.

"Mom?"

"Tea and toast for our tired friend here."

Mark was a nest-making twelve-year-old, precocious in school, nurturing at home. Smith had been divorced from his father since he was two, and his father was with American intelligence, some kind of CIA position, which Smith never wanted to talk about. Wetzon had never met him. There was no contact between Mark and his father, and Mark didn't seem to care.

"Okay," Smith commanded, once Mark left the room. "Let's hear it." She pulled the low-backed chair from her dressing table over to the bed, sat down facing Wetzon, and added her bare feet to the confusion on the bed.

Wetzon took a deep breath, laboring to assimilate the reality of what she was about to say. "Barry Stark was murdered tonight at the Four Seasons."

"Oh, my lord, where were you?"

Wetzon talked for what seemed like hours, filling in the story, answering Smith's barrage of questions.

"He must have said something, Wetzon. Some clue to what was going on."

"He was afraid, I think."

"How did you know he was dead?"

"Smith, for godsakes, believe me, you know. He *oozed* out at me."

Smith shook her head and frowned. "You must have seen *something*."

"Nothing. I mean it."

"Sometimes you amaze me, Wetzon. You don't see things right in front of you—"

"Smith, will you give me a break? Leave me alone. I'm talked out. Barry Stark was stabbed to death, and I found him. I don't need this now."

"Okay, okay, I'm sorry."

Wetzon sighed and closed her eyes. She kept drifting off and coming back. At some point she took off her jacket and lay back again. She could tell Smith was disappointed because she had not been there at the Four Seasons.

Mark reappeared, carrying a pot of fragrant tea, paper tails from the bags hanging down the sides of the pot, and a plate of buttered toast on a tray, and Wetzon sat up and ate, feeling more like herself again as she did.

"Mark, this is very nice," she said.

"Yes, he's become a regular little homemaker, haven't you, sweetie pie?" Smith curled her finger at him. "Come here, I just have to kiss you." Mark came around the bed to receive his kiss. "He takes such good care of me. I don't know what I'd do without him."

The boy swelled with pleasure and settled down on the carpet to listen.

"Wait a minute," Smith said. "The attaché case. Where is it?" She was looking around the room.

"I brought it in. I know I had it with me. . . ."

"It's in the hall," Mark said. "I'll get it." He ran out and came back carrying the case. "Boy, is it heavy."

"I have to call Silvestri right away and let him know about this," Wetzon said.

"Who is Silvestri?"

"A detective I talked to. He seemed to be in charge. He's nice, Xenia," she added.

"You liked him? I can't believe it. You liked a cop? You can't like a cop."

"A detective. And he's sexy."

"Oh, spare me."

"Where did I put his card? I know he gave me his card." Wetzon located her handbag among the chaos on Smith's bed and began looking through it. Finally she swung her feet to the floor, bent over, and emptied its contents on the carpet because the bed was just too much competition. "No card. Never mind. I'll just call the precinct and they'll get a message to him."

She dialed information and then the precinct. It rang and rang. "Thirty . . . thirty-five . . . forty . . . This is ridiculous!" She hung up. "A person could die waiting. I'm sorry I said that. I'll try later." Her head was beginning to throb.

Smith was eyeing the attaché case speculatively. She had that familiar glint in her eye.

"Wetzon," she said, looking at the case, not Wetzon, "while we're waiting . . ."

"Do you think it's right? What if there're fingerprints . . . no, there wouldn't be. I've had it since he left me."

They both looked at the case. It seemed to be alive, bulging, right before their eyes.

"Mark, honey," Smith said, "it's past time for you to be in bed. This is a school night."

"Aw, Mom, I want to see what's in the case, too—"

"We're not going to open it until the detective gets here," Smith said firmly. "So you won't miss anything."

"And I'm sure it's full of papers," Wetzon said reassuringly.

"Aw, you guys are no fun," Mark said.

"Good night, my sweetie," Smith said, offering her cheek.

Reluctantly, Mark kissed her and left. They waited until they heard his door close, then they both sprang toward the attaché case.

Wetzon giggled. This was silly. "Two busybodies," she said. "Aren't we awful?"

"Wait," Smith said. She closed the door softly. "Try the precinct again. One more time."

Wetzon dialed. "Twenty . . . twen—"

"Seventeenth Precinct. Rivera."

"Oh, yes, Sergeant Silvestri, please," Wetzon said. Smith looked disappointed. Wetzon felt relieved.

"Silvestri's not picking up." Rivera's response was mechanical. "I'll have him paged."

"He doesn't seem to be there," Wetzon told Smith. "They're paging him." Smith smiled.

"Ma'am, he's not here right now."

"May I leave a message?"

"Yeah."

"Ask him, please, to call Leslie Wetzon at . . ." She gave Smith's number, spelled her name for him twice, and hung up.

They pounced on the case.

"What do you suppose is in here?" Wetzon asked, running her hands over the thick, luxurious black leather.

"It's locked, dammit," Smith grumbled. "I suppose it was too much to hope that it wouldn't be."

They were sitting on the floor, the case between them.

"Maybe a good old-fashioned hairpin," Wetzon said, reaching up, feeling around, and then taking one out of her bun. A lock of hair slipped and curled around her ear.

Smith laughed her wicked laugh and took the hairpin. The phone rang. "Damn," Wetzon said. "Do you suppose that's Silvestri already?"

"Let it ring," Smith said, working with the hairpin. "I'm making progress."

"No, we can't," Wetzon said, sighing.

Smith stood up. "Here." She handed Wetzon the hairpin. "You try." The phone rang repeatedly. She moved with exaggerated slowness toward it. "Persistent, isn't he?" After the tenth ring, it stopped. "Aha," she said, "that's better." She came back to the attaché case.

"Mom," Mark called loudly, from his room, "it's for Wetzon. Sergeant Silvestri, NYPD."

"Christ," Smith said. "That kid is so compulsive."

Smith and Wetzon looked at each other. Smith took the hairpin and bent over the lock. Wetzon picked up the phone.

"Hello, Sergeant Silvestri."

"What's the problem?" He was curt.

She felt put off by his tone. "It's just that I forgot something that might be important."

"Okay, make it fast."

"I can't make it fast." If he could be curt, so could she. "I have to show you."

"I've got a lot of work here right now, Ms. Wetzon. Can't this wait till tomorrow?"

"No, it can't wait," she insisted. She wasn't going to be left holding the goddam attaché case a minute longer than she had to.

"Where are you?"

"My partner's home. The address is—"

"I have it."

A loud snap came from the floor where Smith was bent over the attaché case.

11

The two women's eyes met with the sound of the lock snapping open.

There was a moment of silence from Silvestri. "How long are you going to be there, Ms. Wetzon?"

"Another hour, maybe. I'm really tired, and I'd like to get home, Sergeant. Ordinarily I'd let this go, but I think it's important."

"I'll get up there as soon as I can, and then I'll take you home."

"Okay." Wetzon slowly replaced the receiver. That was nice. He would take her home. "I think he was still at the Four Seasons," she said. She wondered if he was calling from the same phone booth. She shuddered. In her mind she saw Barry again, sliding out of the booth toward her. "Poor Barry," she said.

"Poor Barry, nothing," Smith sniffed. "The scumbag probably stuck his avaricious nose in where he shouldn't have and got caught." She was no longer interested in Barry, Wetzon could see, but only interested in the case—attaché case—murder case. Smith raised the lid. "And we both know that if there was a profit to be made on this information, Barry was ready to make it, legally or illegally. You have to admit that."

"You're right, of course," Wetzon said, sighing. "But what could he have done to deserve being murdered?"

"Let's just see if we can find out," Smith said with a raunchy giggle. "We'll take everything out piece by piece so we can put it back in the same way we found it."

"Maybe we shouldn't be doing this at all," Wetzon said, but her interest was piqued, and she knew she was in just as deep as Smith. "We are probably breaking the law."

They looked at each other and grinned.

"Let's make a list of what we find." Wetzon took her Filofax out of her handbag and flipped over the calendar and address pages to where she kept the note pages.

"Ready?" Smith asked. "We'll start here and leave this stuff in the accordion file for last."

The attaché case had a large basic compartment and an accordion compartment attached to the inside cover. Smith flipped open the cover to the bottom compartment.

"Okay, here we go. One: research reports and prospectuses from Shearson, Bache, Merrill Lynch, Paine Webber, Alex Brown, his firm . . . my God, he has reams of this stuff here."

Barry had a network of friends at all of the firms, and they were a never-ending supply of research for one another. Brokers with an instinct for self-preservation tended to develop these reciprocal relationships, cultivating sources other than their own firm's research. They had to, because brokers swore that their firms were almost never right, and by the time the stock was recommended to the broker's clients, the institutional investors had already bought and sold the stock and it was on its way down. It was a business of one hand washing the other, in one way or another. A business of tradeoffs, real and psychological.

Smith stacked the reports on the carpet next to the case.

"Two: A Gucci address book. Wouldn't you know. And a very nice one, too," she said, turning it over in her hand. "I'd like to look this over more closely, but we may not have the time."

"What's this?" Wetzon pulled out a large white, lumpy plastic bag. It was stamped YORK HOSPITAL in horizontal blue block letters. "It feels like snack food—M and Ms, nuts and stuff."

"There's another one under here," Smith said, pulling it out.

Wetzon opened the snap and looked in. "Jesus," she murmured.

"What is it?"

"Wait a minute. Give me that ashtray." With rare obedience, Smith reached for the large frosted glass ashtray on the night table near her bed. A fragment of surprise skirted past Wetzon's subconscious. . . . What was an ashtray doing in Smith's bedroom? She didn't smoke.

Wetzon emptied the contents of the plastic bag into the ashtray. Capsules spilled out, a myriad of colors, shapes, and sizes. Pills and plastic vials grew into a huge mound.

"So—the big rock-candy mountain," Smith said softly.

"Do you believe this? What's in the other bag?"

Smith snapped it open and peered inside. "More of the same. And there's another bag back here."

"Don't touch it. Let's just put everything back where it was. It makes me nervous. Hold this for me." Wetzon thrust the empty plastic bag at Smith and, while Smith held it, poured the contents of the ashtray back into it.

For once Smith was silent. She snapped the bags closed the way they'd found them and tucked both bags back into the case. "Your poor Barry was into a lot more than new issues, just as I always said," she murmured. "Not so poor Barry, after all."

"It gives me the creeps," Wetzon said. "Let's quit this."

"Wait a sec," Smith said. "Look." She had pulled out a minicassette recorder. She turned it over. "There's a cassette in it, half-used. We've got to listen," she said eagerly. "It might be important."

She had taken the towel turban off her head. Excitement had brought out her vivid coloring and her dark hair had dried full and wavy.

Wetzon was excited, too. It couldn't hurt them to know what the tape said. She pressed the rewind button on the tiny recorder and waited for the small click. Then she pressed "play" and Barry's voice came metallically into the room.

"Can you make it louder?" Smith settled her back against the foot of the bed.

Wetzon rewound and started again.

"Tuesday, March twenty-sixth," Barry said.

"Today," Wetzon said.

"Shush," Smith said.

There was the sound of a buzzer on the tape.

"Yes," a male voice rasped.

"Mr. Seltzer," a woman's voice responded.

"Good," the male voice said. "Put him through."

"Jake?" The second man's voice.

"Yeah, Art. What do you have?"

"They called again," Art said. "They know something's going on. I put them off again, but they're starting to push, and I'm getting worried. I don't need the SEC nosing around right now. Are you sure you can cover?"

"Yeah. Will you quit worrying?"

"Okay, okay, but what about this Mildred business?"

"That's my department." Jake sounded angry. "You take care of yours. I've got Mildred hogtied and she doesn't even know it." He laughed, and even though the quality of the recording was poor, the downright nastiness in the sound came through to Wetzon, chilling her. "I've got something on her that will take her out. Permanently."

"Yeah, okay, but get the certificates back before you do anything."

"I don't need you to tell me that, pal."

"Yeah, well, my life's on the line here, buddy. I vouched for you in the audit. I could lose everything."

"Okay, okay, but someone knows too much about my business for this to keep happening. We've got a fucking spy here, and if I catch him, I'll kill him. Wait a minute—" Jake broke off at that point and so did the tape.

"That's Jake Donahue," Smith said needlessly.

"I know. Smith, Barry must have been the spy. Maybe he got caught. He looked as if he'd been in a fistfight when he met me tonight."

"If he did, why didn't they get the cassette and the recorder?"

Wetzon rewound the cassette and placed the recorder on the carpet next to the Gucci address book. "I don't know, but it's pretty small. He could have had it in his inside coat pocket. Or maybe he didn't have it on him at all, and that's why they beat him up."

"What do you think he found out?" Smith said. "And who is Mildred?"

"Ah, who is Mildred?" Wetzon said playfully. " 'What is she? That all our swains commend her . . .' "

Smith stared blankly at her. "Really, Wetzon, sometimes you make no sense whatsoever."

"I forgot myself," Wetzon mumbled. She should never try to get literary with Smith. "There's only one well-known Mildred in this business. And she just happened to have once been married to Jake Donahue. Mildred Gleason."

"Ah, yes," Smith said, imitating W. C. Fields. "Let's think about that."

"This stuff looks like more research," Wetzon said.

"Yes, and a 'Standard and Poor's Stock Guide,' " Smith held up a hardcover book. "And *Super Stocks* by one Kenneth L. Fisher."

"No wonder that damn case was so heavy."

A buzzer sounded from the foyer.

"Damn. Your friendly detective didn't waste much time getting here." Smith stood up and stretched, leaving Wetzon to clean up the mess.

Hurriedly, Wetzon put the items back in order and moved the top of the case to close it, but a heavy object that was in the accordion section slipped out, blocking the lock.

"Jesus Christ, Xenia," Wetzon said breathlessly. "Look—a gun."

"What?" Smith was halfway out the bedroom door and returned in a flurry of red and black to stare down at the thick, shiny nose of a small automatic.

The buzzer sounded again. "Don't move, I'll be right back," she said, heading for the foyer. She spoke briefly to Tony over the intercom and was back. Wetzon hadn't moved. She was on her knees, sitting on her heels. Her palms were damp.

They stared at the gun, half in and half out of the attaché case.

"Push it back," Smith said urgently, whispering, although she had no need to. "No, with your pen. Don't touch it."

Gently, Wetzon prodded the nose of the gun back into the case. The case closed by itself from the weight of the accordion file. She pressed the top and the lock snapped into place. She was shaking.

The doorbell rang.

12

Wetzon brought the attaché case into the living room and set it down near the large black marble slab of a coffee table. And there were Smith's Tarot cards spread on the table as if she had just put them down. Great. Silvestri would think she and Smith were flakes.

It was yet another similarity between show business and the brokerage business. Everyone had an astrologer, a personal psychic, a card reader, a numerologist, and was always trying out a new one. A very straight, enormously successful stockbroker had once told Wetzon in total seriousness that he only bought stock that he had checked first with Miranda.

"Miranda?" she had the temerity to ask.

"My psychic," he had replied.

"I'm making a pot of coffee," Smith called from the kitchen.

Wetzon padded back into the bedroom to put on her shoes. She looked at herself in the mirror over Smith's bureau. She was a mess. Haggard. Her hair was coming down. Where had they put her hairpin? She found it on the carpet where they had opened the case, and tried to catch up the loose tendrils of hair.

The doorbell rang again, more emphatically, and since Smith was ignoring it, Wetzon went to the door, smoothing her blouse, straightening her skirt. Her suit jacket lay where she had thrown it when she came in—in the disorder of Smith's bed.

"Now what was so important, Ms. Wetzon?" Silvestri asked when she opened the door. He had his hands in his pockets and he looked tired. The shadow of a dark beard harshened his face. His eyes were flat and dark. Impersonal. Was he annoyed with her for bothering him?

"I'm sorry to have kept you waiting," Wetzon said. "I didn't expect you so soon, and I wasn't dressed. And I'm sorry to make you come up here like this." She was babbling, but she couldn't help herself. "I'm sure you've had a long day, but I didn't feel comfortable about letting this wait. It's in here." She was trying to be professional and brusque, as much as he was.

She led him into the living room, which was not in Smith's normally disordered condition. Well, not quite. There were a pair of Reeboks near the sofa and the usual profusion of magazines—*Forbes, Vogue, Fortune, People, New York,* and *Cosmopolitan*—piled up on the Berber-carpeted floor. Smith's taste in magazines was decidedly eclectic.

The sofa was one of those sweeping L-shaped sectionals covered in a fawn-colored textured velvet.

Silvestri waited expectantly, looking around. The lovely odor of coffee filled the room. His nostrils flickered.

"It's the attaché case," Wetzon said.

"What about it?" he asked.

Smith came sweeping into the room with a tray of coffee and fixings and set it on the marble table. "You must be Detective Silvestri," she said, giving him the royal treatment. "I'm Xenia Smith." She shook his hand. "It's a real pleasure to meet you."

Silvestri was clearly dazzled. He stared at her, still holding her hand. She smiled at him and at her hand. He smiled back at her and gave her hand a little pat with his other hand and then released it. He had not smiled at Wetzon that way.

He looked at Wetzon again, recovering. "The attaché case?"

"Oh, I'm sorry. *That* attaché case."

He looked at it and at her, puzzled.

"I tried to tell you, and then Jimmy Lyons, when he brought me up here, that it isn't mine. It's Barry's."

"I see. And what were you doing with it?" Something in Silvestri's tone made Wetzon feel guilty. He was disappointed in her. She should have tried harder, earlier, to tell him it wasn't hers.

Smith smiled. "Now, Detective Silvestri," she said, "Wetzon doesn't discover a body every day. Particularly someone she knows so well. It was pretty much a shock, don't you think?"

Why had Smith said she knew Barry so well? Smith knew that wasn't true. And it made Wetzon seem as if she were covering up something. After all, she had already told Silvestri she hardly knew Barry.

"Barry left it with me when he went to make the phone call," Wetzon said defensively. "When he kept me waiting so long, I carried it downstairs to give back to him . . . and found him. Then everyone assumed the case was mine, and every time I remembered to tell you, you were busy, or called away, and I just forgot." What she was saying sounded like so many weak excuses—at least to her ears.

Silvestri went over and picked up the case. "Don't imagine there are any decent fingerprints left," he said. "I thought it was a pretty heavy case for such a little lady. I'll have that cup of coffee now . . . black." He smiled at Smith, who smiled back intimately. "It smells terrific."

Smith had made another conquest. Wetzon poured the coffee. There was a

plate of Oreo cookies on the tray. Wetzon hated Oreos and all packaged, pro-
cessed cookies. They were full of chemicals and artificial ingredients. Smith
didn't care about those things.

Silvestri sat on the sofa, and Smith curled up opposite him on the matching
ottoman. "Aren't you going to open it?" she asked eagerly.

Wetzon handed him a cup of coffee. He was looking at Smith.

"No," he said, "I'm going to want my lab people there when we open it."
His eyes drifted from Smith to Wetzon. "You didn't open it, by any chance?"

Wetzon busied herself pouring coffee into the other two cups, contriving not
to be free to look up. "Us? Oh, no," Smith replied innocently. "The case is
police evidence, isn't it? We wouldn't do that."

Silvestri looked dubious but didn't pursue it. He sipped the coffee, checking
out the room. Wetzon was certain he had seen the Tarot cards and wondered
what he thought.

"Who reads the cards?" he asked, as if reading her mind.

"I do," Smith said. "I read danger and death around Wetzon tonight. Danger and death and a dark-haired stranger." She smiled charmingly at Silvestri.
Silvestri smiled back at her. "I'll read yours for you sometime, Detective."

Wetzon suddenly felt de trop. She wanted desperately to be home in her
apartment, in her clean, neat bed. "Do you know anything more about who
killed Barry?" she asked.

With seeming reluctance, Silvestri took his eyes from Smith's. "No . . .
nothing conclusive. Too much data has to be gone through before we can narrow it down. We know he did make a phone call because he used a credit card,
so we were able to trace the number." He looked at Wetzon intently, as if wanting or waiting for her to react.

"But you're not going to tell us whom the call was to," Wetzon said.

"Right." He finished his coffee and stood. "Now I'll thank you, ladies. I
have a long night ahead of me." He looked at Wetzon. "Do you want that ride
home?"

"Oh, no," Smith said, obviously dismayed. "You can't go home tonight,
Wetzon. I really think you should stay here. You don't want to be alone."

But she did, and Smith didn't argue with her. She knew Wetzon was im-
movable when she set her jaw like that. Wetzon went into the bedroom to rescue
her jacket and handbag. She slipped the jacket over her shoulders and examined herself in the mirror again. *Forget it,* she thought. Silvestri wasn't thinking
of her that way. When she returned to the living room, Silvestri and Smith were
still smiling at each other. Wetzon felt put upon and jealous. It was Smith's
incredible magic with men. All men. What was it about her? She wasn't beautiful. She was tall and angular. It was an aura; something she gave off. But
Wetzon had seen Silvestri first. And had even told Smith she liked him. It
didn't seem at all fair.

God, she was bone weary.

Silvestri's silver Toyota was parked illegally in front of the building. Under the streetlight it sparkled. It was probably the cleanest car in New York City—on the outside. He wiped an invisible speck of dirt off the fender, then unlocked and opened the door for her. The inside of the car was even more of a horror than she remembered. The front seat was strewn with papers. On the floor were empty cans of Diet Pepsi. There were empty cardboard coffee containers and napkins, and half a hamburger was graying in another container . . . ROY ROGERS, it said.

"Maybe I should sit in the back," she suggested.

"Naa, just as bad." He was right. The back was filled with the laundry bag she remembered, and several cleaning boxes of shirts she hadn't noticed before. Silvestri collected the papers and books that were scattered on the front seat and dumped them unceremoniously on the backseat. The cartons and soda cans he swept up and stuffed in a crumpled paper bag that also lay on the seat. He leaned over and brushed the seat off with the sleeve of his jacket and helped her in, closing the door, then he carried the attaché case around to his side and put it in the back with his shirt cartons. The night was cool, and Wetzon took her jacket from her shoulders and slipped it on.

"Tell me about her," Silvestri said after he had settled himself in his seat and started the car.

"What do you want to know?" She didn't have to ask him who.

"Is there a husband?" He made a left on Seventy-ninth Street.

"She's divorced. She has a twelve-year-old son, Mark. What else would you like to know?" He was squinting at the lights. He probably needed glasses.

They were taking the transverse on Seventy-ninth Street, going west through Central Park. There was very little traffic. It was well after midnight.

"How did you meet?"

Wetzon settled back in her seat and started to tell him about the chiropractor with the terrible musical about dancers, the imitation *Chorus Line,* when Silvestri stepped on the brakes hard, and if it were not for his arm, which he stretched out in front of her—an automatic gesture from the old days of no seat belts—she would have smashed her head against the dashboard harder than she did.

That's all she remembered clearly. Dizzying pain stabbed through her head. *Hold on,* she thought. *Don't fall, can't fall.* But she couldn't fall. Something shoved her down, mercilessly. "Leave me alone," she said, but she didn't recognize the sound of her voice.

She heard a car door open and close in the distance and then another. She heard voices, shouts. Silvestri, perhaps. Someone yelled, "Police officer!" Then a popping noise, which somehow she knew was a gunshot. And another. "Motherfucker!" someone yelled. Car horns were sounding.

She was being tormented; someone was playing a drum solo on her head. The effort of opening her eyes aggravated the fierce pounding in her head. She was half on and half off the seat of the car. She pulled herself painfully up on the seat, only half aware of the sound of fabric tearing. Everything hurt. Her arms felt as if she'd been on a torture rack. They must have been hit or have hit something.

A cool, damp breeze brushed her face. The door on Silvestri's side was open and he wasn't there. She heard the strident whine of police sirens; lights swirled through the darkness. A white paramedic van pulled up, narrowly missing the open door. More flashing lights. Numbly, she thought, *Silvestri's car must be a mess.* She took hold of the steering wheel and pulled herself with some difficulty toward the open door.

Silvestri, without his jacket, his shoulder holster visible and serious, peered in at her. "Are you all right?" He touched her forehead. She pulled back, wincing. "I'm sorry," he said.

"Everything hurts like hell," she said. "But I think nothing is broken." A man in a blue windbreaker and white pants stood beside Silvestri.

"We'd better take care of that arm, sir," he said. "Miss, can you slide this way?" She saw blood on Silvestri's shirtsleeve, near his shoulder.

Wetzon looked out her right side and saw that they had smashed into a retaining wall of the transverse. God, they'd been lucky. She slid gingerly past the steering wheel, pulling her handbag with her. "I feel as if someone's been stomping on me," she said. No one paid any attention. The paramedic eased her out of the battered car. Poor Silvestri. His precious car. It looked totaled.

The back door was open, too. Everything that had been in the backseat was a big heap of trash. Instinctively, she leaned closer, looking for the attaché case. Silvestri was a few feet away from her, having his left arm bandaged by a female paramedic. He saw Wetzon look inside. They had ripped off one sleeve of his shirt to put on the bandage. Blood seeped through the white of the bandage.

"The bastards got the case," he said.

13

There were a thousand reasons why she didn't want to go to York Hospital, but Silvestri and the paramedics insisted, and Wetzon had no strength left to argue.

Lights from the police cars and the paramedic van spun like a kaleidoscope around her, swirling her up into the madness. Her head continued to complain loudly about the sudden meeting with the dashboard, and although the paramedics had patched the spot, she could feel the warm sensation of oozing blood.

She touched her hair and flinched at the surprising pain that shot through her lower back. Well, why not? Perfect way to end a perfect day: her lower back would go out. She tried to ignore the pain and awkwardly repinned her hair, not as neatly as she would have liked, but well enough.

There was a pseudocarnival atmosphere that belied the fact that there had been an accident, and a shooting. The radio phones in the police cars crackled on and off, issuing and receiving information.

They seemed to be waiting for Silvestri to finish up with the police on the scene before they left. Wetzon saw that the transverse had been blocked by police cars on both sides, and there was probably a car stationed at both the east and west entrances to the Park. The Park grounds above her also seemed ablaze with light, so they must have been searching for whoever had caused the accident and somehow stolen the attaché case.

She was sitting on a stretcher inside the van, concentrating on getting her thoughts together. Her face felt crusty, her lips and tongue thick and dry. She touched her face. Dirt or dried blood. Great. How beautiful she must look. Fumbling in her bag, she took out a small Wash 'n Dri envelope, tore open the wrapper, unfolded the sheet, and carefully dabbed at her face.

"What the hell are you doing?" Silvestri's arrival was so unexpected that she dropped the sheet. The second paramedic was helping him into the van. He carried his gun in its leather holster under his right arm.

"I'm cleaning myself up. What do you think I'm doing?"

"Do you always carry your own wet towel?" He seemed grumpy and annoyed. He sat on the stretcher opposite her. He looked awful.

"Yes." Her tone was snippy. He wasn't the only one feeling grumpy and annoyed.

Someone slammed the doors shut, closing them in. A siren blared.

"It would be best if you laid down," the female paramedic said from the driver's seat.

"I'm sorry," Silvestri said sheepishly to Wetzon, ignoring the paramedic. "I'm grumpy and annoyed."

She gave him a small, stiff smile. "So am I."

"Come on, folks," the other paramedic said. "We know you're tough, but down you go."

Wetzon pulled her feet up and lay back, astonished by how good it felt. She looked over at Silvestri. He had done the same. They stared at each other across the van as if from twin beds. *Aren't you ashamed?* she said to herself. *No,* she replied.

They began to move.

"What happened?" she asked softly.

"Some SOB in a pickup truck passed us and cut us off—"

"I didn't see a truck."

"No, there must have been two of them, because the one driving the truck took off, and the other got the attaché case while we were dealing with the crash."

"Did you get a look at him?"

"Not good enough. He was wearing dark sweats and something over his face, a ski mask. I went after him and he took a shot at me." His mouth twisted, but it wasn't a real smile. "Lucky for me he wasn't any good."

Wetzon looked at his bandaged arm. The dressing was stained red. She had never seen a gunshot wound. On the other hand, she had never seen someone murdered, either, until today. Or rather, yesterday.

"I heard more than one shot, I think," she said.

"Yeah, I got off a couple, but he got away. His buddy with the truck probably swung around and picked him up somewhere in the Park."

"They must have been watching for us when we left Smith's apartment. They saw where you put the case and followed us."

"Yeah." He sounded disgusted. "I'm a real schmuck. I should have been more careful."

"You couldn't think of everything," she said.

"I'm supposed to think of everything. It's my job."

Her head was throbbing and her ears felt strange. Silvestri's voice was funny. His lips were moving, but he wasn't making any sounds.

"What could have been in the case that was so important?" she asked, but the question seemed to come from far away.

She saw Silvestri lean toward her as she started to slip off the stretcher. She fell against a soft but resisting object.

"Oooof," Silvestri said.

This is ludicrous, she thought, but she couldn't move. Silvestri's face was looming over her.

"I don't know," he said as if from a great distance. "You tell me."

"Hey, Pulasky, you know they're searching the lockers?"

"I heard. That's why I'm here."

"You're a little late, man."

"They'll be doing us next."

"It's no joke, man."

"I wasn't kidding."

"Yeah, well, you better get rid of the—"

"Later. We've got company."

Thunderous noise. It was as if she were in a cafeteria, and people were talking loudly and slamming crockery and metal trays. How was she going to sleep? She tried to open her eyes. Her head ached. The sudden light stung her eyes. There were two blurry faces above her, one black, one white, both wearing white coats.

"Ah, there you are," the white-coated black person said. "Welcome back."

She started to sit up, but he put his hand gently on her shoulder. An involuntary groan. She sagged back on the table. "Wait a minute before you try to do anything. Then we'll get you into a wheelchair."

"A wheelchair?"

"I just want to get a few X rays to make sure there are no breaks, cracks, or chips," he said. He had a stethoscope tucked in his upper pocket and a name tag on the pocket that she couldn't read. Doctor something or other. The other man in the white coat winked at her and disappeared. For a moment she thought maybe he had never been there at all.

Silvestri stuck his head through the barely closed curtains, pulling the nurse who was rebandaging his arm along with him.

"One of my uniforms is here for you," he said. "If they spring you, he'll take you home. Intact," he added sheepishly.

In the bright light she could see a muscular arm and lots of dark hair. *Hirsuted,* she thought, feeling silly.

"Sergeant, hold still, please, or you'll start bleeding again," an impatient voice said, and Silvestri disappeared behind the curtain.

They wheeled her through a battery of X rays and what seemed like hours of manhandling and then back down to the doctor in the emergency room.

"You're okay," he told her. "Lucky girl. No stitches, no fractures, just a mighty headache. I'm going to check you in overnight."

"No way." Wetzon was firm. "If I can stand up and walk, I'm going home to my warm bed."

"Okay, okay, you don't have to get tough with me." The doctor threw up his hands mockingly. "Here's something for that headache you're having." He gave her a couple of capsules in a small, white plastic envelope that looked familiar.

"What are these?" she asked suspiciously.

"Aspirin, what do you think? They just have a little codeine added."

"I'm sorry, I don't like to take pills. Do I have to take them?"

"Not if you don't need them."

"Where did you hide my jacket?" she asked. She stood up cautiously. Everything still seemed to be working. "I feel bruised and banged up, but I'm all right." She looked down at her blouse. There was a tear in the shoulder, and there was dirt and blood on her clothes, probably from Silvestri's car floor and her cut head.

"You've had a bad crack on the head," the doctor said, "and you're going to be a Technicolor delight for the next week or so, but I predict you'll live."

A nurse brought her jacket and her bag and wheeled her to the exit, where a uniformed policeman was waiting. As a matter of fact, there were a lot of police in and around the emergency room. Silvestri must have summoned them, but it seemed a little redundant now that the case was gone. She looked back at the doctor to say goodbye, to thank him, but he was already handling the next emergency.

The ride home was fast, and when they got to her building she leaned forward to get out of the car. "You can just drop me here."

"No, ma'am, I have orders to see you into your apartment and check it out before I leave you."

"Oh." She wasn't going to argue with that. She was relieved that Silvestri had thought of it. But, as he had said, it was his job.

Her apartment was dark and quiet. She put on the lights in each room, and the cop walked through, looked quickly around. There was really no place for anyone to hide. The door had been double-locked as she had left it.

"Okay to check the closets?"

"Sure."

"Do you have a fire escape on this building?"

"No."

"A back door?"

"Yes. This way."

He opened the back door. It was clear. He closed it, turning the lock.

"I'll say good night, then," he said. She let him out and double-locked her door. Leaning on it, she kicked off her shoes.

"Jesus, what a night." She glanced at her watch. It took a moment before the hands floated into sight. Three-thirty.

She dropped her jacket and handbag on the bed and went down the hall to the bathroom. She flipped the light switch on, and a hideous black waterbug was revealed in the middle of her bathroom floor.

"Oh, my God," she cried. "This is too much." She knew she had to kill it because she couldn't stand the thought of it being alive somewhere in the apartment.

Considering how battered she was, she moved quickly, stepping on the disgusting creature with her stockinged foot. She felt it squirm horribly under the ball of her foot, but she continued the pressure until her foot touched the cold tile of the floor.

Gagging, she grabbed a wad of tissues from the box on the counter and wiped the mess from her foot and the floor, flushing the evidence down the toilet. She tore off her pantyhose and dropped them to the floor, bent over the toilet bowl, and vomited the remnants of the tea and toast she had had at Smith's all those hours ago. Sweat and tears rolled down her face. She turned on the shower and got into it with her clothes still on, tearing them off under the hot water. The gash in her forehead stung terribly, but the heat and the water were cleansing. Slowly, she began to relax. She took the rest of the pins out of her hair and put them on the side of the tub and let the hot water pour over her.

She left the bathroom wrapped in a big raspberry-colored bathtowel, with another towel around her head. Making a beeline for the bed, she pulled back the quilt and crawled in.

Something clanked on the bare floor. She groaned and peered down over the bed. Her jacket and handbag had fallen to the floor but neither would have made that metallic sound. Something must have dropped out of her jacket pocket. *What now?* she thought.

On the floor near her jacket was a matchbook. It shouldn't have made that noise. She leaned over and reached for it. The effort was agonizing. Her hand closed on the matchbook. She turned it over in her hand. It was gray. Something metallic was sticking out of the matchbook, wedged under the matches. She pulled it out. It was a small key.

14

The loud groan Wetzon emitted was more like a shriek as she threw the key and the matchbook against the far wall. More clatter from the goddam key. She stretched out as best she could under the covers, pulling them over her head. She lay still, breathing hard. Her clenched fists beat the mattress. She was furious.

It wasn't fair. She'd had enough. Really had enough. It was like some weird joke. How shall we torture Wetzon now? What new thing can we do to her . . . now let's see. . . .

Then the memory of poor, crazy Barry came through vividly . . . in living color . . . in dying color.

"You know, I really think of you as my friend," he had said. "You listen to me, you give me good advice, even if I don't take it, and you never even make any money off me."

"Oh, shit, shit, shit." Her voice was muffled under the covers. Deliberately, she eased herself out of bed. She crumpled up the towels she'd wrapped herself in and dropped them on the floor. She stood naked, half-bent, peering at the floor near the far wall, looking for the key.

She found the matchbook near the base of the old oak trunk that served as a television stand. But no key.

Well, there was no way out. She got down on her hands and knees to look for it. With difficulty and some pain, she forced her bruised arms, legs, and back into a pretzel position. She'd heard the key clank, so she knew it was not on the bed. It had to have landed in the same area as the matchbook. But if it was visible, she was going blind, too. She pulled herself into a cross-legged, meditative position and closed her eyes, breathing deeply, deep stomach breaths.

Think nice, calm thoughts, she ordered herself.

What if the key had slid under the chest of drawers? Aha! She lay on the floor, breathing herself flat. It was a feat of no small physical effort. Tentatively, she pushed her hand under the narrow opening at the bottom of the painted cottage chest of drawers. She got, for her efforts, a handful of dust balls.

"Yuk, and thanks a lot. I don't have to be reminded." She pulled herself up into a kneeling position again, every movement agony. *Think this through.* Another great idea: *The flashlight.* It took another eternity to get her body to the linen closet, where she kept the flashlight. God willing, the batteries were still good. They were.

Back to the chest of drawers. She flattened herself out again and put the flashlight next to the opening under the chest, then peered in, cheek to the cool floor. There it was, glinting near the back, amid a mass of more dust balls. She stood, grabbed some tissues from the box near the bed, then tried to push the chest away from the wall. The pain in her back was excruciating. Her head was killing her. She would call Sonya tomorrow to help her work her back out, but right now she'd get the goddam key and call it a day. Or rather, a night.

She gave a hefty push, and the chest inched away from the wall. It was enough. There was the little key, almost lost amid the dust clumps. Very, very slowly, she did a deep knee bend instead of bending over from the hips. She picked up the key, then scooped up all the dust clumps with the tissues, dumping them in the old copper stockpot she used as a wastebasket.

The small key in her palm looked a little like a mailbox key. It was a brass color and had rather squared-off teeth. She stuck it back into the matchbook where it had rested for who knows how long. She knew for sure that neither had been in her suit jacket yesterday morning, because she always emptied her pockets before she hung up anything in her closet. Therefore, it had to have been put in during the day. Yesterday.

She remembered how closely Barry had held her elbow as they climbed the stairs to the balcony at the Four Seasons. He could have slipped it into her pocket then. Very easily, as a matter of fact.

She put the matchbook on the bedside table. She'd think about it tomorrow. She couldn't think of one more thing tonight. She picked up her handbag, considered taking one of those aspirins the doctor had given her, then decided against it and hung her bag on the doorknob.

She turned out the light, crept back into bed, and slid down under the covers. She took two or three deep breaths, and then she slept.

The next thing she knew, she was on the Floor of the New York Stock Exchange, thinking; *What the hell am I doing here?* But everyone was shouting, and no one seemed to be paying any attention to her.

She was still wearing her gray pinstriped suit, and a man came toward her, a name tag on his lapel, carrying an extra large, dripping ice cream cone. As he came closer, she saw it was strawberry. *Who eats strawberry ice cream anymore?* she thought. *And what's he doing on the Floor with such a huge ice cream cone anyway?* She was sure it wasn't allowed. And as she thought that, he walked right into her, and the strawberry ice cream fell in a red glob on the left front of her suit jacket.

"They're searching your gym clothes," he said, winking familiarly. He seemed genuinely upset, taking off his white coat. Why was he wearing a white coat? He began to smear the strawberry ice cream on her breast. She pushed him away, but they kept getting tossed about by the surging humanity around them, yelling stock quotes and waving arms in the air.

She was usually very turned on by the activity on the Floor, but not today. Today she was very angry. She didn't know what she was doing there, and now she'd gotten her clothing in a mess, which was something that never happened to her.

"You got strawberry ice cream all over me," she said peevishly.

"It's not strawberry," he said, wiping her with the sleeve of his white coat. "It's rocky road."

"Oh, for heaven's sake," she said, "who cares."

The man looked grieved. "Okay, okay," he said, "you don't have to get touchy with me."

She began dabbing at the mess with a Wash 'n Dri which she found in her hand. She looked down and saw that she was wearing a leotard under her suit.

"My God," she said, "what's going on?" As if in response, Smith came through the crowd of screaming traders on the Floor as natural as could be, wearing her crimson-and-black flowing robe.

"Smith," she called, waving and jumping up and down. "I'm so glad to see you. Get me out of this!"

"What are you doing here? This is very unfair of you," Smith said, scolding. "You don't belong here. This is my territory. And besides, the closing bell is about to go off."

And just that second, as she said it, it did. But it didn't stop as it always did. It just kept on ringing, and ringing, and ringing.

Wetzon woke to the sound of the telephone.

Moaning, she inched one arm out from under the covers. The pain was unbelievable. *No breaks, huh, Doctor? Little do you know.* The blasted phone persisted. Her head ached. She grabbed the whole phone and pulled it under the covers with her. She picked up the receiver, squeezed her eyes shut, and waited.

"Wetzon? Wetzon, are you there? Answer me!"

"Hello, Smith." Even talking hurt.

"You sound ghastly, Wetzon."

"We were in an accident after we left you last night—in the Park. Someone stole Barry's attaché case."

"Are you damaged?" The toughness in Smith's voice disappeared.

"Only slightly."

"Good. Where was the wonderful Silvestri?"

"He was wounded in the arm."

"This is beginning to sound dangerous, Wetzon. I don't like it."

"And I do? Jesus Christ, Smith, someone's been murdered. Of course it's dangerous." Smith was incredibly irritating.

"There's a purpose to my call, Wetzon. I want you to listen carefully," Smith said, ignoring her partner's bad temper.

Wetzon gritted her teeth. "What time is it?"

"Nine," Smith said. "Listen carefully to me. When we finish talking, put your answering machine on. Then go back to sleep. You sound terrible. I'll talk to you later."

"Wait. What's going on?"

"Your picture is on the front page of all three papers, and very enlarged in the *Post* and the *News*. You're being called the mystery woman in the case."

"Oh, no."

"Oh, yes. And someone else is bound to recognize you."

"My phone is unlisted."

"Don't be naïve. Do you really think that will help?" Smith said impatiently. "We'll talk later . . . when you're really awake."

Wetzon mentally played back *someone else is bound to recognize you.* "Wait, don't hang up," Wetzon groaned. "What do you mean, someone else?"

"I mean," Smith said, "you had a call about fifteen minutes ago from Mildred Gleason."

15

Wetzon pulled on her white terry robe and limped down the hall to the dining room, where she kept her answering machine. The phone began to ring just as she turned it on to auto answer. Shivering, she waited to hear who it was. The apartment always had an early morning chill because she kept the radiators turned off, and it took a little time before the sun took over.

It was a reporter from the *News*. Well, it hadn't taken them long to find her. The reporter very crisply left his name, Calvin Sperling, and two phone numbers.

She leaned against the arched doorway, eyeing her barre warily. In her condition, even with her strong will, she didn't have the nerve.

The phone rang again. It was Silvestri. He left his name and what he called his direct number. She didn't feel like talking to him, either, so she let the tape run and he hung up.

She went into the kitchen. The sun streamed through the dusty window, fine New York City dust here, mixed with a little black soot, and her chipper little basil plant was bending toward the light like an acquiescent woman.

She took the apple juice out of the refrigerator and poured herself a small glass.

The phone rang again. She listened to the voice of Teddy Lanzman, an old friend who worked at Channel 8 local news. She hadn't seen him in a long time.

"Wanna talk, old buddy?" he was saying. There was a long pause. She knew that he knew she was listening. "Okay." He sounded disappointed. "Call me when you feel like."

She steered herself to the front door and waited, alert, then opened the peephole very quietly. Nothing. Just regular noise from the other apartments on the floor and the sound of the elevator on another floor.

She unlocked both locks and the chain, opened the door a crack, reached down awkwardly, gritting her teeth through the pain, took the newspapers from the mat, and pulled them in. Shit, there was a picture on the front page of the *Times* of her coming out of the Four Seasons with Jimmy Lyons, with her hand up in front of her eyes, looking as if they were taking her in for the murder. And there was the beginning of the story, STOCKBROKER MURDERED, to be continued in the B Section, page 35. She sat down on one of the stools in the kitchen and began opening vitamin bottles: one 2,000-unit C, one 400-unit capsule dry E, two calcium pills, and two bee pollen for extra energy—her daily fix.

"I really need you guys today," she said, popping them into her mouth one at a time and swallowing with the apple juice. Her forehead felt stiff and tender where the cut was healing.

She opened the paper. The phone rang again.

"Wetzon"—Smith again—"pick up if you can hear me."

Wetzon picked up and said, "Hold on, I'm here." She waited until Smith responded, then turned off the answering machine. It made a small coo-coo noise, as it always did. And even today, it made her laugh. Even today. Well, why not? She needed the laugh more today than she usually did.

"How are you feeling now?" Smith demanded.

"I'm up and moving. Slowly."

"Silvestri called here," Smith said. "He wants you to come to the precinct at four. Something about a statement."

"I guess I have to do that . . ." she said wearily.

"Why don't I pick you up around three and go over with you?" Smith said it so casually that Wetzon's ears tingled.

"You don't have to do that; I'm a big girl."

"Oh, I'd like to," Smith said, "after what you've been through . . . and besides, I'm having dinner with Silvestri tonight." She giggled suggestively.

Wetzon was silent for a moment, sad about this turn of events. "Aha," she said. "I knew there was more to it. I was sure he had a thing about you. And you, you were turning on the charm. It was *that* thick."

"How did you know he was interested?" Smith asked sharply. "Tell me." It was as if Wetzon had never confided in her that she—Wetzon—was attracted to Silvestri. Could Smith have possibly forgotten?

"Oh, all the questions he was asking about you in the car, before the accident."

Smith's voice came back tense: "What kind of questions? What did you tell him?"

"What do you mean, what kind of questions? Whether you were married, that kind of question. What do you think I would tell him?" She was puzzled by Smith's reaction. But then Smith was eccentric and reacted in peculiar ways to what appeared to Wetzon to be simple events.

Smith laughed now, a hooting, triumphant laugh. "A lot of things are happening," she said. "Guess who called us and wants to talk about a search?" She loved playing I've-got-a-secret, and usually Wetzon went along. At this moment, however, Wetzon was tired and irritated. Probably because of Silvestri. Smith liked conquests, but Silvestri was a detour for her. She usually went after men with a lot of money—money and power. What did Silvestri have? Easy.

Power. And she, Wetzon, had found him attractive in spite of it. Wetzon was not attracted to men because of power, or money for that matter. So was Smith competing with Wetzon? And if so, why?

"Well?" Smith said. "Did you fall asleep? Aren't you going to guess?"

"Oh, I'm sorry." Wetzon had tuned out. Now she was annoyed with herself for feeling resentful. It was petty of her. If Silvestri liked Smith, he liked Smith, and Wetzon wasn't going to make any difference. "I don't know. Tell me."

"Weinberger Brothers." She was very excited. It was an account she'd been trying to land for two years.

"Wow! Okay, I'm impressed. Why do you suppose—"

"We've been summoned to lunch with them on Tuesday. Actually, they wanted to meet Monday, but I put them off till Tuesday because I didn't know how you'd feel."

"You could have gone alone."

"But, my dear, they specifically asked that we both be there." There was an odd coolness in the way Smith spoke that indicated she was not happy that they had asked for Wetzon to be there. Wetzon shrugged it off. Smith considered all clients her territory and didn't like to be thwarted. Well, too bad. For once Wetzon felt a small thrill of pleasure that Smith didn't always get to have everything her way.

"That's really very nice, Smith. I'm sure I'll be fine by next week. Wait a minute . . . what's today . . . I've lost track."

"Wednesday."

"Well, forget my staying home. Carlos comes today. In fact, he should be here any minute, and he'll be nosy as hell if he's seen the papers."

"Are you sure you feel strong enough?"

"I'll be just fine," Wetzon said dryly. "I'll be down in a little while, and we can go to see Silvestri from the office." She stopped suddenly. "Smith?"

"Yes, what's wrong?"

"I found a strange key in my jacket pocket."

"What kind of key?"

"Small. Mailbox maybe. I think Barry must have slipped it to me when I was with him yesterday. I'll bring it with me and give it to Silvestri."

She hung up the phone thoughtfully and went back to the kitchen. She filled the kettle with water, placed the paper filter in the Melitta holder, then measured out the coffee—enough for four cups because Carlos liked his coffee and a croissant before he started cleaning.

Carlos Prince had been her housekeeper since they'd met years earlier in a dance class. They had danced together in quite a number of shows in those days. Housekeeping was his way, as he said, of "keeping the wolf from the door," and he had done very well with it. He had done so well that now he could sit in his Greenwich Village apartment while legions of housekeepers worked for him all over the City.

His very special people he kept for himself. Special people meant people from the old days, good for a gossip. Old friends leading interesting lives. And it was an all-cash business. "Besides, darling, I'm getting a little long in the tooth for the chorus line," he'd say.

She smiled as she took the chain off the front door. She was sure he'd come early today because he'd have seen her picture in the papers, and this was just the sort of thing Carlos loved to be in on. A murder. Intrigue. Money. The Four Seasons.

The hot shower revived her, and when she came out of the steaming bathroom in her terry robe, she heard music.

"Well, good morning glory," Carlos said. He was sitting comfortably in the kitchen on one of the high stools, his legs crossed, all the newspapers spread out on the countertop. The Temptations were singing, "My Girl" in splendid voice. "You've been a very busy little beaver since I saw you last." He shook his finger at her. "Naughty, naughty. And you don't even look too bad."

"Carlos, come on now, it was terrible," she said, drying her hair with the towel.

"Oh, tell. Tell everything. Don't leave anything out," he said greedily. His dark eyes sparkled. Everything about Carlos sparkled. He was slim and dark and strikingly handsome. Today he was wearing a vivid Hawaiian shirt and tight Guess jeans. He had a large diamond stud in his left earlobe.

"I don't know much except a man I was interviewing left me to make a phone call and he was murdered in the phone booth."

"And you saw it—" Solicitously he jumped up and gave her the stool. He pulled over the other stool and sat, watching her. "I brought you a chocolate croissant," he said, beseeching.

A bribe. As if she didn't know. The rich smell of chocolate and butter was overpowering. The little rat. "You're bribing me, you little rat," she said, kissing his smooth, dark cheek.

"But of course, darling."

The phone rang. They both listened attentively.

"Ms. Wetzon, my name is Carpenter, Walt Carpenter, *Wall Street Journal.* I'd like to talk with you at your convenience." It was a very polite, nice voice, entirely in keeping with the professionalism of the *Journal.*

"Mmmmm," Carlos cried, licking his lips. "You're an absolute celebrity. You lucky witch."

Carlos called her a witch because he felt she'd turned his life around since they'd met.

"It's a hell of a way to get celebrity," she complained. "I'd rather have done it with Gower." They both laughed. It was their bitter, black joke, because Gower Champion had been their choreographer, they'd always worked when he'd worked, and now Gower was dead. He had died during the production of *Forty-second Street,* and a lot of people in the theater community felt that David

Merrick had made it seem as if David Merrick himself had done the direction and the choreography. "I've got to get dressed and get to the office," she said, giving Carlos a quick hug.

"Oh no, darling, tell more." He poured coffee into a cup and pushed it and the chocolate croissant toward her on the counter. She was starving, and the croissant looked delicious.

"I don't know more, but stay tuned. I have to give a statement to the detective on the case later this afternoon. This is good, Carlos, you devil." She polished off the croissant and coffee.

"What a joy. Detectives, statements. I love it." Carlos jumped off the stool, wriggling to the music. "Remember everything, and I mean *everything*, so you can fill me in."

She dressed carefully. Dark blue gabardine suit, to match her bruises, and a white silk blouse. She clipped her mother's cameo pin to the blouse at her throat, and, a little defiantly perhaps, put large gold hoops in her ears. She had ruined the skirt to her gray suit by getting into the shower with it. Maybe the cleaner could salvage it.

She could hear Carlos in the kitchen, singing, clattering, beginning his cleaning. The music was playing loudly, Aretha Franklin's "You Make Me Feel Like a Natural Woman." Ha! Right now she felt like an unnatural woman, with all her aches and pains, but her body, seduced by the music and finely tuned from years of dancing, began to move and turn with the beat.

She ran a narrow-toothed comb through her hair and with a couple of twists had it up in its knot, without looking in the mirror. She'd been doing it for so many years, she could do it in the dark. She checked the mirror now as she quickly pinned it in place and applied gray eye shadow and mascara sparingly. She didn't like the look of the bruise on her forehead, so she rolled a silk scarf into a narrow band and tied it around her head. She was ready to face the world.

Wait. The key. Where had she put it? In the matchbook. She found the matchbook on the chest next to her bed, where she had left it last night—or rather, early this morning. She pulled the key out of the matchbook. Innocuous-looking thing. She dropped the gray matchbook, which had a palm tree silhouetted on it, back on the chest.

The telephone rang again. She put the key into her jacket pocket and went to listen to the message. Carlos had turned down the music and was listening, too. She grinned at him. He was such a cutie. So obvious and open. She loved him.

"Hello, Miss Wetzon." The voice had a Middle European accent. "This is Georgette Klinger. We are confirming your appointment with us for tomorrow at twelve noon with Rosa."

After the hang-up and the sound of the machine clicking off, there was absolute silence. Then a guffaw from Carlos.

"How about that for celebrity?" She laughed.

"Well," he said, "you *did* get Georgette Klinger herself." And they both laughed again because, of course, Georgette Klinger never made phone calls herself to confirm appointments. Anyone who called always said she was Georgette Klinger.

"I'll have to break that appointment when I get to the office," Wetzon said.

"Don't you look great in your uniform," Carlos said bitchily, one hip forward, flourishing his hands.

"Oh, shush. And don't answer the phone." She put the *Times* and the *Journal* into a Bloomingdale's shopping bag. Her briefcase was still at the office.

"Don't worry, darling, just keep me informed." He gave her a kiss on the cheek. "And take care of yourself," he said very seriously. "You know, there aren't very many of us left."

"I know," she said, equally serious, closing the door. "I know."

She got off the elevator warily and felt mildly disappointed when no one was around except Larry, the doorman, who was sitting on the sofa in the lobby, feet planted firmly on the marble floor, smoking and reading the racing form.

"Morning, Ms. Wetzon," he drawled, not getting up. He was about ready to retire, so he didn't put out more than minimum effort anymore. "There's a lady waiting for you out front."

"There is?" She peered out the front door.

"Leaning on the car that's double-parked . . ."

Yes, a woman in brown pants and a brown tweed jacket. "Thanks, Larry." She went out the door fast, not looking.

"Oh, Ms. Wetzon, may I speak with you?"

She ignored the call and walked into the street to hail a cab. Several went by, occupied. She grunted and brought her sore arm down to her side. Finding an empty cab at this hour on the Upper West Side was always difficult. The woman came and stood next to her.

"I'm with the *Wall Street Insider*. Julie Davidson. I'd really like to talk with you." She didn't push. She just said it easily. No pressure.

Wetzon turned and looked at her. She had a friendly face, lots of freckles, thick, bleached hair in an old-fashioned flip. A solid figure in her brown pants and jacket. She was a little older than she appeared at first glance.

"About what?" Wetzon asked as coldly as she could.

Julie Davidson looked at her, slightly amused. "About the murder of Barry Stark."

Wetzon nodded, relenting somewhat. "I can't talk about that. The police have asked me not to say anything."

"Perhaps at some point you will be able to talk, and I would really appreciate your giving me some time." Julie Davidson held out a card.

"Okay." Wetzon took the card, automatically slipping it into her pocket with the key. Then she took the card out quickly and put it in her handbag, and checked her pocket again for the key. It was still there.

It was much later than she usually left for the office, and she saw that Sugar

Joe had already pulled up stakes and left his spot on the corner of Amsterdam Avenue near the bus shelter.

Months ago, she had first noticed the addition to the neighborhood of a pile of garbage lying near the bus stop shelter on Amsterdam and Eighty-sixth Street covered by a medium blue wool blanket with a "made in England exclusively for Bloomingdale's" label. Her first thought had been why would anyone cover garbage like that, then the horrific realization that there was a living thing under the oblong clutter. There was also a cardboard container of coffee at one end. The head end? One of those collapsible luggage carriers lay on the ground, like a pillow, probably where the head was under the blanket.

The individual, who had turned out to be a man of indeterminate age, perhaps mid-fifties or older, immediately became a local fixture. Most of the people in the neighborhood, including Wetzon, had never seen him. But those who had tried to help him get to a city shelter described him as tall and very thin, with shoulder-length white hair. He didn't like either the city shelters or the do-gooders. He was always back on the street very quickly. He seemed to go somewhere during the day, but he was in place each evening, and he was there early every morning, for she had seen him at those times. He always returned to the same spot.

Wetzon had begun to think of him as a stockbroker. Maybe he went to his office during the day and came back to his spot every evening. It was a joke, but it wasn't. In New York City these days and in the brokerage business, nothing was too farfetched.

All Sugar Joe ever accepted was coffee, which he liked light, with cream and sugar, three envelopes. Wetzon had discovered this one day when she set two containers of coffee near the lump under the blanket and heard a rough voice say, "Six sugars." Not "thank you." Despite her dismay at his lifestyle, she had laughed.

The kids in the neighborhood had begun calling him Sugar Joe, and the name stuck. It became part of Wetzon's morning ritual to leave him his two cups and for him to grunt at her. How he could see anything from under the blanket, she could never understand.

This was the first weekday morning in months that she did not leave him coffee, and she felt a twinge of remorse.

A cab finally stopped in response to her wave, and she got into it, moving with some difficulty. Everything hurt. Her back was protesting. Sitting forward, she gave the driver her office address and leaned back. She slipped *The Wall Street Journal* out of her shopping bag and unfolded it to the front page. Thank God, the *Journal* didn't use photographs. She saw the small item in the "What's News" section: "Broker slain" and just a small paragraph with the facts as she knew them. Nothing new here. She was relieved. She let her eyes run over the front page. They stopped before she was mentally aware of what they were seeing. Her eyes froze on a sharp headline: COLLAPSE OF KAPLAN, MORAN SECURITIES, INC., datelined Atlanta, Georgia. She read quickly:

Kaplan, Moran, a government securities firm based in Atlanta collapsed yesterday when a great number of clients requested delivery of collateral for their loans to the firm. Official word came from federal banking and securities officials. Clients stand to lose over $7 million. Kaplan, Moran was involved in repurchase agreements, repos, a type of borrowing where a securities firm sells government securities to a client, then buys them back at a higher price on an agreed upon date, from 30 to 270 days. The firm also did reverse repos, where it bought the securities from the client, promising to sell them back later.

A spokesperson for the SEC stated that fraud began after the firm started to have heavy trading losses. It then used money from clients' accounts to cover up these losses. . . .

16

The lunch crowd on Second Avenue was early today, but that was probably because of the balmy weather. It wasn't even noon, and people were already lined up at the sandwich shops and salad bars, buying lunch which they would then eat outdoors in one of the pocket parks that dotted Manhattan's business sections.

Traffic was clogged on Forty-ninth Street between First and Second Avenues because a private garbage-collection truck was blocking the street.

"Stop!" Wetzon commanded. "I'll get out here."

The cabdriver braked to a short stop on the west side of Second Avenue. Tires squealed behind them as another cab stopped short. Wetzon paid the fare, got out, and waited for the light to change. A woman in a black leather trenchcoat, large sunglasses, and a floral silk scarf tied under her chin got out of the second cab and walked in the opposite direction, west on Forty-ninth Street.

The sunlight was dazzling in Wetzon's eyes. . . . Kaplan, Moran . . . She'd never heard of the firm, but they did the kind of business Barry had said Jake was involved in, and they had gone under. Could that have something to do with Barry's murder? Had Barry found out something about Jake Donahue that was bad enough to get him killed?

The light changed, but traffic gridlocked; drivers of cars and delivery trucks leaned on their horns. The burly garbagemen continued to load garbage, paying no attention to the traffic jam they'd created. Two massive men got out of a stalled moving van and began shouting obscenities at the garbagemen, who dropped what they were doing, to respond in kind. The scene was getting ugly. A boisterous crowd gathered, not averse to mixing into the fracas.

Thinking it was as good a time as any to cross, Wetzon was about to step into the street when she saw a bicycle delivery person, in a sleek black jumpsuit with a blue stripe down the side, come barreling down Second Avenue on a lean racing bike, weaving in and out of the traffic and people. She paused. An ambulance siren screamed. Vehicles squeezed right and left to let the ambulance by. Now the figure on the bicycle seemed to be racing the ambulance. Wetzon stood on the edge of the sidewalk, waiting till the ambulance passed. At that moment, she felt a hand on the small of her back, a sudden tremendous pressure, and she pitched forward. Angry, blinded by the sun, she started to turn and was pushed again, harder, directly into the path of the ambulance.

Wetzon tottered, regained her balance, barely, as the ambulance swerved sharply. And as she stepped back, she was grazed by the messenger on the speeding bicycle. He cursed her angrily, so close that she had felt the heat of him and the breeze in his wake. She stood shaking in the street.

"Hey, close call," someone said. A man.

"Are you all right?" asked a dumpy little woman carrying a Saks shopping bag. "Those bicycles! They should be outlawed!"

Wetzon nodded, unable to speak. She touched her forehead. Either she was getting accident-prone, or . . . All at once, she remembered the purposeful pressure on her back and shuddered.

She scanned the crowd behind her, but no recognizable face stood out among the crush of curious bystanders.

She crossed the congested street with care, avoiding the angry citizens around the garbage truck, and walked down Forty-ninth Street to her office.

A man was standing in front of the brownstone. He was wearing sunglasses. Wetzon's heart stopped. She clutched the painted black iron railing of a fence in front of the brownstone two doors away from their office.

It was Barry Stark.

He spotted her and walked toward her. It wasn't Barry. She breathed again. He looked a lot like Barry, though, at least in the first instant. He was not as tall and his hair was long, but not curly, like Barry's, and, the fact was, he hardly looked like Barry at all. What was the matter with her?

As he came up to her he said, "Wetzon?"

He had a large head and a square jaw, and though he smiled at her pleasantly, he did not take off his sunglasses, the mirrored kind, and she couldn't see his eyes, just her reflection in the glasses.

"I'm sorry . . ." she began, backing away slightly.

"I'm Georgie Travers." He held out his hand, and she came forward and took it, thinking how oddly small his hand was. "Didn't mean to scare you. Just spoke with your partner. She's a tough broad. Wouldn't tell me where you were, if you were coming in." He smiled, narrowly opening his lips. "I called you at home, but got your machine—"

"Barry . . ."

"Yeah," he said, putting his hands in his pockets. He was wearing an off-white cotton hand-knit sweater and foreign-looking pants with pleats in the front and narrowing toward the ankles. He had the musculature of a weight lifter, which she could see through the sweater. On his feet were cut-out brown leather sandals and no socks. He looked like an Italian movie star . . . or a gigolo, she thought. "Yeah . . . I heard. Can we go somewhere and talk?"

"I can't now. I have appointments, and the police—" She stopped. It was none of his business.

"How about later? It's important."

"I don't know. Georgie, I can't tell you anything more than what you read in the papers."

"He was my best friend, you know." Georgie stepped closer. She remembered his reputation on the Street, the events that had forced him out.

"I know, Georgie, I know, and I'm sorry. I liked him. I'm really sorry."

"Please, Wetzon. It won't take long. He trusted you. *I* trust you." There was an implication of intimacy in his voice. It was a telephone style that some stockbrokers had, a form of seduction—into a sale. He took her hand in his. He was strong, and she was aware of how small she was. He could easily have pushed her in front of . . . She pulled away. This was crazy. He couldn't have. Georgie had been talking to Smith when it happened. Barry was his friend. Why would Georgie want to harm her?

"How about later, Georgie? I'll call you. Where can I reach you?"

He shrugged. "I'm around. Do you have a piece of paper?"

Wetzon pulled a clean sheet of paper out of her Filofax and gave it to him with her pen.

"These are my private numbers, at home and at the Caravanserie," he said.

"I'll call you late this afternoon. I promise." She edged around him to the door of her office.

He nodded, then walked a few steps in the direction of First Avenue. She was watching him with a vague sense of relief, when he turned unexpectedly.

"Wetzon," he said, a clear warning in his voice, "be careful what you say to the cops."

17

Smith was feeling disgruntled. Wetzon saw that the moment she came flying through the door after avoiding Harold's attempt to waylay her with questions about the murder.

She could tell by the set of Smith's magnificent shoulders, by the slight
declination of her mouth, that things were not going the way she wanted.

"Now look here," Smith was saying into the phone, "don't you dare put me
on hold. I want to talk with your supervisor."

Uh-oh, Wetzon thought. Whoever Smith had on the phone was in for it. She
dumped her shopping bag with the newspapers on the floor next to her empty
briefcase.

Smith turned, phone still at her ear, and gave Wetzon a chilly smile.

"Who's that in the front office with Harold?" Wetzon decided to ignore
Smith's mood. Hell, she was the one with the real problems at this point, not
Smith. Smith was probably in a sulk because she was envious of all the attention
Wetzon was getting thanks to Barry's murder. Smith was usually the center of
activity, representing the public image of their firm, handling their clients,
thriving on the attention.

Well, Wetzon thought, Smith could have it all. Wetzon was very happy
working with the brokers, holding their hands through the interview process
and listening to their problems. She liked the nurturing; Smith could keep the
P.R. Smith was so wrapped up in herself that she hadn't even noticed Wetzon's
bruised head.

"What?" Smith slammed the phone down. "What did you ask me?"

"I'm sorry I asked you anything." Wetzon sat at her desk and looked at her
calendar.

"Oh, now, Wetzon, don't get mad. I've had such a trying morning."

Trying? *She'd* had a trying morning? "How could you have had a trying
morning when Silvestri asked you out to dinner?"

"Oh, that's minor. I knew he would because I did the cards this morning."

Minor. So Smith thought it was minor when—

"What I mean is," Smith continued, riding roughshod through Wetzon's
thoughts, "what I'm saying, sweetie, is that of course I know you find him

attractive, but believe me, he's not for you. You could never handle him. You're so naïve about people. I told him that. I told him how worried I am about you, how anyone can take you in with a hard-luck story."

"Did you really? And what did he say to that, pray tell?"

Smith shrugged. "Truthfully, he was not very sympathetic. He would make mincemeat of you, sweetie. You should thank me."

The intercom buzzed. She snapped up the phone. "What?"

Wetzon turned her back on Smith and growled, "Thank you."

"Later," Smith said, hanging up. "Wetzon, I've told Harold to just take messages for you. The phones haven't stopped. This murder of yours is tying up our lines. Your notoriety is interfering with business."

Wetzon would have responded in kind, but Smith was saved by a knock on the door, and Harold scooted in without waiting for a response.

"Aaaaaa, Smith . . . Wetzon . . ." Harold hesitated. "Our interview . . . he's been waiting. . . ." He was twitchy with barely contained excitement because someone he had talked to on the telephone had been spectacularly murdered, and Wetzon was involved.

Wetzon couldn't help smiling. "What interview? That's what I've been trying to ask, Smith. Who is that young man in our outer office?"

"The cold caller," Harold said. "What do I do about him? Should he wait, or what?" He drummed his fingers on the door frame.

"Oh, that—" Wetzon had forgotten they were interviewing someone to take Harold's place so that they could move him up to associate.

Harold's drumming increased in intensity.

"Harold Alpert," Smith said sharply, "stop doing that this minute. It's very annoying."

"Please, Smith," he had that whine in his voice that she couldn't stand, "what do I do about the cold caller? Should he wait, or what?"

Smith swiveled in her chair and stared at him hard. "Cool down, Harold," she said. "You're making me crazy, and I can't think."

"Oh, I'm sorry, I'm sorry," he stammered. His skinny little body drooped. "But what should we do with him?" He always got depressed when Smith was disappointed in him. He wanted so much for her to think well of him.

"Why don't *you* interview him," Wetzon suggested.

"Of course, you interview him," Smith said, as if it had been her idea, turning on her most radiant smile, warming and reassuring him. "You don't care, Wetzon, do you? Of course you don't. Harold, you know what to ask him, and you can explain to him that we've had a personal emergency. If you like him, we'll ask him to come back and meet Wetzon and me."

"That's great, Smith, gee, that's great," Harold said, his chest expanding, all puffed up because Smith had given him the authority to do an interview.

"Just excuse yourself about having to answer the telephone, and keep screening those calls. Wetzon, that is what you want for now?"

Wetzon nodded.

Smith gave Harold a piercing look. "And tuck your shirt in, if you please."

He started to leave, obediently stuffing in his shirt. "And don't forget your jacket." His jacket hung sloppily half off his shoulders. He straightened his jacket, shamefaced, and tugged at his sleeves. Smith and Wetzon looked him over critically. It really didn't help. He was an untidy mess.

"Oh, here, I forgot." Harold thrust a mass of pink message slips at Smith and Wetzon and closed the door behind him.

Smith sighed. "I don't know why we bother. He's like another son."

"Except that Mark is more mature," Wetzon said.

"One of us is going to have to tell him to shave off his mustache and beard. With that nose and those glasses he looks as if he's wearing a disguise."

"Well, it ain't gonna be me." Wetzon laughed and flipped through her messages, separating the business calls from the personal ones. She knew that Smith was angling for her to do the dirty work.

"Damnation," Smith said, "that rotten Jeff Monahan didn't show up for his appointment in New Haven with Shearson Lehman. These brokers are all alike. You can never depend on them."

"Too bad. That ends him as a viable candidate, I suppose."

"I don't know. I'll have Harold call him and see what his excuse is this time. This is the second meeting the sleaze hasn't shown for. The last time, his car broke down, but he never even called to say he couldn't come."

"Well, we won't be able to show him to Shearson again, that's for sure."

"Wetzon, goddammit, look at this!" Smith waved a message in Wetzon's face. "Elliot Dunham, the branch office manager for Shearson in New Haven, left me a message saying just that, very succinctly. Harold should have told me about it when I walked in this morning, but he's distracted by this damn murder you've gotten involved in."

That's right, Smith, keep dumping on me, Wetzon thought, but she said, "Do you think we can show Monahan to another firm?"

"I don't know if it's worth the bother."

"He's a good producer."

"We'll see," Smith said. "Let's talk about it after Harold calls him and gets the latest excuse. More important, how are you? That's an ugly bruise on your forehead."

So you finally deigned to notice. "It looks worse than it feels," Wetzon evaded. "I'll be a lot better tomorrow." Her head throbbed and she had a burning sensation behind her eyeballs.

"That sleazebag Georgie Travers tried to muscle his way in here this morning," Smith said.

"I know."

"How do you know?"

"Because I just met him outside."

"The nerve," Smith said angrily. "I told him you weren't coming in today. I can't believe he's been hanging around out there all this time."

"What do you mean, all this time? I thought he just got here."

"Did he tell you that?" Smith demanded, hands on hips. Wetzon nodded. "What a creep. He was here over an hour ago. Ask Harold." She laughed. "Harold thought he was applying for the cold caller job."

"I don't understand." Wetzon shook her head, momentarily forgetting her wound. The unwary action brought on another spasm of pain, this time accompanied by nausea.

"You look terrible, sweetie," Smith said. "You should have stayed home today. I could have handled everything."

"But Silvestri—"

"Him, too." Smith patted herself on the shoulder.

I'll bet, Wetzon thought, feeling sorry for herself.

"Do you have the key?" Smith demanded. When Wetzon nodded, she said eagerly, "Let's see."

Wetzon reached into her pocket for the key, her heart fluttering for one moment when she felt for it and didn't find it, until her fingers located it in the corner of the pocket. She held it up in the sunlight that poured through their garden windows. The light made an enlarged reflection of hand and key in Smith's eyes. "Herewith, the McGuffin," Wetzon said dramatically, dropping the stubby key into Smith's outstretched hand.

"The what?" Smith mumbled, studying the key, not really listening.

"The McGuffin. What Hitchcock said was the object of the mystery—that which everyone is searching for, or something like that. You know, like the Maltese Falcon."

"Hitchcock? Are we working with a Hitchcock?" Smith looked up from the key and stared at Wetzon.

"No, no, I'm sorry, just a joke. I meant Alfred Hitchcock. Forget it."

"Mmmm," Smith said, "there are some numbers on this key. Scratched in."

Wetzon put her personal messages under the heavy marble peach paperweight that had been a thank-you gift from Laura Lee Day, a stockbroker she'd placed at Oppenheimer, and went through her business calls again, shuffling the important ones to the top. "Uh-oh, Rudy Reilly. They're zeroing in on me. Help." She slumped in her chair, suddenly tired and depressed. "It's too much . . . it's all too much." She groped for a Kleenex from the box in the desk drawer. Her head hurt, her back and shoulders ached. And she had ruined her favorite suit. "I've ruined my gray suit," she said tearfully.

"It's okay, honey, it's really okay." Smith got up from her chair, the key put aside for the moment, gathered Wetzon up, and patted her head. "You've been through a lot, and you haven't had much sleep. We'll go and have a nice lunch at Café 58, and then we'll let Silvestri handle everything. Okay?"

Wetzon smiled. Smith wasn't much of an intellect, and she could be selfish sometimes, but basically she was a decent, caring person. "I'd like that," she said, gratefully letting Smith take charge. She felt very shaky and vulnerable.

"I'll hold on to the key," Smith said, putting it into her pocket and patting it. "I think we ought to call Leon and try to get him to meet us for lunch so we can get a clear legal opinion on how to approach this."

Wetzon nodded. Smith was right. Smith was always right where business was concerned. She seemed to be so levelheaded, especially in times of crisis.

"I'll get him on the phone. You wash your face and fix your makeup."

Smith was humming when she dialed Leon Ostrow's office. Wetzon could see she felt much better now that she was taking charge. She was not at all good at being swept along in someone else's life.

"Oh, my God, I almost forgot," Wetzon whispered. "Take a look at this." She put the *Journal* article about Kaplan, Moran on top of Smith's desk. "This is what Barry started to tell me about, only he was talking, I think, about Jake Donahue's."

Smith stared at her, then glanced absently at the paper. She put her finger to her lips. "Oh, yes, is Leon there, sugar?" she said sweetly into the phone. "Yes, Xenia Smith. Well, hi there, you old sweet thing. How're you doing? I know." She became cool and professional. "*Everybody* recognized her. No, she's okay. No, I hadn't noticed your call, sweetie, we've had so many calls this morning. Listen, Leon, dear, we were wondering if you'd be able to join us for lunch. We have a four-ish appointment with the detective who's working on the case. How's one o'clock? Café 58. See you . . . What?" She looked startled. She stared at Wetzon. "You do? How interesting. We can talk about it when we see you, sweetie pie." She hung up.

"What did Leon say just now?" Wetzon asked.

"Wait a minute." Smith buzzed Harold.

"Yes, Smith." He sounded harassed.

"Reservation for three at one o'clock at Café 58."

"Ohhh, you're not going to leave me all alone here to handle the calls? What if the phones get tied up and I lose some calls?" He was whining again.

"You do the best you can. You've handled things alone before. This is no different. Don't be such a baby," she said icily.

"Right, Smith, I'm sorry. Gee, I didn't mean it. You know that. Smith, I liked Bailey Balaban."

"Who is Bailey Balaban?"

"The candidate for cold caller for us. You know, the one I interviewed. He just left."

"Okay, we'll talk about it tomorrow and arrange for him to come back and meet us next week." She looked at Wetzon. Wetzon nodded. "Do we have anyone with appointments to be confirmed today?"

"Yes. George Mallow with Alex Brown, after the close, at four-thirty."

"Well, you do it. And call Monahan and find out what the hell made him miss the second appointment. But take care of the reservation first."

"Okay."

Smith hung up the intercom. "I don't know what we're going to do with him."

"He's feeling left out." Wetzon was standing with her back to Smith, looking at their pretty, sunny garden with the white cast iron chairs. It seemed such a long time ago—and it was only yesterday—that the garden furniture was delivered.

"Who cares how he feels," Smith said. "It's his job to adjust to us."

"What did Leon say that was so interesting?" Wetzon turned back to look at Smith.

"Oh, nothing much," Smith said casually. There was a long pause. After Wetzon had turned back to the garden, Smith added, "Just that he represents Jake Donahue."

18

They were only nine blocks from Café 58, a small French restaurant just off Second Avenue, so they walked up Second Avenue. It was a glorious spring day.

They often ate at Café 58 because the food was good, the service even better. There was something rather homey about it—its attempt at East Side chic, thwarted by the inapt red-and-black houndstooth upholstery on the banquettes and chairs, probably left over from a previous incarnation at the same address.

They were greeted effusively when they arrived, Smith leading the way. The sharp contrast from the bright sunlight of the street to the muted lighting within made Wetzon dizzy, and she rested her hand on the warm, smooth wood of the bar to steady herself.

"Good afternoon, mesdames." The maître d' bowed. "Table for three today . . . how is that in the corner?" He knew that was where they preferred to sit, so it was like playing a charade, but they always went along with it.

"Perfection, as always," Smith said.

He led them to their table. "I would like a Lillet," Smith announced, after she was settled.

"And you, madam?"

"Diet Coke."

"Oh, really, Wetzon," Smith said, "don't you think you should have a light drink to help you relax?"

"No, I don't want to relax that much. I'd rather have the caffeine until we get Silvestri over with," Wetzon said testily. She hated it when Smith tried to take over her life, too, but she was usually less vulnerable and thus able to sidestep before Smith started on her.

Smith, who had been watching her closely, patted her on the arm. "Whatever you want, sugar."

"What did you see in the cards today?" Wetzon asked as their drinks were set in front of them.

"I didn't spend as much time with them as I would have liked," Smith replied evasively, not meeting her eyes.

"Now, come on, Smith, tell me."

"A strong, dark man has entered my life." Smith smiled.

"Silvestri, I guess," Wetzon said. "The cards are right again. And what else? What about me?"

Smith was busy studying the menu.

"Smith, you know that menu by heart, and you always have the cold poached salmon, so tell me. What did they say about me?"

"Danger for you, I'm afraid, my sweet." Smith seemed reluctant to elaborate. "Oh, good, there's Leon."

"Well, girls." Leon folded his lanky body in his standard baggy suit into a chair and peered at them through thick hornrimmed glasses. As usual, his glasses caught the wisps of hair around his ears and threw them every which way.

"Ladies," Smith and Wetzon corrected in unison. Leon shook his head solemnly. It was their long-standing joke that Leon could never get used to the difference between girls and women and ladies, what he called "the language of lib."

The maître d' brought Leon scotch on the rocks so quickly that he must have asked for it when he walked in the door. They watched him do his scotch ritual. He took a small swallow of the drink and held it in his mouth for a few seconds before swallowing. "Aaaaah," he said, not disappointing them. "Wetzon, what's a nice girl like you doing involved in a murder?"

"Leon, it was about an hour after we—"

Leon put up his hand. "Just tell me what actually happened," he said sharply. "The rest will keep."

Smith's eyes widened and she frowned at him. He shifted awkwardly in his seat as he caught Smith's reproof.

"Forgive me, Wetzon, business pressures. . . . Please continue." He moved his hand toward her, palm up, motioning her to begin. And he listened. Leon was the best listener. He scratched his head vigorously. Wetzon spoke; Smith interrupted a few times. Leon rubbed his forehead, scratched his nose. When Wetzon finished, he was silent for a few moments. He took off his glasses, cleaned them with his napkin, and put them on again. "Where is the key?" he asked.

"Here." Smith produced it.

"Looks like a safe deposit key. Except they're usually heavier than this." He handed the key back to Smith. "Of course . . . you have to give it to the police. What time is your appointment?"

"Around four," Smith answered.

The waiter was hovering. A busboy using tongs placed a fresh, crisp baguette on each bread plate.

"I'll have the poached salmon," Smith said, "and a salad with vinaigrette dressing."

"Same for me," Wetzon said.

"The liver," Leon said. "And the salad."

Wetzon broke her baguette into pieces, buttering each. She was starving. She realized she'd had almost nothing to eat in the last twenty-four hours, just the chocolate croissant that Carlos had brought her. And she could hardly remember eating it.

"I'd like to go with you, but I think you can handle it yourselves," Leon said, looking at Smith. "Unless, Wetzon, there's something you haven't told us . . ."

Wetzon shook her head.

"Just tell them what you know. They don't have reason to suspect you, do they, Wetzon?" His eyes, behind the thick glasses, were solemn.

"Leon, for godsakes," Smith said.

"That's all right, Smith," Wetzon cut in. "It bears asking, I think. No, Leon, I don't believe so."

"You'll do fine. I have a rather important meeting this afternoon, otherwise I would go with you."

"Jake Donahue?" Smith's voice was coy.

Leon poked at the slivers of ice in his glass with his index finger. "There's no harm in telling you now, because it went out over the wire about an hour ago. Donahue had a relationship with Kaplan, Moran . . . you know about that firm?"

"Yes," Wetzon said, eyes wide, her mind working.

"Kaplan, Moran?" Smith repeated, trying to place it.

"Yes, the Atlanta bond house that went belly up because of repos. They were closed down yesterday," Wetzon explained.

"There's an investigation going on now. The SEC is involved." Leon's tone was noncommittal, but his face was grim.

"How serious?" Wetzon asked.

"Serious."

"You know, don't you, that Barry Stark worked for Jake Donahue?" she said.

The luncheon plates were put in front of them.

"Another Lillet, please," Smith said.

No one picked up a fork or even looked at his plate.

"I know," Leon said. "Speaking for my client, Mr. Jacob Donahue, we would be very interested in what that little key unlocks." He looked from Smith to Wetzon, cutting a slice of liver and placing it in his mouth. He chewed very slowly and swallowed, enjoying the rapt attention of both women. "Because, my dears, and this is for your ears only, there is suddenly a great deal of money unaccounted for at my client's firm."

19

They sat at the table dawdling over coffee after Leon left. Wetzon felt the caffeine begin to revive her. Sometimes one needed a little artificial lift, she rationalized to herself, because she tried to stay away from most chemicals. This thought reminded her of the pills the doctor had given her. What had she done with them?

"Interesting," she said, wiping crumbs around distractedly. The little bits of bread bounced about on the white linen tablecloth as she moved her coffee spoon back and forth. "Smith—"

"Wetzon—"

They laughed.

"Leon seems upset," Wetzon said.

"Yes." Smith was thoughtful. "I suppose it's about Jake Donahue, but he really shouldn't have taken that tone with you."

"It's funny about his being there," Wetzon mused. "I wonder if he was there when it happened."

"Where? What are you talking about, Wetzon?"

"Leon. He was there. He was at the Four Seasons last night. I ran into him before I met Barry."

"Leon? He was *there?* I can't believe it." Smith was indignant. "Why didn't he tell me? Who was he with?"

"I don't know. It was crowded and I couldn't see—and now that I think of it, he wasn't anxious for me to see, either—" She remembered the way he'd stood, deliberately blocking her view of the bar area, how he had walked her to the chairs.

Smith patted Wetzon's hand. "Leave it to me, sweetie. I'll find out. Don't say anything to anybody about Leon being there . . . not even to Silvestri. . . ." She took the key out of her pocket. "Right now, we have more important things to think about."

They both stared at the key.

"What do you think it was—" Wetzon started.

"What if we—" Smith said. "What if we *didn't* give the key to Silvestri?"

"What do you mean?"

"I mean . . . not right away."

Wetzon was quiet for some moments.

"Wetzon?"

"We couldn't do that," Wetzon said. "It's evidence in a murder."

"Of course, we can't *keep* the key, but that's not the point. We could just *hold* it for a while and see if we can find out what it unlocks. What could it hurt? And we might even make some money while we're doing it—let's say a finder's fee." Smith was smiling her crooked smile, being very sweet and persuasive. "Listen, sweetie pie, you're tired now, and you've been through a lot. Why not wait until you're thinking clearly? I really could handle this for you. For *us*."

"No, Smith," Wetzon said firmly, taking the key. "I don't want to withhold evidence. It's bad enough I walked off with Barry's attaché case without thinking."

"Now, now, sweetie, I wasn't suggesting anything about withholding, just waiting. But of course we'll do whatever you want." She patted Wetzon's hand again, obviously humoring her.

Sometimes Wetzon wondered what she was doing in this kind of work. Although she denied it vehemently, Smith seemed to be motivated only by money. "The object," she always said, "is to get the money out of his pocket and into mine."

In fact, everyone in this business seemed to be motivated only by money. Oh, the brokers gave lip service to how they protected their clients, but when push came to shove, and the commissions were not rolling in, even the best had sold a stock to someone who had no reason to buy it. And the headhunters? They were no different, although Wetzon had never sold anyone on a move she didn't think was a good career choice. But she wondered about herself, too. It wasn't that she didn't like money. She did. But the securities business was surrounded by an almost overpowering aura of greed. It was as if making money wasn't enough. It was a contagion, this money, and greed was the disease. How much was enough?

"More coffee, mesdames?"

"Let's have another cup," Wetzon said. "We have time, and I'd like some dessert, something very chocolate."

"Okay. What do you have?" Smith asked the waiter.

"We have a very fine chocolate mousse cake or a zuppa inglese, fresh strawberries, plain or with zabaglione sauce."

"Mousse cake for me. That's an easy one."

"I'll have the strawberries with zabaglione," Smith said.

Wetzon opened her palm and looked thoughtfully at the key again. There were definitely numbers scratched in it. "If this were a safe deposit key, I think it would be heavier and more official-looking. Mine has 'Yale' in big, important letters across the front. This looks more like a jewelry box key or a mail key."

"Well, the police have probably gone over Barry's apartment by this time.

Maybe it unlocks a cabinet or a storage box there." Smith sighed. "You know what the problem is? We're too honest. Anyone else would have taken Leon's hint and sold the blasted thing to Jake Donahue."

The mousse cake was a heaping mound of dark, rich chocolate intersected with chocolate sponge cake, just what Wetzon wanted right now. "Oh boy," she said, brightening. "This is going to make me very happy."

"Such small things make you happy." Smith smiled indulgently.

"I can be bought for a big piece of dark, rich chocolate anything." Wetzon laughed, letting a forkful melt in her mouth. "See how easy I am?"

But Smith was gazing off in the distance, not really listening. Wetzon's eyes followed hers. Nothing. She was looking at nothing.

"What's the matter, Smith?" she asked.

"Wetzon!" Smith grabbed Wetzon's hand. "I just had a brilliant idea. What time is it?"

"Two-thirty."

"Let's go. Let's get out of here."

"I want to finish my cake," Wetzon protested. "Tell me your idea." She really didn't care about Smith's idea. She was enjoying the essence of chocolate melting deliciously over her tongue. For the first time since Barry's murder, she was feeling like her old self. She was not going to let Smith draw her into one of her schemes.

"Oh, poof, Wetzon." Smith jabbed her fork at a strawberry. "You're no fun."

"We have time before we see Silvestri. Why rush out of here? I don't want to go back to the office."

"I don't want to go back to the office either," Smith said, signaling the waiter for their check. "I want to go to a locksmith."

"Oh, no—"

"Oh, yes. Who would it hurt? We'll just make a copy of the key and hold it. If it turns out the police can't find what it unlocks, maybe we can. And besides," Smith laughed her mock wicked laugh, "think of all the grateful people. . . ."

20

After all, Wetzon told herself, how wrong was it? They'd wait and see what the police came up with. . . . No, it was wrong. All wrong. It smelled wrong. Smith was always so good at turning things around. She was the most seductive of creatures. She could spin flax into gold just by talking.

"No," Wetzon said, bristling. "It's wrong."

"Oh, honestly, Wetzon, you're such a priss," Smith said. "Very well, I'll be responsible . . . if something happens . . . but really, what could possibly happen?" She was the picture of innocence.

"Okay, okay. I give up. You win." Wetzon hated being called a priss and Smith knew it.

They were standing in front of Sy's Locks on the corner of Second Avenue and Sixtieth Street, under the Roosevelt Island aerial tramway. Sy had a storefront business, a sliver of space the width of a door. In fact, it was a door. The upper part opened like a Dutch door, and Sy had made a plank of a tabletop that fitted over the top of the bottom half of the door. On his left, on the side wall, were nails, hundreds of them, row upon even row, with thousands of keys. A bare bulb hanging from the ceiling lighted the ridiculously narrow space. A business created in an alley. It could only happen in New York, where space was at such a premium.

A framed photograph of Milton Berle stared out at them. *To Sy, best locks in town after the Carnegie Deli. Love, Uncle Miltie.*

"What can I do for youse ladies?" Sy was a runty little man with a pungent Brooklyn accent. His face was a mass of seams and warts, with white and gray beard bristles sprouting through all that activity.

"The key, please, Wetzon." Smith held out her hand. It wasn't a request, it was a command.

Wetzon sighed and handed over the key.

"Turn your back, Wetzon," Smith instructed. "This is all my idea. Remember, I'm taking the responsibility."

"Let's just get it over with," Wetzon said through clenched teeth.

"We'd like you to copy this key."

Sy took the key and squinted at it. "Uh-huh," he grunted, moving back into his narrow space, searching. "Here we are." He held up a key, placed them both into the vise of the machine on his front shelf, turned on the motor for a second or so, then opened the vise. He held up both keys to the light, took a large metal file, and made a few passes at the new key. "Uh-huh," he grunted again, feeling the new key for rough spots with his deeply callused thumb.

Then he set both keys in front of Smith on the little shelf. Smith put them together. A perfect match.

"Perfection," she confirmed.

"What do you think it was made for?" Wetzon asked.

"Strongbox," Sy said, taking off his cap and scratching his bald spot. "The kind you get in a hardware store, maybe. Or a cabinet, like an architect's or a dentist's."

"How much?" Smith asked.

"Three dollars."

She handed him three dollar bills and took the keys. "One for you, Wetzon, and one for me," she said, slipping hers into her pocket. "Leave it to me. We'll put this in a nice safe place and I'll talk to the cards."

"It's three-thirty. We'd better get going." Wetzon was now certain that the police would find what the key unlocked in Barry's apartment. The key had been too easy to reproduce. If it was a safe deposit key or a mail key, Sy would have said something . . . or would he?

She looked up above the giant concrete structure of the tramway at the clear, blue sky. Everything would be all right. She watched as the aerial tram, a bright red car, pulled into the docking area. It seemed to float in.

"Come on, let's call Harold and see what's happening in the office," Smith said.

They stopped at a pay phone near the Fifty-ninth Street entrance to the D&D Building, and Smith called Harold collect.

"I wish you wouldn't do that," Wetzon complained.

"I know, but I'm not going to carry a lot of change in my pockets," Smith said.

"You could carry a handbag like other people."

"I am not like other people," Smith replied. "Hello there, what's happening, sweetie pie?" She waited, listening. "Lots of calls about you, star," she said to Wetzon. She listened again. "That's the best story I've heard yet." She looked at Wetzon. "Monahan said he did the interview and was made an offer."

"Unbelievable," Wetzon said. "But believable," she added.

Smith listened again. "He told Harold he was there for over an hour. Thought Elliot was a hell of a nice guy."

"Garbage," Wetzon said.

"Guess what Wetzon just said? Right, garbage. Did he tell you what this mythical offer was?" She shook her head at Wetzon. "He told him he would think about it and get back to him."

"Think about what?" Wetzon said. "This is great. Another crazy." Carlos always broke down "crazy" into three categories: nice crazy, crazy crazy, and vicious crazy. At this point Monahan was just plain crazy crazy.

"Anything else? No, we'll tell Elliot about it tomorrow. Let him cool off a little. Wetzon, Mildred Gleason called again."

"My new best friend," Wetzon said, watching a city tow-truck driver attach a towline to a black Audi while the woman in the driver's seat screamed hysterically and shook her fist at him.

"Harold, please call her and tell her Wetzon will have to get back to her tomorrow. And about six or seven reporters called. And Carlos." Smith licked her little finger and stroked her eyebrow in a mincing imitation of a homosexual.

Wetzon ignored her. Smith could not tolerate homosexuals, and it was a subject of contention between them. Wetzon, from her years as a dancer, had a great many gay acquaintances and a few close gay friends.

"And me?" Smith was asking. "Uh-huh, uh-huh, uh-huh. Who? Well, really. He's got a lot of nerve. Okay. Give me the number." She motioned to Wetzon for pen and paper, which Wetzon gave her. "Anyone else? Ah, that's nice. Just hold the rest for me. I won't be back today, but I'll be in first thing in the morning." She looked enormously pleased with herself as she hung up the phone.

"Anything I should know about?" Wetzon asked.

"Leon," Smith said with a smug smile. "Dinner tomorrow night."

"Not with me."

"No . . . just little ol' me." Smith threw her arms in the air triumphantly and spun around, wild-eyed, bursting with a strange energy, pulling an astonished Wetzon with her.

21

The cab dropped them off in front of a low, modern building, a construction of pale tan bricks and lots of glass.

"This can't be it," Wetzon said. She had expected the station house from *Hill Street Blues,* an old, battle-worn, gray stone fortress, worse for the wear, high stone steps, NYPD carved in the stone above massive doors. What a disappointment. That style of precinct house had much more verisimilitude.

"It looks like Mark's first school in Virginia," Smith said. "Spoils the magic."

When they opened the door, the inside, too, looked like a school. Stone floors, tiled walls, fluorescent lights, a pay phone on the right amid a forest of plants.

Definitely disappointing. Hard to believe that real crimes were solved in this atmosphere.

There was noise, a lot of it, but it was more like men's-locker-room noise. In fact, Wetzon thought, the whole place looked and smelled like a gym. There was a battered old metal desk in institutional gray at the door, but no one sat there, and uniformed cops came in and out, brushing by Smith and Wetzon without paying the slightest attention to them.

They walked straight a few paces until they came to a large opening on their left, and turning, they entered an immense room, definitely like a gym. On their left, running the full length of the room, was a low railing, behind which were desks, computers, a switchboard, and men, some in uniform, some not. Everything was painted the same ugly green.

"Help you, ladies?" a uniform asked. He stopped typing.

"Yes," Wetzon began, "I—"

"We're here to see Detective Silvestri," Smith interrupted, smiling that smile again.

"Sure," the uniform said. He was a nice-looking young man, with a bushy mustache and hair that touched the back collar of his shirt. His name tag said *Gallo.* "Wait a minute and I'll tell him . . ." He paused.

"Smith and Wetzon," Smith drawled, for effect.

The nice young man smiled politely, not sure if he was being made fun of.

He picked up the phone, holding the receiver with his shoulder as he resumed typing, and said, "Tell Silvestri there are a couple of ladies here to see him."

"He's expecting me," Wetzon said. "At four."

"You're a little early. He's in a meeting. Take a seat." He motioned toward the long row of plastic and metal chairs, green again, lined up on the opposite wall. They were unoccupied except for an elderly woman sitting forlornly in the middle of the row, who seemed to be carrying on a running conversation in heavily German-accented English with someone who wasn't there. She had a large shopping bag at her feet and she kept rummaging around in it.

"Charming," Smith said. "Let's not sit. We can look around."

"I'm too achy not to sit when I have a chance." Wetzon made a beeline for one of the plastic chairs. "You look around, if you want to." She took a mirror out of her handbag and looked at herself. Awful. Dark circles under her eyes, drooping lids, raw scabby bruise on her forehead. She put the mirror away and leaned back, closing her eyes.

Restless, she opened them again in time to see Smith disappear in the direction from which they had come. Uniforms came and went, dropping off papers, picking up radios. Steady action with no sense of urgency. She counted three policewomen.

Smith came back and sat down next to Wetzon. "You look rotten, sweetie. After you finish here, go home and get to bed—"

"Gee, Ma, do I have to?" Wetzon said with a faint grin. She saw that Smith had combed her hair and put on lipstick. She looked very attractive in her black suit and burgundy silk blouse. There was a vivid spot of color on each cheek. She had obviously found a bathroom on her tour.

"Ladies, you can take the stairs on the right or the elevator out in the hall on your left."

Wetzon turned right when they left the big room.

"Where are you going, Wetzon?" Smith demanded. "You're so tired you can't stand, but you're going to take the stairs?"

"Never ride when you can walk," Wetzon replied. "It's good for the calves."

"Thanks, but I'll take the elevator."

More space with more green desks; telephones ringing. The desks were piled with papers. Men in street clothes lounged around, standing, sitting, talking to one another and talking on the telephones. The staccato clatter of typewriters took the place of the tickertape, but it seemed familiar territory to Wetzon.

"It looks like the boardroom of a brokerage house," she whispered to Smith when she got off the elevator and joined her. "A lot like Jake Donahue's, as a matter of fact."

Smith was positively luminous. Was it Silvestri, the environment, or just the excitement? The more Smith glowed, the drabber Wetzon felt.

Silvestri came out of an office in the back of the room and waved them toward him. He was wearing the same rumpled brown suit, and he didn't look as if he had a dinner date planned for that evening.

"Ms. Wetzon," he said formally, shaking Wetzon's hand. "How are you doing today?"

"All I need is a full night's sleep," she answered. "How is your arm?"

"All I ever need is a full night's sleep," Silvestri said, but he was looking at Smith.

"It's a little crowded in here," Smith remarked, looking over Silvestri's shoulder. Two desks and several well-worn metal chairs were squeezed into a tiny room. One desk was occupied. Wetzon recognized Metzger from last night at the Four Seasons. His eye pouches looked even worse in the light of day. Metzger was on the phone, making notes in a dog-eared notebook. "I'd better wait downstairs, or out here," Smith said, pointing to the "boardroom."

"Are you sure?" Silvestri seemed a little disappointed. "We can bring in another chair."

"No, I'm fine. I want to call the office anyway."

"Well, you can use one of the desks out here."

"I'll go downstairs to the pay phone," Smith said cheerily. "Don't you two bother your heads about me."

Wetzon looked at Smith suspiciously. Smith was up to something. It was when she was most innocent-looking and -sounding that she was up to the most mischief.

"Here, Ms. Wetzon, sit down, and I'll get a stenographer." Silvestri went into the main room and spoke to a neatly dressed man in a plaid sports jacket and gray pants. The man picked up a metal carrying case and followed Silvestri back to the office. He set up his stenotype unit on its stand and waited. Silvestri slid into the chair behind the desk and motioned to Metzger, who ended his phone conversation.

Wetzon saw Smith wait until they were settled, then turn quickly and disappear toward the staircase. She was wearing slingbacks, and the noise of her clicking heels on the steps carried all the way back to Silvestri's office. Why had she insisted on using the elevator to come up and had now taken the stairs down? Sometimes Smith was such an enigma.

Wetzon turned her attention to Silvestri and felt a wave of warmth rise from her fingertips to her cheeks. She was so attracted to him that she was afraid it showed. She looked down at her hands. She wanted so much to make a good impression. He cleared his throat politely, and she looked up. Silvestri was waiting expectantly, as if he'd just asked her a question.

"I'm sorry." She was flustered. "Did you say something?"

"Yes. I asked if you were ready to begin."

Wetzon nodded, swallowing with difficulty.

"Try to relax," he said sympathetically. "Just answer the questions as carefully as possible. I'm not going to give you the third degree. Would you like some coffee or a Coke?"

She shook her head, feeling very much alone. "Just water, please, and I'm ready."

22

Silvestri took off his jacket with exaggerated care, one arm at a time, and put it on the back of his chair. He was wearing a blue-and-white-striped shirt and a tan lambswool sleeveless sweater, and Wetzon could see the bulge of the bandage beneath his shirtsleeve near his left shoulder. There was no gun in view. *Why isn't his arm in a sling,* she thought. *He has to be having some pain.* When he went out into the squad room to get her the water and himself some coffee, she noticed another bulge under his sweater near his waist in the middle of his back. His gun.

Nervous, Wetzon looked around. The room she was sitting in was smaller than the office she and Smith shared, but it gave the illusion of more space because it was glass from midway up. There were blinds all around on the half-windows, so privacy was obviously available if needed. A large map of the City was on the wall behind Silvestri's desk and a calendar hung from a nail on the side wall. The calendar was still on February.

Everything needed a coat of paint. There was an ugly brown spot on the ceiling from what looked like a leak, where the plaster had puckered and dried, and there were scuff marks and chipped places on the walls. Someone had written a phone number on the wall with a magic marker.

Hanging from the low ledge around the office, where window met wall, were clipboards. Cases, probably. She saw that out in the squad room Silvestri had stopped to talk to another detective, who had his pants leg up, his foot on a chair. He was adjusting his sock—no, it wasn't his sock, it was an ankle holster. She was so fascinated that she got up out of her chair and came close to the window to get a better look.

Metzger eased himself up as if to see what she was looking at so intently, and muttered, "Goddam cowboy."

The other detective rolled down his pants leg, picked up a black leather jacket, and left the squad room.

Metzger's phone rang once. "Yeah?" He listened, made a note in his book, opened his desk drawer, and closed it hard. "I'm on my way." He hung up the phone and nodded at Wetzon. Then he went out to meet Silvestri, who was precariously carrying two cardboard cups by their lips in his right hand. Metzger relieved him of one of the cups. They put their heads together and looked around at her once. Metzger returned to the office with the cup he had taken from Silvestri and set it on Silvestri's desk. Steam rose in a delicate cone from the cup. Metzger went back to the squad room and beckoned to one of the other detectives, who scooped up some material from his desk and left the squad room with him.

The clock on the opposite wall of the squad room said four-thirty. Silvestri stood in his doorway, glanced at it, and sighed. He handed Wetzon the cup of water and sat down at his desk.

"Thanks," she said, taking the water. She was anxious to tell him about the key and get rid of it. She felt it was literally burning a hole in her pocket.

The stenotypist, who had been reading a battered copy of *New York* magazine, totally disinterested in the activity in the small office, put it down on the floor under his chair and readied himself.

Silvestri leaned back and studied her. She shifted uneasily in her chair. She hated being looked at like that, as if she were a specimen.

The stenotypist cleared his throat. Silvestri nodded. "Are you ready?" he asked her again.

"Before we start about last night, I want to show you . . ." She took the key out of her pocket and held it out to him. Her hand shook. "I found this in the pocket of my suit jacket after I got home last night."

He leaned forward with an almost unobtrusive wince and took the key, his hand brushing hers, completely unaware of her attraction to him. She wondered what kind of vibes she gave off that were so different from Smith's. Or did she just give off no vibes at all?

"Well, well, well," Silvestri was saying, concentrating on the small key. "You say this was in your pocket?"

Didn't he believe her? "Yes, Barry must have put it there when he took my arm at the Four Seasons. I don't know how else it could have gotten there."

"Did you take your jacket off at any time before you got home?"

That was a thought. Of course she had. "Yes . . . at Smith's, which is ridiculous because why would Smith—" She stopped.

"Yes?" Silvestri was watching her thoughtfully. His eyes were flat, revealing nothing. His manner was totally professional.

Why would Smith want a copy of the key if it was her key? Of course she would want a copy of the key if it was hers. No, it didn't make sense. "There's no reason for Smith to have put a key in my pocket and not tell me," Wetzon said firmly.

"Okay." He spoke slowly, running his fingers around the edge of the key. "What about York Hospital?"

"Yes, my jacket was taken off when we got there, but what reason would anybody have to put a key in my pocket?"

"I don't know, but I'll check it out. Meantime, let's assume that Barry Stark put it in your pocket."

"Okay."

"Why?"

"You mean, why would he? I don't know, maybe because he was afraid of someone."

"Good. Did he react to anyone at the restaurant or at the bar when he came in?"

She strained to remember. He had looked over at the bar several times. "I don't know. He looked over at the bar . . . it was very crowded. But Barry was the kind of guy who was always looking around in a room, looking for the next possibility, the next sale. He had this nervous energy, like a motor that was always racing. A lot of brokers have it."

"And after you were seated?"

"He kept talking to me, but looking around. I think he either saw someone or thought of something, because all at once he looked as if he'd seen a ghost. He turned a ghastly white and jumped up, saying he had to make a phone call."

"Did you notice anyone looking at him?"

"No. It was very crowded. Unusually crowded." And noisy. The bar had been jammed with people—

"Did you see Jacob Donahue there?"

"Jacob Donahue? Was he there? I didn't know that." She was puzzled. Surely Barry would have said something if he'd spotted his employer in the crowd? "I've never seen him in person, only in newspaper photographs, so I'm not sure I would have recognized him. *Was* he there?" she asked again.

Silvestri ignored her question. "What did Stark say to you? Start at the beginning, when he phoned you yesterday."

She concentrated, wanting to be accurate. "He said he had a problem, that he wanted to see me. I thought it was a problem in his office. Barry always had problems. He made a lot of money, but he was always complaining about not making enough. And the new-issues market is dead." And so was Barry.

"Explain, please."

"New issues are companies that are brought public. They're known as I.P.O.s—Initial Public Offerings. All of the major brokerage houses are involved in this, more or less. To put it simply, a private company pays a brokerage firm big money to bring them public, sell their stock to the public. The salesmen—the brokers—of the firm then sell these shares for the company that's going public. The big houses like Shearson and Merrill usually syndicate the best of these, offering chunks of shares to other, smaller brokerage firms. Firms like Donahue's take on the smaller, more marginal companies that want to go public, those with more risk to the future shareholders, the ones the more established firms are wary of." Wetzon leaned forward as she spoke, engrossed, relaxing visibly.

"Donahue's normally does not syndicate shares in what they bring public. They keep everything in-house and that's what their brokers sell almost exclusively. When these new issues come to market, the firm puts a price on the stock, and if the market is down, the price is low. Therefore, a company often waits to go public to get a better price on its stock. When the market is bear and sinking rather than rising, the new-issues market goes dead, and brokers at firms like Donahue's, who have built their books with just new-issue clients, don't make any money. This is all very simplistic, I'm afraid," she said apologetically.

"But they can sell other stock besides these new issues, can't they?" Silvestri asked, frowning. "They could be doing that at the same time, couldn't they?"

"Yes, but most of them don't. I know, it doesn't make sense to specialize, but a lot of brokers do it. They shift into whatever product they perceive they can make big money in. Barry was like that. Many brokers look on this as a long-term career. They want to build a client base and do well for their clients and keep adding to that base over the years, through referrals, building up a decent, steady business. But others, like Barry, say they're in it for the short haul. They want to make the big killing—make their million and get out before they're thirty-five."

Silvestri's eyes widened. She continued, a little guilty about enjoying herself. "And some of them do. Others make their million and live up to it. Cars, houses, alcohol, drugs, gambling, women, divorces. A million dollars doesn't go very far with the government and the mob as your partners. A lot of these brokers are burnout cases by the time they're thirty-five. I've interviewed guys of twenty-four or twenty-five who sat with me, literally shaking—high on stuff—I don't know what." She was gesturing, showing him. "These kids are taking home three-quarters of a million dollars, more or less. What does a twenty-five-year-old kid do with all this money? 'How much do you need?' I always ask, because I'm curious. I never get a straight answer, but I know the answer is, 'More, more, more, as much as I can get.'" She paused. "'If it kills me.'"

The stenotypist looked up.

Silvestri was staring at her. "Gosh," she said, "I'm sorry. I get a little carried away, I guess. See what you started." She smiled at him ruefully.

"I don't know much about the stock market," Silvestri said. "It always struck me as being a crapshoot."

She smiled at him again. "This is a business where most people—even those at the top—are looking for the quick buck, the big killing. I'm repeating myself, but it's about money. It's about greed."

"Didn't the SEC institute all kinds of checks and balances after the Crash in '87?"

"Sure, but you can't legislate away greed. I'm sure you see it all the time."

"You must be good at your business," Silvestri said, showing dark-rimmed turquoise eyes.

She considered that. "I am. Funny about the language of making money.

All death words. Dead market. Big killing. Barry Stark was always looking for the big killing.''

"Tell me about when you met him last night."

"He was a little late, and he seemed nervous, almost frantic. He kept talking about repos."

Silvestri looked at her quizzically.

"Repos are repurchase agreements," she said patiently. "I didn't know either. He explained it to me. It's a financial transaction—in this case, with government securities. It's pretty tricky, and it sounded as if he'd stumbled into a compliance problem."

"Compliance?"

"Compliance to the SEC and federal law. Every brokerage firm has a compliance department to protect it from doing anything wrong. It's like internal affairs in the police department."

Silvestri nodded.

"It sounded as if Barry had come on something that for once he couldn't handle."

"Meaning?"

"Meaning, I'm tired," she said wearily, "so I'm telling you that this is a whore's business. People will do anything for money, including breaking the law, if they think they can get away with it, or leaking or selling information, selling speculative stocks to their own grandmothers. Anything. And Barry was not one who would let a little illegal action bother him."

"So?"

"So this problem that he had stumbled onto had to be life-threatening. He was scared."

"Okay, what happened when he left?"

"He jumped up, said he had to make a phone call, that he'd forgotten something and would be right back. And he left, practically on the run. That was it." She was getting tired of repeating it.

"And what did you do?"

"I waited. Oh, yes, and when I stretched my legs under the table I bumped his attaché case. Otherwise I would have forgotten about it. I waited about twenty minutes or so. I was getting edgy. I couldn't imagine what was taking him so long, and I wanted to go home. So I paid the bill and took the case with me downstairs to the phone booths. I was going to tell him I couldn't wait, that I had another appointment."

"Did you see anyone follow him down the stairs?"

"No one specific. People were going up and down constantly."

"Did you see anyone around the phone area when you got there?"

"No."

"Then what did you do?"

"I went straight to where Barry seemed to be talking on the phone. He was all hunched up over the receiver."

"You couldn't tell something was wrong with him?"

"No."

"Didn't you think he was in a strange position?" Silvestri's voice was skeptical. Maybe she *had* been too wrapped up in herself. She should have noticed, now that she thought about it, how odd Barry had looked, all scrunched up like that. She shrugged.

"I can't explain why I didn't get suspicious except to say that I've never seen someone dead before, let alone violently dead."

"Okay, then what?"

"The rest you know."

"Tell me."

She shuddered, reliving it. "I knocked on the glass to get his attention, but he didn't move. I was getting really annoyed. I pushed the door open slightly, and he . . . his body . . . slipped toward me, out, almost falling on me . . . I had to get out of the way. It was horrible." She choked. She pushed back her chair as if to get away from the thing that Barry had become.

"Take a deep breath," Silvestri said loudly. "Keep breathing deeply. Come on now. Slowly."

She broke out in a cold sweat, but kept breathing deeply. She was afraid not to. Tears came awkwardly. "Oh, God," she gasped, "I'm sorry. This is so tacky."

Silvestri stood up and sat on the front corner of his desk, near her, his right hand resting lightly on her shoulder. "Keep breathing," he said.

There was an agitated knocking on the glass, and Wetzon and Silvestri looked up to see Smith, furious, eyes flashing. "What are you doing to her?" she mouthed to Silvestri, pointing to Wetzon.

"It's okay," Silvestri said. His hand left Wetzon's shoulder. "No more questions for now." He shrugged lopsidedly at Smith, an I-didn't-do-anything expression on his face. Nodding to the stenotypist, he opened the door.

"What are you doing to her, Silvestri?" Smith demanded. "Don't you see she's ready to collapse?"

"I know, I'm sorry. We had to finish it."

"It's okay, Smith. I'm okay." Wetzon's voice trailed off, high and distant.

"I'll have one of the men take you home," Silvestri said, turning to look at her.

"I'm going with her," Smith said. "You can pick me up there."

It was only when they got to Wetzon's building that Wetzon remembered she hadn't asked Silvestri if they'd found out anything about the missing attaché case.

23

"I'm all right, I really am," Wetzon insisted. "Please stop fussing over me." They were on the sidewalk in front of her building. Larry, the doorman, his coat off, was leaning against the building, smoking, talking to one of the locals, ignoring them. "It was just talking again about finding Barry that did it."

"You looked as if you were about to pass out," Smith said. "You didn't tell him about the other key, did you?"

"Of course not. I wouldn't do that without telling you first."

One of those new Honda scooters pulled up to the curb near them, and a man in a huge gray crash helmet and goggles, wearing a white lab coat, tie slightly askew, got off and looked curiously at Smith and Wetzon.

He removed the crash helmet, revealing curly gray hair, and, taking off the goggles, crossed the sidewalk to talk to Larry. Larry, bored, pointed vaguely at Smith and Wetzon and went back to his conversation.

The man in the white coat turned and came back to them. "Miss Wetzon?" he asked, looking from Smith to Wetzon.

"I'm Leslie Wetzon," Wetzon said, dodging Smith's elbow. "You were looking for me?"

"Yes, I'm Dr. Pulasky, Rick Pulasky, from York Hospital." He smiled at her. He had a nice smile and warm, dark brown eyes. His hair was tousled. Too old to be an intern or even a resident. "I handle outpatient supervision for Emergency Services at York."

"Oh, how nice," Wetzon said, impressed. "I didn't know hospitals had such a service."

He flashed her another smile. "It's experimental, and we're the only ones in the City who are trying it right now. I'm here to monitor how you're doing."

"Oh, I'm fine," she said lightly. "No problems." *Liar,* she thought, "As you can see." She spread out her arms and stifled a gasp.

"Dr. Pulasky," Smith said in her soft, breathy voice, emphasizing "doctor." She smiled seductively and offered him her hand.

Wetzon wondered if Smith was attracted to Pulasky, too. Or was it just second nature for her to do this with all men? Odd that she had never noticed this about Smith before, but then they had never been very social together, despite their business partnership. Or maybe it was just that she was so tired that everything was annoying her. She was beginning to feel like an observer in her own life.

"I'm sorry," she said. "This is Xenia Smith."

Pulasky took Smith's hand for a moment, then dropped it. "Nice to meet you," he said carelessly, eyes on Wetzon. "You look shaky. You should have spent the night in the hospital. . . . Head injuries are deceptive, you know. You can't jump back into the thick of things as if nothing had happened to you." He was very intense, and attractive. His eyes were gypsy eyes, so dark, and he was lean, the way Wetzon liked men.

"Well, you're right there, she should definitely be in bed," Smith said, "but she can be so stubborn." She was smiling that crooked little smile.

"I'm feeling very tired right now," Wetzon said irritably. She turned away, resentful that Smith was talking about her as if she weren't there.

"Thank you, Doctor, but we have no need of your services," Smith said coldly, dismissing him. "All Ms. Wetzon needs is some rest."

Wetzon felt a small, hot kernel of anger rising to her throat. She was sick and tired of Smith's interference in her life, sick of Smith's constant attempts to manipulate. Turning to Dr. Pulasky with a flirtatious smile, Wetzon asked, "And what treatment would you care to suggest, Dr. Kildare?"

"Maybe I should look in on you tomorrow," he said, playing along. "Strictly professional, of course."

"Of course." Wetzon narrowed her eyes at him.

"Oh, come on." He grinned. "Give a guy a break."

"Okay, call me."

"No, how about tomorrow? And how about if I bring dinner? I come off duty after eight-thirty."

"I hate to interrupt . . ." Smith said haughtily.

"Well, how about it?" Pulasky said, ignoring Smith. His eyes crinkled when he smiled.

"Okay," Wetzon said. "Twelve B."

"I hope you like ribs," he said, starting the Honda. "Nice to have met you, Miss . . ." He'd forgotten Smith's name, Wetzon thought triumphantly. He'd actually forgotten her name.

"I do," she called after him.

Smith was angry. "I don't like him," she said.

"Why? I think he's nice." They were in the elevator, and someone had been next door using the health club swimming pool because on the floor of the elevator was a small pool of blood. Blood? Where was her head? Small pool of water. It was the woman in 9A. She did it all the time.

"He's not trustworthy," Smith was saying. "You don't understand body language, and I do. He doesn't look you in the eye. And he has very strange eyes."

"Who cares about body language," Wetzon said cheerfully. "Just give me a nice body." Smith probably didn't like him because he wasn't a pushover for her.

Wetzon unlocked her door and saw the shadow of a man in the sunlight streaming through her living room windows. Her heart rose up in her throat. She clutched Smith's arm, backing away.

"Don't be scared, darling, it's only me," the shadow said, coming toward her.

"My God, Carlos, you gave me a fright." She stood aside and let Smith through while she pulled her key from the lock.

"Well, hello, Carlos," Smith gushed with phony enthusiasm.

"Hello." Carlos was civil. Barely.

The tiny hairs on the back of Wetzon's neck prickled a warning. She wished they would both go away and leave her alone.

"You're here late, Carlos," she said, dropping her bag in the foyer and stepping out of her shoes. She shrugged off her jacket and left it on the floor.

"I was worried about you." He was very serious, not at all like her Carlos and not like this morning when he was being so curious and bitchy.

"Does anyone mind if I collapse?" she asked. She sank into the sofa and put her feet up. Every bone in her body felt one hundred years old.

Smith sat in one of the plushy club chairs and smiled brightly at Carlos. "I'd love something cold to drink," she said.

"I can't get up, Smith, just help yourself," Wetzon said.

"Oh, I'm sure Carlos will get us something, won't you, dear boy," Smith said condescendingly. "I'd like a Diet Coke with lots of ice."

Carlos gave her his full fish eye. "Your hands have been in so many people's pockets lately, they must be tired." He turned his attention to Wetzon. "What would you like, darling?"

"The same, please, Carlos."

When he went for the Cokes, Wetzon reproved, "Smith, please."

"He's so disgusting and degenerate. You never know who's good for you. You have terrible judgment about people."

Wetzon closed her eyes. *Give me a break,* she thought.

Carlos returned with one of her old Coke trays and three glasses of iced Coke. And a dangerous look in his eyes.

"Listen, Les," he said, "I waited for you because just as I was about to leave . . . I was standing in the foyer as a matter of fact . . . someone tried your door."

"What?" She sat up.

"Really?" Smith sounded dubious.

"I know someone tried to break in," he said impatiently. "I began banging and thumping around, and he must have heard me and went away."

"How could he get past the doorman?" Smith asked.

"Larry is not always one hundred percent on the job, Smith," Wetzon said.

"Why didn't you look out?" Smith demanded of Carlos.

"Are you crazy?" he said. "He could have had a gun. . . . He could have shot me through the door."

A cold knot started deep down in Wetzon's stomach. She shivered, staring at Carlos, trying to take in what he was saying.

"Well," Smith said, "any *real* man would have gone after whoever it was."

"Smith . . ." Wetzon warned. "Carlos—"

"Listen, you barracuda," Carlos said amiably, leaning close to Smith's face, eyeball to eyeball, "don't try to manipulate me. It won't work, and it makes me—"

"Carlos! Xenia, for *Godsake*," Wetzon cried.

"That's quite enough." Smith stood up. "I don't have to sit here and be insulted by a dirty fag."

The buzzer sounded.

"I'll get it," Carlos said. "Maybe *she'll* have slimed out of here by the time I get back."

Smith was in a fury. "That's it, Wetzon. I have nothing more to say to you. You sit there and let me be insulted by that *degenerate* you claim as a friend—"

"Your date is waiting in the lobby," Carlos called maliciously from the foyer. "Don't forget your broomstick, dear."

Smith stomped out of the apartment without looking back, without saying a word. The door slammed behind her.

"Oh, shit. Shit," Wetzon cried, burying her head in the sofa pillows.

"Gee, birdie, I'm really sorry," Carlos said, sitting next to her, hugging her. "But there's something wrong with that woman. Don't you see that? She's not your friend if she tries to alienate you from your friends. And she's always putting you down. She never even got upset about someone trying to break in."

"Oh, please, Carlos, not now. I'm scared."

"Come on, not to worry. I'm here. Carlos is not going to let anything happen to you. Who would I *dish* with?" He kissed her on the top of her head. "That's why I waited. I'll sleep on the sofa tonight and get you a chain bolt in the morning."

"Thank you, friend," she said.

"I really wish you'd get out of this sleazy business," he said, "and come back to us where you belong. You're too nice for them. They're all such sharks, and they're going to eat you alive."

24

At that moment Wetzon agreed with Carlos—that she was being eaten alive—but she was certain it was only because of Barry's murder.

She changed into jeans and a soft brown-and-aqua plaid flannel shirt.

The truth was, she liked headhunting because it was fun. No day was like any other day. And she *liked* making money. She had stopped dancing because she was tired of going from one show to another, many of which closed after opening night. She was tired of the injuries, which came with the territory of being a dancer, and she'd seen that in time she would be just another broken-down, aging chorus girl.

"What do you want for dinner, my love?" Carlos asked.

"Chinese. Beef in orange sauce—very spicy."

"What else?" he asked, prompting, because he knew she rarely varied from what she liked.

"Shrimp fried rice . . . cold noodles with sesame sauce."

"By George, she's got it!" Carlos cried, mocking her, mocking *My Fair Lady*.

Georgie, she thought. She had forgotten to call Georgie.

"I'm going to stop at the Food Emporium and fill up your larder," Carlos said.

"It's okay. I have to make some phone calls."

"Oh, birdie, you never know when to let up."

She pushed him to the door. "Out with you. And don't rush."

The paper with Georgie's phone numbers was in her purse. She found it and called the first number.

"Yeah."

"Georgie? Wetzon."

"The cops were just here." He sounded rattled. "Where are you?" His voice was slurred, as if he'd been drinking.

"I'm at home."

"I'll be right over."

"Wait . . . no. Not good." She thought for a moment. Carlos would be gone for at least an hour.

"Okay," Georgie said quickly, "I'll meet you at Amsterdam's in fifteen minutes."

"Wait—" But he'd hung up. Damn. She had hoped to avoid seeing him again. He made her uncomfortable. The hell with it. Best to meet him and get it over with.

She took her denim jacket from the hall closet and scrawled a quick, innocuous note to Carlos that she'd forgotten to do something and would be right back.

Georgie was hunched over a beer at the far end of the bar, which was just starting to fill up. Amsterdam's did a big business with the "happy hour" groupies that spilled over into the yuppie crowd after seven o'clock. The real diners didn't come until after eight.

Georgie was still dressed as she had seen him earlier in the day, even to the Ray-Bans, and he was smoking a stub of a cigarette.

"I'll have one of those." Wetzon pointed at his beer and slipped onto the high, black stool next to him. She saw her reflection come into focus in the dark mirrors of his glasses. "If we're going to talk, Georgie, you'll have to take off those sunglasses," she said testily. There was something about people who wore dark glasses that hid their eyes—a hostility, something threatening. And she'd had quite enough of that for today. She ran her fingers lightly over the chipped enamel surface of the bar counter.

Three brightly dressed young women came in, laughing, and one took the stool next to Wetzon, while the others stood, chattering.

Georgie shifted the sunglasses to the top of his head, and Wetzon shivered. His eyes were bloodshot, his look glazed but wary. "Come on," he growled. He took her beer and the one he was drinking and nudged her to one of the small blue-and-white checked cloth-topped tables.

She was sorry she'd come out to meet him. He was mean and scary-looking. His face had the stubble of a reddish beard. She sat reluctantly. "What do you want, Georgie?"

He rubbed his eyes. A waiter brought two more beers. He finished the one he was drinking and started another.

"I want to know what Barry told you last night." He tilted the bentwood chair back precariously and lit another cigarette.

Cigarette smoke floated in the air between and around them.

"Nothing. He told me nothing," she said impatiently. "He didn't have a chance to. He sat down with me, jumped up, and I never saw him again—I mean—alive." She wasn't afraid of Georgie now; she was angry. She felt she was being used. "What's going on, Georgie?"

"Listen, Wetzon." Georgie drank more than half of the second beer in one swallow. "I don't want to make you suffer, but Barry was my best friend. I wanna know what happened and who killed him."

She softened, looking at his wasted face. "Okay, I'm sorry. I'll try to help."

"The cops came to see me. Asked me a lot of questions, where I was at the time—I was in the middle of a session with my ad agency—so I'm clear."

Wetzon hadn't thought of Georgie as a suspect, but now she considered it. Could he kill someone? No question about it.

She changed the subject. "Did you know Barry from Merrill?"

"Naa, longer than that. Forever. We all grew up together, in the North Bronx . . . went to Science together. Then we split up . . . and after college Barry and I ended up at Merrill. Jesus, it was fun." He finished the second beer and started a third.

"Can I get you anything?" the waiter asked.

Wetzon shook her head. "Another round," Georgie said. "You didn't know us then. It was so fucking exciting. We were desk partners . . . we shared a Quotron. We cold called together, vied to see who could open the most accounts." He stopped. "I always beat him out," Georgie said, with a chilly half-smile. "The market was so crazy—Jesus." He lit another cigarette, dropping the match on the floor. "We thought it would never end."

Wetzon nodded, remembering. It was three years ago. She and Smith had just started their firm.

"Yeah, and the headhunters were all over us—like vultures. Yeah, even you, Wetzon." He pointed his finger, yellowed from nicotine, at her.

She blinked, taken aback by the accusation. "I thought I was different," she blurted, hurt, in spite of her mistrust for Georgie.

"Don't kid yourself, Wetzon. You're a salesman, just like us. You're out for the buck. You like the money. But you *were* different. You give great phone. You didn't push, you listened. Barry liked you. Shit, I liked you."

"You gave me Barry's name and phone number," she said, somewhat mollified.

"I did?" He looked surprised. "I don't remember."

"You said, 'Call this guy, get him out of here, then I'll get all his accounts.'"

"I said that?" Georgie laughed suddenly, a weird neighing laugh, and his small eyes folded up and disappeared. "Man, was I funny."

"You guys made a lot of money that first year in the business." She looked up at the yellow globes that lit the restaurant. Smoke hung in the light, suspended. Everything had a dreamlike quality to it. Slowly, she brought her attention back to Georgie.

"Yeah, more than we'd ever seen. I bought a Jag and Barry got himself that red Porsche. Christ, it was unbelievable." He seemed to have forgotten her, staring into his beer. "It was even better the second year. Barry bought his big loft in SoHo, and I picked up the old church for a song, and the health club . . . I had plans. I wasn't gonna sit around and be a fucking stock jockey the rest of my life. The market could come apart any frigging minute—"

"You were right."

He turned to her and nodded. "Yeah. But before it did, we were going to have one hell of a roller coaster ride. We took a whole house ourselves in East Hampton the second summer. The place was crawling with gorgeous women. . . ." Roughly, he pulled the sunglasses off his head and tossed them on the table, running his hands through his hair. "I broke the record for opening new accounts, and they gave me an award and a week in L.A. They had me talk to all the new trainees . . . then . . . ."

"Then the market took a nosedive." Wetzon sipped her beer, remembering how badly shaken all the relatively new brokers had been. They had never seen a bear market.

"Yeah. Happy clients became unhappy assholes overnight. The bitching started. Complaints up the wazoo." He shrugged. "That's when I quit."

Wetzon didn't challenge him. She knew for a fact that there had been a lawsuit, that Georgie had sold a deep tax shelter to an eighty-year-old widow. The widow's family wanted restitution and had gotten it. Georgie had been fired. "Barry had a problem at that time," Wetzon said. Barry had been accused of unauthorized trading in two of his accounts.

"Who didn't?" He jammed his cigarette out in the ashtray and lit another. "They all love you—management and clients—when you make money for them, but the minute the well runs dry, they forget. For me, it was good riddance. I never wanted to hear another complaint from a frigging client that I lost him a few thou when only last year I made him twice that. By that time I had the Caravanserie going—"

"Barry called me around then." She kept trying to turn the conversation back to Barry.

Georgie squinted at her. "He was my friend, but he was a schmuck. He was making big bucks, but he was blowing it away. I told him, schmuck, put your money in real estate. He never listened."

"He told me he was ready to make a move, but he'd cut a deal for himself with Jake Donahue."

"That he did." He stared at Wetzon hard. "Don't kid me. He must have told you something yesterday."

She shook her head. "Only that he had been close to something big and had . . ." she stopped to think again, "that he'd overplayed his hand . . . something like that . . . and they were on to him. Do you know what he meant?"

"He was doing some kind of business deal with Mildred Gleason," Georgie said. "He wouldn't tell me what. Said it was the opening he'd been waiting for, just what he needed to get going again."

"The new-issues market is depressed, dead in the water. He told me Jake was getting into repos—"

"I don't know anything about that crap, and I don't want to know, but if you're talking depressed, Barry was it. Christ, he was even thinking about getting married."

"Barry?" She didn't know why she was so shocked. Somehow she couldn't imagine Barry as a married man. "Who was he going to marry?"

"I told him he was out of his fucking mind. I didn't get it. He was making it with this sharp-looking piece from Connecticut—someone he worked with—but he was talking about marrying Buffie." Georgie shook his head in disgust. "He said, can you believe this, none of us was getting any younger."

"Buffie?"

"Yeah. She was one of the crowd—from the neighborhood—the four of us—" He raised his hand. "Same again here," he called out to a passing waiter.

Surreptitiously, she looked at her watch. Carlos would kill her.

"Georgie, I've got to go—"

"Wait a minute, Wetzon. Barry had some stuff of mine he was holding." She could hardly hear him. Amsterdam's had begun to fill up. People were standing three-deep at the bar.

"I don't know anything about that." She started to stand.

He clamped his hand on her shoulder and held her down, hurting her. "I went through his locker," Georgie grunted, leaning beery-breathed into her. "Nothing. Not a goddam thing but old sweats and jogging shoes."

"Goddam it, Georgie." Wetzon was furious. She'd had enough. "Kindly remove your hand," she said through clenched teeth.

Georgie took his hand away slowly, surprised by her reaction. His mouth twisted, jeering. "You're a killer, Wetzon."

"I accept your apology, Georgie," Wetzon said, standing. "One question."

"What?" He restored his Ray-Bans, covering his terrible eyes.

"Is there going to be a funeral?"

"Funeral? Barry?" Georgie laughed that high whinnying laugh. "Barry was a donor."

"A donor?"

"Yeah. He signed one of those things on the back of his driver's license that said you can have his organs. He loved the idea. He wanted everyone to have a piece of him, he used to say." Georgie snorted. "Yeah. He wanted to be cremated and told me to spread his ashes along Wall Street and dump a little on the floor of the Exchange. Isn't that a laugh?"

"Very funny," Wetzon said, not laughing. "I'll see you, Georgie." Her reflection looked back at her from his glasses.

"Wetzon," Georgie said, "if you remember anything, tell me first. And don't talk to any strangers."

She didn't answer. She was wondering why he had suggested Amsterdam's on Eighty-second and Amsterdam, how he had known she lived on the West Side.

25

There were so many messages on her answering machine that the tape had run out, but she didn't care. Carlos had pulled the plug on the phone in the bedroom, and she'd gotten the best night's sleep since Barry's murder. She had awakened peacefully in cool sheets, bright sunlight filtering in slatted patterns through the venetian blinds. She'd managed to get back to the apartment only minutes before Carlos last night, so mercifully there'd been no involved explanations.

Carlos was crooning "Singin' in the Rain" in the kitchen, and the apartment smelled of fresh coffee and croissants. It was wonderful to be taken care of. All she really needed was a good wife. The warm sense of security she felt almost made her forget the events of the last two days. Almost.

She moved Carlos's towel off the shower rod and took a hot shower, acutely aware, now that she was rested, of her aching body. The bruise on her upper arm, in glorious shades of purple and yellow, was still quite tender. The one on her forehead was scabby and ugly. She rubbed shampoo into her hair and stuck her head under the steaming water. Then she turned off the hot water and took a final icy rinse, getting rid of the soap and closing her pores.

She towel-dried her hair and put on her terry robe, padding barefoot into the kitchen, drawn by the magnetic smell of the coffee.

"Coffee . . . coffee . . ." she moaned, like a wanderer in the desert calling for water.

"Thought you'd never wake up, sleeping beauty," Carlos said, breaking off his song. "The papers are full of the murder story, and you—the mystery woman in the case—you haven't even told me anything about it."

"I don't know anything more than I've told you." She suddenly remembered why Carlos was there, why he'd stayed the night, and the small knot in her stomach came back, only bigger this time. "Did you hear anything during the night?"

"No. Maybe it was all conicidence, no connection."

"But, Carlos, this building is pretty secure. Even small burglaries don't happen here."

"Well, someone goofed, that's all."

"Whatever, it's pretty scary," she said, pulling the terrycloth robe about her tightly.

"I'm going out to get a locksmith, and I'll get it done for you before I leave," he assured her, "so not to worry. Then I have to get back to *my* life." He smiled, excitement surfacing. "Marshall thinks there might be something for me in his new show—"

"Oh, Carlos, that's wonderful! Does he want you to audition?"

Carlos nodded. "I'm picking up the script this afternoon."

"Great. What a super thing to happen. Have you been working out?"

"Faithfully, darling," he said, "even today. Used your barre. But let's not get our hopes up. It hasn't happened yet."

"I could do with a little workout myself this morning."

"Go ahead. I'll be back as soon as I can."

She listened to the elevator door close and finished her coffee with her usual line-up of vitamins. She even took a big bite of Carlos's half-eaten croissant, then, shrugging, finished it. She'd work it off. She changed into her leotard and did some stretches at the barre. Her body creaked a little, protested a lot. She was very tight.

The phone rang. She took the towel from the barre and slipped it around her neck. She'd have to get it. The tape was out, and it might be important.

"Hello."

"Leslie Wetzon? Is this Leslie Wetzon?" The voice was gravelly and coarse, somewhat familiar.

"Yes, who's calling?"

"Mildred Gleason. I'm so glad I got you."

"Oh, yes, Mildred. I'm sorry I didn't get back to you. It's been pretty hectic . . . because of the murder—"

"I know— Look, that's what I want to talk to you about."

"Okay, we're talking."

"No, not on the phone. I can't talk on the phone. In person, please, one on one." The older woman sounded uncertain, not at all like the Mildred Gleason she had met that night at Harry's. "I'll come to you," Mildred said, "wherever you say, whenever you say." There was a hint of pleading in her voice. Mildred Gleason was not a pleader. "Please, it's very important to me."

Wetzon thought for a minute. She vaguely remembered an appointment, an interview on her schedule downtown for tomorrow.

"Hello, hello, Wetzon, are you there?" High anxiety.

"Yes, wait a minute, Mildred. I want to check my appointment book." She opened the Filofax and saw she had a meeting with Howie Minton at five o'clock the next day at the bar of the Vista Hotel at the World Trade Center. She could cancel, but why get backed up? He was a potential candidate. She could go downtown earlier and see Mildred Gleason around two-thirty, and look in on Shearson's broker training program in the World Trade Center before she met

Howie Minton. "Today is out, but I can come to your office tomorrow around two-thirty. Is that all right?"

"No, it's not all right. It must be today—as soon as possible."

Wetzon was taken aback by the imperiousness of her tone. "I told you I can't do it today," Wetzon said stiffly.

There was no response for a few seconds, then, ". . . I see. Well, it will have to do. Look, I'm very grateful . . . you don't know. . . ."

"It's okay, but there really isn't anything I can tell you—"

"Thank you for this," Mildred Gleason said hurriedly, whispering. "I'll see you at two-thirty tomorrow."

Curious and intrigued, Wetzon replaced the receiver. The phone rang again. She picked it up and said hello cautiously.

"Wetzon, this is Smith." Smith's response was cold. "We have to speak seriously."

"About what? What's the matter, Smith? What's happened? Are you okay?"

"It's that animal. Carlos. I've been up all night . . . sick about it. He's a very bad person and he has a terrible effect on you."

"Oh, come on, Smith. Carlos has been my closest friend for almost ten years. You can't bait him and expect him not to fight back."

"You'll have to choose between us, Wetzon," Smith said, beginning to cry. "I can't be treated like that."

"I'm not going to do anything of the kind, Smith, so pull yourself together. You're forgetting that I have heavier things on my mind right now."

"We'll talk about it when you're feeling better," Smith backed off, fixing blame. "When you can handle it."

"I *am* handling it," Wetzon insisted. "And we're never going to talk about this again." She hung up. What in hell had gotten into Smith lately? Wetzon felt as if her life had been turned inside out in the last twenty-four hours.

Then she remembered the key. Did Smith's odd behavior have anything to do with the key?

26

The office was a beehive of activity. It was Thursday morning, and the business of making money continued.

Smith was on the phone with Loeb, Dawkins. "Jerry Matthews. Yes. The first invoice is dated October twentieth. I sent a duplicate in December." She was making a major effort to keep her voice pleasant. "It is now over five months . . . I would like to send someone down for the check." Exasperation was creeping into her voice. "All right, Kathy. I hope so." She slammed the phone down.

"Standard procedure for them," Wetzon said. "They're not about to let us send for the check. They might lose some interest on the money."

Smith's eyes glinted dangerously. "If they want a fight, we'll give 'em one." She was wearing a deep plum knit suit with black braided trim, gold chains, and pearls. Around her throat was a long, narrow wisp of a band, a silk print tie of deep mauve cabbage roses. Her olive skin glowed.

"You're wearing a new suit," Wetzon said, admiring. "Something special going on today?"

Smith didn't respond. She pressed the intercom. "Harold? Send another duplicate invoice on Jerry Matthews to Loeb, Dawkins, attention Kathy Cramer. Mark it fourth notice on the bottom." She paused. "Just do it, please. No editorial comments." She looked at Wetzon, who smiled. Harold was getting out of hand.

"Seriously, Smith," Wetzon said, "don't you think we should drop Loeb, Dawkins as a client once they've paid us? Their slow payment is chronic. We're a small business. If we were waiting for payment on a lot of placements from Loeb, Dawkins, we'd have no cash flow whatsoever, and we'd be out of business."

"Let's think it through carefully," Smith said, "when things have quieted down a little."

Wetzon nodded. Was that a dig? Maybe not. She'd give Smith the benefit of the doubt and try not to be sensitive. She looked at her watch. "Steve Switzer interviewed at Hallgarden this morning."

Harold opened the door. "Steve Switzer for Wetzon, on nine-o." He stood in the doorway.

"Come in and listen, if you want," Wetzon said. She thought it was a good idea to give Harold as much exposure as they could before they moved him up to associate.

"Steve? How did it go?" She heard horns honking, street noises. He was calling from a pay phone.

Steve Switzer was the biggest producer at Murray, Allen, a disreputable penny-stock house that, rumor had it, was about to be closed down by the SEC. Switzer had been referred to Wetzon by a former Murray, Allen broker whom Wetzon had placed at Pru-Bache last year.

Normally, a move would take a month or more from the initial interview to the start date at the new firm. And Wetzon always suggested that a broker see more than one firm, as a basis of comparison. But with Switzer, there was an undercurrent of urgency, and Wetzon was worried.

"It went great," Switzer said, shouting over the background noise. "I like this guy Garfeld. I want to go there. But I can't talk now because I'm on my way to Bache."

"Bache?" Wetzon groaned silently.

"Yeah. Warren set me up with his manager. Get me some feedback from Garfeld and I'll call you later."

"Shit!" Wetzon said, hanging up. "He's on his way to Bache—Warren set him up there. That's rotten. Wouldn't you think Warren would have let me do it? They'll love Switzer at Bache."

Smith shook her head and pointed a well-manicured scarlet finger at Wetzon. "I told you, you can't ever trust them."

"But what about Hallgarden?" Harold interjected.

"Oh, right now he wants to go there, but let's face it, Hallgarden is a small firm. Bache can make him a better offer. Let's see what Andy Garfeld has to say."

Wetzon dialed Hallgarden and asked for Andy Garfeld.

"I like him," Garfeld told her. "He's coming back tomorrow at nine o'clock to meet Gordon Kingston, our chairman."

"Well, we're going to have to move fast with him, Andy, because he's talking to Bache right now. And not through me."

"I'll work something out. Have him call me when you hear from him again. Oh, and listen . . . talk to him on how to dress."

"What do you mean?" She cringed. "How was he dressed?"

"Sportjacket, striped shirt, red socks. It'll never wash with Gordon."

Wetzon hung up the phone. She shook her head. It was all perception, how you looked at it. If your appearance was right and you said the right words in a forthright and confident tone, no one would doubt you. Brokers didn't, as a rule, wear polyester, but every once in a while a client would reject a broker as unfit, and it was often because he wasn't dressed properly. She remembered one broker who had lost his license because of unauthorized trading in several accounts. He had worn cowboy boots with his three-piece pinstripe, and after he had left the business in disgrace, everyone said, "Well, there, you see. He really didn't fit in." You could be forgiven a little cutting of legal corners, but only if you dressed properly. So much for individuality in an industry that prided itself on entrepreneurship.

But for all the unwritten rules of dress, or the so-called dress code, if the broker's numbers were big enough, if he made enough gross commissions for his firm, individualistic behavior was considered slight eccentricity, and the heads of firms looked the other way. One of the biggest producers at a major Wall Street firm wore jeans to the office.

She sighed and looked at Smith. "I see it's going to be that kind of day."

Smith turned. "Now what?"

"Would you believe that Switzer went to his interview at Hallgarden in a sportjacket and red socks?"

"Yes." Smith's attitude was so superior.

"Oh, Smith."

"Wetzon, you are such a Hallmark card." Smith smiled. "I'd really love to sit Switzer out with you, but I have a lunch appointment, and then after that—"

"Something special?" Smith had made no further mention of Carlos, or Silvestri, for that matter, and Wetzon was not about to bring up either of them.

"No," Smith said, nose buried in her appointment book. "Obligatory lunch. Appointment afterward at Mark's school." She crossed to the bathroom and gave herself the once-over in the full-length mirror on the inside of the door. She added rouge to her cheeks and fluffed out her short, dark curls.

Wetzon watched her curiously. Something was up. She could sense it. It was the same feeling she'd had yesterday at the precinct when Smith surrendered her to Silvestri.

After Smith left, Wetzon sent Harold out for lunch and asked him to pick up an egg salad sandwich for her.

She was worn out, but her mind ricocheted from question to question. Who had murdered Barry Stark? And why? What was Barry holding for Georgie? Had Georgie killed his friend? What did Mildred Gleason have to do with Barry's murder, and why did she want to see Wetzon? Georgie had said Barry was doing a business deal with her—could she have killed him? What did that key open? And what about Leon Ostrow? He had been at the Four Seasons that night. Had Jake Donahue been there, too? Why else would Silvestri have asked her if she'd seen Donahue there? And Leon represented Jake Donahue and Jake Donahue was Barry's boss. They wanted the key. . . . Always back to the key. Circles within circles within circles.

And why was Smith behaving so strangely?

Wetzon had thought of Barry as just another broker, perhaps a little crazier, a little greedier, than most, but now, in his death, he seemed to be taking on new dimension. There was Buffie, the girl he was going to marry, and the other girl—the one from Connecticut Georgie had mentioned—who worked with him at Donahue's. Did Silvestri know about them? Had Georgie told Silvestri anything? She doubted it. Was Georgie the one who had tried to break into her apartment? Was it even connected with Barry's death? And, she had almost forgotten . . . who had stolen Barry's attaché case? What was Barry doing with all those drugs from York Hospital? She had a pretty good idea what that was about. She remembered now that several brokers had told her Barry was a connection for drugs on the Street. Was Barry's murder drug-related?

It was too confusing.

The phone rang. "Smith and Wetzon," she said, grateful for the interruption.

"I loved it," Steve Switzer said, fresh from his meeting with Pru-Bache. "They took me to the trading floor. I think I could work there." He was flying. "Cancel me at Hallgarden tomorrow."

"You can't do that, Steve," Wetzon said firmly. "First, what if Bache doesn't come through with the deal you want? You can't put all your eggs in one basket." She meant what she said, and she was speaking calmly, sure of her territory. "But more important, Steve, this is a career decision. Bache is a behemoth organization. Prudential owns it. You would just be another fish in a big pond over there. You want to be with a firm that might still be bought by another company. You want to accumulate stock and stock options in the firm before this happens. When Primerica bought Smith Barney, I saw some brokers and longtime employees become millionaires overnight." She knew, based on experience, that Steve Switzer would have a tough time going from being the top producer at his small firm to being one of many at Pru-Bache. That and culture shock would zap him. He would be starting all over again as a rookie in a new environment.

"Can I get stock options at Hallgarden?"

"You can ask for them now and you can accumulate them when you're there."

Switzer paused. "I'll keep the meeting tomorrow."

"Andy wants to talk to you, so give him a call." She paused. "And by the way, Kingston is very corporate. That means pinstripes, white shirt."

"Wetzon, come on, you know who you're talking to? I always look great. I just bought a new suit. Cost me a thou."

She hung up and called Andy Garfeld, who listened to her report on Switzer's reaction to Bache, taking audible, impatient drags on his cigarette. "Doesn't he know that Bache is the wrong place for him?"

"Andy, brokers are suckers for other good salesmen."

A long moment of silence, then: "Unfortunately, you're right."

Harold came back with her sandwich. "No calls." She was emphatic. "I want to have my lunch in peace."

She went out to the garden and ate her lunch sitting on their new garden furniture.

Her thoughts drifted magnetically back to Barry Stark. Barry the sleaze, to Smith. Hyper, money-crazy Barry, who characterized himself as a poor kid from the Bronx. Barry, who had sent her a list of brokers, with phone numbers and background notes, without asking for a kickback on a placement. Opportunistic Barry, looking for the big killing, going to marry a girl he grew up with, but having an affair with someone he worked with.

Warm and drowsy, she nestled into the hard seat of the chair, remembering that Georgie had made fun of Barry as an organ donor. Organ donor. Maybe that was why Wetzon had liked him. There was something about Barry . . . something soft . . . something boyish. Bad boyish sometimes, but definitely boyish. He'd had a kind of rough charm. And he had chosen to be an organ donor. An oddly humanitarian thing for him to do. She shook her head. Georgie, on the other hand, had little charm that she could see. She shuddered. Georgie frightened her.

"Wetzon?"

"Harold."

"Steve Switzer."

Wetzon sighed and reluctantly left the sweet solitude. When she picked up the phone to take Switzer's call, she was back in the marketplace.

"I spoke with Andy," Switzer said. "He offered me seventy percent payout for a year."

"Incredible." It was incredible.

"And they'll make a market for me in any stock they can do diligence on."

"Fantastic." It was.

"Senior vice president title, private office, sales assistant, cold caller."

"Good, good."

"What else should I ask for at the meeting tomorrow, besides some upfront—"

"Steve, I don't think you should ask for the world. They're a small firm. You'll put them off."

"Wetzon, I know what I'm doing. If you don't ask, you don't get. Tell me what else I can ask for."

Wetzon rubbed the itchy area around the scab on her forehead. What the hell, maybe he was right. Maybe that's what her trouble was—she tended to accept, not demand. "You could ask for an expense account. At your production level, it could be one percent of your gross. And stock options."

"That's what I want. That'll do it."

"I'll talk to you tomorrow, after the meeting. Good luck."

If Steve Switzer made a deal with Hallgarden, Smith and Wetzon would have to take a fee-forward deal, one weighted heavily on Switzer's production for the coming months, two to thirteen, against a small down payment. It was like rolling dice. Sometimes it paid off dramatically, and sometimes it was what the traders called a dead cat bounce. Nothing.

The phone rang. She hoped it was for Smith because she'd had it for the day. She cleaned off her desk and with her fingertip rubbed a whitish spot from the rough surface of the marble peach paperweight.

"Wetzon, that was Howie Minton's sales assistant confirming your appointment tomorrow at five o'clock at the Vista Bar."

She nodded. Howie was getting carried away with himself, too. Trusting a sales assistant to confirm an appointment with a headhunter. Had he forgotten who paid the sales assistant's salary? Not very smart. Unless, of course, he wanted his firm to know he was talking to Wetzon. Now that was diabolical, but knowing Howie, a definite possibility. She laughed out loud.

The sun had moved around to the south and was brightly beckoning her outdoors.

She pulled on cotton socks over her pantyhose and laced up her pink Reeboks. It was such a beautiful day, she would walk home, window shop, get some exercise, think about clothes, food . . . Silvestri. Damn him. Damn Smith. Spend a nice quiet evening . . . Oh lord, she had forgotten about her date with the good doctor, Rick Pulasky. What a brain.

She flipped through her old phone messages—reporters—nothing urgent, dropped them on her desk, and put her black pumps in her briefcase, along with the suspect sheets on Howie Minton and Steve Switzer.

"You're leaving early." Harold was accusing. He always took being left alone personally.

Wetzon ignored his displeasure. "I'm working from home tomorrow morning. I have appointments downtown in the afternoon. I'll talk to you tomorrow."

"Is Smith coming back?"

"Don't know. I doubt it." She walked to Smith's desk and looked at her appointment book. Next to two-thirty were the distinct initials G.T.

G.T. Wetzon frowned. Mark's teacher? No. Mark's teacher had a funny name—they had laughed about it—what was it? Oh yes, Alice Littlejohn. Who was G.T.? She waved to Harold and walked out into the gentle afternoon sun.

She stood for a moment on the sidewalk in front of their office and then walked briskly toward Second Avenue. She stopped dead in her tracks.

G.T.

Georgie Travers.

27

What would Smith be doing with Georgie Travers, whom she loathed? And who said G.T. had to be Georgie Travers?

Wetzon hesitated on the corner of Second Avenue. Which way should she walk? She decided to take the scenic route up Fifth Avenue to Central Park South.

If you think too much, you'll get crazy, she told herself. *Look at the people on the street, look in the store windows.* She looked at a leggy young woman with a disarray of long, dark hair held up in places with plastic combs and clips, and dangling, mismatched earrings—contrived SoHo-ian havoc—who was leaning against a big blue mailbox on the west side of Forty-ninth Street, lacing high white boots. She wore a short black tunic, mid-thigh length, over black tights. She straightened up and stared back at Wetzon, who had not realized she was staring. Abashed, Wetzon moved hurriedly toward Fifth Avenue.

You are forgetting your manners, old dear, she thought. Which reminded her of Carlos. Wouldn't it be wonderful if his career was born again. He missed the gypsy life more than she did. He missed the excitement and the gossip and the camaraderie. It seemed not to have worn him down as much as it had her.

She eyed the display of short metallic evening dresses in Saks's Forty-ninth Street window skeptically. Who would ever wear anything like that? Certainly no one she knew.

A cool breeze came out of the sun-drenched clouds and caught her unexpectedly. She felt a chill and then the sudden, odd sensation of being watched. She swung around, remembering the previous day's terror of the hand shoving her into the traffic.

Shoppers, gawking tourists hung with cameras, messengers, Senegalese peddlers with their knockoffs of designer watches, the usual Fifth Avenue mix of people and costumes. Out of the corner of her eye she saw the girl in the Robin Hood costume—boots, tights, tunic—staring into another Saks window nearby. But she was paying no attention to Wetzon. There was no sense of recognition, or menace, for that matter.

Wetzon shook her head. She was getting jumpy. She continued on her way, but this time she moved faster.

I. Miller on Fifty-seventh and Fifth was having a sale on Ferragamo shoes. She marched herself right in and tried on a pair of black patent leather pumps with her usual two-inch heels. They were wonderful. She bought them in patent, white, and navy and arranged to have them delivered. As she waited for her American Express Card to be returned, she looked out past the display window onto Fifty-seventh Street and saw, once again, the girl with the tousled dark hair. She seemed to be waiting for someone.

When Wetzon left I. Miller, the girl was gone. She crossed Fifty-seventh Street and walked toward The Plaza and Central Park South.

"Do you want to go Trumping?" she heard a woman carrying a Bergdorf's shopping bag say to another with a Bonwit's bag. Trumping. That was a new one. They were referring to the shops in the Trump Tower across Fifth Avenue from I. Miller. Tiny, expensive shops and boutiques clustered amid pink marble. It was a beautiful, if slightly voluptuous, place, with its tall waterfall, the expensive noshery nearby, and the grand piano with a cocktail pianist in the lobby.

Whenever she passed The Plaza she thought of the scene in *The Way We Were* where Robert Redford comes out of The Plaza with a very white-bread–looking woman, and Barbra Streisand, very ethnic, is across the street asking people to sign "ban the bomb" petitions. It made her feel very sad, as if she really knew those people. She was thinking about Katie and Hubbell, the Redford and Streisand characters, as she walked up Central Park South. She paused at the St. Moritz's Café de la Paix, where tourists were having iced drinks outside, and caught another glimpse of the girl in the tunic and tights, who, seeing Wetzon, scurried into the St. Moritz lobby.

This was too coincidental. For some peculiar reason, the girl was following her. Was she angry because Wetzon had stared at her when she had first seen her leaning against the mailbox?

As Wetzon stood mulling this over, she watched a man pedal by in the barrel seat of a sports car—just the seat, not the car. He was steering with a rod that came up like a joystick between his feet. Momentarily, the strange contraption almost made her forget her bizarre shadow.

As soon as the light changed, Wetzon plunged into Central Park. Her briefcase seemed to be getting heavier and heavier, a sure sign that she was tired. From behind the stone wall she watched the girl come out of the St. Moritz and look around.

Unexpectedly, the girl crossed the street and headed in Wetzon's direction. Wetzon, feeling a stab of fear she knew was irrational, took off, aiming for Central Park West, dodging nannies with babies in carriages, screaming children with dripping ice cream cones, joggers, the elderly who sat sunning on park benches. A big black dog braced his massive paws and began barking furiously at her as she came out on Sixty-fifth Street.

She had literally raced through the Park, not breaking pace until she made the turn onto Columbus Avenue and was back on her home turf, the West Side. Panting and sticky, she stopped to catch her breath in front of Trocadero, with its wonderful window of French-style sportswear, when, to her consternation, she saw the girl she was running from, now loitering in front of Furla's, acting for all the world as if she were casually looking at the handbags in the shop window.

Damnation, Wetzon thought, more angry than frightened. She'd put a stop to this. When the girl looked away for a moment, Wetzon tucked her briefcase under her arm and bolted up the street to Sedutto's, the ice cream shop. She went through the back of Sedutto's into Diane's, the burger house attached to it, and around to the front doorway of Diane's. The girl came up the street after her, looking right and left; when she reached the entrance to Diane's, Wetzon jumped out, grabbing her arm.

"I've got you now," Wetzon said indignantly, shaking her, as the girl tried to pull away. "Who are you and why have you been following me?"

The girl stared at her and, to Wetzon's horror, her face crumpled and she began to cry.

"Oh, shit," Wetzon said, instantly feeling like an ogre.

"Oh, God." The girl sobbed, tears gushing down her thin cheeks. "I'm so sorry. I didn't mean anything. I wanted to talk to you, but I didn't know how." Her accent was basic Bronx.

"Come on now," Wetzon said, distressed. Everyone was looking at them curiously, sliding past, warily. She put her arm around the surprisingly muscular shoulders of the sobbing girl. "Café La Fortuna's around the corner. Why don't we just sit down and you can talk to me there."

The girl sniffed noisily, drew a yellow Kleenex out of a tiny, hot pink shoulder bag, and blew her nose. They sat at an outside table. Wetzon was embarrassed by the mountain of fear she had built out of nothing. And now she felt mean, even a bully. "How about a cappuccino?" the mean bully asked.

The girl nodded. Tears had streaked her mascara and black eyeliner, which ran unevenly down her face. She looked like a little girl who had put on her mother's makeup and made a mess of it.

Wetzon ordered two cappuccinos and said to the girl, "Do you know me?"

The girl snuffled. "You're Wetzon."

"Okay. Do I know you?"

The girl groped in her pink bag for another Kleenex and gulped and hiccuped as the tears returned. She shook her head. A purple comb slipped from her hair and landed at her booted feet.

Wetzon took a small pack of tissues from her handbag and gave it to the girl.

"Oh, I'm so sorry," the girl mumbled, mopping up her face.

"Who are you?"

The waiter put two cinnamon-dusted frothy cappuccinos in front of them and discreetly departed.

"My name is Ann Buffolino."

"Ann Buffolino?" The name meant nothing to Wetzon. Then a little glimmer of light flickered in her mind. "Wait a minute. Are you Buffie?" she asked, knowing the answer before it came.

28

"Barry and I were going to get married." Ann Buffolino's pale brown eyes watered up and tears dribbled down over rouged cheeks.

"I know." In response to the question on Buffie's wan face, Wetzon added, "Georgie told me."

"Oh, you know Georgie." It was more a statement than a question.

"Very slightly." Better than she wanted to know him.

"We all went to school together." Buffie looked down at the wads of damp Kleenex next to her untouched cappuccino. An immense teardrop rolled slowly down her nose and teetered on the tip, ignored. "We were a team. All for one, one for all. Like *The Three Musketeers*—we love those old movies."

"Without D'Artagnan?" Wetzon asked. Buffie probably wouldn't know the reference.

But Buffie surprised her. "Barry was D'Artagnan." She swiped the tear from her nose with the back of her hand. "He's so handsome. I mean, he was, wasn't he? I can't believe he's dead." She pressed her palms to her face and rubbed her swollen eyes. She looked like a hurt child.

Wetzon, commiserating, patted her shoulder, noting at the same time how large Buffie's hands were for such a small girl. Her fingers were ringless; chipped, bright pink polish covered long oval nails. "I'm so sorry. Do you have family? You really shouldn't be alone now."

Buffie gulped and made a small burp. She licked the cappuccino foam from her lips. "I have my work," she said. Her dangling earrings swung back and forth as she moved her head. "This is good. And the boys have been wonderful to me—especially Georgie."

"What kind of work do you do?" Something warm and living brushed Wetzon's leg. Startled, she looked down and saw a huge, orange-striped cat, purring loudly, rubbing against her. Wetzon sneezed. She was allergic to cats.

"Oh, there's a sweet thing," Buffie said, picking up the cat, stroking it. "I teach aerobics at Body Beauty by Rita on Seventy-ninth Street." She fell silent, her eyes expectantly on Wetzon.

"Why did you want to talk to me?" Wetzon wouldn't have matched Barry with Ann Buffolino—not in a million years. The girl was strange, flaky, but maybe it was because she was still in shock. She wondered if Barry would really have married her. The orange cat undulated luxuriantly against Buffie's black tunic, leaving a trail of short orange hairs, and then curled up contentedly in her meager lap and went to sleep.

Buffie, hands folded neatly over the orange pillow that was the cat, became clear-eyed. "Barry said he was going to take care of me if something happened to him. He told me he wrote his life story and that I was to call this lady— Mildred Gleason—and she would pay me the insurance money."

Wetzon closed her eyes. She couldn't believe this was happening. Buffie had just, perhaps unintentionally, perhaps deliberately, disclosed a whole new facet of Barry's murder. "Haven't you talked to the police?"

Buffie looked at Wetzon as if Wetzon were crazy. "Oh, yes, yesterday, but I wouldn't tell them anything about this."

"Why not? It might help find out who murdered Barry."

"Then I wouldn't have anything," the girl said plaintively. "And he meant for me to have it. I loved Barry, but there's no way I can bring him back. Georgie told me you had to know where he hid it because you were the last person he talked to."

"I told Georgie that Barry didn't say anything to me about anything. I didn't even know about you until Georgie told me. You have to tell the police what you know." Wetzon was beginning to suspect that Georgie had set her up.

"I don't know what to do." Without warning, Buffie put her head in her hands and started weeping again. The cat awoke and jumped off her lap, tail twitching.

The shadows on the brownstones around them had lengthened. They were now sitting in the shade, and the air began to cool.

"Buffie, please don't cry." Wetzon looked at her watch. It was almost four. "Tell me what Barry said about this life story of his. Maybe I can help you find it."

Buffie dried her eyes with the remnants of her Kleenex, not using the pack Wetzon had offered. She sniffled and coughed. "It was after his boss started hassling him."

"Jake Donahue?"

"Yeah. Jake said to him, 'I've been known to put bullets in people's heads.' Once he even got a gun out of his desk and pointed it at Barry. Barry went crazy."

"Why would Jake say something like that to Barry?" No wonder Barry had a gun in his attaché case.

"I don't know, but Barry said Jake would be sorry when he and Mildred Gleason got through with him."

"What else did he say about Mildred Gleason? Georgie told me Barry was doing a deal with her." The light was dawning. Mildred Gleason would have to get on line behind Georgie and Buffie and everyone else who was determined to find out Barry's last words to Wetzon.

"I guess." Buffie dipped her head and began to pick at her chipped nail polish. "He didn't talk much about business when he came up."

"You didn't live together?"

"Oh, off and on." Tears welled up in the puffy eyes. "I don't understand how it could have happened, and why he didn't tell me where it was."

"It must be in your apartment—or his."

"It's not in his." She was very matter-of-fact.

"How do you know?" *What are you doing?* she thought. *You are interviewing her like a detective.* On the other hand, she had noticed that lately people were telling her things that they might not have told the police. Maybe she could put all the information together and help Silvestri—

"Because Georgie and I went down and looked."

"I'm really sorry, Buffie, but I don't know anything that could help you." Wetzon looked around for the waiter. "Maybe Barry changed his mind about writing it." Somehow she couldn't see Barry sitting down and writing his autobiography. "Or maybe he left it with someone else."

Buffie became agitated. "No! No! He wouldn't have given it to her. He couldn't. It was mine, my insurance. He promised!"

"Her? I'm sorry." Did Buffie know about the other woman, the one from Donahue's, whom Georgie had said Barry was seeing?

"I saw him with her—"

"Who was she?"

"How would I know?" Buffie seemed annoyed that she'd been interrupted.

"I'm so sorry," Wetzon said for the umpteenth time, not knowing what else to say. "When was this?"

"It was last fall, October, around Halloween because I remember the jack-o'-lanterns. . . ." Buffie dabbed at her eyes. "He used to meet me at my place. . . . My last class didn't end till nine o'clock. He was always on the phone—you know Barry—but this one time he sort of turned his back when I came in. He was acting kind of funny." Her lower lip pursed querulously.

"What do you mean, funny?"

"Well, you know, kind of secretive, like he was hiding something."

The waiter drifted in their direction. He moved like a dancer, which he probably was. "Can I get you anything else?" he asked. He had a nice voice. Wetzon shook her head.

"Anyway," Buffie continued, wound up, "I asked him if something was going on I should know about." There was a faint suggestion of anger in the swollen brown eyes. Her large hands clenched and unclenched on the table. "And he said it had nothing to do with me, that he was doing a special deal and it was secret, that it was the thing he'd been waiting all his life for. He would tell me about it when it was done."

"I still don't understand how you know there was someone else." Damnation. She was getting more deeply involved, felt herself being dragged into the maelstrom that had led to Barry Stark's death.

"Because he got up real early the next morning and told me he had to meet someone before work." The small face hardened. "So I followed him." She smirked, singularly unwaiflike, almost cunning.

"So you saw what the woman looked like?"

"Not really. He left my place real early, around eight. I waited a few minutes, then I went after him. It was cold, colder than I thought, and I only had a sweater on over my leotards, but I had to see. He was walking fast down Central Park West and then he went into the Park at Seventy-second Street. There were some people around, you know, so I just pretended to be a jogger and kept out of his sight." She laughed, all involved in the drama of her story. Color crept back in her face. "He was cold, too. I could tell because he kept clapping his hands together."

Across the street, the car alarm on a white Porsche went off. Two teenagers, leaning on the car, dropped their beer cans and took off, yelling curses in Spanish. A gaunt black man came out of the brownstone closest to the car and walked around it, patted the gleaming hood lovingly, then turned off the alarm and went back inside.

Buffie leaned forward, sat back, pulled at her tunic, and crossed her legs. "When he got to the Tavern on the Green, he cut downtown, and I don't ever remember being in that section of the Park. We went down this steep hill, and he stopped to look at, you know, some statue of a dog. I began to smell something funny and then I remembered about the zoo being there. He went right in, but I couldn't follow him—it was too open. The only person around was this fat old lady with a supermarket cart stuffed with bundles and bags. She smelled worse than the animals." Buffie's nose wrinkled. "I sort of hid behind her. Barry kept looking at his watch and walking back and forth like he was trying to keep warm. Once I thought I lost him but then I saw him with a container of coffee." She twitched nervously in her chair. "He didn't see her coming, but I did—"

"How did you know—"

The waiter brought the check, and Wetzon put five dollars on the table, anchoring it under her mug. The late afternoon shadows had lengthened almost grotesquely. Wetzon shivered.

"I don't know . . . she didn't fit there, I guess. They walked a little while. At first I thought they were arguing. Then he put his arm around her, and they went into one of the animal houses. There was nobody around and I thought they were going to do it right there. I hid near the entrance—and I saw them talking real close, but I couldn't hear anything except the monkeys screaming. And all the time he was holding her hand." Again, decidedly unwaiflike, Buffie glared at Wetzon. "I could have killed him."

Wetzon stiffened. In spite of everything, she was shocked by the confession and by the sudden change in Buffie's personality.

"But I didn't—I couldn't," Buffie said hastily.

"I know you didn't." But Wetzon couldn't help wondering just how upset Buffie had been. She reached for her briefcase. She wanted to run away, get home, hide. "I have an appointment," she murmured.

Buffie was staring down at her hands, rubbing the protruding knuckles of her thumbs. "Barry always said he could trust you. He *must* have told you where he put his stuff."

Wetzon sighed. Why was everyone continually carping at her about this? "But he didn't. If it's not in his apartment and it wasn't in his locker, as Georgie claims, where else could it be?"

Buffie stood. "Please, Wetzon, it won't take long—I live near here—could you come up and help me look again? Barry always said you were real smart. Maybe you'll see something we didn't see."

Why did she always have such a tough time saying no? Wetzon mused as she walked with Buffie up Columbus to Seventy-fourth Street. If she had said no to Barry in the first place, she would never have gotten involved in this mess. But as Carlos said, *no* wasn't in her lexicon.

"Buffie, how do you know Barry was still seeing this woman? That was at least six months ago. Maybe it was just a—"

"Because he was still talking to her on the phone and making dates with her last week, that's how," Buffie responded belligerently.

"What did she look like? Could you see her from where you were standing?"

Buffie played with the strap of her pink shoulder bag, swinging it as she walked. "I could tell she was tall, almost as tall as Barry. And she was wearing this long, black leather trench coat. I couldn't see her face because she had big, dark glasses and a scarf on her head, tied under her chin."

29

They turned west on Seventy-fourth Street toward Amsterdam, Buffie talking distractedly about Barry and "her insurance." Wetzon listened halfheartedly. The woman Barry had met wore a black leather trench coat and a scarf tied under her chin. She had seen someone dressed like that recently.

In the middle of the block, several yards away, Wetzon noticed a man getting into a cab. Tall, awkwardly thin . . . glasses, smallish head . . . Leon Ostrow. "Leon," she called. "Leon!" The cab door slammed shut and the cab pulled away. She saw the dark shapes of two heads in the back seat. No. She must be wrong. What would Leon be doing in this part of town at this time of day?

Buffie was staring at her. "I thought I saw someone I know," Wetzon explained. "Guess I was wrong."

Buffie lived in an old residential hotel that had been converted into tiny apartments. The lobby was small and rundown, with ugly imitation wood paneling, linoleum floors, cheap Danish modern furniture. A sign on the concierge's desk said: ALL VISITORS MUST BE ANNOUNCED, but the concierge was conspicuously absent, while the switchboard next to the desk buzzed, unattended.

There were two elevators at the end of the shallow lobby. One had an out-of-order sign on it. They took the other to the sixth floor and started down a long narrow hall with dim overhead lighting, red-flocked wallpaper. The entrance to Buffie's apartment was in a particularly dark alcove. As Buffie started to unlock the door, Wetzon noticed something lying on the floor, partially caught in the doorjamb. She bent to pull it out. It was a narrow silk tie with mauve cabbage roses, like the one Smith had worn today. Wetzon bit her lip, perplexed. What the hell was going on?

"That's funny." Buffie backed away from the door.

"What's funny?"

"It's unlocked. I know I locked it when I left. . . ."

"You were upset. Maybe you forgot." Distracted, Wetzon looped the tie around the shoulder strap of her purse, thinking only that she wanted to get this over with and be on her way.

"Maybe," Buffie concurred, uncertain.

Wetzon moved around her and pushed the door open. A hideous odor hit them with the force of a sledgehammer, driving them back, unwittingly, against each other.

"My God! What's that?" Buffie cried.

Wetzon gagged. It was an animal smell but not like the zoo as Buffie had described. It was a dead animal smell—like on the farm, when her father had slaughtered. . . . She couldn't bear to think about it.

Buffie looked stunned. She pushed the door open tentatively. The stench was overpowering. The apartment was in violent disarray, furniture overturned, drawers hanging open, an imitation oriental rug flung back, exposing the stained wooden floor.

The two women moved gingerly into the room, hands over their noses. In a doorway to what might be the bedroom Wetzon saw a brown leather sandal. She moved forward, mesmerized. The sandal was attached to the foot of an individual who lay twisted unnaturally near the bedroom door. "Oh, no!" she gasped. She pivoted, instinctively trying to shield Buffie, just behind her, from seeing.

"Georgie, oh, God, Georgie!" Buffie shrieked, frozen. She covered her face and began to wail.

Wetzon willed herself to turn. Georgie's frightening eyes were now vacant. He seemed to be floating in a mass of congealed brown slime . . . there was so much of it. . . . She swallowed hard, put her hand over her mouth. One arm was twisted abnormally behind him. The long wooden handle of what appeared to be a butcher knife was in his hand, half out of his back, as if he had been trying to pull it out. Her stomach lurched. *Slaughtered,* she thought. The smell was ghastly.

"We've got to get an ambulance, the police. Come on!" Wetzon yanked Buffie away, stepping over the mess on the apartment floor, slamming the door. In the hallway Buffie doubled over and began to vomit. Wetzon pressed her lips together to keep from joining her. She had to get out of there. "Buffie," she whispered hoarsely. The girl seemed not to hear her. "Buffie," she implored, "please, we have to go downstairs and call the police." The girl looked shattered. The jaunty hair drooped, the funny earrings seemed freakish, the outfit, bedraggled. Vomit was spattered on her white boots.

Wetzon, who felt the way Buffie looked, had no recourse but to take charge. They took the creaking elevator back to the lobby, where there was still no evidence of the concierge. Wetzon left Buffie on the black-and-white tweed sofa and went behind the desk and picked up the phone.

"Here, here, you can't do that!" an angry voice yelled. A fat man in a tight blue T-shirt came out of a back room. The missing concierge. His gross belly protruded over dirty gray uniform pants. Wetzon saw a greasy gray jacket that matched the pants hanging on the back of the chair behind the desk.

"I'm calling the police," she said. "There's been a murder upstairs."

"Are you crazy, lady?" When Wetzon didn't respond, his face blanched. "You're serious. Jesus! I'd better get the building manager."

She took a deep breath and spoke to the 911 operator, gave her name, Buffie's address, and reported what had happened. Then she hung up and sat next to Buffie to wait for the police. It was a kind of déjà vu. She had been here before. It was getting like quicksand. Wherever she placed her small pointed foot, she sank deeper and deeper.

She had a sudden, urgent thought. "Buffie," Wetzon asked, "how did Georgie get into your apartment?"

Buffie made a mewing noise and looked at her, dazed. "He had a key. They all did." She mewed again and swayed. Her head slipped to Wetzon's shoulder. Wetzon put her arm around Buffie and held her. That's when Wetzon noticed the silk tie on her handbag. She had forgotten it. She untwisted it awkwardly, so as not to dislodge Buffie, who was probably beyond feeling anything. She sat still and closed her eyes, trying to clear her thoughts. It appeared to be a duplicate of Smith's. What if it was Smith's? Smith had written "G.T." in her appointment book. Smith was her partner. Murder. Two murders, maybe. It was more than she could cope with right now. She pushed the tie into her purse.

"Are you Ms. Wetzon?" She opened her eyes and saw a burly, overweight black man in a short-sleeved white shirt, tieless, dark pants, sportjacket over his arm. "You the lady that called about a murder?" Amber lights danced on the street. A police emergency van was parked in front of the building.

"Yes," Wetzon said. "In six-o-five, this woman's apartment—" She shook herself mentally. Why was she speaking like a moron? "He's a friend of hers, Georgie Travers. I think he's dead."

Another man in street clothes motioned to several uniformed policemen and one policewoman. They started cordoning off the entrance to the building.

She was learning more than she had ever wanted to know about police routine.

The black detective sneezed and blew his nose.

"God bless you," Wetzon said.

"Rose fever," the black detective said. He spoke with an asthmatic wheeze. "I'm Walters." There were beads of sweat on his high forehead. He mopped his brow with the handkerchief he had sneezed into. "This is Conley. We're going upstairs. We'll want to talk to you and—" He pointed to Buffie.

"Ann Buffolino," Wetzon said.

"I'm going to leave you with Bellman." He nodded to the short policewoman, who looked almost comically overburdened with the gun belt, book, billy club, and other paraphernalia that were standard-issue to uniformed police in New York City. The large hat with its patent leather brim hid most of her face. "If there's anything you need, ask her."

The fat concierge hovered like a toady, muttering, "Mr. Goldstone is coming, he'll be here soon, you'll see, he'll be here," as if it were an incantation. The switchboard buzzed and buzzed and buzzed. He made no move to answer it.

Silvestri should be told, Wetzon thought. She struggled to her feet and Buffie tumbled onto the couch, half-conscious. "Detective Walters," she called. Was he a sergeant like Silvestri? "Georgie Travers, the—uh—dead—the man upstairs—is involved in another murder case."

Walters looked impatient. His stubby finger was on the elevator button. The elevator door opened and two men got out. "What's this? What's this?" the taller, older one asked.

"You have to call Silvestri, Sergeant Silvestri, at the Seventeenth Precinct," Wetzon insisted. Her voice cracked.

Walters ignored her. "There's been an accident," he told the two men. "We'd like you to stay, if you would, and answer a couple of questions."

"How exciting," the younger man said sarcastically. The taller man poked him in the ribs, and the younger man clamped his mouth shut.

Walters raised his arm to one of the uniformed policemen. "Just get verification from the doorman," he said. "The nervous fat guy. And keep them here till I get back." He looked at Wetzon for a moment, thinking. "Conley, Silvestri at the Seventeenth. See if he can get over here." He sneezed again.

"God bless you," Wetzon said. She went back to the sofa and Buffie and waited. It was six o'clock. She would never get home in time for her date with Rick Pulasky, and even if she did, she was in no mood to see him, or anyone, for that matter.

Policewoman Bellman smiled at her kindly. She had crooked front teeth. She was perched on the arm of the sofa, trying to comfort Buffie, who was sobbing into a fresh clump of Kleenex.

"Oh God, oh God," Buffie keened, rocking back and forth. "I don't understand what's happening."

People were beginning to come home from work. They were identified by the concierge and allowed in, their names and apartment numbers noted on a list. A flustered, balding man in a checked suit turned out to be the managing agent, Mr. Goldstone. He took over the switchboard, which had been buzzing incessantly.

Wetzon, watchful, saw Silvestri through the glass front doors before he saw her. Her heart did a jeté. He was wearing a dark blue suit, just as rumpled as his brown one. He flipped his I.D. at the policeman at the door, and stood aside to let a tenant in. Silvestri had a slight hook in his nose which Wetzon hadn't noticed before. It made him even more attractive.

My knight in shining armor, she thought. Would that he were. She remembered Smith's possessive smile.

"Ms. Wetzon," he said, coming forward, hands in his pockets, acknowledging her with a slight nod.

And without a morsel of feeling, she thought.

"I'm Silvestri," he said briskly to the policewoman. "Seventeenth. Where's Walters?"

Bellman got to her feet respectfully. "Six-o-five." She moved away slightly as if to give Silvestri a chance to talk with them.

"Ms. Buffolino," Silvestri said, his voice matter-of-fact. Buffie blubbered into her wet Kleenex. Silvestri looked at Wetzon with cold, slaty eyes, taking in her suit and Reeboks. "What's the story here?"

"Georgie Travers is dead," Wetzon said. "He has a knife in his back. Buffie and I found him in Buffie's apartment a little while ago."

"Well, Ms. Wetzon, for a little lady who says she hardly knew Barry Stark, you seem to be pretty thick with all of his friends."

"That's not true," Wetzon protested, bewildered. "I didn't even know about Buffie until Georgie told me about her."

Silvestri raised a thick, dark eyebrow at her. Why did she always feel defensive with him, as if she had to prove something?

"Things are not always what they seem, Sergeant," she said, indignant. He had no right to treat her like a suspect.

"I'm eager to hear about it." He turned on his heel and went upstairs.

Forty minutes later Georgie's body was removed in a big blue bag, strapped to a rolling stretcher. Wetzon and Buffie watched, holding hands tightly.

They went with Silvestri, Walters, and Conley to the Twentieth Precinct on Eighty-second Street, where Buffie asked tearfully for the ladies' room. Wetzon went with her and watched, impressed, as she put herself back into a semblance of the contrived kookiness she'd had when Wetzon first saw her, and then dashed out of the room. Wetzon wetted a paper towel with cold water and stared at her drawn reflection in the mirror, then held the cold towel to her face and throat. She thought about changing back into her pumps, but rejected it as too much trouble. Besides, Silvestri had already seen her in the Reeboks.

When Wetzon came out of the ladies' room, Buffie was speaking intently to someone on the pay phone. She hung up as soon as she saw Wetzon.

"Do you have anyone—a friend—you can stay with?" Wetzon felt an odd sense of obligation, knowing with a sinking realization that she would take Buffie home with her, if the girl had nowhere to turn.

Buffie nodded. "I just spoke with him. I'm going over there after we're finished."

So, Wetzon thought, Barry was not the only man in Buffie's life either.

It was after eight when a blue-and-white dropped Wetzon off outside her building. Dr. Rick would have come and gone. Too bad. She dragged herself to the elevator.

"Was anyone here for me?" she asked the night doorman, who emerged from the back hall when he heard her footsteps.

"No, Ms. Wetzon."

Once inside her apartment, she double-locked the door and played back her messages.

"Leslie Wetzon, this is Rick Pulasky. There was a big pile-up on the FDR Drive tonight. Emergency is on O.T. Forgive me, please. Same time tomorrow night?" He left his service number. "Call me only if it's not good. Ciao."

She went into her bedroom and closed the blinds. In the dark she stripped down to her underwear, dropping purse, briefcase, and clothing onto the floor. Then she crawled into bed.

"Go away, world," she said.

30

Rain clattered on the bedroom window in uneven gusts, waking Wetzon before her alarm. The bedroom was dark and cool.

Friday.

A blessed dreamless eight hours of sleep. And it was almost a relief to know it was raining, as if, with the change in the weather, all the bad things that had been happening would stop.

She got out of bed slowly. Her suit lay where she had dropped it, limp and smelling of cigarettes and other things—vomit and death. Damn. It would go to the cleaners. But she would never be able to put it on again without remembering Georgie.

Hands on the barre, head bent, she meditated, breathing deeply. *Think good thoughts. Bad thoughts out, good thoughts in.* She worked through her standing exercises and felt better.

Was she getting tougher, more inured to murder? Or was it Georgie? She had been afraid of Georgie. She'd felt threatened by him. Had he been the one searching Buffie's apartment, or had he surprised someone there and died because of it?

She made coffee, showered, brought in the papers. Georgie was news, as the owner of the Caravanserie, only it turned out he wasn't the real owner. According to the article in the *Times,* he had sold it to a British company at the end of 1986, to take advantage of the old tax law, and had been under an agreement to manage it for five years.

Wetzon put aside the papers to blow-dry her hair. For an instant, in the bathroom mirror, she saw once more Georgie's small, cold eyes and cruel mouth. Who had killed him, and why? And why was everybody trying to find out what Barry had said to her?

She sat down suddenly on the edge of the tub and turned off the hair dryer. She was avoiding something. The silk tie that was identical to the one Smith had been wearing. Smith's appointment with G.T., her obvious secrecy. Leon outside Buffie's apartment building. Had Smith arranged to meet Georgie behind Wetzon's back? Georgie's back . . . Coolly detached, Wetzon watched her hands begin to tremble and then shake violently.

She dropped the hair dryer on the bright raspberry bathmat. Oh, shit. She felt as if she were drowning. Two people she knew had been murdered. It was apparent that Silvestri thought she knew more than she did, and he liked Smith, and Smith was being weird. Carlos was too busy resuscitating his old career to be around. Wetzon felt lonely and frightened. And there was no one in her life whom she could turn to for physical comfort. No man for protection. Unless she could count on Rick Pulasky, M.D.

Yesterday, for the first time in her life, she had sized up a situation quickly and had taken charge when she saw she had to. *So, Wetzon, old girl, we will not have any self-pity here.* She threw her hair forward over her face and turned the dryer back on, running the warm air through her hair, shaking out the dampness.

Come to think of it, what did she even know about Rick Pulasky? He'd entered her life abruptly, and she'd made the date with him to spite Smith. But hadn't he been in the emergency room that night?

She stood, determined, went into her bedroom, and dialed information for the number of York Hospital, then dialed that number.

"Can you tell me if you have a Dr. Rick Pulasky on staff?"

"Dr. Pulasky? Hold on a moment, please."

"No, wait—" Damn, they were transferring her to him.

"Emergency." A woman's voice.

"Dr. Rick Pulasky, please." She would hang up if he came on the line.

"He's with a patient. Who's calling, please?"

"Oh, that's wonderful," Wetzon blurted, her fears assuaged. "Never mind. Thank you. It's not important."

But it was important. He was who he had said he was. Now that she had settled that in her mind, she would deal with Smith.

She dialed Smith's home number. It rang and rang. No answer. Smith didn't own an answering machine. She didn't like them.

Wetzon hung up and dialed the office. Harold answered after the second ring. "Smith and Wetzon. Good morning." And to Wetzon's question: "She said she'd be in after ten. She had to stop at Bloomingdale's to return something she bought for Mark that didn't fit."

"Okay, tell her to call me. It's important. I'll be home till one. And let me know if anyone calls. Switzer, in particular."

It would be nice to have Switzer a wrapped-up, done deal this morning.

She took her dark gray suit out of the closet and looked at it critically. Three years old, very severe, but okay for a rainy day. She'd put on the pale blue silk shirt with the white collar and cuffs. It was very feminine but still professional. She made the bed neatly with tight hospital corners and laid out her clothes.

Smith called while Wetzon was popping vitamins with her apple juice.

"Did you see what happened to that scuz, Georgie Travers?" Smith asked without preamble.

"Smith, I found him."

"You what?"

"I was with Buffie—"

"Who?"

"Oh, hell, it's too long a story—"

"Tell!"

Wetzon ran through the bare events. She decided to leave out the silk tie because she did not want to deal with it over the telephone. She'd rather see Smith's face when she told her. She did, however, casually mention seeing Leon outside Buffie's apartment.

"Oh, you couldn't have seen Leon," Smith said, a little too quickly.

"How do you know? Maybe he was talking to a client in the neighborhood." Smith was always so positive she was right about everything. "Or maybe he's having an affair with someone who lives there," she added mischievously.

Smith was outraged. "Wetzon, how can you say a thing like that? You don't know Leon the way I do."

What an interesting remark, Wetzon thought. "Well, I know I saw him."

"I'll find out."

"Smith, do me a favor. Forget it."

"No. Leave it to me. I'll find out if he was there." Smith's voice was breathy. "Did you tell the police?"

"No, but—"

"Don't." She hung up.

Wetzon hadn't told the police about Leon because she had forgotten to, and no one had bothered to ask her if she'd seen anyone suspicious. But then, Leon wasn't suspicious . . . or was he?

At eleven o'clock Harold phoned to tell her that Switzer had just called. "How did he sound? Excited?"

"Angry."

"Uh-oh." With trepidation, she dialed Switzer.

"There was no offer." Switzer was in a rage. He was at his office and it was hard to catch every word. People shouted and phones shrilled in the background.

"I can't believe it. I thought this was a hi-there-how're-you-seal-the-deal meeting."

"So did I. That Garfeld is a schmuck. He just stood there like some fucking asshole."

"I don't get it. What did you talk about if there was no offer?"

"Me. What I did before. I told him how I made a mil in the moving and storage business."

Switzer had skipped college, built a profitable moving business, and sold it to one of the conglomerates. He'd come away with a huge profit. In his mid-thirties he'd looked around for a new career and had fallen into the netherworld of selling penny stocks.

Wetzon had heard that Gordon Kingston, chairman of Hallgarden, was a snob about background, and Switzer had at least two strikes against him: he was not a college graduate, and he came from a blue-collar business.

"Steve—"

"Stay with me, Wetzon, I want to put this order in. I'm having a wild day. I should be sitting here making money instead of wasting my time at all these meetings with assholes."

"Steve, let me talk to Andy and get the whole story. Maybe they're going to let him make you the offer after they talk."

"This really pisses me off, Wetzon. My time is money. I'm out of the office, I'm not making money. No more meetings. I know it's not your fault, but I don't have to go anywhere. I get respect here. And I have a new opinion of Garfeld. He's a wimp."

She hung up and groaned loudly, smacking her quilt with both hands. How could it have gone wrong? What a question. At any time, in the process of any deal, anything could go wrong. But they should have made Switzer an offer, then and there, this morning, and had a done deal.

She phoned Andy Garfeld. "Andy, I just spoke with Steve. What's going on?"

"Well, truthfully, Wetzon, Gordon didn't think he was quality enough for us. And Switzer has a client complaint on his U-Four."

"Quality. Jesus, Andy. You knew his background. He didn't try to hide anything. He told you about the complaint. And he won that arbitration."

"Wetzon, I think Steve should call Gordon this afternoon and tell him how much he'd like to work here."

"Do you really think he'd do that?" Wetzon didn't think Switzer would, but he might. "I think it's insulting. Do you honestly think Kingston will change his mind?"

"No." Garfeld was copping out. "But it doesn't hurt to try."

"In that case, Andy, I think I'll tell him to forget it."

"I'm sorry, Wetzon. Send me some other people. And tell Steve I'm sorry."

Switzer was right. Garfeld was really a spineless wonder. She made careful notes on her conversations with Garfeld and Switzer on the back of Switzer's suspect sheet and returned it to her briefcase. She would let it cool for the weekend and go back to work on Switzer on Monday. If she lived that long. She smiled ruefully. *Nice, Wetzon. Good day for black humor.*

Her detachment unsettled her. Here she was doing business as usual. Had she gotten hard? Was her bottom line money now and not people? Was it, oh, okay, Barry died, Georgie died. Too bad. Next broker, please.

No, no, it wasn't like that at all. She never treated a broker as if he were a piece of meat the way other headhunters did. Each was an individual with problems unique to him. She always listened carefully, and she had always prided herself on the fact that she never knowingly sent a broker to a firm that was wrong for him in personality and style of business.

Wimp. Speaking of wimps, will the wimp in this room stand, please. You know who you are.

She took the crumpled silk strip of mauve cabbage roses from her purse and stretched it out on the bed, staring at it. It surely looked like the same one. She turned it over. In spite of all her doubts, the Bloomingdale's label caught her unprepared.

31

Wetzon usually hated the subway ride to Wall Street. The IRT was a garbage bin. The floors of the old train were worn and pieces of the linoleum were pulled up, and filth was everywhere you looked, pieces of newspaper, candy wrappers, discarded food. Graffiti covered the windows, seats, and doors, as well as the subway route maps. Pity the poor tourists, who thought graffiti was so quaint. There was usually at least one can of soda rolling back and forth with the jerky motion of the train, its probable partial contents spilling out on the dirty floor of the car, making contact between floor and shoe sticky. The subway noise was even worse. The screech and shriek from the wheels on the tracks were deafening.

At the far end of the car a bum lay on his back, sleeping fetidly on several seats, having the whole side of the car to himself, isolated from and ignored by the rest of his fellow passengers. No one appeared outraged by his scent or his behavior. New Yorkers seemed able to blank out what they didn't want to see and deal with. It was like holding your breath around a putrid odor. Or seeing a real war on television. Perhaps.

The train stopped at Fourteenth Street, and only one of the doors opened. Someone clumped on and sat across the car from her. On first view, the new rider was a man, tall and broad-shouldered. What made her—forced her—to look was the shock of hair which stood straight up and ran down the middle of the head, to the nape. The sides were shaved clean. The remaining hair was about three inches in width, if that. Like an Iroquois brave. Only purple. The eyes were heavily made up with black liner and mascara, and the skin was ashen. The ear that was visible to Wetzon had four safety pins piercing it, starting at the lobe and moving upward. Attached to the safety pins were pieces of scrap metal that appeared sculpted, or at least planned. The eyes did not focus but looked downward.

The legs were encased in wide fishnet stockings, full of additional holes and tears and held together, up the side of the one leg that could be seen, by more large safety pins, all the way up into the short, cut-off pants. The feet wore bulky, brown army boots, halfway laced, very polished, and with what appeared to be the tongue of the boot extended.

The body wore a white T-shirt with a faint, faded pattern and a worn work shirt over that, unbuttoned, with the sleeves rolled up. There was no evidence of breasts, but, under close scrutiny, something about the enigma began to give off female vibes. The nails had bright red paint, but that didn't mean anything these days in regard to sex.

In a city where everyone had a statement to make, this one was a thunderbolt. She was somebody's daughter, God help whoever it was. The defiance that emanated from the stiff figure was palpable.

Wetzon shuddered. Her life was in turmoil. She was filled with doubts about herself, her work, Smith, Leon. She was glad Rick Pulasky was coming over tonight. It would be diverting and she wouldn't be alone. For the first time she felt an unease about living alone that she'd never felt before. But this was foolish. It was impossible to live in New York City and not feel vulnerable at times.

The car emptied out at Chambers Street, including the defiant one, and three black teenagers got on and sprawled across from her. They wore high white athletic socks and gym shorts and New Balance running shoes with the big pink N on the side. Expensive shoes for teenagers. She didn't know if they were just ordinary teenagers or if they would jump her and grab her purse. Her usually good instincts were askew. She stood up when the train pulled into Park Place, but the sharp stop threw her back into her seat. Two Guardian Angels got on when the door opened, looking efficient in their dark red berets, and Wetzon relaxed visibly. The teenagers continued talking, paying no attention to either Wetzon or the Guardian Angels.

Boy, her imagination was on overtime. She got off the train at Wall Street. The rain had stopped, but the air was damp and chilly. She buttoned her Burberry. Mildred Gleason's office was at 61 Broadway, not far. It was just short of two o'clock.

The sky overhead grew threatening as she walked down Wall Street, congested with people despite the weather. Originally built as a wall in the seventeenth century to defend the then Dutch city against the English, by the turn of the twentieth century the street had transmogrified into *the* financial district of the country. Over the last fifteen years, the financial district, now known as the Street, had become a mix of old and new: here where Wetzon walked, stolid, concrete buildings were aged and stained with soot and the streets were dark, narrow caverns; and down by the East River, on the southernmost tip of Manhattan Island, where the buildings were all giant towers of marble and glass.

Wetzon was always amazed by the otherworld atmosphere in lower Manhattan. Everywhere, office workers mingled with executives and messengers, salesmen, traders, arbitrageurs. There were very few tourists with cameras in this section of the City. The denizens scurried about the cramped, grimy streets, dwarfed by the sheer mass of structure, real and symbolic.

Perhaps that was why so many of the companies had moved to Water Street and The Battery area, drawn to open space and light. But that light brought discovery with it. The dark old buildings had kept many secrets, and the crooked little streets invoked a sense of mystery. The bright light was almost like an invitation for the SEC to take a look.

Wetzon turned down Broad Street, which in the Dutch days had been a canal. She loved the historical aura of this section of New York. Because of her business she always found herself rushing down for a meeting or an interview and then rushing back to midtown. One day she would walk the streets with a guidebook like a tourist.

It started to rain. She opened her umbrella and turned into the short, narrow warren of Beaver Street. These old streets were dark in normal daylight because even not-too-tall buildings blocked out light. The street was barely the width of a limousine, having been designed for carts and carriages, with slivers of sidewalks added later, and hardly space for more than one person at a time. And when everyone carried umbrellas, as now, it became an obstacle course.

Wetzon was trying to negotiate her way around a fat, bearded man devouring a slice of pizza, oblivious to the rain, when she collided with a woman in a shiny red, wet-look raincoat carrying a huge red-and-white striped umbrella.

"Good lord, it's Wetzon! Why aren't you in your office dialing for dollars?"

Wetzon had been so rapt in thought that she had not recognized Laura Lee Day, a petite woman about Wetzon's age, who held a black violin case in her arm as if she were holding a baby. Laura Lee's brown hair was also in a wet-look and stood up, short and spiky, with blonde tips, but neat. Two years ago Wetzon had recruited her from Merrill and placed her at Oppenheimer.

A refugee from Mississippi, who still spoke with a thick southern drawl when it suited her, Laura Lee Day had come to New York to study violin at Juilliard, but her daddy felt she should either get married or have a serious career, so after a few months he had stopped paying for lessons. She'd gone to work for Merrill as a stockbroker, just to earn money for her music studies. Four years later she had become one of the top producers on Wall Street. She had a beautiful apartment right across the street from Juilliard and paid for her own violin lessons with one of the best teachers in the world.

"Laura Lee Day, as I live and breathe," Wetzon responded in a southern accent. Her words came back at her: *as I live and breath*. Why were all her words death words lately?

"Wetzon, now, Wetzon," Laura Lee scolded gently. "I know what you're doin' to yourself and you're to stop, y'hear?" She stepped into the street to let someone pass. "Shut your baby umbrella and come under mine."

"Laura Lee, I'm a mess," Wetzon confessed, folding her umbrella and ducking under the huge red-and-white one. "I've been a mess since—"

"Not another word, Wetzon, darlin'. Y'know, I was thinking about you today. Let's move on off the sidewalk. We are causing a perfectly frightful traffic jam."

Tiny, ancient Beaver Street, where the Cotton Exchange had once been headquartered, almost gave one a feeling of optical illusion. The buildings rising high above it seemed to tilt in, like trees, over the people far below. A car crept slowly toward them, forcing them back onto the sidewalk.

Wetzon looked at her watch. "I'm late," she said, without her usual obsession to be on time for appointments.

"Where are you off to?" Wetzon held Laura Lee's umbrella arm and they walked toward Broadway.

"I have an appointment at Sixty-one Broadway."

"Where to after that?"

"The Vista Bar at five o'clock."

"Good. After you finish at Sixty-one Broadway, you come right on over to my office and pick me up." Laura Lee was ebullient, even on a dull day, and she was bubbling with energy today.

"What are you up to, Laura Lee? Where are we going?"

"Century Twenty-one is having a big sale on silk lingerie."

"Laura Lee," Wetzon laughed, "you're crazy. I don't wear silk lingerie." They stopped on the corner of Beaver and Broadway.

"Well then, darlin', it's time you did," Laura Lee said emphatically. "It'll do wonders for your self-image." She chortled. "And your sex life. See you."

What sex life? Wetzon thought, watching Laura Lee's cheery red figure sashay off in the direction of the World Financial Center.

32

Sixty-one Broadway was one of those wonderful old art deco buildings. The main doors were inlaid with geometric designs in brass on bronze, like the Frank Lloyd Wright stained glass windows that were in the Metropolitan Museum. The lobby had obviously been recently restored, all the brass polished to a high shine, the trim and borders sharply defined. She waited for the elevator in the lobby. There was not much traffic in and out at this time of day. When the elevator doors opened, a girl in a sedate denim dress started off, then, seeing Wetzon, sidled away, eyes and head down. Buffie. It was Buffie. Wetzon went after her, cornering her near the newsstand.

"Buffie. What are you doing here?"

Buffie looked at her insolently, tossing her hair, which was in a ponytail today. "It has nothing to do with you."

"Did you find Barry's material? Are you coming from Mildred Gleason's office?"

Buffie shook her head stubbornly. Her mouth was a thin hard line.

"You fool. Two people have been murdered." The girl's greedy stupidity infuriated Wetzon. "Let the police handle it. I hope you told them yesterday about the 'insurance' and Barry's writing?"

"Leave me alone," Buffie said, pushing Wetzon away. "It's none of your business."

Shocked by Buffie's violent reaction, Wetzon stumbled against the magazines and dropped her briefcase. When she looked up, Buffie was gone. She wasn't behaving at all like the Buffie from yesterday. No weakness, no tears. Nothing fragile about her.

"I'm sorry," Wetzon said to the newsdealer, an old man with white hair and faded eyes, whose bulbous nose was liberally decorated with broken blue veins. She picked up her briefcase.

"Takes all kinds these days," the newsdealer said in a faint brogue.

She got on the elevator, so deep in thought that she forgot to press the fifth-floor button, and the elevator stopped to pick someone up on ten. Oh, well, she would stay on for the ride up, and she waited impatiently for the elevator to pick up others on the remaining floors. The elevator, too, was a work of art, bronze and brass, fine geometric lines, a sense of history and pride revealed in the fact that it had been cared for so well for all these years. It said, "old money," and, "you can depend on us." *Sure,* Wetzon thought. Then, *You're getting cynical, old girl.*

The reception area of M. Gleason & Co. also had that look of trust-me about it. Wood paneling, English antique furniture, mahogany and walnut, dark wood, and an oriental rug on the floor. The receptionist, an attractive older woman with a lot of white hair rolled in a traditional chignon, greeted Wetzon warmly but professionally. "Good afternoon. May I help you?"

"I have a two-thirty appointment with Mildred Gleason."

"Your name?" She had a large agenda book open on her desk.

"Leslie Wetzon."

"Oh, yes." She checked off Wetzon's name in her book. "I'll take your coat for you, and if you'll just have a seat for a moment, I'll let Ms. Gleason's assistant know you're waiting." As the woman rose, her phone rang.

"That's all right," Wetzon said. "I'll do it. Is that the closet?" She pointed to a closed door near the entrance.

The woman nodded. "Mildred Gleason and Company, good afternoon," she said into the phone.

The closet gave off a faint floral scent. Wetzon hung her Burberry next to a black leather trench coat and settled into a large chintz-covered wing chair. *The woman's touch,* she thought chauvinistically, but she didn't care. The world of investment banking was like one great private men's club, a fraternity that grudgingly permitted some women to enter, but only because, in these times, they couldn't keep them out physically. But psychologically and in reality, women were and would always be on the outside. Everything about the industry, down to the decor, was male-oriented. She mentally congratulated Mildred for being her own person.

The receptionist seemed to be having trouble getting through to Mildred Gleason's assistant. She dialed several times and let it ring. Finally she said, "I can't seem to locate Ms. Bancroft, Ms. Gleason's assistant, so I'm going to ring Ms. Gleason. . . . Oh, Ms. Gleason . . . yes. I can't seem to get through to Bobbie . . . oh, she is . . . Ms. Wetzon is here to see you . . . yes . . . all right." She put down the phone and smiled at Wetzon, standing. "If you'll come this way." She opened the door, revealing a wide, well-lit hallway carpeted in rich, plush gray. "Down this hall, make a right at the end, and walk straight back. Ms. Gleason's office is at the far end of that corridor." She stood aside and let Wetzon through. The door closed behind her with a soft click.

How different this was from Jake Donahue's. The walls were lined with old prints, Currier and Ives type of prints. Maybe even the real thing. After all, Mildred Gleason's father had been a major rainmaker on the Street back in the forties. Wetzon walked slowly, looking into the offices that opened off the corridor. The fairly spacious offices held one or sometimes two brokers. All the doors were open, and the market activity came in a quiet flurry, not in an uproar as at Jake's. All very professional. People talked in moderation, and even the phones rang with muted *brrr*s.

She turned right and walked down another pleasant space, more Currier and Ives prints, doors opening off the hall. The quiet buzz of voices followed her. The door at the end of the hall was half-open, and Wetzon paused. She heard angry voices. Women's voices.

"You are not going to pay anything. I won't let you. Don't you know she's lying? It's obvious she doesn't have it."

"*You* won't let me? Hold on here. Aren't you forgetting who you are? Who I am?" The deep, rasping voice was Mildred Gleason's.

There was a long moment when no one spoke. "I could never do that. You never let me forget—not for a minute." Something, a book perhaps, slammed on a hard surface. "Oh, God, my head is killing me."

"Bobbie dear, please don't be angry." Gleason's voice was pleading. "You know it only makes the pain worse. This has been such a mess. And I have—*we* have—so much at stake." There was another long pause. "You mean so much to me."

The other voice responded, "Sometimes you have a strange way of showing—"

The voices quieted into murmurs.

Wetzon felt a pang of guilt at eavesdropping. It was a peculiar conversation for two women to have, unless they were having a relationship. Actually, she had never considered Mildred Gleason as sexual even though she had been married to Jake Donahue, who had a reputation as a womanizer. She knocked on the door.

"Come in, come in." Mildred Gleason rose and came out from behind her desk, hand outstretched. She wore a tailored black wool gabardine skirt, a rose silk shirt, and a wide black alligator belt with a large gold buckle. "I'm so grateful you were able to come. Here, please sit on the sofa. . . ."

Wetzon entered a room full of antiques. A beautiful old partners' desk stood in front of the windows and a very large oriental rug lay on the floor. The jacket to the black gabardine skirt lay oddly out of place on top of the desk, as if Mildred had just taken it off. The window blinds were angled down, leaving the room in dim light.

The other woman was sitting in the far corner, in a wing chair similar to the one in the reception room. She wore an outfit of deep olive green and did not get up. Wetzon was barely able to see ropes of pearls of varying lengths over a full bosom. It was difficult to tell the woman's age because she wore dark glasses and a patterned silk turban that picked up the green in her dress and completely covered her hair. Ignoring Wetzon, she gave a soft moan and pressed a long, thin hand on the side of her head.

"This is my assistant, Roberta Bancroft. She suffers terribly from migraine." Gleason gave the word the English pronunciation, *meegraine.* "I hope you don't mind if she stays while we talk. I have no secrets from Bobbie." Mildred smiled fondly at her assistant, who moaned again. "That's why we've drawn the blinds. The light is agony for her. I hope you don't mind."

"Not at all," Wetzon said. She looked at Roberta sympathetically, careful not to stare. There was something . . . about her. . . . "Have we met before, Ms. Bancroft?"

"I don't believe so," Roberta responded in a low voice. "Forgive me, it is painful for me to speak." She did not offer her hand.

Wetzon seated herself on the sofa, and Mildred sat slightly to the right in a Chippendale side chair. On the butler's tray coffee table was a silver trivet holding a crystal pitcher of what looked like lemon slices floating in water. Nearby were a small, silver ice bucket and some handsome crystal goblets, probably all Waterford.

"I keep a pitcher here all the time," Mildred said, gesturing toward the water. "It's so much better for me than coffee. I get too wired on coffee. Will you have some? It's just water, good old New York City tap water."

"Yes, I'd like that. This is a beautiful room, Mildred."

"Thank you. It's my sanctuary, isn't it, Bobbie?" Despite her air of poise, Mildred's hands trembled as she raised the crystal pitcher, and a little water splashed over the side of the goblet. Her eyes were sunken and red-rimmed. "Oh, my, I'm just not myself today," she continued wearily, mopping up the spill with a linen napkin. She looked drained, white and tense, though, in a strange way, not as bad as she had looked when Wetzon first met her in Harry's. Her nose had seemed thicker then, her chin less defined. Now her face seemed fuller and younger.

Of course, Wetzon realized, wondering if she was gawking, Mildred must have had a face lift. Wetzon leaned her briefcase on the floor against the sofa and took a sip of lemon water. It was good.

Roberta shifted her position several times, crossing and recrossing slim ankles, not speaking, sending out waves of impatience. Mildred Gleason, watching her anxiously, stood up, the gold bracelets on her narrow wrists clinking. Her fingers played with the heavy gold chain around her neck. Two small, dark perspiration spots stained the underarms of the rose silk blouse. She closed the door to the hallway and leaned against it as if to catch her breath. A Bunker Ramo on her desk burbled and bleeped like a stew pot. Wetzon hadn't seen one of those machines in a long time. Most of the firms had switched to Quotrons. She had good legs, Wetzon thought, her mind drifting.

"I . . . ah . . . Barry . . ." Mildred began. The phone rang. She whirled and picked it up. "No calls . . . didn't I say no interruptions? . . . Oh . . . why am I being bothered, Bobbie?" Bobbie didn't answer. Mildred looked, as she spoke, more and more disordered, standing there leaning over her tremendous desk, her hair on end, her makeup smeared, the perspiration stains on her beautiful blouse. She lit a cigarette, still bent over the desk. "Who? Oh . . . I'll have to call him back . . . what was the name? . . . Tell him four-thirty will be fine. Now, *no* interruptions." She hung up. "I'm sorry about this . . . uh, these last two days. . . . My God, where was I?" She straightened up as she spoke. Ashes dotted her dark skirt.

"Barry."

"Yes. Barry. That was the police, you know. A detective named Silvestri wants to see me at four-thirty today." Wetzon had the distinct feeling that Mildred was speaking to Bobbie even though she was looking directly at her.

"You? Why?" Wetzon asked.

"Don't you know? You must know. . . ."

"Of course she knows." Bobbie's voice was dipped in scorn. She didn't move.

"I'm sorry. You're confusing me. I don't know why you wanted to see me. Perhaps if you could tell me what this is all about?" Mildred's nervousness was contagious. Wetzon found Bobbie, in spite of her migraine, sitting stonelike with her dark glasses and her arms folded, intimidating.

"I *heard* it," Mildred Gleason said distractedly. "I heard him being murdered and I couldn't do anything. I knew they would trace it. I've been expecting them. Oh, God, it was horrible. I *heard* him being murdered."

In the corner, Bobbie made a coarse noise that was a cross between a cough and a laugh.

"You . . . Barry? *Barry* was calling you when he was murdered? Why?" Wetzon was baffled. What did it mean? One thing it meant for sure: if Mildred *had* heard Barry being killed over the phone, she had not murdered him.

Mildred strew more ashes with a quick, restless gesture of her hand. "He was working for me. We were working on something, a deal, on the side. . . ."

"I told you not to trust him. He was a lying scumbag." Bobbie made no effort to hide her contempt. "He double-crossed us."

Mildred lit another cigarette from the remaining tip of her butt, then stubbed the first out convulsively. She shot an angry look at Bobbie. "It was a secret." She drew closer to Wetzon. "You've got to help me, Leslie. May I call you Leslie?" She sat on the arm of the sofa, not waiting for an answer. "I know you can, and I'm desperate. I'll make it worth your while. I'm a very wealthy woman, you know . . . and I'm very good to my friends."

"Oh, my, yes," Bobbie said. "She certainly is."

Wetzon was revolted by both of them. "I'd like to help you, Mildred, but I don't know what I can—"

"You can tell me what he told you. I know you were close. He always spoke so highly of you."

"But he didn't tell me anything, just that he was in big trouble, serious trouble. And we were not close," Wetzon corrected, annoyed.

"You're holding something back. That can't be all. Try to remember,"

Mildred cried, leaning toward Wetzon, flourishing her cigarette. Its smoke stung Wetzon's throat. "Or maybe you're playing games with me." There was menace in her voice. The tendons in her neck twisted. "I don't like games."

Bobbie half-rose, moaned, and sank back in the chair. Gleason moved quickly to her and grasped her hand. "Mildred had high hopes for Barry, I'm afraid," Bobbie said softly. "She's such a kind person. He was having trouble with Jake, wasn't he, Mildred? We all know Jake's a liar and a thief. Barry came to see Mildred, as a friend. Jake hadn't kept his agreement with Barry. No surprise there. I think that's what it was, right, Mildred?" Bobbie's hand still clasped between hers, Mildred grew visibly calmer. Bobbie went on. "We think Barry found out something about Jake and that's why Jake killed him. He's a violent man who will stop at nothing to get what he wants." She spoke with a fevered vehemence. Her features were blurred in the dusky light.

"Yes," Mildred said, pulling away, pacing the room restlessly. "Jake could have done it. He's capable of anything. Trust me. That's why I have to know where Barry—" She stopped short and sat near Wetzon on the sofa.

Roberta gave a whimpering sigh.

"Really, Mildred, I don't know. He started talking about repos. . . ." Wetzon fidgeted, trying to move away from her. This close, Mildred Gleason seemed incredibly malevolent, like a child's image of a witch, come to life. And Roberta's persistent moaning was eerie. If she was in this kind of pain, why was she sitting there with them?

"Go on . . . that's not it, but go on," Mildred urged, her potent cigarette breath enveloping Wetzon. Wetzon drew back.

"That's all. He asked if I knew what they were and I said no and he started to explain."

Mildred's face spasmed. "No, there *has* to be more. He must have said *something* else. Did he mention *what* he was doing for me?"

"No. He never mentioned you at all. He was very upset. More than that, he was frightened. He said he had to make a phone call, and he left."

"He didn't mention the tapes?"

"The tapes? What tapes?" Wetzon remembered the cassette from the attaché case that she and Smith had listened to. So it had been made for Mildred Gleason. And there were more of them somewhere. "No." Wetzon shook her head. She wished Gleason would put out that horrible cigarette. "No, he never mentioned tapes, or you."

Roberta rose, a tall and slim-hipped shadow, and leaned on the back of the chair, as if she was about to leave the room.

"Did he have *anything* with him?" Mildred's attention floated disconcertedly between Wetzon and Roberta.

"Just his attaché case."

"Where is it? That's it," Mildred said, excited, clawing her arm. "What did you do with it?"

"Please, you're hurting me," Wetzon said, pulling her arm away. She thought fast. She didn't want to get into an explanation of the accident in the park and the robbery. "Why would I have it? The police have it."

"God damn it!" Mildred's gravelly voice cracked. "It was my big chance. I'll never get another one like that." Her nervous fingers tore at the gold buckle on her belt.

"This is a colossal waste of time," Roberta announced in a loud voice.

"What did Barry say to you over the phone?" Wetzon asked, watching Roberta uneasily.

"I don't want to have to hear this again," Roberta said. She opened a side door and went through, closing the door behind her.

"I'm sorry," Mildred said. "She doesn't mean to be rude. It's just that dreadful migraine, and she's so upset about everything that's happened." She took a long pull on her cigarette, choked, venting acrid smoke.

"I understand," Wetzon said, trying to be sympathetic, but failing. Nausea swept over her. She shook her head. "You were telling me about what Barry said." Her voice was strained.

"He didn't finish . . . he said . . . 'The bitch, we're fucked . . .' then he laughed this weird laugh . . . 'but I've got the tapes.' I said, 'What tapes, Barry?' He never told me *how* he was going to do it, you see. Then he said, 'What are you . . . are you crazy?' Then he made some noises, awful noises, then nothing."

A toilet flushed. Wetzon started.

"I couldn't disconnect," Mildred continued, not reacting to the sound. "I kept trying to hang up. I didn't know what to do. I knew something terrible had happened. I knew the police would get to me eventually . . . I needed time . . . to think . . . I couldn't call them, you see. . . ."

"You should have done it right away."

Mildred's thin-lipped mouth twisted over smooth, white, capped teeth. "Oh, what difference does it make now? I've got to get those tapes before . . . they were my last chance. . . ." Her voice drifted off. Her face sagged with hopelessness and defeat. Her skin tone had faded to a yellow-tinged gray.

Wetzon stood up. "Maybe the police have them," she said. She had been there long enough.

"No, Barry was too smart for that . . . he would have hidden them somewhere. Oh, God, I was so close— One more week, he said, and we'd have Jake just where we wanted him. He'd been working on it all winter. He didn't tell me what or how. He was so smart. I didn't want to know. I didn't even know about the tapes until the phone call."

"I'm afraid I don't understand."

"Don't you see? The tapes. They would have finished off that double-dealing son of a bitch Jake Donahue, don't you see? It would have been all over. Over." She put her face in her hands.

Loud voices could be heard outside. A woman shouted angrily, and a door slammed. The noise came down the hall, closer.

Despite her repulsion, Wetzon felt a twinge of pity for Mildred Gleason. She put her hand on Mildred's bent and bony shoulder. "I'm sorry I couldn't help you, Mildred." She moved toward the door. Sure, Barry had been so smart he had gotten himself murdered.

The door burst open without preamble, and a powerfully built man stood there in a purple rage. His face was distorted with fury and a thick vein throbbed in his forehead. "You fucking cunt!" he screamed, shaking his fist at Mildred, who sprang to her feet, equally enraged. Jake Donahue.

Wetzon backed out of the way. Lately she always seemed to be in the line of fire.

Brokers and staff spilled from the bright hallway into the murky room, the men grabbing Jake and pulling him back, away from Mildred.

Wetzon drifted toward the door. She certainly didn't want to run into Silvestri here.

"I'll kill you, you hear, you fucking bitch! You stay out of my business or I'll kill you!"

"Bastard, bastard!" Mildred shrieked. "Get out of here!" She clutched at him, hands like claws, raking his face, before she was pulled back.

There were so many people crowded into the office now that no one saw Wetzon duck out. Jake wasn't going to kill Mildred, and everyone would calm him down and send him home. He had brooked Mildred's sanctum sanctorum, and that was enough to drive her over the edge. Wetzon could hear Mildred screaming incoherently as she slipped unnoticed out of the office.

The saddest thing in all of this was that no one was mourning Barry Stark, not even she, Wetzon thought, as she pulled her Burberry from the closet in the reception room. The black leather trench coat that had been next to it was gone.

33

Laura Lee Day's office in Oppenheimer Tower of the World Financial Center was the dream of almost every broker Wetzon had met. It was deeply spacious, with velvety taupe carpeting, and an extraordinary view of lower Manhattan, including the Statue of Liberty.

"You sit right down here, darlin', and rest yourself," Laura Lee said. "I just have one more phone call." Laura Lee was wearing a deep purple wool crepe suit with enormous shoulder pads, a white silk blouse which fell in folds from her throat, and huge mabé pearl earrings. Her slim legs were in sheer black hose, and she tottered slightly on extra-high heels. She was a little woman who thought big.

Wetzon curled up in a peach and milk-chocolate striped club chair in front of Laura Lee's expanse of black lacquer desk, on which papers, reports, and files in multicolored folders were neatly stacked next to a Quotron and a small calculator.

Laura Lee pulled a lavender folder out of the rainbow stack, then pressed a button on her phone without picking it up.

"Yes, Laura Lee," Laura Lee's sales assistant said.

"Get Harry Cleveland for me, please, Joanne. Then no more calls. Wetzon and I have an important business appointment outside at three-thirty." She flashed Wetzon a dazzling smile.

Wetzon wondered vaguely why Laura Lee was so specific about the time. Her phone buzzed.

"I've got this little old seven-figure trust fund to deal with," Laura Lee intoned, taking some papers out of the lavender folder and settling into her desk chair. "And then we'll get some silk next to our skin. Wetzon, you have no idea what a difference it—" She smiled a cool, professional smile. "Yes, Harry, I'm just fine. I hope y'all are well? Good." She became brisk, losing most of her southern accent. "The check arrived this morning. I have studied the portfolio, and I am in the process of writing out an analysis, but why don't I share a few ideas with you now? As we discussed, I think we should sell the oils. I don't think we'll see a lot of movement there for the present. No. The area can be volatile, too much so for this portfolio. There should be more play in the food group or the consumer group. Maybe P. and G. Yes. I'd get out of the banks. If we see interest rates blip up in the next few months, that group will suffer, as will your utilities. I will go through your utility holdings and make some decisions about which ones to keep. No. Wrong timing. We want to stay away from anything that is interest-rate sensitive. I have to think that through carefully. I like the drugs at this juncture so we'll keep them for the time being. Yes, I agree. They are undervalued."

Laura Lee looked up and smiled at Wetzon. "Harry, I'd like to reallocate some of the assets because I think you are overweighted in certain categories," she continued, "and I think the portfolio could use a conservative real estate investment. The rest I think we should keep liquid, either in money market or T-bills. But all of this will be much more complete when you receive my analysis." She listened intently, then punched some buttons on her quotron. "Mmm. Yes. I just checked. Forty-eight and an eighth. Near its low. Good time to buy, I think." There was a pause as she listened again. "No, I don't like it. It's too much of a high flyer for this type of account. . . . Why thank you, Harry. I'll call you after I hear from him. Not at all. The pleasure is mine." She hung up, eyes bright. "What a doll. He's referring Jerry Goldwater to me. Jerry Goldwater, the real estate mogul, who just bought himself a movie company!"

"Laura Lee," Wetzon said, impressed. "I am simply overwhelmed. You are fantastic."

"There. Now that that's settled, Wetzon darlin', suppose you tell Laura Lee what this is all about." Laura Lee plunked herself down in a loveseat covered in the same peach and milk-chocolate fabric as the chair in which Wetzon was sitting. On the small chrome coffee table between them was a huge glass bowl filled with anemones in various shades of purple. "You're looking downright frayed and not your usual bright and cheery self."

"I don't feel like my bright and cheery self," Wetzon said dryly.

"It can only be that dear old Barry is reaching back from the grave."

"Laura Lee, don't joke."

"I'm not." Her round face was solemn. "Don't forget, I knew both of them—Barry better than Georgie, of course. We were all in the same training class, but I was sent to a different branch office."

"I'd forgotten—or maybe I never knew." Wetzon was weary. She had not had a chance to mentally process her meeting with Mildred and Roberta. "I feel as if I'm getting pulled into something I don't understand and I can't seem to stop it." She sighed. "I feel as if I've lost control of my life, that I've failed in some strange way."

"Listen to me, Wetzon. You are a genuinely nice person, and there aren't many people I can say that about, let alone headhunters."

There was a soft knock on the door and the door opened a crack. "I'm going for coffee, Laura Lee," Joanne said. "Do you or Ms. Wetzon want anything?"

"Not for me. How about you, Wetzon?"

"No, thanks anyway, Joanne."

"Now, where were we?" Laura Lee asked.

"You were telling me how nice I am," Wetzon said. Laura Lee was funny in her serious mode.

"Don't make fun of yourself, Wetzon," Laura Lee scolded. "I wouldn't be here and have all this"—she waved her arm around her office—"if it weren't for you. I was ready to leave the business when I met you. Remember?"

Wetzon nodded. She remembered. Two years ago, Laura Lee had been discouraged and depressed. The stock market plunge on Black Monday had devastated her, as it had every broker, particularly those who had never seen the market do anything but go up. Laura Lee felt her business wasn't developing in the right direction, and she was being harassed by someone she worked with. Wetzon had asked her, "Did you like it when you started out in the business? Do you like the act of selling? And do you like making money?"

Laura Lee had answered yes to all three questions, and Wetzon had suggested she look at Oppenheimer, Bear, Stearns, and Alex Brown, three classy boutiques, where all the paperwork, posting, recordkeeping were done by qualified assistants, where all a broker had to do was sell, where the products were super-sophisticated, designed for the high net worth individual.

"You changed my life, Wetzon," Laura Lee said. "I don't know where I'd be now if it weren't for you. You told me I was terrific. You gave me confidence. You believed in me. I love what I do, and I'm really good at it. I am a professional. I help people. And you do, too. Which brings me to—" She pressed the button on her phone. "That's it, Joanne. I'll be back in an hour." She stood up and pulled Wetzon up. "Let's go, darlin'. I want to talk to you about a friend of mine. She's meeting us at Century Twenty-one at three-thirty."

34

"What did you think of Barry?" Wetzon asked curiously as they walked up crowded sidewalks, past clogged traffic, on Broadway to Cortlandt Street. Cortlandt ran into historic Trinity Place, behind Old Trinity Church. Cortlandt to Trinity, Dutch to English.

"Barry? A handsome devil," Laura Lee said, knotting the belt of her shiny red raincoat. "Dimples, cleft chin. Great body. All in all, a hunk."

"Oh?"

"Don't 'oh' me, Wetzon. I've got the same kind of hormones every girl has. He came on with me, but he wasn't my type."

"What's your type, pray tell?"

"Barry Stark was a *boy*, Wetzon. And dumb. I like men. Successful men. Smart men. What do you like?"

What *did* she like? "You're right about Barry," she said. "He was a boy—"

"Come on, Wetzon, don't try to wriggle out. What do you like?"

"Brains, I guess. Humor." *Silvestri*.

"Well, the late Barry Stark didn't fit any of our categories, but he had no trouble attracting other women. They loved him."

Wetzon nodded. "I'm not surprised."

"Actually, to be frank, Wetzon, he was a loudmouthed animal with no class, and he did a big business selling drugs—both he and Georgie did—until Georgie got into the disco business."

"I'd heard that rumor about Barry."

"It's the godshonest truth. Take it from me, darlin'. I was there. Everybody knew. Eventually, he would have gotten caught. It was only a matter of time . . . with the insider trading scandals, and all . . . everyone is looking for dirt."

"Maybe that's why he was killed."

"Maybe. Who knows?" Laura Lee frowned at a pushcart chef who was creating billows of acrid smoke as he grilled shish kebab over hot coals. "He wasn't all bad, though. He was real nice to me, even after he knew I wasn't buying—him or the drugs. He used to help some of us in the class with our cold calling pitches. He was really good at it. So was Georgie, but Georgie wouldn't help his own grandmother if she was in a wheelchair barreling down a hill." She made a face. "Georgie was a pig." She took Wetzon's arm. "You know, once, after he went to Donahue's, Barry even referred a big account to me. Someone who wanted to buy half a mil in bonds. It knocked me out. I called to thank him, and he said I should take good care of the guy. I think he was embarrassed. Can you imagine Barry Stark embarrassed?"

"No," Wetzon agreed.

"I still have that account," Laura Lee mused.

"What a strange thing for him to do."

"Not so strange. He knew I wouldn't burn the guy out."

Laura Lee opened the door to Century 21, and they entered what at first looked like a job-lot store. Shoppers, mostly women, were milling among piles of merchandise. A stubby, middle-aged woman and her look-alike teenage daughter were systematically going through the boxes of shoes that were stacked in tottering, uneven rows against a wall. Tables overflowed with merchandise, and women jostled one another for positions.

"Ah, here we are." Laura Lee began sifting energetically through a table of silk lingerie. "Aren't these gorgeous?" She held up a pink teddy, Christian Dior tag still on. "Wetzon, this has your name on it. It's your size. Treat yourself."

Wetzon laughed. "Okay, but I'll never have the nerve to wear it." She moved on to the next table, to slips and camisoles, dodging the elbow of a sleek black woman, who murmured, "Sorry."

"Wetzon," Laura Lee said, at her side, arms full of lustrous silk. "My friend—you know the one I mentioned I want you to help? She's going to meet us here."

Wetzon groaned and shook her head at Laura Lee. "You'd better tell me about her."

"Her name is Amanda, Amanda Guilford, and she's *really* good."

"I know her name. I may have talked with her. Where is she now?"

"She was at Shearson until last summer." Laura Lee held up a white camisole with pale blue embroidery across the breast. "Isn't this precious?"

"That's why I know her name."

"It's not my size," Laura Lee said, disappointed.

"I'll take it." Wetzon reached for the camisole as Laura Lee shook a mocking finger at her. "Where is she now?"

"Donahue's."

"Oh, shit, Laura Lee—"

"Wetzon, what difference does it make, honestly? Amanda needs help and I know you can help her."

They were reaching under piles of lingerie, scooping, holding up to each other what they found. The feel of the silk, the humidity, and the hum of other women around them struck Wetzon with a strange intensity. She remembered the moment in *Moby Dick* when Ishmael is working the ambergris with another sailor. It was hypnotic and sensual, as now.

"Wetzon? Hello, darlin', are you there?" Laura Lee was waving a pair of violet silk panties at her. "This is my friend, Amanda Guilford."

A beautiful young woman with long, sun-streaked blonde hair and a peaches-and-cream complexion, a golden look that Wetzon envied, stood at Laura Lee's side. She was a full head taller than Laura Lee.

"Hi. I'm really grateful to you for talking to me," Amanda said, smiling with pink lips over perfect teeth. She had a flat, New England accent.

"It's going to crowd up as soon as the market closes, girls," Laura Lee said briskly. "So I'll pay for everything, Wetzon, and we can settle up later." She grabbed the items in Wetzon's arms and rushed off to the checkout counter, leaving Wetzon with Amanda Guilford.

Amanda flipped aimlessly through the silk panties on the table. She had the athletic build of a swimmer or tennis player, enviably broad shoulders, a narrow waist, under her belted Burberry, china-blue eyes, a square chin, and a throaty voice. Clean good looks. Very little makeup.

"I suggest we sit down over a cup of coffee, if that's okay with you," Wetzon said. Laura Lee thrust a small bag at her, which Wetzon put into her briefcase.

"I've got to get back, girls, so have a good talk," Laura Lee bubbled, full of bonhomie. "I'll check up on y'all later." Smiling like the Cheshire cat, she left them with a fading remembrance of darkly outlined eyes and bright red lip gloss.

"Why did you leave Shearson, Amanda?" Wetzon asked, when they were settled in a booth of a nearby coffeeshop.

Amanda shrugged her glorious shoulders. "Bored, I guess. I like selling stock. My manager at Shearson wanted me to sell mutual funds, unit trusts, product . . . you know, Shearson product." She deftly squeezed the Lipton teabag around her spoon and dropped it on the saucer.

"But why Donahue's? There are a lot of firms that don't push you to sell product. Oppenheimer, for one." Wetzon sipped the decaf brew that tasted like caramel-flavored water.

Amanda nodded. "I know. I made a terrible mistake. I met Jake Donahue at a party." She looked at Wetzon. "He's an exciting man. He made it sound like a lot of fun. He promised he'd feed me with a lot of his stocks and I'd make a ton of money. He was very convincing."

"If he kept his promise, you probably made a ton of money."

"I did in the beginning." She unbuttoned her raincoat and slipped out of it. She was wearing a simple camel wool jersey dress and a string of pearls. Very Connecticut and not very much like the other brokers Wetzon had seen at Donahue's. "Then Jake asked me to do him a favor."

For the first time Wetzon noticed the faint, dark smudges under her eyes. She wondered suddenly if Amanda knew Barry. She had to. But what if she was the girl from Connecticut Georgie had mentioned, the one Buffie had seen Barry with at the zoo?

"What kind of favor?" Was it sexual, or was it something that would compromise Amanda and make it difficult to place her at another firm?

"Not that." Amanda's reaction was immediate, getting Wetzon's drift. "Well, not exactly." She smiled a self-deprecating smile. Pale golden freckles trailed across her small nose and fine cheekbones, looking almost painted on. She was exquisite. "He wanted me to come on to a broker there, get close to him and tell Jake what he was doing."

"Spy?"

"Spy, I guess."

"What did you say?"

"I said no, of course, what do you think?" She reddened, a touch offended.

"I'm sorry."

"Don't be." She cut the air between them horizontally, with her hand. "I had to in the end because that bastard Jake began to starve me out on his stocks."

"Who was the broker he wanted you to spy on?"

Amanda shook her head.

"Let me guess," Wetzon said. "Barry Stark."

Amanda looked startled. She nodded. "He was a great-looking guy," Amanda said. "I liked him. It was easy. We had some good times." Her blue eyes filled. "But I had to make a choice, and I know if Barry had to make the same choice, he would have done what I did." She took a handkerchief from a brown leather clutch bag and blew her nose meticulously.

"Did you find out what Jake wanted to know?"

She played with her pearls, rolling them through her fingers. "Barry was taping Jake's calls. He and his partner were trying to get something on Jake."

"His partner?" Mildred Gleason, of course.

"He would never tell me. God, it's been awful these last few weeks. Barry said Jake threatened to kill him. And the day he was murdered, he and Jake had a terrible fight—"

"Did he know how Jake found out?"

She shook her head. "No. Oh, maybe he suspected. He told me he had a diary. He called it his insurance policy. I heard him tell Jake, too, that last day."

"Have you talked to the police, Amanda?"

"Yes, two detectives came to the office this morning, but I didn't tell them anything except that we spent a lot of time together."

"But why not?" Wetzon found everyone's reticence exasperating. "You should have told them the whole thing."

"I couldn't—I can't—" Now the china-blue eyes spilled over. "Jake said he'd ruin me. He'd see to it that I'd never get clearance to work anywhere on the Street again. I'd lose my license."

So it wasn't simple after all. She was right. Jake could do what he had threatened. Amanda could tell all and, as with every whistle-blower, find herself on the outside. Blackballed by gentlemen's agreement, banished from the Street.

Wetzon pulled a small yellow pad and a pen out of her briefcase.

"Okay, Amanda, tell me this. What was your gross production at Shearson for the twelve months before you moved to Donahue's?"

"One hundred seventy-five thousand. My second year in the business."

"That's good. How about since you came to Donahue's—nine months, is it?"

"Around three hundred thousand, but most of it is on Jake's stocks."

"Get your runs together, and we'll have you out on interviews first thing Monday."

"I've already Xeroxed my books," Amanda offered eagerly, perking up.

"I'll call you on Monday, but I want you to be prepared to interview immediately. Do you have any preference about firms?"

"No wire houses. What about Alex Brown? I've heard nice things about them." She fixed her eyes on Wetzon and smiled.

"We'll start there." Wetzon's watch said four-thirty. "Have a calm, restful weekend, and don't worry. It'll be fine. You'll be fine."

"Oh, Wetzon, I don't know how to thank you." Amanda wrung Wetzon's hand. "Laura Lee said you're wonderful, and you are."

Wetzon picked up the check. Amanda waited for her at the door.

"Amanda, did you ever meet Barry early in the morning at the zoo?"

"Me?" She looked confused. "No. I never go near zoos. I blow up like a balloon. I'm horribly allergic to animals."

35

Wetzon was waiting for Howie Minton in the lobby bar of the Hotel Vista, thinking what a big waste of time it was to meet him again. Howie Minton had a brainstorm every year, during which he thought he wanted to leave L. L. Rosenkind. Last year it had been because of a new manager. How strange men were about change. If something was displaced in their environment, they felt threatened instead of challenged to make it right again. It happened all the time. The new manager had a different approach, or perhaps the chemistry between him and Howie was wrong.

She had come across only one broker who moved every few years because he felt it was good for him to have a change. Saul Mossberger claimed it made him work harder and kept him interested and on his toes. She could see his point. It was an easy business to plateau in. Many brokers reached a certain point of growth and then stayed there. Saul had been in the business twenty-five years and had moved four or five times and now was getting ready for another move. But he was decidedly different from anyone she'd met in the brokerage business. He'd spent his developing years in a Nazi concentration camp. Now over sixty, he didn't take Wall Street machinations very seriously. He had a big trading business, mostly immigrant refugee clients who had come here with nothing and made good. They were gamblers at heart, loved to play the market. . . . "Do you want to order something while you're waiting?" the waiter asked.

"Yes, Perrier with lime." She wondered how the Mildred Gleason–Jake Donahue confrontation had been resolved. If they'd been let loose on each other, there surely would have been a double murder. She was sick of the whole business. And then there was the beauteous Amanda Guilford. It never ceased to amaze Wetzon what a small world the brokerage community was. Everyone seemed to know everyone else.

She looked at her watch. Ten after five. Brokers were rarely on time for appointments. Most of them were drowning in details—paper, information. There was so much to do before they shut down at the end of the day. So much they were responsible for. She took a sip of her Perrier and thought about Mildred Gleason again. If Mildred *had* been Barry's partner, and if Barry *had* been taping Jake's phone conversations, it was to use in some way against Donahue. But not officially. Wetzon didn't think unauthorized tapes of phone calls could be used in court. Even more curious was the fact that Barry had not told Mildred about any tapes until almost his last words. For some reason, he wasn't feeding her the tapes all along.

Well, eliminate Mildred as Barry's murderer. Mildred hadn't killed Barry because she had been on the phone with him when he died, so maybe Roberta was right—Jake Donahue had done it. Donahue certainly had the best motive. The last thing he would have wanted was to let his embittered ex-wife get her hands on something she could use against him. And hadn't Silvestri asked her if she had seen Jake that night at the Four Seasons?

Until today, Wetzon had only seen photographs of Donahue in newspapers and magazines. He was always good copy. But it was nothing like meeting him in person, especially when he was in a rage. He had a tough, jowly face with the jaw of a streetfighter. Not someone you'd ever want to be angry with you. He had been incredibly successful, all the while leaving bodies behind him. What a thought—leaving bodies behind him. Astonishing what the subconscious could come up with.

And what about Roberta what's-her-name, Mildred's assistant? Her bizarre behavior must have had to do with their personal relationship, not business. Still, why did Wetzon feel they had met before?

"So, Wetzon, it's really been nice seeing you again. Bye-bye. Keep well."

She looked up to see Howie Minton standing over her, laughing at her.

"My God, Howie, how long have you been standing there?" Feeling like an idiot, she slid over on the banquette. "Here, sit down. I'm really sorry. I was thinking about something and lost track of where I was."

"It's all right. I'm easy. So tell me," Howie said, sitting down, adjusting his white French cuffs, flashing gold cuff links, "why did you murder Barry Stark?"

"Oh, Jesus, Howie, that's awful."

"Oh, come on now, I'm joking . . . see . . . it's a joke. Ha, ha. You know it's a joke," Howie said sincerely. "Besides, everyone who ever knew Barry Stark wanted to murder him at one time or another."

"What are you saying, Howie? I didn't even know you knew him." There it was again. The Street was a family, for better and for worse.

"Sure I knew him. He was a slug, a real lowlife. He turned a lot of nice people into veggies. Listen, this is my philosophy, there's so much money to be made legally, who needs to—"

"You should talk to the police, Howie. You could give them some leads, maybe," she responded, equally serious.

"Yeah, I could tell them about Mildred Gleason." Howie flicked some lint from his sleeve.

"Mildred Gleason?" Wetzon sat up. "What about Mildred Gleason?"

"Promise you won't say anything, Wetzon, and I'll tell you."

"Oh, Howie, you know I don't talk. If I told what people tell me, I'd be out of business." She slipped her hands under the table and crossed her fingers on both hands. "Okay, I promise." God, what had she come to?

"Vodka tonic," Howie told the waiter. "All right. Remember at the end of September last year, right around the Jewish Holidays, we had this record-breaking heat wave? Every day for a week the temperature was around a hundred?"

Wetzon nodded. The waiter returned with Howie's drink and a bowl of popcorn.

"So I have a good client—a Greek—and he has a chain of coffeeshops. He likes to trade, big, but it's all—let's put it this way—I have to go pick up the money."

"Oh, Howie," Wetzon said, knowing he meant it was cash money. "That's so damned dangerous."

"Don't worry, Wetzon. It's under control. My manager and I have it all worked out." He stirred his drink with the yellow plastic stirrer. "Anyway, at this point the market is laying there like a beached whale, so dead that I'd go all the way to Greece for the money, if I had to." He laughed a little too heartily.

A group of bronze-skinned men in expensive suits came into the bar and sat at a table across from Wetzon and Howie Minton. They were talking passionately, rapidly, in Spanish.

Howie lowered his voice; Wetzon bent toward him to hear. "I come in the back way, as always, through a private entrance, and Kostos's brother has it all ready for me. So I sit down in the back office and start counting. Nickie—that's the brother—brings me a Turkish coffee, and when I go to put the money in my briefcase, I knock the damn cup over and get a spot on my tie." He looked at his tie as if it had just happened. "I'm telling you I'm really bugged—it's a new Paul Stuart tie. I take my case and come out of the office to look for the men's room. You know these coffeeshops—they have two rows of booths with a common partition. Well, on the upper half of Kostos's booths, there's a mirror, so I lean into a booth to check out my tie, and damned if I don't hear—" He licked the popcorn salt on his fingers. "Do you want to hear the rest?" He was teasing her.

"Howie, come on," Wetzon protested. "Give."

"Okay, okay, I'm as nosy as you are. The first thing I hear is that foghorn voice of Mildred Gleason, and she's doing a number on someone about what a bad move he made. And I'm dying to know who it is and pretty soon she calls him Stark so I know damn well who she's crapping on."

"What do you mean 'a number'?"

"Oh, you know, about the new-issues market being dead and Jake going back on his deal. Then she tells Stark how good her business is, and he gets more depressed by the minute. Says his life is falling apart and his air-conditioner conked out, and you can tell she's loving every minute of it. She says to him he can work for her and he lightens up right away and then she gives him the old one-two. Not as a broker, she says, you have no book—like he's not good enough to shine her shoes. You've got all your clients in Jake's crummy stock, she says, and I don't give freebies to brokers to rebuild their books. Jesus, what a bitch. I'm almost feeling sorry for the poor bugger. By this time, Wetzon, old buddy, I gotta tell you, I have my nose to the goddam partition."

Wetzon was so engrossed in Howie's story that she did not see the waiter until he said a rather loud, "Ahem."

"I'll have another vodka," Howie said, checking his solid gold Rolex.

"Perrier," Wetzon said. "What happened next?"

"Well, she says she'll pay him big bucks for information about Jake that she can use to get back her father's firm. You know, of course, that Donahue's was her father's company and Jake took it over and changed the name?"

"I know."

"Anyway, she gets him interested. Papers, tapes, wiretaps, whatever, she says, but she wants enough inside dirt to bury Jake. Ha! Knowing Jake, he's probably doing the same thing with her."

The waiter brought their drinks and took away the empty glasses.

"So," Howie continued, "Stark picks up on it right away and gets her up to a hundred and fifty thou and a limited partnership before he's finished. She agrees to give him ten thou on account and then she tells him it's all going to be handled by her assistant. Boy oh boy, Stark made some deal," Howie said enviously.

"Yes, he did, didn't he?" Wetzon was unable to keep the sarcasm out of her voice.

"Oh, well, so it goes," Howie said nonchalantly. "When you play with fire, you gotta know you're going to get burned."

"Did you hear anything more?"

"No, because she called for the check. I took off before they stood up."

"What a story. Didn't you tell anyone about it?"

"Who was I gonna tell? Jake? I'm an observer on this one, Wetzon. My motto is, don't start something you can't finish. I saw Stark about a week later, and he was on top of the world, prancing around Harry's in his Vuarnets with that tall blonde broker from Donahue's."

"Don't tell me you don't know her name, Howie?" Wetzon joked.

"I don't, Wetzon," he said, taking her seriously, looking chagrined. "Do you?"

"No." She was trying to keep a straight face. "About Barry, though, I think you should tell that story to the police."

"Not on your life. I don't want to get involved. It wouldn't look good. And it wouldn't be healthy. Who knows why he was aced? It could have been a lot of different things. Believe me."

"Okay, let's talk about you. How's Ellen feeling?"

"Great, great. The baby's due in six weeks."

"Wonderful."

"And we bought a house. In Manhasset."

"So you've become a commuter."

"Yeah, and it's not so bad. I read the papers on the train in the morning, read the financial reports and the ten-Ks on the way home."

"And how are things in the office?" Wetzon asked, steering him to the crux of what had brought him out to meet her once again.

"Well, that's what I wanted to talk to you about. You know I think of you as my friend."

Whoever said that dishonest people can't look you in the eye? she thought instantly, meeting Howie's sincere ones.

"Okay, I'm listening," she said.

"Another one of my good clients, I put him into one of our high-tech stocks, you know, an R.R.R., a Rosenkind research recommendation, and he went in heavy, because it looked really good—" Howie paused and reached for his drink.

"And?"

"And the stock took a nosedive—a big one—and he was in the hole fifteen thou—" Little beads of sweat had formed on Howie's upper lip.

"So? That wasn't your fault. The company recommended it, and he bought it."

"Right. My client said he didn't blame me, but he was writing a letter to the company to complain about the stock and the way it acted after they recommended it, and he wanted me to know that's what he was going to do."

"Okay, very nice of him."

"Right. So he writes the letter, and Compliance calls me in and the head of retail is there, and my manager, and the head of research, and they tell me they're going to give this guy his fifteen thou back. They don't want lawsuits and publicity, and then they drop it on me. They're going to take the fifteen thou they give him back out of my future commissions."

"That's terrible. Unfair. What did you say?"

"I said that's terrible and unfair and you're making me very unhappy."

"And what did they say?"

"They said, that's too bad for you."

"So you want to look around again?"

"Yes. And this time I'm serious, Wetzon. I'm ready to make the move. I want to show them they can't do it to me. I'm not in this business forever, you know. I want to lay away some equity and get out by the time I'm forty. You know what I mean. One big killing and I'm out of this rat race."

There it was again. The big killing. They were all looking for it.

"So what do you say, Wetzon, my friend?"

She smiled at him. "Let's go for it. How much do you have in so far this year?"

He pulled a folder out of his briefcase and showed her his runs. "This is a very important step for me, Wetzon. So I feel good that we're going to work on it together."

It was after six when Wetzon and Howie Minton shook hands.

"I'll call you Monday and let you know what I'm doing," she said.

"Start with Shearson," he said.

"Okay."

"Thank you, my friend," Howie said. "I'm going to run for my train." He got up, ignoring the check, which the waiter had left on the table. "Wetzon," he said, taking her hand again, "keep well. And take my advice, as a friend, don't get involved with this Barry Stark business. And stay away from Jake Donahue. There's something bad coming down there."

"Wait, Howie," she called after him. "Tell me—"

"Gotta run, Wetzon. Stay well." Howie strode away, straightening his French cuffs: a well-dressed man of twenty-eight whose yearly income was well over $150,000. It was amazing. Yes, Howie was right. In what other industry could such young men make so much money so quickly and so legally?

She paid the bill, left the waiter five dollars, and went down into the belly of the World Trade Center to take the IRT back uptown. Rush hour was almost over and the platforms and trains were much less crowded than they would have been an hour earlier. She got a seat on the #2 train, the express, which she could take up to Seventy-second Street and switch to the local.

She would stop at Zabar's and buy nice uncomplicated things like coffee and cheese. She had not forgotten about her date with Dr. Pulasky.

36

Zabar's on a Friday night. Not the best time to try to rush in and out. There were three limousines double-parked in front. She could remember when Zabar's was just a small neighborhood fancy deli-grocery, with pots and pans and kettles and gadgets hanging from the ceiling. Now it had tripled its size, adding prepared foods and salads and knishes, fresh cookies, a chocolate shop, many more unique breads and rolls, and a second floor that undersold every housewares shop in the world. People came to New York City now with the request to see Zabar's, as if it were a landmark like the Statue of Liberty.

She took a number from the machine near the cheeses: 99. The number on the light box was 80.

She walked around the aisle of prepackaged cheeses, looking at the different types from all over the world, and picked up a soft, creamy French brie. There was no prewrapped Royal Province with peppers, so she would have to kill time until her number was called.

Kill time. More death words, she thought, as she went to get the coffee, which was now in the renovated addition of the store. Here were the coffee beans, big wooden barrels full, set in a semicircle. The grinders were all going full speed. Although they didn't give numbers here because the lines were usually shorter, that was not the case tonight and she would have to wait. But in general, people on the coffee line were polite and didn't push. She wondered if coffee drinkers were less hostile. The cheese people were impatient, and the fish and meat people were often pushy, even angry.

The two coffee clerks were moving in almost a syncopated rhythm, filling the treated paper bags with beans, tossing the scoops back into the burlap sacks in the barrels with a soft *whoosh-swoosh*. The smell of ground coffee was intoxicating.

It was almost another fifteen minutes before she walked back through the rear of the store and into what had once been the main store, passing the hot and cold foods, pasta salads on her left and the smoked and other fish counter on the right, walking to the front, toward the cash registers, alongside of which were the breads, rolls of infinite variety. The croissants, muffins, and scones were piled up on trays on the counters next to the rugalach, which were not always available. There were long lines at each register.

"We have a special, ladies and gentlemen, on croissants tonight, sixty cents each. Take some home with you for tomorrow's breakfast," the metallic voice over the speaker urged. She took four.

She was beginning to feel the strain of the day. She half-wished Dr. Rick wouldn't come, so she could just put her body into bed and forget about the last two days.

Wetzon, you dope, she chided herself. *There are no men in your life, and here's this adorable doctor who likes you, and all you want is to be alone. You should have your head examined.*

A sharp breeze had sprung up when she left Zabar's. Fewer people were on the darkened street and those were hurrying home to dinner. There was a line at the Loew's theater complex for the seven o'clock show.

On the corner of Eighty-third Street and Broadway she stopped at the Burger King and bought two coffees, with three sugars each, to go. It might be too late, and Sugar Joe was probably already under his blanket at the bus stop on Eighty-sixth Street, but she owed him the coffee because she'd missed him for the last two days.

She walked up Broadway, balancing her briefcase and the paperbag with the hot coffee in one hand, the small Zabar's shopping bag in the other, and her shoulder bag on her shoulder, the strap of which kept slipping off because she had both hands occupied. Her open raincoat flapped in the wind, catching at her legs.

"Hi, Joe, sorry I missed you," she said, bending to place the hot coffee next to what she decided was the head of the blanket-shrouded body. As usual, no movement, no evidence that anything was alive under there. She straightened up. There was a faint grunt from the blanket. "Good night, Joe," she said softly, mostly to herself, and headed across the street.

At this time of day, particular to this time of year, when daylight vanished all too quickly, leaving a certain rawness in the air, a peace-filled silence settled over the City. Shops were closed, grillwork up, streets emptied, children were home at dinner; yuppies were either not home from offices or home and preparing to go out to dinner. Traffic and noise in all of the City's middle-class neighborhoods faded gradually. Wetzon loved this special quality of New York. It was as if the magnificent machine that was New York wound down and literally came to a rest for a short time before the crew of the night shift came on.

Right now, as grateful as she was for the stillness, her thoughts moved inexorably back to Barry Stark and the ultimate stillness of his death.

A giant crane stood at the far side of the avenue where a building was under construction, surrounded by the usual on-site clutter: dumpsters, a concrete mixer, stacks of bricks and cinderblocks, and an assortment of large black metal drums. The deep shadows of unfamiliar objects were reflected in the hazy light from the street lamps.

Her shoulder bag slipped off her shoulder again as she was crossing to the north side of Eighty-sixth Street, shifting her center of balance. Her abstraction was pierced by a peculiar, hollow cry that echoed distortedly, bouncing off the sightless glass windows of Lichtman's Bakery on the southwest corner of Eighty-sixth and Amsterdam.

"Out—out—out—*out!*"

She pivoted, catching a whiff of a familiar scent, and something tore at her coat. A sharp blow on her side from another direction winded her, spun her out of control, rendering her unable to scream, and threw her across the avenue. Her instincts all the while messaged her to relax, relax in flight, for she was flying, no brakes, no help. She rolled over and over in the dirt and refuse, slamming into something solid.

Stunned, tangled in the raincoat and shoulder strap of her handbag, she half-crawled toward the dull light. Her hair had come loose and was hanging in her eyes. Had she been mugged? Is this what it was like? She looked up cautiously from her crouching position to get her bearings. She was half under the construction crane. Dirty, filthy, torn hose. Awful mess. Car horns blaring.

On her knees now, in the distorted shadows cast by the streetlights and car headlights, she saw what appeared to be two figures dancing grotesquely in the middle of Amsterdam Avenue. Rigid, breathless, she watched in horror as one of the dark figures separated from the other, arms raised skyward. The streetlight caught on something, glinted, something in the hand, coming down hard on the other figure. She heard a short cry, like that of a small animal in pain, and then a gurgling sound, as if someone was choking. One of the figures broke away and ran toward Broadway. The other figure, spinning briefly, staggered, then toppled over in the street. Traffic was at a standstill. An oncoming bus came to a shuddering halt. The cabdriver behind the bus hit his horn, adding it to the others. From the shadows, people began to gather.

Moving with bruised precision, like Coppelia, Wetzon pulled herself up, trying to grasp what had happened. Her briefcase lay with the torn Zabar's bag in front of the crane. She must have held on tightly until the last moment. She was missing a shoe.

The avenue was alive with voices, horns, lights, people. Limping, holding her purse by its long strap, she wove her way to the front of the group of people and saw the crumpled body of a man lying on the street. His long white hair fanned out over the pavement. Someone in uniform, a doorman from one of the adjacent buildings, bending over him, cried, "He was mugged, he was mugged!"

"Terrible," someone said.

"Ordinary people can't go out at night anymore."

Approaching him, Wetzon took off her raincoat, rolled it up, and slipped it under the fallen man's head. She didn't know if he was alive, but his eyes, in a long, cavernous face, were closed. The last two dead people she had seen had open eyes. *My God,* she thought, *where am I? Am I having a nightmare?* She straightened up, confused, and limped back to the crane. Where were the paramedics? She crawled around on her hands and knees looking blindly for her shoe; then, not finding it, she picked up her briefcase and what was left of the Zabar's bag and walked the short distance to her building.

Javier, the night doorman, was standing in front peering behind her, toward Amsterdam Avenue. "What—" he started. He stared at her as if she were an apparition.

"Quick, Javier, call the police," she cried. "Someone was just mugged. He's lying in the middle of the street." Javier hesitated, then raced to the phone at the back of the lobby.

Then a new sound, the *putt-putt* of a Honda, came west across Eighty-sixth Street. The Honda pulled up directly in front of her—it was Rick.

A sharp cry rose from someone in the small crowd gathered at Amsterdam and Eighty-sixth.

"What's going on?" Rick asked, turning off the motor and unloading a big shopping bag. "What happened to you?"

"Not me, Rick, hurry, someone's been mugged. Can you see—"

He dropped the shopping bag unceremoniously at her feet. "Wait here," he ordered, and raced to the corner.

The Zabar's bag, her briefcase, everything she was holding slipped out of her hands without her being aware. A siren sounded and then two blue-and-whites sped past her, screeching to a stop on the corner.

Wetzon leaned awkwardly against the door of her building, wondering why she couldn't straighten her body. She was listing to the side. Oh, she had lost a shoe. She took off the remaining one. That was better. From where she stood she could see the rolling police lights bouncing off storefronts and an eerie yellowish reflection in the dark sky. The crowd was strangely mute. Car and bus noises had subsided. Traffic was probably being detoured.

Another siren shrieked and a white emergency medical truck came up Amsterdam and pulled up beside the two police cars. Helplessly, she felt herself being drawn back to the accident, unaware that she was shoeless. There was something she was trying to remember . . . before she was pushed. She caught the thought and held it. Pushed? Had the mugger—

Rick emerged from the crowd and walked toward her, slowly.

"Rotten business," he said, shaking his head, putting his arm around her.

"What was it? Is he all right?"

"No, he's dead. What happened to you?" He was looking her over professionally.

"I don't know. I got caught in it, I guess. It was almost me. I think I was . . . someone pushed me out of the way. Who was the man? Do you know who he was?"

"A derelict. Apparently he slept in the bus stop on Amsterdam and Eighty-sixth. Someone recognized him."

Wetzon felt sick. She couldn't breathe. "Oh, no. Sugar Joe."

"Sugar Joe? You knew him?"

"Yes. He liked his coffee with a lot of sugar," she said, distraught. "Oh, God. I'm so sorry. Who would have wanted to kill him? He didn't hurt any-body. I've been bringing him coffee. . . ." Her voice broke. "Why would any-one want to kill him?"

"Who knows? There are some really crazy people out there. Come on, babe, let's go upstairs. I want to get a better look at you. I think you've had enough for today. Listen to your doctor." Rick picked up the shopping bag and, bracing her with one arm, led her to the elevator.

Javier followed with her briefcase and the shopping bag, handing it to her as she got on.

"Hey, what's this?" Rick was staring at the back of her jacket. "How did this happen?"

"What? Oh, I don't know," she said wearily. "I felt something and then someone hit me or pushed me—"

"This is bad stuff," he said, putting down the shopping bag and inspecting her back. "Your coat was slashed—this isn't a tear. This was done with a knife. But it's only the coat that's cut. You were lucky." He ran his hand gently down her back.

She collapsed against him, and it felt good. He was wearing a crisp, freshly laundered blue shirt under his jacket, and his body was hard and fit. He smelled of antiseptic. Clean and pure. She needed that right now. She couldn't stop shivering. He pressed the Up button and the elevator door opened.

"How was he killed, Rick?" she asked, unable to let go of it.

"The last question about this?" He looked down at her sternly.

"Oh, yes," she said. "I promise." But that didn't mean she wasn't going to think about it.

He kept his arm around her and pressed 12. He hesitated for a moment. "He was stabbed," Rick said.

37

She was back on the Floor of the New York Stock Exchange, but it was full of exercise equipment, and the traders and specialists were working out on the equipment. Everyone was going at a frenzied pace on bicycles, treadmills, and rowing machines. The floor was thick with order slips and ticker tape, and as she moved, the pieces stuck to the bottoms of her feet and between her toes. *Wait a minute,* she thought, *where are my shoes? For that matter, where are my clothes?* She realized, appalled, that she was walking entirely naked on the Floor of the New York Stock Exchange. Naked except for her best string of pearls.

"Oh, for heaven's sake," Smith said, exasperated, coming out of the pool. She was wearing a black pinstripe suit and was oblivious to the rivulets of water pouring from her. "You don't know how to take care of yourself, Wetzon. You're really impossible. You can't walk around here like that. You just don't understand this business. Here, put this on." She wrapped Wetzon in a big towel that said CARAVANSERIE in giant red letters. Turning to her companion, she said, "Leon will take you home, won't you, sweetie?"

"Of course, dear heart," Leon replied. He had come out of the steaming pool wearing a bikini. "Anything you say . . ."

Wetzon giggled. A scarecrow in a bikini.

"Here," Wetzon said to the dripping Leon, handing him the towel. "I think you need this more than I do."

"No, no, you can't do that!" Smith cried, furious. "Look at yourself. Take this." She took off her wet jacket and put it on Wetzon's shoulders. Wetzon, resigned, slipped her arms into the wet sleeves, shuddering from the clamminess of the material.

"Shall I take her home now, dear?" Leon asked Smith.

"No, I'll take her home," Silvestri said. He was running in place on a moving treadmill. "Come on board," he said, holding out his hand to her. Decidedly relieved, Wetzon took his hand, a workman's hand, strong and thick, and she jumped up behind him on the treadmill, which moved off through the Stock Exchange.

The door to the ladies' lounge was wide open, and Wetzon caught a glimpse of a copper-haired woman sitting in front of a dressing table in a negligee, peeling an apple with a large paring knife.

Wetzon put her hand in the jacket pocket hoping to find a token for the subway so that she could get home, but the only thing there was a matchbook.

A Good Humor man in a white jacket was running along beside them. "What'll you have, babe?" he asked.

"I don't know," she said.

"Come on, I don't have much time. Pick a flavor. You've got to tell me. It's getting late." He looked at a huge Mickey Mouse watch on his wrist.

"Why do I have to?"

"Don't ask so many questions. Just do it."

"Okay, I'll have a toasted almond," she said. She always had a toasted almond if she ate a Good Humor. He ought to know that.

"Sorry," he said. "All I have is rocky road."

"But I don't like rocky road, and I don't think it's a Good Humor flavor."

"I'll get you toasted almond if you give me the key," the Good Humor man said craftily. His dark eyes looked familiar to her.

"The key to what?"

"Nothing," Silvestri said gruffly. "The key is not the key."

"I have to get going, babe. Last night was terrific."

"Mmmm," she said.

"Hey, open your eyes, princess."

She opened her eyes. Rick. She'd been dreaming that weird dream again. It was getting to be like a soap opera. Every time she closed her eyes, a new chapter.

"Welcome back to the world," Rick said, smiling at her.

"Thank you for putting me together again," she said, remembering.

"Comes with the white coat," he said, bending over her. Beads of water from his hair, still wet from the shower, sprinkled her. She reached up and pulled him down on top of the quilt, on top of her.

"You're very nice," she said, kissing his ear. "Come back."

"I will," he said, stroking her through the quilt.

"Mmmm," she said.

"Duty calls," he said, getting up reluctantly. He kissed her on the lips lightly, touched her cheek. "Lock up behind me, babe."

She heard the door close and sighed. He'd cleaned her up, calmed her down, fed her, and made love to her. She had been so needy. She got out of bed and walked naked into the foyer. The apartment smelled of fresh coffee. What a doll. He'd made coffee. She peeped into the kitchen. God, he'd even cleaned up everything from last night and put out the garbage.

The newspapers lay on the floor near the door. She locked the door, left the papers where they were, and got into the shower. The shower curtain was damp, and there was a subtle change in the atmosphere of her usually pristine bathroom. She smiled. Lovely Saturday. Lovely, quiet Saturday. Healing time.

It was miraculous that she'd escaped injury last night. Poor Sugar Joe. She felt as if almost all the violence of a lifetime had been telescoped into the last few days.

She wrapped herself in a towel and was struck by the sense that she had just done this same exact thing. Had she already taken a shower this morning? No. Then what was troubling her? It was that damn dream.

Too quiet. Very strange. Her phone had not rung since she'd come home last night, and she had not checked the machine. She picked up the phone in the bedroom. Dead. What the hell . . . She went into the dining room and picked up the phone on top of the answering machine. Dead. Crazy.

She played back her messages. The newspaper people again, every last one of them. She'd heard all that before. Smith. Carlos. Jake Donahue. Jake Donahue? Just that, Jake Donahue and a phone number. Then Smith again, sounding agitated.

"Where are you? Call me right away."

The downstairs buzzer sounded. "Yes?"

"Ms. Smith coming up."

"Shit," Wetzon said, hanging the wet towel back on the rack in the bathroom and putting on her terry robe. There went her private, quiet Saturday.

Her doorbell rang imperiously several times. "Okay, okay, I'm coming," she grumbled.

She opened the door and Smith, in snug, straight-legged jeans and a shapeless, yellow Shaker knit sweater, was standing there, arms full of newspapers. "Jesus, Wetzon, what's with your phone? Do you know there's something wrong with your phone?"

"Yeah, I just tried to call you," Wetzon lied.

Smith walked past her, dumped the newspapers on the floor, and picked up the phone in the dining room. "Dead," she said unnecessarily.

"I know," Wetzon said, rolling her eyes, humoring her.

Smith got down on her hands and knees and looked behind the old pine dry sink. She groaned. "Did you ever think of plugging it in?" She plugged in the phone and stood up, dusting off her hands. "Your wonderful treasure of a maid does not clean behind furniture. He's certainly not good for much."

"Now how could that have happened?" Wetzon said, puzzled. "And with both phones, too."

"You lead a wild and unpredictable life, Wetzon." Smith pulled off her bulky sweater, draping it over the barre. She was wearing a yellow T-shirt with a lot of black question marks across her breasts.

"I love you, Smith, but what the hell are you doing here?"

"Haven't you seen the papers or heard the news, you dummy?" Smith sounded miffed. "Look." She bent and picked up the *New York Post* from the floor. "Look at this."

Wetzon stared at the familiar face in the photograph that covered most of the front page but didn't focus on the headline for a few brief seconds. It was Mildred Gleason, one of those "before" pictures, before facial surgery, but definitely Mildred Gleason. And the headline said: SECOND WALL STREET MURDER.

38

"I still can't believe it," Wetzon said.

They had spread out all the papers on the living room floor. The clear northern light coming through the windows made the blaring headlines seem unreal. There were pictures of Jake Donahue, old pictures of Mildred Gleason in a Joan Crawford outfit with the shoulders out to here, when she'd been one of the first women members of the New York Stock Exchange. There was even a stiffly posed picture of Jake, Mildred, and her father, Joseph F. Gleason, all in a group of officers of the Joseph F. Gleason Company. Mildred's and Jake's faces were singled out with black rings.

Mildred Gleason, president of M. Gleason & Co., the investment banking and brokerage firm, was stabbed to death sometime last night in her elegant executive suite at 61 Broadway. According to police spokesman Edward McCarthy, Ms. Gleason's body was discovered by a cleaning woman about 11:00 P.M. last evening. There were no signs of a struggle. The body was found face down in the doorway leading to her private bathroom. The wound was in the back, and there appeared to be no sign of a struggle, indicating that Ms. Gleason may have known her attacker. The report of the medical examiner noted that Ms. Gleason died at approximately 9:00 P.M.

"I just can't believe it," Wetzon said again. She flipped through the papers for an item on Sugar Joe. Nothing.

"What are you looking for?" Smith asked suspiciously. She was sitting cross-legged on the floor, her eyes bright and excited.

"Just more on Mildred Gleason," Wetzon said, not ready to tell Smith about last night. She got to her feet. "I should get dressed. Come on, talk to me. Do you know there was a message from Jake Donahue on my machine?"

"How would I know that?" Smith asked innocently.

In the bedroom Wetzon bent, reaching behind the nightstand, and reattached the telephone. Smith followed her, kicked off her shoes, and lay down on the unmade bed, inhaling deeply. "Mmmmm," she said, "there's been a man in your bed."

"Oh, shush," Wetzon said, opening her lingerie drawer. "That's odd."

"What's odd?"

"I don't know. Something's stuck in here." She put her hand into the partly open drawer as far as it would go and groped around. "What the hell is this doing here?" She pulled out a white half-slip trimmed with lace.

"Very pretty."

"I must have moved it without thinking. It's usually on the bottom of everything. I haven't worn it in years." She refolded it and tucked it away on the bottom of the drawer, took out clean panties and a bra, and closed the drawer smoothly.

"So how was the good doctor?" Smith asked, plumping up Wetzon's pillows.

"Good. How was Leon?" She pulled a new Ralph Lauren red sweatshirt over her head and looked at herself in the mirror. Not bad, considering all that had happened.

"Leon." Smith looked at Wetzon disapprovingly. "That's much too big on you."

"I like things big," Wetzon said, irritated.

The phone rang. "Hello," Wetzon said, adjusting the elastic on her old gray sweatpants, which were also probably too big in Smith's eyes.

"Hi, babe, just checking up on you. How are you feeling? Good medicine last night?"

"Good medicine, Rick." She felt herself blushing.

Smith closed her eyes and sighed audibly. Wetzon turned her back on her.

"How about tonight?" he asked. "Movie and pizza or sushi?"

"That would be nice. Either. What time?"

"I'm off earlier today and on late afternoon and night tomorrow. Let's see. Do you like old movies? *Notorious* is at the Regency."

"Oh, I'd love to see it again," she said. "It's my favorite Hitchcock."

"Great. I'm going to do a workout first. Do you want to come with me?"

"Where?"

"The Caravanserie . . . we get a membership through the hospital."

"Ordinarily, I'd join you, but . . ." She flexed her knees. "Ouch," she said. "Forget it."

He laughed. "Okay, meet me at the Regency at five-thirty. There'll probably be a line, so whoever gets there first should get on line. Oh, and, babe, leave your hair down. I like it that way."

She hung up the phone, smiling. She turned around and saw Smith laughing.

"The cards say two dark men for you," Smith said. "*Two*, you pig." She got up and stretched.

"Oh come on," Wetzon said. "It's either feast or famine with me, not like you."

"And they say one of them is not so nice."

"Oh yeah?" Wetzon said. "Well, I only know of one dark man in my life, and he's very nice, and he's not really dark—he has gray hair. Let's have some of the coffee that nice gray man left for me." Still barefoot, she moved into the kitchen, Smith at her heels.

"I had such a deep sleep," Wetzon said, pouring the coffee, "and now that I think of it, such a strange dream. You, Leon, Silvestri . . . people I didn't know . . ."

They took their mugs of coffee and went back to the papers on the living room floor.

"It's related to Barry, isn't it?" Smith said, sitting on the floor, leaning against the coffee table and reading the accounts of Mildred Gleason's murder again.

"It has to be. She kept asking what he'd said to me. Can you imagine, Smith, she said she was talking to him on the phone when he was being murdered. . . ."

"How awful. But she must have figured out who did it. That's why she got taken out." Smith actually had a gleeful expression on her face, as if she were talking about a placement, not a murder.

"Barry was working for her. He'd made some tapes, and she was going to use them to get Jake Donahue. That piece of tape we heard must have been one of them."

"No kidding," Smith said lightly.

Wetzon eyed her friend. How strange. There it was again: the odd feeling that Smith already knew about the tapes, what they meant. How could she? Wait a minute. Leon. Leon represented Jake Donahue. The key. *The key.* How could she have forgotten?

"What did you do with the key, Smith?" Wetzon demanded.

"The key?" Smith asked vaguely. "Oh, yes, the key. It's in my desk. I decided you were right. We should stay out of it."

Not we, Wetzon thought. *You.* "Oh, Smith, that's great," she said, breathing easier.

"I'll give you the key on Monday, okay?"

"Sure, that's wonderful. We can throw it away and forget about it."

"I wonder if there's anything more about the murder on the radio," Smith said.

"Let's see." Wetzon walked on her knees over to the stereo, wincing at the tenderness from last night's escapade. "It's eleven o'clock. There should be some news." She switched on the radio.

They listened to a rundown of the world news, then: "Locally, police report no further developments in the Wall Street murders. The second murder, that of investment banker and socialite—"

"Socialite," Smith snorted.

". . . Gleason, took place in her executive suite at approximately nine o'clock last evening. Employees of M. Gleason and Company have reported a violent altercation earlier in the day between Gleason and estranged husband Jacob Donahue, noted Wall Street guru. An employee, who did not wish to be named, declared it had stopped just short of blows and that there had been bad blood between them."

"Bad blood, Jesus," Smith said. "Who writes their copy?"

". . . reported but not confirmed by police that stockbroker Barry Stark, who had worked for Jacob Donahue, had been talking to Gleason on the phone at the time he was murdered. We will continue to follow up on this case as events unfold. . . . The sanitation workers, who have been working without a contract for—"

Wetzon snapped off the radio. "Sooo . . ." she said. "I saw some of that violent altercation."

"Oh, tell."

"Jake broke into Mildred's office screaming and yelling. He was angry enough to kill her."

"Aha!"

"Damn, now Silvestri will find out I was there."

"Probably."

"And want to question me again."

"Probably."

"He'll think it's a little weird that I've been close to three murders . . . *I* certainly do." Wetzon was silent for a moment as Smith watched her. Then she said thoughtfully, "You know, Smith, I bet if we put the pieces together right, we can solve this before the police do. Everyone I've talked to has told me something he or she hasn't told the police."

Smith waited, eyes veiled.

"I'm sure Barry must have told me something that I haven't remembered. He wouldn't have just given me the key without an explanation. . . ."

"I'm starving," Smith said. "What do you have to eat?"

"You know me. Bagels."

They went into the kitchen, and Wetzon took a bagel and sliced it in three pieces. They sat at the counter with their coffee.

"What are you doing tonight?" Wetzon asked.

"Leon is taking Mark to the Planetarium this afternoon and then we're having dinner at Tavern on the Green." She made a face.

"I thought you didn't like Tavern on the Green."

"I was outvoted. They're supposed to have a new chef."

"What happened to Silvestri?"

"Oh, he's around, but after all, he's just a cop. An attractive cop, I admit, but he's not really for me. Mark needs a role model."

"Silvestri would be a good role model."

"Wetzon, don't be obtuse. You know what I mean," Smith said, not looking at her.

"Yes, you mean Silvestri doesn't make enough money for you."

"Well, he can't take me to the Four Seasons."

She had stopped listening to Smith. Something had skimmed across the surface of her memory, eluding her again.

"Mildred's assistant, Roberta, sat through most of the meeting," Wetzon said, thinking out loud.

"So?" Smith opened Wetzon's refrigerator and took out a bag of dried papaya.

"I don't know. There was something creepy about her." Wetzon wrinkled her forehead, eyes distant. "Tall, very chic, but covered up."

"Covered up?" Smith bit into a piece of papaya and chewed gingerly. "Not bad . . . the papaya, I mean."

"Dark glasses, turban—you know—no eyes, no hair. Peculiar relationship."

"Well . . . Mildred Gleason . . . she was a notorious dyke—"

"I didn't know that. But anyway, what does that have to do with anything?"

A curious expression formed on Smith's face. "Oh, Wetzon, you are so dumb sometimes, I don't know what we're going to do with you."

39

Wetzon busied herself making more coffee, so as not to let Smith know she was hurt. *Dumb.*

"Oh, by the way," Smith said, "Harold told me about Switzer. Maybe we can work it out on Monday. I'll talk to Gordon Kingston. I met him last month at the Economic Round Table luncheon. Remember, it's not over till it's over."

"And even then, it's not over," they both said together.

Smith took a piece of paper from the notepad on the counter top. "Okay," she said, choosing a pencil from the pressed glass spooner. "What do we know?"

"We know that Barry was murdered at the Four Seasons," Wetzon said, "while he was on the phone with Mildred Gleason." She put the bagel slices in the toaster oven.

"Right," Smith said, making two columns on the paper and labeling them KNOWN and UNKNOWN. "And we know that he was working for Mildred, taping phone conversations at Jake Donahue's."

"None of which could be used in court," Wetzon said slowly. "But Mildred could have made trouble for Jake with the SEC, couldn't she?"

"Blackmail," Smith said, writing *blackmail??* under UNKNOWN.

"Okay, Barry got something on Jake that could hurt Jake, so say Jake kills Barry?"

"But how does Jake know Barry was working for Mildred?" Smith asked. "He has no motive unless he knows."

"That's where Amanda Guilford comes in," Wetzon said absently.

"And who is Amanda Guilford?" Smith demanded, throwing down her pencil. "You're not telling me everything you know, Wetzon."

"Amanda Guilford is a friend of Laura Lee Day—"

"That flake—"

"Let's not start anything, Smith," Wetzon warned. "You know how I feel about Laura Lee."

"You are totally undiscerning when it comes to friends, Wetzon."

"Drop it, Smith," Wetzon said sharply.

"Okay, okay, don't hit me." Smith tried to make a joke of it.

"So if Jake knows Barry is spying on him, he has a motive."

"Wetzon, you don't know Jake Donahue the way I do." Smith ran her fingers through her hair, preening. "Jake would never resort to murder. He doesn't have to."

Wetzon gave her a sidelong glance.

The toaster oven clicked off. She opened the door and turned over the slices, burning her hand on the hot top of the door. "Damn," she said, slamming the door closed, "why do I always do that?" She turned on the cold water and let it run on the burned spot, then took an ice cube out of the freezer and held it to her hand.

"Does that really help?" Smith asked, scribbling notes. "There must be a connection we're not seeing. Georgie—"

"Georgie could have killed Barry—but don't you think Barry, Georgie, and Mildred had to have been killed by the same person? You know, modus operandi—the knife?"

"What about Barry's little girlfriend?" Smith put the head of the yellow pencil in her mouth.

"She was with me when Georgie was killed, but wait, Smith—I think she was up at Mildred's office before I got there yesterday because I ran into her coming out of the elevator." Could Buffie have gone back later and murdered Mildred?

"What would her motive be?" Smith took the pencil out of her mouth and rubbed the lipstick mark off its yellow coating.

"Barry is supposed to have written his autobiography."

Smith burst out laughing. "You can't be serious! Barry Stark could hardly tie his own shoelaces, Wetzon, let alone write a sentence."

"Oh, come on, Smith, he went to Bronx Science and he graduated from college."

"Humpf."

"Buffie was supposed to sell it to Mildred for big dollars, but she couldn't find it."

"That's because it doesn't exist," Smith hooted. "How do you know all this?"

"Buffie told me."

"Maybe Mildred wouldn't pay her so she went back and stabbed her."

Wetzon took out the bagel slices and put them on a plate between her and Smith. "Cream cheese? Butter?"

"Cream cheese. No to all those earlier questions."

"It has scallions in it."

"Better still."

"No, that doesn't make sense. As long as Mildred was alive, Buffie might be able to get money for the autobiography, if there was one."

"What about this Amanda person?"

"What about her? I don't think she knew Mildred. She's a broker at Dona-hue's. Jake, with his infinite powers of persuasion, induced her to spy on Barry." Wetzon gave Smith a piercing look. "I expect you to keep this confidential, Smith. That means not telling Leon or Donahue."

"Wetzon, you hurt me," Smith said. "Would I break a confidence?"

Would she? Wetzon was far from certain. "Anyway, we're going to quickly and quietly outplace Amanda next week."

"You can trust me," Smith said, her face artless.

"I wonder if Jake has an alibi for any of the murders," Wetzon mused. "And if he hasn't, why haven't the police arrested him? Didn't Silvestri say anything about it?"

"I tried to get it out of him, believe me," Smith said, smiling, smearing her piece of bagel liberally with scallion cream cheese. She laughed. "But he's not much on shop talk. . . ." She trailed off suggestively.

Wetzon took a bite out of her bagel, covering up a twinge of envy. Smith was not interested in Silvestri, but she was not letting go of him, either. And she seemed to be taunting her with him. Or maybe it was just Wetzon's paranoia. Silvestri had come into Smith's magnetic field, and he was going to be another orbiting planet, like Leon, like the other men in Smith's life. She poured more coffee into their mugs. It made her sad.

"Hello, hello," Smith said, elbowing her in the ribs. "Where are you? Where did you go just now? What are you thinking about?"

"The key, of course," Wetzon said quickly, feeling guilty. After all, it wasn't Smith's fault. She didn't do it on purpose. She had a kind heart and she meant well.

"Right. The key. It must unlock where the rest of the tapes are. Maybe it unlocks the hiding place of the mythical autobiography."

"Did you ever find out what Leon was doing at the Four Seasons and near Buffie's apartment?"

"Oh, it was nothing—as I told you—" Smith said easily. "He was meeting with an M & A specialist from Montgomery re one of his aging clients who is looking to sell his company and retire. He left long before you found Barry, so you shouldn't be thinking bad things about Leon."

"Well, of course, I never thought he had anything to do with the murder, but what about his being near Buffie's apartment?"

"But, Wetzon sweetie, he was never there. You probably saw someone who looked like him. Remember how tired you were, what you've been through. You couldn't have seen him." She patted Wetzon's cheek.

"I don't know, Smith. It sure looked like him. I just don't know. I've had such a terrible week, and then last night that derelict, Sugar Joe, was mugged—killed—on Amsterdam and Eighty-sixth and I almost got caught in it. . . . Actually . . ." She looked down at the scraped skin on her hands.

"Actually, I lost another suit last night. The mugger tore the jacket of my dark gray suit."

"You're kidding," Smith said, putting her coffee mug down with a thump. "Why would anyone want to murder a derelict?" She stared hard at Wetzon. "How was he killed?"

Wetzon stared back at Smith. "I don't want to be paranoid . . . but Rick thinks—"

"I don't give a fuck what Rick thinks. How was he killed?"

"Oh, Smith, it's just a coincidence." Smith glared at her. "Okay, he was stabbed, and my jacket was slashed."

"Jesus Christ, Wetzon, there's a nut out there with a carving knife, who's already gotten three people you knew and possibly a fourth. How do you know he wasn't out to get you and the bum just happened to get in the way?"

"Of course, I don't, but—"

"Did you call Silvestri?"

"No. Now really, Smith, it's nonsense. Why would anyone want to kill me? I don't know anything."

"It's not nonsense, Wetzon. You're in danger. I knew it. The cards have been saying so. Someone thinks you know something. It's that key—"

"No, it couldn't be. No one knows I had it except—" Wetzon floundered. "Except you, Silvestri . . . and Leon. Leon?"

"No," Smith said hotly. "Leon is totally trustworthy. You ought to know that."

"But Leon represents Jake Donahue."

"I know, but . . ." Smith looked down at the counter and absentmindedly brushed some bagel crumbs onto the floor. "There'd be no reason. . . ."

"Oh, Smith you didn't. . . ." Wetzon was furious.

Smith's face reddened. "I did it for us," she said defensively.

"Did what? Just say it—did you give Leon the key?"

"Well, not exactly." Smith did not meet Wetzon's eyes.

"What exactly?"

"I sold it to him."

"Oh, no, Smith, my God, how could you?"

"It's okay, it really is. No one will ever know about it. I did it for us. Twelve and a half thousand each. Come on, Wetzon," Smith said, smiling seductively. "It was easy money."

"Illegal, unethical money, Smith!"

"It's done. We'll buy ourselves something nice. You can buy a fur coat," Smith said, cajoling. "You've always wanted one, and now you can get yourself a big, beautiful, dark mink." She was being cloyingly sweet. "We deserve it. We work very hard. It's only right." Seeing Wetzon's anger, her face hardened. "Come on, you *knew* what I was going to do when I made a copy of the key, so don't get holier than thou with me."

"I don't want the money, Smith. It's dirty. It's not the way I live my life, and it's not the way I want to live."

"Money is money. You'll change your mind."

"No, I won't. Where did you put it? Not in the office, I hope."

"No, I have it at home. I'll hold your share for you. You'll come around. It's part of doing business. A lot of cash always changes hands. I don't see why we shouldn't get some of it. You're so naïve, Wetzon. And smug. Grow up. Everyone has a price. Even you."

Wetzon felt sick to her stomach. She pushed away the rest of her bagel. "I'm tired," she said, "and I'm scared."

"But you shouldn't be scared of Jake. Don't you see, there wouldn't be any reason for Jake to try to kill you. He already has the key. But I think someone else is scared that you may know something." Smith stood up. "I've got to get home before Leon and Mark do." She took Wetzon's hand gently. "I want you to promise me something."

"What?"

"I want you to call Silvestri and tell him about that derelict. It may be nothing, but let him make that decision. He knows more about the case than we do."

"Oh, Smith—" At this juncture Wetzon didn't think Silvestri knew more about the case than she did. How could he possibly put all the pieces together?

"Promise me."

Wetzon looked into Smith's eyes. There was honest concern for Wetzon in them and Wetzon accepted it. "Okay, I will."

"Now," Smith insisted. "As soon as I leave."

"Okay."

"And lock your door after me."

"Okay." *Just leave.*

Wetzon poured the rest of the coffee into her mug and turned off the burner. She had forgotten to tell Smith about Howie Minton. And she had forgotten the silk tie with the cabbage roses. Or maybe she was too chicken to deal with it. She had just wanted to be alone, as quickly as possible. She took her mug of coffee into the bedroom, setting it on the old painted washstand she used as a night table. She opened her closet door and stared at her shredded jacket.

Enough. Where had she put Silvestri's card? She could never find it when she needed it. Screw it. She picked up the phone and asked information for the precinct phone number and then punched the buttons.

"Seventeenth Precinct, Dombrowsky."

"Detective Silvestri," she said, then waited for the switchboard to put the call through.

"Hollander." There was laughter in the background.

"Detective Silvestri, please."

"He's not here right now. Can I help you?"

"Please just tell him Leslie Wetzon called."

Wetzon hung up the phone. All right, she'd done what she'd promised. She started to make the bed. Stopped. Gave a little cry, got into bed and pulled the covers up over her head. She'd done what she'd promised. She always did what she promised. She always did the "right" thing.

She thought about the money Smith had taken for the key. It was wrong. It was dirty. And it was immoral. How could Smith not see that? Or did she see it and just not care?

Wetzon had thought, until lately, that their partnership was good, worked well, and that they were well suited, but now she didn't know. She felt besieged. By the murders. By Smith's peculiar behavior. By her own sexuality. She was hopping into bed with Rick, but she lusted for Silvestri.

She reached out to turn on the radio and caught her finger on the edge of the washstand, tearing her nail. Damn. She sat up, opened the drawer, and poked around for her emery board. It wasn't there. Damn, where was it? She gave up and leaned over. Oh, there it was, on the other side of the drawer. Carlos must have decided to clean out the accumulation of junk for her. She raised her pillows and leaned back, putting on the radio.

The weather would be cool today. But fine. Clear. Fine.

". . . A new development in the murders which have stunned Wall Street this week. This station has received information from a source in the district attorney's office that investment banker Jacob Donahue has been taken in for questioning in the recent murders of stockbroker Barry Stark and Donahue's estranged wife, Mildred Gleason, also an investment banker. The police have refused comment. We'll have more information on this case as it develops. Stay tuned. On another local issue, the district attorney's office has announced that the investigation of massive drug thefts at New York City hospitals has been completed and arrests are imminent. They are denying that the thefts are widespread, constituting a conspiracy, as the *Daily News* has asserted, and have indicated that only one hospital is involved. In Washington today—"

Wetzon turned off the radio. One word from the newscast kept ringing in her mind. *Estranged*. It had been mentioned before, but somehow she hadn't picked up on it. Jake and Mildred were not divorced—they were *estranged*.

40

Wetzon ruffled her hair through her fingers. It was almost dry. She combed away the wildness and stared at her reflection in the bathroom mirror. A very serious face stared back at her. "Smile, kid," she said, "you're on *Candid Camera*," and her reflection smiled back at her, dutifully. That was better. She needed a trim. She needed a new hairdo and a fresh image. That's what she needed. She took a hairband and pulled her hair into a ponytail.

Estranged. Estranged meant separated, didn't it? Everyone had thought Mildred and Jake were divorced. Maybe estranged could also mean divorced.

She put the *Swan Lake* cassette in the player and stood at the barre. Breath. Positions. One and two and three and four. And stretch and lift and pain. And extend, extend, extend, slowly stretching. Pain. Demi-plié, grand plié, relevé. Terrible shape.

If Mildred and Jake were still legally married, and Mildred was dead, Jake inherited Mildred's firm. Which was a hell of a lot more solvent than Jake's. What a kicker.

Still, it would have been stupid and obvious of Jake to murder Mildred after that scene in her office. And while Jake also had the best motive to murder Barry, he had to have had the opportunity. Had he been at the Four Seasons that night? She changed positions, watching herself in the mirror. And what about Roberta? Wetzon did not remember seeing her when Jake had burst into Mildred's office.

The police must have some idea, she reasoned.

Plié, one, two, three, four, and relevé, one, two, three, four. Her neck and upper back were very tight. She felt tormented. By Barry and his goddam key, by Smith and her greed, by the revelation of the twenty-five thousand dollars. By Smith's larcenous soul. Why hadn't she realized that about Smith? She had been lazy in letting Smith copy the key, and now she was as guilty as if *she* had made the deal with Leon. She would have it out with Smith, and they would return the money to Leon, get the key back, and destroy it. But what would stop Leon from copying the key, too?

Silvestri would have to be told. There was no other way. She would insist. What a mess. Life had been much less complicated when she was a dancer.

Because there was no money, stupid. The focus was on the work and the art. They had all thrived on their creativity and poverty. *As soon as money arrives on the scene, it becomes the focus. It becomes about money.* She would tell Silvestri everything everybody had told her. Divest herself of all of it. Cleanse herself.

She was sweating now, but loosening up. She'd have to take another shower before she went to meet Rick. She opened the mat on the floor and, lying down, rolled back into the plough, then raised her legs slowly into a shoulder stand.

Smith had been raised as a foster child in poverty on the south side of Philadelphia. She thought of money as the answer to everything. Wetzon had never realized that before.

Rick. She liked Rick. He was cute and boyish, in spite of his prematurely gray hair. Boyish. The operative word about Rick was boyish. *Thank you, Laura Lee Day.* Even his name was boyish. Boyish as opposed to manish. An interlude in the interim. Okay. But was she, perhaps, that desperate for a lover, a relationship? Was the loneliness of being self-supporting in New York City finally getting to her?

Her doorbell rang. Doorbell? Who the hell was that, and how had he gotten past the doorman without being announced? She felt a stab of fear. She carefully changed her hand position and came out of the shoulder stand slowly into the bridge, then lowered herself vertebra by vertebra to the mat.

The doorbell rang again. She tiptoed to the door, opened the peephole as quietly as she could, which wasn't quiet enough, and found herself looking at Silvestri, who was looking at her.

"Blast," she said, aware of her damp state and workout clothes. She unlocked both locks and opened the door.

"You might have called," she said testily.

"I thought you called *me,*" Silvestri said, looking at her appraisingly. He seemed a bit unsettled, taken aback. She knew her face was flushed from the exercise, and perspiration marks showed through her sweatclothes. Her wet hair curled around her forehead and the sides of her face.

Wetzon brushed the damp swirls out of her eyes self-consciously. "Oh hell, Silvestri, come on in. You caught me in the middle of my workout. Where was my doorman?"

He smelled of coffee and cigarettes. And her father's aftershave. Woodsy. A working man's smell. Rick smelled of antiseptic.

"I didn't see anyone," he said.

"Nice."

She led him into the living room, still strewn with newspapers where she and Smith had left them. "Make yourself comfortable," she said.

The strains of *Swan Lake* billowed and flowed around them. They stood for a moment watching each other. Then Silvestri sat on the sofa and made no bones about surveying the room.

Wetzon dropped to the floor, arms forward, hands around her ankles, elbows on the floor, stretching her legs, flexing. "I'm sorry," she said, not meaning it, but wanting to break the silence. "I don't want to tighten up." Now he was openly studying her, not saying anything. "I used to be a dancer," she said, uncomfortable, knowing she had told him this before.

"I know," he said, settling back on the sofa, waiting.

"I called you—" she began.

"You called me," he said at almost the same moment.

"Did Jake Donahue kill Mildred and Barry?"

"What were you doing at Mildred Gleason's office yesterday afternoon?"

She stared at him. "She called me and begged me to see her," she said warily.

"So you were with Stark and Travers *and* Gleason shortly before each died."

She didn't like the tone of his voice. "Wait a minute, Silvestri," she said, frightened. "Should I get a lawyer? Am I a suspect?"

They stared at each other, locking eyes.

"Naa," he said finally. "You could be, but you're not. No motive. Too many witnesses clear where you were."

"Jesus, Silvestri, what are you doing to me?" She sat up, hugging her knees, chilled. "I called you because Smith thinks someone is trying to kill me—"

"Talk to me." Silvestri took a pad and a pen out of his inner pocket, giving her a glimpse of his gun and shoulder holster. He was no longer compensating for the gunshot wound.

"The derelict that was killed last night—down the block from here—"

"Yeah?"

"You know about it?"

"I read the report. What does it have to do with you?"

"Nothing, I think. But I knew him. His name was Sugar Joe. At least that's what we called him. I've been leaving him coffee for a long time, almost a year now. He slept in the bus stop." She paused, watching him. He didn't react, so she went on. "I was pushed or thrown out of the way only a second or so before it happened. Smith thinks the mugger was after me."

"What makes you think it has anything to do with you?"

"I don't. I think I just got caught in the crossfire. Coincidence. Why would anyone want to kill a derelict?" *Swan Lake* came to a concluding crescendo around them.

"This is the eighties, and it's New York City. Why indeed," Silvestri said, impassive. "Why would Ms. Smith think the murderer wanted you?" He rose and looked at the books she had stacked on the side table, picking them up, one at a time.

"Because of my jacket," she said. "Wait, I'll show you." She jumped up and went to her bedroom, took the jacket from the closet, and brought it to him.

He took the jacket by the collar, letting it hang down while he studied it. It looked even worse than she'd remembered. The second suit she'd ruined in two days, she thought regretfully. She'd have to get a whole new wardrobe if things kept up like this.

"I'd like to take this with me," he said.

"Why not? I can't wear it, can't even have it repaired."

He tucked the remnants of her dark gray suit jacket under his arm, and she felt a lovely little thrill. *Masochist,* she thought. *Stop it.*

"Why did Mildred Gleason want to see you?" Silvestri asked.

"She wanted to know what Barry said to me. She said Barry had been working for her, that he'd called her just before he was murdered. *While* he was being murdered." She hesitated. This was her opportunity to tell him everything. "Silvestri, I'd like—"

A beeper went off. Silvestri's.

He reached into his breast pocket and turned off the beeper. "Did she say anything else?"

"Yes, that Barry had said something about tapes."

"Can I use your phone?" She hadn't realized how tall he was. Or possibly, how small she was.

"Yes, in the other room, where I work out."

He didn't move. "That's all?"

"Yes, that's all. Then Jake came in, and they started screaming at each other, and I left." She led him into the dining room and waited while he placed the call.

"Silvestri," he said into the phone. He listened. "I'm on my way back." He put down the phone.

"What about the key?" she asked. "Did you find out what it unlocks?"

He shrugged. "It's a standard key used for medical cabinets in hospitals and, more than likely, elsewhere. Does it make any sense to you?"

"No," she said. "But Barry must have told me something that I can't remember, something I haven't been able to put together. What would Barry be doing with a hospital cabinet key, and why would he give it to me?" She stopped, thinking. "Was he murdered for the key?" Both hands to her head, she frowned. "It's not logical. None of this is logical."

"What makes you think murder is logical?" Silvestri said.

41

She went down in the elevator with Silvestri to get her mail.

"I almost forgot—" she began, and wondered why she kept doing that. She had something to tell him and then she'd go off somewhere and lose track of where she was. "I almost forgot," she said again, feeling cotton-brained and stupid.

Silvestri looked guilty, as if she'd caught him out. He'd been leaning against the back of the elevator, eyes on the trellis effect of the dropped ceiling, whistling under his breath. He turned to her. His eyes were deep, deep turquoise again.

"Yes?"

"I'm sorry," she said, heart pounding, distracted, shaking her head, ponytail swinging. "I don't know where my mind is." She was taking shallow, quick breaths.

Neither seemed to notice at first that the elevator door had opened and they were in the lobby.

"You were going to tell me something," he said, taking her arm. She felt a small shock where he touched her, which became a strange tingle spreading up and down through her body, and looking at him, she saw that he'd felt it, too. He dropped her arm, and they left the elevator and stood in the lobby. The moment was gone. There had been a pull, an attraction, between them, for a brief instant, and they'd both felt it. And while Silvestri appeared to have been taken by surprise, Wetzon's attraction to him dated to their first meeting. It was his response that she hadn't expected.

She cleared her throat and her voice cracked when she spoke. "I saw Buffie—Ann Buffolino—when I was going into Mildred Gleason's building. She was leaving the building and tried to avoid me."

Silvestri waited. The poker face revealed nothing. The eyes were slate again. "Was Gleason's assistant there when you saw Gleason?"

"Yes. She left a few minutes before I did."

"Left the room or the building?"

"The room, for sure. The building? I don't know. Is it important?"

"Possibly." He was noncommittal, but Wetzon sensed a heightened energy.

She thought hard. She remembered the sound of a toilet flushing. "Does the other door in Mildred's office lead to a bathroom, and if so, does it open to another room?"

"Yes and yes. It leads to Ms. Bancroft's office."

Wetzon nodded. "Well, if she owns a black leather trench coat, she probably left the building."

"Why do you say that?"

"Because there was one hanging in the closet when I got there, and it wasn't there when I left. Does that help?"

"Possibly," he said again.

"Okay, I get it."

She watched him leave. He looked like a college professor, slightly rumpled but tweedy, with brown suede elbow patches on his jacket sleeves. But he was a rumpled, tweedy police sergeant, with a tattered gray jacket under his arm, and he was moving fast. She wished she knew what his question about Roberta Bancroft meant.

Curiouser and curiouser.

She unlocked her mailbox and sifted through her mail, throwing away the Lancôme and Estee Lauder special offers from Saks and Bonwit's, and the L. L. Bean catalog. She wrapped the letters and the Williams-Sonoma catalog in *Business Week* and got back on the elevator with the twins from the fourth floor and their galumping golden retriever. Portia, the retriever, was dancing and panting and carrying on like a puppy after her walk. The twins were having a tough time holding her down. When they came to the fourth floor, Portia jumped up and gave Wetzon a messy, wet kiss and bounded out.

"Thanks a heap, Portia," she said to the empty elevator, wiping her face, but smiling. It was hard not to smile.

Something was really nagging at her about the key. A hospital cabinet. It was all so confusing. She dropped the mail on the counter in the kitchen, took a Granny Smith apple out of the refrigerator, and cut it into slices. Her lovely afternoon was gone. She went through the letters and pulled out what looked like an invitation in a square white envelope. The apple was tart and good.

It was an invitation to a Wall Street Night at the Caravanserie on Monday evening at six o'clock. Barry Stark again. Barry had told her about these evenings; he must have put her on the mailing list. She slipped the invitation back into the envelope. It was funny about Barry. He just didn't stay dead. He kept coming back in one form or another. Over and over again.

She took a quick shower and put on a quilted denim skirt with a red silk work shirt. A modern irony, that—an expensive silk work shirt. She smudged her eyelids with gray shadow, used a bit of black mascara on her lashes, then shook her hair out of the ponytail and let it fall around her face. Rick had said to wear her hair down, and it had been years since she'd done that. Her hair, fine and slightly curly, hung down well below her shoulder blades. Too long. Her face looked unexpectedly soft and vulnerable in the mirror. She turned away. No good. She couldn't walk out looking that unprotected, no matter what Rick liked. She would compromise. She brushed her hair, parted in the middle, and pulled it over on one side, banding it under her left earlobe. Okay, so now she looked a little like Emily Dickinson. What the hell. It was quarter to five and she'd better move a little faster. Some Ombre Rose behind the lobes and on the wrists, and finito.

She straightened up the bedroom, putting things away, closing the venetian blinds to the departing light. On the chest of drawers she saw the small white plastic packet with YORK HOSPITAL written across it in blue that the emergency-room doctor had given her. She emptied the contents into her palm. Four aspirin look-alikes, with codeine.

She dropped the pills in the toilet bowl, flushed, and looked again at the little packet in her hand. Then she froze. The plastic bags of pills and drugs she and Smith had found in Barry's attaché case were much larger than this one, but they were identical. Those, too, had said YORK HOSPITAL. She felt a pinch of fear, as if someone had just walked over her grave. Was the medical cabinet the key opened at York Hospital?

Okay, that's it, she told herself sternly. *Time out. No more deducing.* She started to throw away the packet, then changed her mind and put it in her medicine cabinet with the various colored, aging bottles of nail polish which she bought and never used, preferring to stick with conservative translucents.

In the dining room she rolled up the exercise mat and took the towel from the barre where she'd left it and put it in the washing machine in the kitchen. She opened the rest of the mail quickly, discarding everything but a bill from Con Ed, which was insanely high for someone who lived alone and didn't cook much, and the networking invitation to the Caravanserie. She'd think about it for Monday. Maybe there would be brokers. . . . She took the invitation out of the envelope again. *Six dollars and a business card and this invitation . . .* She put it back in the envelope, and for the first time noticed the emblem on the back flap: a silhouetted palm tree. She'd seen that before, somewhere. Anyway, it looked familiar. She was having recurrent déjà vu. She shook her head thoughtfully, as she put *Business Week* and the Sonoma catalog in the basket in her foyer, and dropped the invitation on her desk in the living room. She gathered up the newspapers and piled them neatly on the floor of the foyer.

She looked for her Burberry in the hall closet, couldn't find it, and made a quick tour of the apartment. That was funny. Then she flashed back and saw herself rolling it up and putting it under Sugar Joe's head last night, only she hadn't known it was Sugar Joe. All that long white hair. She was glad she had done it. She put on her denim jacket and opened the outside door, hesitated, went back and turned on her answering machine.

God, it was taking her a long time to get out of the apartment. Almost as if she didn't really want to go. But why the hell wouldn't she want to go? She liked

Rick. He was nice. He liked her. She loved *Notorious*. It was her favorite Hitchcock movie. She closed the door firmly this time and turned the key in the lock.

No doubt about it, something was troubling her. A lot of things were troubling her. Inconceivably, she was involved with three, possibly four murders. Her partner, Xenia Smith, was behaving strangely. Her lawyer, Leon Ostrow, had done something unethical— She pressed the elevator button. And Leon and Xenia had suddenly gotten very close. Or had they always been close? She didn't think so. And on top of everything else, she was having those peculiar dreams.

And what about Silvestri, the first man she'd been strongly attracted to in a long time. Smith seemed to have ensnared him. And Smith didn't even want him.

And she, Wetzon, was on her way to meet another man—a handsome doctor, who obviously liked her, who was a good lover, so why was she not zipping right down to the Regency, thrilled to be spending time with him again?

42

Wetzon walked toward Broadway, sidestepping the spot on Amsterdam Avenue where Sugar Joe had died—maybe in her stead—passing the bus stop that had been his home. There was no trace of his metal cart of possessions or his blanket. Either the police had taken them or the Sanitation Department or another street person had. What was the difference? Things got swallowed up in New York. Things and people. If you let up for one minute . . . Sometimes keeping it all together made her tired.

On Broadway she paused in front of the Korean market to look at the neat arrangements of fat, red strawberries and sliced fresh pineapple. It was one of the hundreds of immaculate small markets that had been opened in the last few years all over the City by Korean immigrants moving into the mainstream of the American system. Just as the Indians had moved into the newsstand business and earlier immigrants had—Chinese with laundries and restaurants, Jews with dry cleaning stores and tailor shops. It was the best of America, and their children would become the next generation's doctors, lawyers, and scientists.

Broadway had become a bazaar over the last year. There was an entrepreneur on every corner with a tablecloth or blanket, selling old books, phony designer watches, glitzy jewelry, sunglasses, leather pocketbooks, and belts. Everything and anything. Without a license and without overhead.

She stopped at Zabar's and, seeing that it wasn't jammed with people, went in and bought two chocolate croissants and continued down Broadway.

In front of the Baptist church on Seventy-ninth Street a jazz quintet had set up and was playing, very professionally, "String of Pearls." The alto saxophonist caught her eye and held it, flirting. She stopped and listened, and then, for no reason at all that she could figure, she remembered her recent dreams, both of which had taken place on the Floor of the New York Stock Exchange. The Good Humor man in the white coat with the Mickey Mouse watch and the rocky road ice cream. What had reminded her of them? She stood watching the quintet, no longer seeing them. The connection had disintegrated.

She put a dollar into the bass drum case, which already contained a decent amount of change and bills, saluted the alto saxophonist, and pulled herself away. She'd be late if she didn't hurry.

Rick was on line when she got there, watching for her. He waved; the line was beginning to move. She saw the Honda parked on the corner, chained to the street sign.

"Mmmm, nice," he said, greeting her, putting his arm around her waist, sniffing her hair. He had an oversized duffel in his other hand.

"I was dawdling on Broadway," she said. "It's like a giant flea market. You don't know what to look at next."

"What did you buy?" he asked, poking the Zabar's bag.

"Chocolate croissants."

"Aha, just the thing to take the edge off the appetite. That and a tub of popcorn."

"Make that a giant tub of popcorn, and you're on," she said.

The hush of the audience was immediate as soon as the lights dimmed and the credits came on.

Wetzon's sharpest memory of *Notorious* was the long kissing scene between Bergman and Cary Grant, and it was as she remembered. Sensual, sensuous. Rick's arm was around her, and she could feel the heat of his body through the thin silk of her shirt. She imagined that it was Silvestri she was sitting there with, and a warm flush ran through her. She struggled to concentrate on the film, and in spite of everything she was soon swept into the story.

The key! She had forgotten that the climax of the film was Bergman's theft of the key to Claude Raines's wine cellar for Grant, and because of it, the Nazis' discovery that she was a spy.

Damnation. It was inescapable. Just as she had gotten immersed in the mood of the film, she was jerked back to reality by the coincidence of the keys.

"I've lost you somewhere," Rick complained mildly when they left the theater.

Broadway was a hive of activity. Couples dressed for dinner, restaurants busy. The line for subway tokens on Seventy-second Street stretched out of the station, mostly high-school- and college-age kids. It was Friday night, the beginning of a spring weekend. Joy to the world. "I know, Rick, you're right. I'm sorry," she said. "My mind keeps going back to the murders. I can't help it. There was another one last night."

"I know," he said, taking two white crash helmets out of his duffel and handing her one. "Are they connected?" He unlocked the Honda, put on his helmet, and sat down. Wetzon put on hers and sat behind him, arms around his waist, hands clasped in front. "That's real nice," he said, patting her hands. They rode up Broadway, the wind whipping up her skirt. His body felt good under her arms, taut, with no excess.

He pulled up to the curb in front of Sakura, and they looked over the take-out menu, settling on a big order of tekkamaki, the sushi deluxe, and vegetable tempura.

"Something to drink?" she asked.

"I just happen to have a six-pack of Heineken right here." He winked and patted the duffel bag.

When they arrived at her building, Rick chained the Honda to one of the metal poles that held up the dark blue canopy in front of it. He picked up the duffel and the bag of food. "Hey, babe, you there?" He snapped his fingers at her.

Wetzon flinched, embarrassed. Where had she been? Something kept slipping away. She'd almost had it. She handed Rick the crash helmet.

"Come on." She smiled and took his arm. "Let's have our sushi feast." She must try to keep her mind on him.

They had a picnic on the floor of her living room, plucking the food from containers with chopsticks, drinking beer from the bottle.

"I've lost you again, babe," Rick said, breaking her reverie, a touch of impatience creeping into his voice.

"I'm rotten company, I'm afraid," she confessed, feeling a pang of guilt. "I keep thinking I'm missing something. It's that damn key."

She was lying on the living room floor, her head in Rick's lap. They were listening to George Benson, drinking beer. He had loosened her hair and fanned it out around her head, sifting it through his fingers. "Hey, ouch!" He'd pulled her hair as she was talking.

"Oh, sorry," Rick said in a silky voice. He massaged her temples. "Okay, then why don't you tell me about this key? Maybe it'll help to talk about it."

"The key?"

"Yes, you said 'that damn key.'"

"Oh, yes, I did—"

"You're so tense," he said, rubbing her neck and shoulders. "Maybe you should just talk it through. A fresh opinion might help . . ."

"I don't know, Rick. I hate to drag you into this mess, and the more I talk about it, the more confused I get."

"Come on now, babe. I'm a scientist, uninvolved, clear-headed as they come. Try me." He unbuttoned the top button of her shirt. "What about this key?"

"Barry put a key in my pocket before he was murdered."

"Why would he do that?" His hands were warm and strong. The massage felt so good, she could just drift off right now.

"Don't know . . . unless he wanted to get rid of it quickly."

"What does it look like? Do you have it here?" There was no change in his soft, pleasant voice, but a slight change of pressure in his massaging fingers made her open her eyes.

"I don't have it," she said. "The police have it. Why?"

"Just curious," he said indifferently.

"I guess I should just leave it for the police to figure out."

Rick took his hands from her shoulders. "I may be moving out to the Coast soon," he said.

"How come?" She looked up at him, upside down.

"I've had an offer to head emergency medicine at a hospital in San Diego."

"Gee, Rick, that's really nice." She rolled over and leaned on her elbows, facing him. "You're going to take it, then?"

"Yes. I did my first residency in internal medicine, and then did another one in emergency medicine. I've been at York for over four years, so this is it. I was out in San Diego about two months ago, and I liked them and they liked me. And I love the lifestyle. Great weather all year round."

"I'll miss you," she said, patting his knee.

"I haven't made it definite yet. Don't pack me off." He pulled her to him and kissed her hard. A little too hard. Not like Cary Grant and Ingrid Bergman. She felt herself tensing up and so did he. With sure hands he began to massage her neck and shoulders again, and she felt her body relax into his. "Come on," he said, his voice a sexy whisper, "it's Pulasky's prescription for well-being."

"Pulasky . . ." she heard herself murmur. Or maybe she didn't quite say it out loud. Maybe she thought it and didn't say it. But just before she let her mind go and gave in to her body, she thought of the Pulasky Skyway in New Jersey and remembered the jagged rocks that ran like the cut-out center of a mountain along the side of the road just past the Skyway, and her last flicker of thought was, *rocky road.*

43

She was making a big platter of French toast when the phone rang.

"Damn," she said under her breath. "Rick?" No response. She turned off the heat and moved the pan. Her machine should have grabbed it, but the phone kept ringing. "Damn." She picked up the phone, still holding the spatula in her left hand. "Hello."

"Guess what, guess what, guess what!" Carlos shouted into the phone.

"What? What? You crazy person," she said, immediately forgetting her irritation. He must have gotten into the show.

"I got it! I got it! How do you like that?"

"I like it a lot. *What* did you get?"

"Oh, come on, you know what I got! And it's not chorus either—it's assistant choreographer. Marshall sprang it on me when I got there. Get that, *assistant choreographer!*"

"Oh, Carlos, that's super!"

"You're damn right it's super! And we do Boston and Washington pre New York."

"When do you open in New York?"

"September fourteenth."

"Happy Washington summer."

"Who cares! Now, as to why I'm calling you at this ungodly hour, madam. I wanted to get you before you were completely booked socially. We're going to celebrate, you and I. Dinner tonight—on me—my celebration—and the biggest and the best of the clubs, the Caravanserie, afterward. We'll really do it up nice. Dance up a storm. You could use the exercise. What do you say?"

"Hold on a minute, can you?"

"Ho ho, we're not alone and celibate anymore." It always amazed her how intuitive Carlos was where she was concerned.

"Shut up, you nut." She put her hand over the mouthpiece. "Rick?" she called.

"Yo?" he said, sticking his head out of the bathroom. He had shaving cream on his face and a razor in his hand. So the duffel had held a lot more than beer.

"When do you go in today?"

"Four. Trying to get rid of me?"

She felt her face redden. "No, don't be silly. . . ." But he was back in the bathroom again. "You're on, Carlos. What time?"

"Seven-thirty. We'll do dinner at Mezzaluna, and you can tell me all the delicious details about your new lover."

"Carlos, you're impossible."

"Listen, darling, I'm happy for you. And a little jealous, too. Now what's with all these Wall Street corpses?"

"I'll tell you all about everything tonight."

She opened the outside door and picked up the Sunday papers from the mat, dropping them on the floor in the dining room. The dropleaf table was open and set for two. It was after one o'clock and she was starving.

The sun had awakened her early that morning, and she'd taken a hot shower and slipped quietly into a leotard and tights, bunching leg warmers around her ankles, for the apartment was chilly and there was no heat. She was aching mentally and physically for a workout. She hadn't taken class in over ten days, and with the good, strong sunlight coming through her windows, she felt more energy than she had in a week. She had worked quietly, without music, letting Rick sleep.

Her concentration was so pure that she hadn't noticed Rick standing in the doorway until she'd completed most of the workout. He was naked except for his blue bikini underwear, which she found funny and not at all sexy, sort of like the old Calvin Klein ad in all the bus stops, androgynous. He had a smooth, almost hairless body, in prime shape. She knew he worked out with weights because he'd told her so.

"Don't stop, babe," he'd said. "I like watching you."

But she hadn't been able to go on. And she was very confused by her reaction to him. She felt strangely invaded and uneasy and couldn't say why. "How long were you standing there?" she'd asked, trying to hide her confusion.

"Only a little while," he'd said, backing off a fraction.

There, she'd done it again, and she didn't know how or why. She'd sensed that he wanted to make love to her again, and she'd been incomprehensibly afraid. Afraid.

"I'm finished." She'd stopped abruptly. "I'll get breakfast."

"No," he'd said, "I'm going to shower and shave." He'd disappeared down the hall, and she suddenly knew that it was over. She had clicked off. It was something she did, some defense mechanism she carried with her all the time. She didn't know why, but the funny little knot of fear was still there.

They lingered over coffee and the papers, both pretending that nothing had changed. And maybe it hadn't. She was depressed and tired again, and she felt she couldn't trust her reactions. She'd had almost no time to herself since Barry was murdered.

"It's almost three," Rick said. He was wearing his jeans but was bare-chested.

"Do you want more coffee?" she asked.

Her doorbell rang. "Damn, who can that be?" She was still wearing her tights and leotard, but she'd pulled on an oversized sweatshirt after she'd finished her workout. She peered through the peephole. "Oh, for godsakes, it's Silvestri again."

"Who's Silvestri?"

"The detective on the case." She unlocked the door and pulled it open angrily. "Don't you ever call?"

"I knew you were home," he said placidly. "Good afternoon."

"How could you know I was home?" she demanded.

"Your line was busy. Aren't you going to ask me in?" He was still wearing the rumpled sports jacket.

"Jesus, Silvestri," she said, "and where was my doorman this time?" She opened the door wide.

"He was there. He said good afternoon to me." Silvestri walked in and then stopped, seeing Rick's shadow against the light coming through the dining room windows behind him. "Of course, I didn't mean to interrupt," he said, squinting at Rick. There was something about the way he said it that implied just the opposite.

"This is Rick Pulasky. Dr. Pulasky, Sergeant Silvestri," she said, mortified. Her cheeks felt on fire. *Oh shit.* She felt as if she'd gotten caught in the act.

"Doctor," Silvestri acknowledged, without changing his expression.

"Oh, don't mind me," Rick said. "I was about to get going. . . ." He went down the hall toward her bedroom, proprietorial, shirtless, flexing his muscles.

Nice, she thought. It was humiliating. They were acting like two roosters. "Would you like some coffee?" she asked Silvestri, who stood looking after Rick. "Silvestri?"

"Oh, yes, what? Coffee? Oh, sure." Silvestri was still staring after Rick.

"What can I do for you today, Sergeant?" She decided she wasn't going to let him provoke her. She put a fresh mug on the table and poured the coffee. Silvestri sat down in Rick's chair.

"Known him long?" Silvestri asked, contemplating his coffee.

"I don't think that's any of your business, Silvestri," she said, annoyed. He looked at her without expression. Dammit, she had let him get to her. "Oh, all right, if you must know, he's from York Hospital. He came over the other day to check up on me, and we hit it off."

"Check up on you—?"

"Yes, after the accident. York has this experimental program where they assign doctors from Emergency to follow up patients after they've been treated and sent home. Rather an admirable program, don't you think?"

"Admirable," Silvestri said, echoing her, but faintly ironic.

"I'm going, babe." Rick stood in the doorway, fully clad. "Don't get up, Sergeant." He was making a big show of his duffel.

"I had no intention," Silvestri said, putting milk in his coffee.

Excusing herself, Wetzon followed Rick into the foyer.

"I'm sorry about this," she said.

"No problem, babe," he said. He put his arms around her. "We'll talk." He pulled her close and aimed a kiss for her lips, missing because she'd turned to see if Silvestri was watching. He was.

44

"So?" Wetzon was annoyed with Rick for being presumptuous, annoyed with Silvestri for barging in without calling, and annoyed with herself for not handling the situation better.

"I hope I wasn't interrupting anything important," Silvestri said, looking immensely pleased with himself.

"You weren't, but you wouldn't care if you were, right?"

"Right," he said, helping himself to more coffee. Today he wore a dark blue turtleneck sweater under his jacket. He looked less official, and sexy.

"So this isn't a social call, I take it." She stood with her hands on her hips.

He reached into his inside pocket and pulled out some papers, and again she caught a glimpse of his shoulder holster. It jolted her right out of the cat-and-mouse sexual play and into harsh reality.

"I want to go back over a few things," he said, avoiding her eyes.

"Okay . . ." She was getting very strange vibes from him.

He looked at his watch. "Metzger is late," he mumbled. He seemed to be procrastinating.

"That's nice." Wetzon was totally confused. "Shall I make more coffee? And is Detective Walters coming, too?"

"No. The case belongs to the Seventeenth." His eyes met hers, and she felt a peculiar pull, like an undertow. Weak-kneed, she sat down.

"That's you. . . ." Her voice was barely audible; she was finding it difficult to speak. So Georgie's death and Barry's *were* linked.

"That's me."

"What—" She seemed to have lost her voice. Clearing her throat, she said, "What do you want to know?"

"You said George Travers asked you to meet him Wednesday night."

She nodded.

"You also said you hardly knew him, yet you went out to meet him. Why?"

"Because he seemed very upset and wanted to talk." Silvestri was right. Why had she gone to meet Georgie? She hadn't even liked him.

"Is that the only reason?"

"What other reason could there be, Silvestri?" she asked impatiently. Should she tell him she had trouble saying no?

He leaned toward her. "What's your stake in this, Ms. Wetzon?"

She rocked back as if he'd slapped her. "Stake? I don't know what you're talking about."

"Come on now, just what did Barry Stark tell you? I think you know far more about these murders than you're telling us, Ms. Wetzon. You are with-holding vital information. There have been four deaths."

She clenched her jaw, digging in. *Damned right, Silvestri, and when I put it all together, I'll let you know.* Instead she said, with as much ice as she could muster, "All I can tell you about Georgie is what I told you before. He said Barry was holding something for him, and it wasn't in his locker at the Caravanserie."

"We're talking obstructing justice, Ms. Wetzon."

She had wanted to get out from under, tell him everything she knew, but how could she now? It would seem as if she had purposely kept information from the police. Her head reeled. What had she gotten herself into?

"Go away, Silvestri," she said, very upset, standing.

He sighed, put his papers in his pocket, getting ready to leave, and she thought about the key again. She could not let him leave without telling him about it.

"Silvestri—wait—"

"Yes?" He moved closer and she took a step back, leaning against the barre. He frightened her when he looked at her like that.

"Silvestri," she said, plunging in, "there *is* something I have to tell you." She felt his eyes, piercing her, appraising her, as if he already knew what she was going to say. But how could he?

He waited.

"There's a copy of the key . . ." she began haltingly.

"I know," he said, not letting up.

"How do you know?" She was stunned.

"I have it. You gave it to me."

She frowned. "No. You don't understand," she said. "I gave you the key. . . ."

"No," he said gently, as if he were talking to a child. "You gave me the *copy.*"

"I'm sorry, I'm confused," she said, crowding the barre.

"The one you gave me had never been used," he said. "It was freshly cut."

"How could you tell that?" She felt exposed, as if it had been her idea to make the copy. "It could have been the key Barry gave me." *Damn Smith,* she thought. *I'm out on a limb because of her. No. Because of me. I always go along because it's easier.* "I thought it was when I gave it to you."

"But you'd made a copy."

She stared at him. "How do you know for sure?"

"The edges were still rough, and I'm a good guesser."

"The other key is in my office," she said, defeated, unable to look at him. Why did she feel so ashamed?

"Why did you do it?" he asked.

"I didn't," she said, facing him, "but I went along with it, so I am guilty." For a moment, a quick moment, an odd expression glimmered in Silvestri's eyes.

"Oh?"

"You think otherwise?" she asked defensively.

"As I understand it, it was your idea, and Ms. Smith persuaded you to let her hold it in the office." Silvestri's eyes were hard slate.

Wetzon was shaken. "Smith told you that? I can't believe she said that—" She stared at him, upset and dismayed.

"But she did," he said.

"How could she have said that?" She felt herself babbling. "It's not true, it's just not true. It didn't happen that way at all. She's my friend, she's supposed to be my friend—"

"I'll be on my way now. Think about what I said. This is not a game, Ms. Wetzon. I expect to hear from you—and soon."

"You're a hard man, Silvestri," she said, fighting tears.

"I'm a detective," he said gruffly. "I'm nosy. I ask questions. Things that don't fit bother me."

She did not hear him leave. She was holding on to the barre for dear life. Why hadn't she told him about Smith and the twenty-five thousand dollars. What was Smith trying to do to her? What the hell was going on? She had to confront Smith first thing in the morning.

And worse, she was mortified by the fact that Silvestri had believed Smith. She felt small and cheap, like a piece of garbage. Automatically, she went into first position, left hand on barre, head high, shoulders low, tears starting.

45

"So what do you think, Carlos?" Wetzon said.

They were in tiny Mezzaluna on Third Avenue in one of the window seats on the platform. Every table was full, and there was a noisy waiting line on the white ceramic tile floor and out into the street. In spite of the din coming from the open pizza kitchen and from the music, they seemed to be sitting in a pocket of acoustic perfection. They were in a storefront café of wild clutter, tables close together, surrounded with floor-to-ceiling paintings.

Crowded on the minuscule table were a gigantic bowl of steamed mussels and two small pizzas, a tuna with anchovy and the standard margarita, with tomatoes and mozzarella. They were halfway through a wonderful bolla.

"What do I think?" Carlos said. "You really want to know what I think? Are you ready?"

She nodded. "Come on, Carlos, this is serious."

"I know it's serious, buddy mine, and I want to tell you what I've said before: that nutcase broad you're in business with is bad news."

"Oh, Carlos, I don't know. I can't say that. She's been behaving strangely lately, but . . ."

"Strangely? Hey, come on, that's an understatement." Carlos pointed a long, double-jointed index finger at her. "And if you don't dig in, I won't continue with my incisive analysis of your situation." He cut the two pies into narrow sections and announced, "Remember, this is my celebration. So let's celebrate. I demand it. I command it." He raised his glass and crossed his eyes.

Wetzon raised her glass, reached across the small table, and clicked hers to his, laughing. "You are incorrigible," she said. "And look at you." She studied him seriously. "You're becoming a distinguished gentleman on me. Do I actually see gray at the temples?"

"Oh, please, don't remind me. I'll have to get one of those magic combs." He groaned theatrically, lifting his eyes to the ceiling, the back of his hand to his forehead.

"Assistant choreographer, how about that? Name on the poster, royalties and everything."

"And everything. And since Marshall is also directing, I get to be very creative." Carlos was wearing a scarlet satin shirt, open low in front, enough to show cleavage in a woman, but in Carlos's case, plenty of bare chest and lots of heavy gold chains. "It's about fucking time," he said with a touch of the old cynicism. "It's only taken twenty years. They'll probably call me an overnight success."

"From your mouth to God's ears, my friend," Wetzon said. "I salute you, my dear friend," sentimentally, her glass high.

"Thank you, thank you," Carlos said, eyes downcast, in mock modesty. "But now let's get back to you."

"Me . . . yes . . . well, I seem to have gotten in over my head everywhere. I don't understand what's happening. I feel as if I need a trot to my life. . . . Everyone, including the police, thinks Barry told me something before he died, and an assortment of certifiably crazy people keep telling me things about each other they refuse to tell the police, and I haven't told the police what they've told me, and oh, God, I don't get Smith. . . ."

"Hold on there, sweet thing." Carlos set down his glass to take her hand. "You always think everyone is as good and honest as you are."

"Like you?"

"Now, there's what I'm saying. I'm neither good nor honest."

"Oh, Carlos, come on now, I've known you for ten years, and you are a faithful, honest friend."

"True."

"And you would never do anything to hurt your friends."

"True."

"So why would Smith have told Silvestri such an out-and-out lie about the key?"

"To save her ass, of course." Carlos shook his head. "You are such a trusting soul. How long have you known Xenia Smith?"

"Almost three years. She's my partner, for godsakes."

"And what do you really know about her before that?"

"Well, she has a Ph.D. in psychology from Columbia, and she worked on the staff of the Menninger Clinic for five years."

"And how do you know all that, pray tell?"

"She told me, you foolish person."

"Ha! Which one of us is the foolish person?" Carlos said triumphantly. "I rest my case." He threw up his hands dramatically.

"Maybe she felt trapped. Maybe Silvestri cornered her."

"The cop, you mean?"

She nodded. "The detective on the case."

"Tell me more. I'm dying to hear—get it?"

"Stop being so crazy for a minute. Yes, I got it. Seriously, do you agree I should confront Smith tomorrow?"

Carlos's eyes flashed. "Damn right. I'd be furious with you if you let her get away with this. You're already starting to make excuses for her—listen to yourself. Let me tell you, there's no way she can weasel out of this. Now, enough about her. I want to know all the delicious dirt about the slayings."

"Okay, I'll begin at the beginning. This stockbroker I know—Barry Stark—calls me about some trouble he's having and wants me to meet him at the Four Seasons, which I do. He looks as if he's been in a fistfight and he's nervous as hell. We sit down and right away he jumps up, says he has to make a phone call, and doesn't come back. He leaves his attaché case with me. The rest you know."

"Only what I read in the papers. I want it from the eyewitness. It sounds like a real whodunit." Carlos rubbed his hands together in anticipation and ran his tongue over his lips lavishly, in a broad, villainous caricature.

Wetzon reached across the table and punched him gently. "Carlos, stop licking your chops, you bum. This is serious. And I'm not the *National Enquirer.*"

"Oh, do go on." His dark eyes with their gorgeous dark lashes teased her. "Don't be so touchy. I leave you alone for two days, two more people get iced, and you've lost your sense of humor. How are we going to solve these murders if you can't see the forest for the trees?"

"Maybe you're right," she said, crinkling her eyes at him. "I'll accept that under advisement."

"Good girl!" He gave her an abundant, loving smile and opened a mussel. "Continue."

"Okay, so I wait and wait and finally I go down to the phone booths and open the door and he falls out at me with a knife in his chest. No more questions about that scene, please," she said as Carlos opened his mouth to ask for more gory details. "Unless you want me to embarrass you and barf all over this lovely table of food."

"I give up," he said, making a face at her. "Then what happened?"

"I get interviewed by Silvestri—"

"What's he like?"

"Who?"

"Silvestri."

"Why?"

"Because you get all fussy and blushy every time you mention him. Who are you kidding, darling? I know you better than anyone in the world. Is he the new interest?"

"No. He likes Smith."

"Too bad, no taste. Erase him."

She felt her face flush, and she took a nibble of pizza, avoiding Carlos's eagle eyes.

"Anyway, I ended up at Smith's with the attaché case."

"Did you open it?"

She nodded guiltily. "How did you guess?"

"Simple. I know you and I know Smith. But honestly, I would have been desperate for a look-see myself. I hope you were smart enough to use gloves."

She shook her head, chagrined. They hadn't even thought of it.

"Jesus! Your prints are probably all over everything. Don't you ever watch television, darling? Even a six-year-old knows better than to muck with evidence."

Wetzon sighed. The pizza suddenly tasted like cardboard. "It was a dumb move, I guess, but it seemed harmless. All except for the gun."

"Gun? What gun?" The joy on Carlos's handsome face disappeared and in that moment he looked every bit of his thirty-eight years.

"Barry had a gun in the case." She was depressed again. She'd picked up the change in Carlos's humor immediately. "There's more," she said. "Drugs, blackmail, I think. More murder . . . Georgie Travers, Sugar Joe, Mildred Gleason . . ."

"I'm sorry I teased, birdie," he said, taking her hand. "What can I say? This is the real world, and you have every reason to be upset."

"I know, but you were right before. I have lost my sense of humor. I've lost all sense of who I am and who everyone else is." She gave him a miserable smile.

"Let's make a detour, darling," Carlos said. "Who is the new love interest?"

"Not much of a detour. When Silvestri was driving me home, someone cut us off, stole Barry's attaché case, and we ended up in the emergency room at York Hospital . . . that's how I met this very nice doctor. . . ."

"Aha, the new love interest."

"Well, sort of." She picked at an anchovy on the pizza and kept her eyes down.

"Look at me for a second," Carlos said knowingly. She raised her eyes reluctantly. When they met his, he said, "But you prefer the cop."

"The detective." She blushed.

"Oh, now I do rest my case." He looked smug. "Go on."

"You already know about the key I found in my jacket pocket, but what I didn't tell you is that Smith sold it for twenty-five thousand dollars to Leon Ostrow, presumably for Jake Donahue."

"Christalmighty, she's really a low-level cunt."

"Carlos, come on, she had a lapse. It's because she was so poor when she grew up."

"Sure." Carlos's voice dripped sarcasm.

"I told her I wouldn't touch the money, that she's to give it back."

"Very likely she'll do just that," he said even more sarcastically. "But do go on."

"Then I'm accosted by one of Barry's girlfriends, who wants me to help her look for a diary of some sort that Barry's supposed to have hidden, and we go to her apartment and find Georgie Travers there, dead."

"Who—" Carlos began.

"You wanted to hear the whole story," she grouched, "so don't interrupt. I'm on a roll. Then Mildred Gleason pleaded with me to come see her, so I did, and it turned out that Barry was working for her as a spy while he was also working for Jake Donahue. She told me that he was on the phone talking with her when he was murdered."

"And you think show business is sleazy?"

"I know. You're right. While I was talking to Mildred Gleason, Jake Donahue crashed in and threatened to kill her. That's when I sneaked out."

"Oh, joy. Delicious. Better than *Dynasty*. Why didn't you stay and watch?"

"Because I had an appointment with a broker, silly," she said. Carlos had such a mad sense of humor that she was starting to feel good again. He made her laugh. At the situation. At herself.

"Okay," Carlos said, devouring another slice of pizza. Nothing ever seemed to hurt his appetite. "I've got another question for you. Who wasted Georgie Travers?"

Wetzon stared at him. "Wasted . . . You've been watching too much television, Carlos."

"I knew him, birdie." A trace of a frown crossed his face as he poured the last of the wine into their glasses.

"You did? How?" Carlos always surprised her.

"Through the Caravanserie—some people he and I both knew."

"You must have some interesting little black book."

"Oh, boy, do I." He laughed. "I'll leave it to you in my will. You can auction it off."

"Jesus, don't say that." She shuddered. "It's almost what Barry did." She filled Carlos in on Buffie and the mysterious autobiography. "But I'll bet there was nothing in writing. Maybe he was just trying to keep himself alive. He figured the story was his insurance."

"What about the tapes?"

"I think there really may be more tapes hidden somewhere."

"Maybe the police have found them."

"Maybe."

"So who killed Barry Stark?"

"Jake Donahue . . . One of his clients? One of his girlfriends? And who killed Georgie?"

"One of his boyfriends."

"Oh, Carlos. Don't be bad. What about Mildred Gleason?"

"Simple. Jake Donahue."

"No. Wrong. But they're all related. I know it. I feel it."

"Okay. Smith did it. Believe me."

"Which brings us back to the key," Wetzon said, ignoring him.

"The key is easy. The key unlocks the safe where the tapes are."

"No, I don't think so. Silvestri said the key was to a medical cabinet."

"Hey, wait a minute. I know," Carlos said. "The key belongs to Silvestri, the cop with absolutely no taste, who likes Smith. It's for his little tin box, where he keeps his loot."

"Loot?" She shook her finger at him like a schoolteacher. "Carlos, what are you talking about?"

"You know, the payoff money cops always get."

"That does it," Wetzon said, slapping her hand on the table. "Carlos, you are truly demented. I think it's time we hit the Caravanserie before you overdo it." She felt sad. "And you were doing so well there for a while."

"Trust me, my love, Carlos knows. Carlos has second sight," he said, waving for the bill. "And now that I've done all this head work, I truly feel we should be dancing our little hearts out."

46

It was business as usual at the Caravanserie, no matter that the man who had created it had been brutally murdered only two days earlier. The entrance line stretched all the way down Sixty-fifth Street to First Avenue, but there was very little jockeying for position. Some hopefuls were absolutely straight types in business suits and simple dresses and others were a little more colorful. A tall man in a pink polo shirt with I'M THE CATCH OF THE DAY written across it and a Mets cap on his head chatted with another man, slightly younger, in a white cutaway and black tuxedo pants chopped off at the knee, wearing rolled white athletic socks and high, black Reeboks. There were girls in sequins and glittery miniskirts, and a middle-aged man and woman in black leather and chains. And there was the usual crowd of slummers from SoHo, writers, show-biz folk. Everyone was an original, one step removed. A touch of punk, a little Madonna, and a smattering of S&M.

"Andy Warhol was right," Wetzon said when they got out of their cab in front of the Caravanserie. The door was manned by two stunning women, one black and one white, and four big, big men in the uniform of a private security service.

"What?" Carlos said, paying the driver.

"That everyone would be famous for fifteen minutes. Georgie the celebrity. Georgie who?"

A massive woman in a long gray skirt and a gray cape pulled over her head, shroudlike, was howling in front of the line, "The broadcast is over! God says everyone can leave the country!" No one was paying the slightest attention to her, and she paid no attention to anyone else.

Carlos took Wetzon's hand and gave a square invitation card to the black woman at the door, who was wearing a white knit suit, very Chanel, with cascades of gold chains.

"Hi, Carlos, what's doing, baby?" she said, giving him a high five.

"Hi, Gwen. Meet my friend, Les Wetzon."

"How do, friend Les." Gwen winked at Wetzon and dropped the invitation into a huge metal bin that was painted in Picassoesque blue period, clowns and all.

"Hey, Carlos," the other doorkeeper said, allowing a couple wearing matching gold lamé T-shirts and denim overalls through. "Doctor Schweitzer, good to see you again."

The setting was the great old Episcopalian church, St. Eustis, which had received landmark status. Years earlier, most of St. Eustis' parish had moved on to Queens, and the church had been used by a succession of other denominations, including the Hari Krishnas and even the Jews for Jesus, but not for very long, and it had actually been empty for some time when Georgie Travers got the idea to make it into a disco, and then added on his exclusive health club above and behind the ornately baroque church building with its large, round rosette stained glass window in the front. There was something almost obscene and sacrilegious about it, and groups of Moral Majority types still picketed from time to time.

Inside the wonderful church was an elaborate glass-brick stairway that split in the middle and curved upward, not so high so you would lose the effect of the beautiful vaulted ceilings with their art nouveau frescoes. At the top of the staircase was a ballroom with banks of seats around, built up like a three-tiered bleacher, but upholstered in velvet.

The startling blend of modern mixed with Deco, melded with the basic baroque of the old cathedral, was breathtaking. Wetzon had never seen anything quite like it, including the sets of the Broadway shows she had done. The noise was equally breathtaking. Music throbbed from massive speakers, like columns, and the lighting effects carried the two of them back onto the stage again. When they joined the multitude on the dance floor, Wetzon felt the music, the lights, and the undulating crowd sweep away the events of the past four days, almost as if they had never happened.

"What a turn-on!" she shouted to Carlos as she gave herself up to the music. God, she and Carlos hadn't danced together since she'd gone straight, as he was fond of calling her decision to leave show business. And this was wonderful, wonderful.

As they danced, she tilted her head back to watch the fantastic simulation of a fireworks display on the whirling ceiling, changing rapidly like a kaleidoscope, and saw a piece of the ceiling begin to move, descending toward them. She glanced around. No one seemed at all panicky, they just began to back away, slowly, keeping to the beat of the music as if it were expected, and then a set piece—incredibly, a real set piece of what looked like an Asian Eliza and Little Eva crossing the ice from *Uncle Tom's Cabin*—came down and settled on the dance floor. The scene was like one of the pantomimes in pre-World War I theater. *Uncle Tom's Cabin* by way of *The King and I*. Its creator was a dancer or choreographer, for sure. There was applause and laughter as Topsy and Eva jumped out of their setting and were immediately claimed as dance partners. The set piece floated back up to the ceiling and disappeared into the spinning fireworks, and the beat went on, with Wetzon and Carlos and the rest twisting and weaving, improvising, through the glittering, multicolored light show, the air a rich incense of smoke and frenzy and perfume.

"Isn't this the greatest place in the world?" Carlos cried. "See what you've been missing." He looked beatific.

Streamers in Day-Glo colors spilled from overhead. The beat changed, quickened. She was electrified, more alive than she had felt in a long, long time. Had she been sleepwalking in those years since she left the theater? It was something she would have to think about.

"Dear Carlos, you're right, you beautiful man," she said, hugging him, their bodies weaving with the music.

Later, much later, downstairs, in a gallery that seemed to run the full length of the building, beginning under the glass staircase, they sat at the longest bar she had ever seen and sipped champagne with fresh peaches crushed in their glasses—Bellinis, Hemingway's drink. The music swelled overhead, but here one could speak and be heard.

She leaned into Carlos and planted a big kiss on each of his cheeks. Her unexpected move almost knocked them off their high stools. Giddy laughter followed. She was unable to come down. Her heart still pounded, her body heard the call of the music and responded.

"You look ten years younger," Carlos told her. "Come home. Marshall said he'd find something for you. We could play—"

She put two fingers to his lips, stopping him. "Hush," she said. "You're spoiling it."

"No?"

"No. I am not Annette Funicello and you are not Frankie Avalon. And now, I regret to inform you that, even as we speak, my coach is about to turn into a pumpkin."

"See what I mean?" Carlos said, mocking her. "All right, party poop. Stay here and I'll settle up."

She swiveled on the tall stool and, facing the bar, saw her face reflected in the smoky glass of the long, ornate mirror behind it. Her hair had come loose and fallen around her shoulders. She looked happy and young. If only Silvestri could see her now.

Cut that out, she scolded herself grimly. She drummed her fingers on the bar, keeping time, humming under her breath.

Idly, she picked the book of matches out of the ashtray on the counter and thought about what it would be like to have Silvestri make love to her. Jesus, this place was having a weird effect on her. She glanced absently at the matchbook in her hand, saw the silhouetted palm tree, and felt her heart stop.

Déjà vu. She had done this before, seen this before. Somewhere, sometime. Important.

She saw Carlos coming back for her, and she slipped off the bar stool and went to meet him, clutching the matchbook.

"What's the matter?" he asked. "You look as if you've seen a ghost."

"I think I have," she said. "I've just figured something out."

"What?"

"Come home with me and I'll show you. Can you?"

"My darling, that's the best invitation I've had in months."

"Come on, crazy," she said fondly, pushing him past a couple in sequins and toward the glass staircase. "I just want to make a quick stop. . . ." The real night people were beginning to crowd in, and the hypnotic, thumping beat of the music could be heard, luring them back. It was as if they were in the middle of a tribal rite. Voodoo. ". . . in the ladies' room." She tucked the matchbook safely away in her little string bag.

"That's easy," Carlos said. "It deserves a visit anyway. . . . Wait till you see it. Come with me."

Taking her hand, Carlos led her back into the gallery with the endless bar. They cut in and out through the boisterous mass. At the end of the bar—it actually did come to an end—was a door that led into a small lounge, which was painted in waving lines of Day-Glo pinks and blues. The lighting was muted. There were three glass sculptured doors in the lounge. One said GENTLEMEN and one said LADIES and the third said PRIVATE CLUB, MEMBERS ONLY.

"That's the entrance to the health club upstairs," Carlos said.

"Now how would you know about that?"

"Oh, I have my sources. Not everyone in a three piece business suit is hetero, you know," he said, stretching his vowels.

"Why, Carlos, you sly one. I never knew suits turned you on."

"Never the suit," he said, twisting his shoulders, turning his head, "always the man."

"Okay, man," she said, touching his cheek. She studied the door marked PRIVATE CLUB, MEMBERS ONLY. Unlike the other two doors, this one had no knob, only a narrow slot where the knob would be. It was one of those horizontal locks that could only be unlocked with a special magnetic card. "Shucks," she said.

"What 'shucks'?"

"I just had the thought that maybe the mystery key unlocked that door."

"Think again. This was one of Georgie's special touches. Adds cachet. You can only get in with a special card, a magnetic card programmed for this door, like a bank card. *Anyone* could have a key. . . ."

"Georgie, yes," she said, thinking out loud.

"What about Georgie?"

"His murder must have something to do with Barry's. Maybe it was for the stuff Barry was holding for him?"

"Who knows? Georgie had his enemies—might have nothing at all to do with Barry the sleazolo."

"I don't think so. Let's go," she said abruptly, pulling him to the door.

"I thought you wanted to use the facilities?"

"I'll wait till we get home."

47

Her apartment had a warm glow from the light of the pale orange art glass globes of the Mueller Freres chandelier in the foyer. It played softly over the off-white walls, highlighting the old "Geese in Flight" patterned crib quilt framed on the right hand wall, and spilled onto the worn oriental rug, once rust colored, now faded, of undefined pedigree.

"I love your apartment, especially at night," Carlos said. "It's like a cocoon."

"It's my safe haven, and I wouldn't have it if I hadn't gone straight," Wetzon said, putting the string bag and her coat down on the small white park bench. "So there."

"I know, I know." Carlos threw up his hands. "I give up."

"Coffee?" she asked.

"Naa, how about a tall Perrier and a slice of lime," Carlos said, taking off his shoes and settling himself on the sofa, feet up.

"I don't have any limes."

"Oh yes you do, darling, look in the bin."

She brought the two Perriers, set them down on the coffee table, and sat opposite him, on the floor.

"You're terrible, you know," she began. "You spoil me." Her voice cracked suddenly. "Oh, God, what am I doing? I'm falling apart." She saw Carlos sit up, worried, saw him come around the coffee table, a blur through her tears. "I'm sorry, I'm such a dope. You're my friend and my family. What would I do without you?" He put his arms around her and kissed her forehead. "And I love you very much, you know," she said.

"I know. And I love you," he said. "And it'll be all right. Honest. Not to worry. You'll see. Here." He handed her a black silk handkerchief from a back pocket of his tight black pants.

She looked at it and laughed, sniffling. "I can't use this, you nut. It's much too elegant for nose and eye wiping." She went into the kitchen for a Kleenex. When she came back, Carlos was once more majestically ensconced on the sofa.

"Now, my girl," he demanded, "let's talk about this brainstorm of yours."

"God, how could I forget?" She tapped her forehead with her forefinger.

"Wait a minute." She brought the string bag from the bench and pulled out the Caravanserie matchbook. "Look at this."

"Wow! Gee! Oh, golly! It's a matchbook from the Caravanserie." He fluttered his dark lashes over his wicked eyes.

"Will you stop? I know that. Just wait a minute and you'll see." She went into the bedroom, put on the light, and fished around in the drawer of the washstand. Then she looked on the top of the chest of drawers, in the basket where she kept odds and ends. Nothing.

"I know this is crazy," she moaned, coming back into the living room, scratching her head, dismayed.

"Do you want to tell me what's going on?" Carlos watched her shrewdly.

"Okay. When I found the key in my pocket after the murder, it was sticking out of a matchbook like this one."

"So?"

"So I threw it across the room because I was angry and upset."

"The matchbook?"

"The matchbook and the key."

"And?"

"I don't remember what I did with the matchbook. All I thought about then was the key." She felt weepy again. God, what was wrong with her tonight?

"Are you looking for that matchbook, is that what you're trying to tell me?" He was grinning now.

"Yes, and this is not funny."

"Well, birdie, if it was a perfectly good matchbook, where would Hazel put a perfectly good matchbook when she was cleaning up the next day?"

"Carlos! You! Of course. You came the next morning." She dropped to her knees, took the tall, pressed glass celery vase that stood on the coffee table and tipped it over. Matchbooks of every variety tumbled out.

With maddening ease Carlos reached over and plucked up the duplicate matchbook to the one in her hand. "You were looking for this, Sherlock?"

"Yes," she said, grabbing the matchbook, staring at it intently, turning it over. "It's just like this one," she said, disappointed.

"Well, what did you expect?"

"I don't know. Answers. Something. Anything. A message maybe." She opened the matchbook, and choked. Written on the white inside flap, in ink, were some numbers: *2105-14R-28L-2R*. The matchbook trembled so violently in her fingers that she almost dropped it. "I knew it!"

"What is it?" Carlos leaned forward, serious.

"Look at this." She extended the matchbook to him across the coffee table. "Like in my dream—the key is not the key. Silvestri said it. It was staring me in the face all the time." She was rocking back and forth on her knees, gulping with excitement.

"Well, well, well," he said, drawing out his words. "The notorious Barry Stark's last will and testament."

"Written in a matchbook. How typical. What does it mean, do you suppose?"

Carlos squinted at the numbers. "It looks like a lock combination."

She frowned. "For a safe?"

"You'll make lines," Carlos warned, reaching across the coffee table, smoothing her forehead reprovingly.

"Oh shush. Well, it's not for his locker at the Caravanserie."

"How do you know?"

"Because Georgie told me he'd searched it. All it had was workout stuff."

"I don't know, then, but it sure looks like a locker number and a combination to me, old dear."

"Damn, so near—" She scrunched up her face. "The key is not the key. The locker is not the locker." She scrambled to her feet. "What if Barry had a second locker—that no one knew about?"

"I think she's got it!" Carlos said, doing his imitation Pickering again, English accent and all.

"What do you suppose we're going to find in the locker?" She was dancing around the room excitedly.

"We're not going to find anything, birdie," Carlos ordered. "We're going to let the police handle it."

She danced over to the sofa. "No, we're not, my sweet," she said, tickling him. "I'm going to make points with my detective. Come on, I'll bet the tapes are there. And his autobiography—maybe? And Georgie's stuff. God, it's mind-boggling."

"I don't approve," Carlos said, worried. "I think it's too dangerous. Someone's murdered three people for this—" He held up his hand to stop her interruption. "And tried to get you, too."

"No. I think that was pure coincidence." She felt a surge of confidence. "No one's going to kill me until he gets this." She touched the matchbook to the tip of his nose.

"Now who's crazy?"

She sighed, suddenly exhausted. "If I'd only put it together sooner, Mildred Gleason might still be alive."

"You can't do that to yourself, you know. Forgive yourself for not being perfect. You would have had to tell the heart-throb cop if you had found it. You wouldn't have given it to Mildred Gleason regardless."

"You're right, I guess." Her manic feeling of triumph deteriorated, leaving her with an oppressive sense of sorrow. So much death and for what?

Carlos yawned. "Oh, well, I guess the excitement's over. Listen, my love, I've got an early meeting with Marshall tomorrow."

"I've got a full day tomorrow, too," she said. She stared wearily at the matchbook.

"Let me know what you're doing, will you?" he said, putting on his shoes.

"I will," she replied, her thoughts meandering. "We're a great team, you know . . . Annette and Frankie. . . . We could—"

"We are a great team. We always were." He smiled sleepily. She knew he was deliberately misunderstanding her. His second yawn was extravagant.

"I'm sorry I'm keeping you up," she said.

He chucked her under the chin. "Be nice. Remember I have the key card to the health club."

"Yes, and I have an invitation to a networking party at the Caravanserie tomorrow."

"Hmmmmm. How convenient."

"I'll call you tomorrow," she promised.

She closed the door, satisfied. She put the matchbook on the table in the dining room and then noticed the little blinking light on her answering machine.

Sighing, she turned it on to answer-play. When would the reporters give up?

"Hi there, it's me, your pal." The sweet voice of Xenia Smith filled the quiet room. "I just want to tell you I'm thinking about you and I love you."

48

Wetzon prepared to leave her apartment the next morning bent on confronting Smith and clearing the air between them. Or, closer to the truth, to clear the air between Wetzon and Wetzon. "Did you forget Howie Minton, Wetzon?" one of those Wetzons asked.

No, she hadn't forgotten Howie Minton. Amidst all this blood and gore and confusion was still the need to do business, to make money. What else was it all for? She had it, too—the same greed they all had. Would she be a headhunter if there weren't all this money in it? She couldn't honestly answer that question. She didn't rightly know. She'd had nowhere to go as a dancer. That's what happened after you hit thirty. And the truth was, money or no, she loved her work.

So she had not forgotten she had to deal with Howie Minton. And Steve Switzer. And Amanda Guilford. Yes. Amanda.

She would call Silvestri at some point, but she was reluctant to tell him about the matchbook. The incident with the key still stung. He thought she was unscrupulous—dishonest—and how could she blame him? Now she was determined to get the tapes herself and deliver them to him. To make amends. No—to show him.

She would go to the networking meeting at the Caravanserie tonight. Carlos would meet her, and Carlos would be able to get the tapes out of Barry's locker. She'd show Silvestri.

She opened the door to her apartment and walked into Silvestri.

"Oh, Jesus Christ," she said, juggling her briefcase. "Are you harassing me?" *Get you, Wetzon,* she told herself. *When what you really want to do is throw yourself at him, tell him . . .*

"You're holding out on me, Ms. Wetzon," he said bluntly, looking down at her. "Do I have to remind you we're dealing with murder?"

She backed away, into her apartment, unable to meet his accusing eyes. "Would you like to come in?" Her words came out sharper than she'd intended. She walked into her living room and sat down. He followed her.

"Would you prefer coming to the precinct and talking to the Lieutenant?"

"Now?" She looked at her watch nervously. It was almost eight-thirty.

He ignored her question. "I'll give you till noon tomorrow. I want you at the precinct by then, if not before." His tone was cold and hard.

"Gee, thanks." She wondered how it would have been if Metzger had handled the case. Whenever she and Silvestri met, whatever they said to each other took on a personal tone and went wrong. Her lips trembled. *I'm having a breakdown,* she thought. She brushed the wetness from her cheeks with her fingertips and stared defiantly at Silvestri.

His eyes were hard to fathom.

"Take a look at these," he said, pushing aside the books on her coffee table and spreading a group of photographs, all different sizes, black and white and color, dealing them out and lining them up as if he were playing bridge.

She watched his face as he put each out, but he gave her no hint. *A poker face dealing to the dummy,* she couldn't help thinking. Smith was right. *You are a dummy,* she told herself sternly. She studied the photographs, acutely aware of him, the smell of him—his aftershave, cigarette smoke on his clothes, the coffee on his breath. "What is this for?"

"We're looking for someone you might have seen at the Four Seasons who didn't turn up during our initial interrogation."

"Oh," she said, looking at the pictures. "Wait a minute. This one is Dinah Shore. What's she doing here?"

"I always include her," Silvestri said pleasantly. "She's a very special lady. You'd be surprised how many people pick her out as the person they saw—"

"Oh, great," she said sarcastically. "It was a test and I passed." She put the photograph of Dinah back in its place. "Well, I didn't see her that night. I like her, too," she added, not smiling.

"Keep going," he said, serious again.

She pulled another photograph from the arrangement. "I think I saw her in the ladies' room, only she was wearing dark glasses, but I'd remember that hair. It's the most amazing color, like copper." She thought for a moment. "I know her, I think. Who is she?" The eyes of the woman in the posed color photograph looked back at Wetzon suggestively.

"Are you sure?" Silvestri asked, ignoring her question.

"Positive. Are you going to tell me who she is?"

"Don't you know?"

"No. Would I ask you if I knew? How would I know?" She studied the photograph. "Who is she?" Silvestri raised an eyebrow at her. "I guess you're not going to tell me."

"I guess I'm not going to tell you," he said, scooping up the rest of the photographs and stuffing them back in his inside pocket. "Not if you don't already know."

They both stood.

"Are you going to your office?" he asked. "If you are, I can drop you."

"Okay, you can drop me on Second and Forty-ninth."

He had another car, a green Plymouth Valiant which had seen better days. "New car?" she asked facetiously.

"Borrowed."

That was all they said to each other. He drove in silence, concentrating on traffic.

Wetzon felt her resolve wavering. She was growing more and more uneasy about everything. He pulled into the bus stop near Forty-ninth Street and turned to her. "Wanna talk?" he said, not shutting off the motor. She looked at him, uncertain. "The Lieutenant's a mean son of a bitch," Silvestri said. "Nothing like me."

"Sure, you're a pussycat, Silvestri." She opened the door and stepped out, then leaned back toward him and spoke quickly. "Georgie told me Barry was holding something for him and it wasn't in Barry's locker. Buffie told me Barry had been threatened by Jake Donahue, that he'd written his autobiography as insurance and stashed it away somewhere, that if anything happened to him she was to present it to Mildred Gleason and Mildred would pay his insurance to Buffie." Silvestri leaned both arms on the steering wheel, chin on arms, giving her his profile. She rattled on, peeved as hell by his bland reaction. "Mildred told me she'd hired Barry to get dirt on Donahue. Jake hired a broker named Amanda Guilford to spy on Barry. Leon Ostrow, my lawyer, was at the Four Seasons that night and outside Buffie's apartment building before we found Georgie." She stopped, breathless. "Okay? Thanks for the ride." She slammed the car door.

Silvestri leaned over and rolled down the window on her side. "That's a start," he said. "You're not off the hook yet. Noon tomorrow."

"Ingrate." She pulled herself up proudly, angry that he wasn't satisfied, and walked away from the car. If her guess was right, she would present him with the stuff from the locker before noon tomorrow. That would do him.

She hadn't even looked at the business section of the *Times*. Usually she thumbed through it over her morning coffee, but she had been in a hurry this morning and too jumpy to concentrate. She'd had her apple juice and all the vitamins and had skipped the coffee. She'd have it in the office. And for the time being she would block Silvestri from her mind.

The magnolia trees were thickening with pale magenta buds, and the humid mist was just starting to clear. It would probably be a nice day. The weekday morning smells of New York—coffee, danish pastries, croissants—came from the shop on the corner of Second Avenue. There was one like it on almost every corner in New York now. She walked past the line-up of secretaries, clerks, and executives in business uniform, lured by the enticing odors.

When she opened the door to the brownstone office, she was greeted by the unmistakable aroma of brewed coffee. It wasn't like Harold to have made coffee, but there he was pouring himself a cup, so he must have. Wonders would never cease.

"Good morning," she said. "Just what I need this morning, fresh coffee."

"Good morning," he said, drowning his coffee with milk and sugar. "Smith had it made before I got here." He looked at her with concern. "How are you feeling? Did you see the papers this morning?"

"I'm feeling fine," she said genially, her back to him, going through her mail. "Why?"

"Smith says . . ." He faltered.

She turned and smiled at him encouragingly. "Don't stop now, Harold, tell me what Smith says." This was really annoying. It was as if Smith had deliberately set out to make her feel defensive this morning.

"Well," Harold said, lowering his voice, "Smith said that we have to be very gentle with you because you've been so depressed since Barry's murder, and we're not to worry you about business problems or anything."

What business problems? she thought. "Isn't that sweet of her. But she's a mother, and," she said, with the air of sharing a confidence, "you know how mothers are, Harold. They just hover too much."

"Oh, don't I know," Harold said fervently, as she knew he would because he had one of those mothers. "But she's awfully worried about you."

"She enjoys worrying about me, so let's let it be our secret, Harold. I'm really fine." She flung out her arms and did a little shuffle tap routine.

He laughed, applauding.

"Now what was that about the papers? Don't tell me someone else has been murdered." She took the *Times* out of her briefcase as she spoke and opened it to the business section. "Uh-oh."

The headline read: GOVERNMENT CLOSES DOWN BROKERAGE FIRM.

She leaned against the outside door, stunned. *So the Feds finally make their appearance,* she thought. Long overdue. It was almost as if they'd been hanging around the perimeter all along. The government almost never shut down brokerage firms. Usually if it was a matter of sudden loss of capitalization, the firm's underpinnings, the government gave the industry time to rush in and try to remedy the situation—arrange a merger with or a buy-out by another securities firm. Because if word got out, it soured the client on the whole industry. But if the firm was thought to have been doing something illegal, the industry had to stand aside. It was shattering news for investors, bad for the market, bad for headhunters, bad for the industry. She folded the paper in half lengthwise, New York style, and read the article.

Government agents padlocked the brokerage firm of Jacob Donahue & Co. late last night. Sources close to Donahue claim investors began demanding their money and stock certificates because of the publicity about the recent murders of Donahue's estranged wife, Mildred Gleason, and Donahue's employee, stockbroker Barry Stark. Carole Sue Wright, a spokeswoman for the SEC, stated that because Donahue & Co. held the securities instead of transferring them to the lender, when the investors demanded the return of their securities, it was uncovered that Donahue & Co. had used these same securities in several repos agreements.

"What happens to the people who have accounts there?" Harold asked.

"The accounts automatically go into SIPC," she answered, rereading the article. She looked up and, seeing the blank expression on his face, added, "Securities Investors Protection Corporation. It's insurance for up to half a million dollars per customer account."

"Oh." Harold nodded. "And what happens to the broker if he hasn't done anything wrong? Can he move those accounts?"

"Not easily. The government appoints an overseer. It all takes time. So a broker is better off finding another firm and rebuilding his book. And that's not easy either, because most of the firms are wary of hiring a broker from a disreputable firm and without a book."

"Did you see where it says that Jake and Mildred were never divorced?" Harold loved gossip.

"I can't believe Mildred would have been that stupid, unless she felt she could somehow hold on to her father's firm by not divorcing Jake. All of which means he will probably inherit her company, unless they prove that he's a murderer. Poor Mildred. She even loses after she can't lose anymore."

"But won't the Exchange and the SEC take away his license?"

"Yes, if he's convicted. Otherwise, they might slap his wrists for a short time or fine him, or maybe they'll say he can't trade for thirty days or sixty days, or ninety days, but then he'll be back—if he's not the murderer. And in this business, maybe even if he is."

"What's going on? Am I missing something?" Smith poked her head out of the main office. She was wearing the silk tie with the cabbage roses as a band around her dark curls, tied in a bow at the nape of her neck. Wetzon stared at it, flabbergasted. Was it the same tie Smith had worn the day Georgie was murdered, or was this a brand new one she'd bought at Bloomingdale's this morning? And if it was new, did Wetzon have the old one, because Smith had been at Buffie's apartment with Georgie and had lost it there after— No, she couldn't let herself think that.

"We were just talking about Jake Donahue," Wetzon said. "I need to talk to you, Smith." *But not about the silk tie, obviously*. Smith would wriggle out of that.

"First let me get you a cup of my fresh brewed coffee," Smith said sweetly, sounding like a television commercial. "I knew you would need it this morning. Where were you last night? I called."

"At the Caravanserie."

"You went to the Caravanserie? Really?" Harold was agog. His mouth dropped open and his eyes all but popped from behind his glasses. "Did you see any stars?"

"Later, Harold, please," Smith said sharply. "We have work to do now." She handed Wetzon the coffee.

"You had some calls, Wetzon," Harold said, cowed.

"Who?"

"Sid Ashencraft from Thomson McKinley in Palm Beach."

"Probably about Angela Buttenweiser."

"You can call him back, he said."

"Who else?"

"Steve Switzer. Smith spoke to him."

Smith nodded. "It's dead with Hallgarden, but I talked him into looking at Oppenheimer."

"He wants up-front. It's a waste of time. They won't give it to him at Oppenheimer."

"Wetzon, you know as well as I do that these brokers never know what they want."

Wetzon sighed. Smith had a point. Sometimes things fell into place for all the wrong reasons. And maybe sometimes people got murdered for all the wrong reasons.

"Any other calls?"

"Yeah, a Dr. Pulasky."

"Did he leave a number?" Harold looked stricken, his bearded face funereally grave, flooded with concern. "Don't look so worried, Harold, Dr. Pulasky is a personal friend."

"Yes," Smith said mischievously, "*very* personal."

Harold smiled, tentative, not understanding. "He said you couldn't reach him, that he would call again later."

Wetzon closed the door to the office she shared with Smith and put the coffee cup down on her desk. Her briefcase went under the desk. She took a sip of the coffee, and a deep breath, then turned to face Smith, who was smiling indulgently at her. It was downright disconcerting. Smith was sending out waves of love.

Wetzon sighed and took another swallow of coffee. It was unusually good. Probably a new blend of decaf.

"Smith," she began.

"Yes, dear." Smith's big dark eyes were moist. Actually, she looked more exotic than usual this morning. Her olive skin was set off by the vivid blue and mauve colors in her silk dress, and she'd made herself up to emphasize her high, broad cheekbones and doe eyes. Her dark hair was a curly wimple for her face, cut by those damn mauve cabbage roses. . . .

"Smith." Wetzon closed her eyes against Smith's wide-eyed innocence, knowing that Smith well realized its impact on her. "Smith, why did you tell Silvestri that it was my idea to make a duplicate of the key?" It made her angry all over again just thinking about it, and saying it out loud, she found herself shaking with fury.

"What did you say? *I* told Silvestri it was your idea to make a copy of the key?" Smith's face reflected nothing but indignation. "I did no such thing. How could you possibly think I would?" She paused, waiting for Wetzon to cave in, but Wetzon kept silent. "Actually," Smith said, smoothly placating, "he wanted me to say that, you should have heard how he phrased it, but I wouldn't. I think he was trying to trick us, to get us to say something incriminating about each other."

"Incriminating? Smith, what are you talking about?"

"Well, you know, that whole business with the key." Smith's voice radiated goodness. "You know I would never have said such a thing to Silvestri. I'm your friend. I love you. We have a history together. You know you can trust me. We've been together too long for that." Smith put a hand on each of Wetzon's shoulders, staring into her eyes. She was sincere.

Wetzon felt sick. Here was her friend and partner, Xenia Smith, meeting her eyes unflinchingly and telling her that Silvestri had set a trap for them, and maybe he had, because he had guessed the key had been copied. Of course he had. And he had caught them both. It had all been a silly mistake. "Oh, I know, Smith," she said. "I'm really ashamed that I could have thought you would do that." She was surprised to discover that she was shaking.

Smith's eyes fluttered as if she were going to cry. She was full of compassion. "You're just overwrought by this whole thing, dear. Just look at yourself, you're trembling. Maybe you should get away for a few days. Why not take my country place—"

"No, no, I'll be all right, and besides, I hate the country. I'd just get stir-crazy there. But thank you. Now where is that damn key?" But she wasn't all right. Her heart was thumping and she felt waves of panic in her chest.

"You really ought to go home," Smith said. Her eyes narrowed solicitously. "You look terrible." She opened her desk drawer and took out an envelope. "Here it is."

"I'll give it to Silvestri tomorrow." Wetzon put the envelope in her handbag.

"Why tomorrow?"

"He wants to see me at the precinct tomorrow at twelve."

"What for?"

"More questions, I guess. Smith, about that money from Leon—"

"Don't say another word," Smith said. "I gave it all back to Leon last night. You were right, of course." She smiled her crooked smile.

"I'm so glad, Xenia." Wetzon, feeling fiercely relieved, squeezed her partner's hand. "Just let me sit here for a minute. I feel as if I've been running miles."

"Okay, sweetie, you just sit there and relax and I'll fill you in on what we've been doing about Donahue's. You don't have to worry about anything right now. First, Harold pulled all the names. We have home phone numbers for some of them, but who knows if they're at home. They're probably all scattered around looking for jobs."

"And their accounts will all go into SIPC and be frozen for who knows how long, so what firms are going to be willing to hire them, especially through us? We'll have to see, but we may just end up spinning our wheels," Wetzon said, starting to feel better.

"I put Harold on it. He'll let us know if he comes up with anyone."

"Good. Now I have to set up appointments for Amanda Guilford and Howie Minton."

"Oh, no," Smith groaned. "Not him again. He'll never leave Rosenkind."

"This time I think he will. They've decided he has to pay for a customer complaint about their bad stock picks."

"So *he* says, the sleazebag."

"Now, Smith," Wetzon said, and they were back in motion again, grinning at each other. But her heart still pounded and she couldn't quite shake the feeling of panic. The last time she had felt like this, she'd drunk regular coffee by mistake. Smith had made the coffee this morning and Smith knew she drank only decaf, so it had to be something else. The shock of everything that had happened to her over this past week was probably starting to tell.

Harold opened the door. "Smith, call for you from Gary Enderman."

"Oh, please, give me a break," Smith said. "And it's only Monday."

"Al Catella for you, Wetzon."

They retreated to their corners and picked up their weapons. So the day began.

49

Somewhere near midmorning, Carlos phoned. "We've got a problem about tonight, darling," he said. "My main man with the entry card is out of town until tomorrow, and I haven't been able to round up someone with another."

"Shit," Wetzon said.

"And Marshall called a creative session for tonight. I'm really sorry, birdie."

"That queers everything," Wetzon bitched.

"I resent that implication."

"If the foo shits," she said, laughing. She sat back in her chair and caught a glimpse of Smith looking at her inquiringly. She shook her head, indicating it wasn't business.

"Very funny, very funny," Carlos replied. "Listen, we can do it tomorrow night."

She lowered her voice. "But the networking thing is tonight. I wanted to do it tonight."

"Well, we can't, Miss Compulsive."

"I know, I know." She thought for a second. Hadn't Rick mentioned he had a membership at the Caravanserie through the hospital? She'd have to ask him. Maybe he would do it for her.

"Hello . . . hello, have I lost you entirely?"

"Carlos," she whispered, "I think I just remembered someone telling me he was a member of the club."

"And I wanted to play cops and robbers with you, spoil sport."

"But you 'wanna dance' a lot more, right?"

"True! ' 'tis true, 'tis pity and pity 'tis, 'tis true.' Well, go ahead, but you have to tell me *all* about it."

"Goodbye, Carlos, you idiot."

"But that doesn't make me a bad person," he said. "Be careful," he added, becoming serious. "Do you trust this guy?"

"Of course." Why shouldn't she trust Rick? She hung up; her hand remained resting on the receiver.

"What was all that about?" For some reason it always seemed to make

Smith paranoid when she couldn't hear Wetzon's conversations with her friends. Even when she eavesdropped, Smith rarely understood what she heard. One thing always amazed Wetzon: Smith had no sense of humor, unless she made the joke.

"Just Carlos being silly."

"Who did you go to the Caravanserie with—the Good Humor man?"

A little bell went off in Wetzon's head. Smith meant Rick, of course. The Good Humor man, all in white. "No. Carlos. We were celebrating. He's going to be assistant choreographer on Marshall Bart's new musical."

"Humpf," Smith said. "And are you seeing the Good Humor man tonight?"

"Yes. Why?"

"Oh, I thought we could have dinner together, just the two of us, the way we used to."

"Maybe later in the week," Wetzon said, suddenly feeling sorry for Smith. She'd been left out of things since Barry's murder. Smith liked to be the star, and here was plain little Wetzon getting all the attention, and not even wanting it, either. "Later in the week, okay?"

She didn't want to tell Smith about the Caravanserie and Barry's locker, or the networking night, because she knew that Smith would try to take it over, as she had done with the key. This was Wetzon's idea and she felt proprietary about it.

"Wetzon, dear, one more thing," Smith said with a big, sweet smile.

"What?"

"Jake Donahue would love to meet you. He saw your picture in the papers and—"

Wetzon felt herself getting angry all over again. "Oh, yes, he saw my picture in the paper and he was overwhelmed with my beauty. Right? And just in passing, he'd like to know what Barry told me before he died."

"Wetzon, why are you being so difficult? It's just that he's heard a lot about you—"

"How?"

"Well, from Leon, from me . . . and he'd like to meet you." She was positively glowing with sincerity. "Leon can arrange it. Come on now, Wetzon, Jake's a very attractive man, and he knows a lot of important people."

"Smith, are you crazy? Donahue's a crook, and he's probably going to jail. And he could be a murderer. He figures I know what Barry had on him. Just as Mildred did."

"Honestly," Smith said, with a light laugh, throwing up her arms. "You are such a hardhead. I was only trying to do something nice for you. Forget it—it was just an idea."

Surprised by Smith's easy capitulation, Wetzon smiled warily. Smith was so unpredictable.

Harold opened the door. "They're closing the Dean Witter office on Sixth Avenue and giving the brokers two weeks to choose another office in the system."

"Do we know anyone there?" Smith asked.

"Everyone. Wetzon's talked to at least ten brokers there. I've pulled the names."

"Yes," Wetzon said, taking her update folder from the drawer of her desk. "And one of them is Joe Stotner. I'll go after him and the rest after I take care of Amanda Guilford." She pulled her yellow pad with the notes she had made on Amanda's history and business out of her briefcase.

"Oh, I forgot," Harold said, "there's a woman on the phone for you who doesn't want to give her name. She's holding on line three. Jesus, I'm sorry."

"One of Wetzon's waifs, no doubt," Smith said sweetly.

Wetzon smiled back sweetly and picked up the phone. "Wetzon." She heard clamor in the background, but no one responded. "Hello? Wetzon speaking."

"Hello." Wetzon could barely hear the woman's voice over the noise. Subway noise? "Can we speak confidentially?" the woman asked.

"Yes, of course." Another paranoid broker, probably from Donahue's, she thought.

"This is Roberta Bancroft. I must see you tonight."

The sudden intrusion of Mildred's assistant triggered an anxious pulse in Wetzon's throat. "I'm very sorry about your loss, but—"

"Please, I'm begging you. My life is at stake." Her voice faded. The connection seemed bad. Wetzon strained to hear. Her voice came back, very low. ". . . something crucial . . . you're the only one . . ." The sound of a jackhammer obliterated her words. ". . . who can verify—"

Wetzon's heart began to race. "No, please. Call Sergeant Silvestri at the Seventeenth Precinct. Here," she fumbled in her handbag, "I'll give you the number."

Now Roberta's voice crackled. "I tried. He wasn't there. Please. My life is in danger. I can't go home. Please help me. You must help me—"

Wetzon closed her eyes, listening to the muffled sobs, agonizing. She'd be crazy to get involved. "Okay," she heard herself say. She looked at her schedule. "Can you come to my office later today? Around five-thirty?" At least that would give her plenty of time to get to the Caravanserie.

"Oh, yes, anytime, whatever you say." Roberta's voice grew stronger, eager. "I'll call Sergeant Silvestri again. I'll tell him to meet me at your office. But please, please, do not tell anyone else. If you do, it may be the wrong person—" The connection was cut off, leaving Wetzon speechless. Roberta must know who had killed Mildred and Barry. It had to be Jake, or maybe someone Jake had hired to do it. Who else could it possibly be? She looked up and saw Smith watching her suspiciously. "What's up now?" Smith asked, an odd tightness in her voice.

"Amanda Guilford . . .she's so nervous," Wetzon fabricated. "I told her I'd meet her late in the afternoon."

"At the Four Seasons?" Smith asked, tongue in cheek.

"God, Smith, I don't know if I have the guts to go back there this soon. Just the thought makes me shiver."

"Switzer for you, line one," Harold interrupted.

"Switzer? Now what?" She picked up the phone. "Steve? What's happening?"

"I'm starting at Hallgarden in two weeks."

"You're what?" Wetzon mouthed, *He's going to Hallgarden,* to Smith and held up two fingers for weeks. Smith jumped up and crossed over to Wetzon's desk, clapping her hands together soundlessly. "How did it happen?"

Switzer's voice was bursting with contained excitement. "About an hour ago it came over the tape that that asshole Gordon Kingston resigned. I called Garfield and he said, 'When are you coming on board?' "

"You firmed up the deal already?" Wetzon was flabbergasted. All the terrible things Switzer had said about Andy Garfeld seemed to have been forgotten, at least for now.

"Wetzon, you know you gotta move fast in this business." Switzer laughed. "We're doing a kiss contact."

That was a new one on her. "Kiss contract?"

"Yeah, 'keep it simple, stupid.' "

"Well, okay then! Congratulations."

The phone rang and Harold came running back. "Andy Garfeld!" he whispered.

Wetzon put her hand on the mouthpiece. "Hold him."

"Listen, Wetzon," Switzer said, "Andy explained it all to me. I know he was under the gun. I don't hold it against him. He's a terrific guy. Later, huh?" The phone clicked.

Wetzon shook her head and punched the button releasing Garfeld from hold. "Congratulations," she said.

"You know already?" He sounded disappointed.

"Just spoke with Steve. You got yourself a great producer."

"I hope so. My ass is in a sling if he's not a winner. I gave him the best deal I had. I want him over here this week."

"He said two weeks."

"Wetzon, I leave it to you. Get him here by Friday."

"Yes, sir," Wetzon said, saluting, putting down the phone.

"It's not over till it's over," Wetzon and Smith said simultaneously.

Smiling, Wetzon slipped her fingers into the outside pocket of her suit jacket. They touched the smooth cardboard of the matchbook.

And even when it's over, it's not over.

50

She talked to six brokers from Dean Witter and set up appointments for two of them; the others wanted to stay within the firm and had made arrangements to move to other branch offices. She arranged for Howie Minton to see three firms during the week, and for Amanda Guilford to talk with Alex Brown that afternoon after the close. Her stomach was telling her it was just about ready for lunch when Rick phoned again.

"I'm so glad you called back. Hold on a sec." Wetzon turned, looking for Smith, but Smith was already sitting in the garden with a foil sun reflector under her chin, working on her tan. "Rick, didn't you tell me you had a membership at the Caravanserie?"

"Yeah," he said, ". . . through the hospital."

"Well, I need your help. . . . Can you—would you—check out a locker there for me tonight?" She was talking so fast into the mouthpiece of the phone that her tongue kept tripping on her teeth.

"Hey, hold on, whose locker? Tell me slowly, babe."

"Rick—I think I figured it out. I mean—last night—Barry told me—"

"Barry's dead, babe."

"I know, I know. But he left me a message . . . in a matchbook. The key was caught in the matchbook—"

"The key? You have the key?"

"No, don't you see?" she said, impatient. "The key was never important. What was important all along was the matchbook. It had a locker number and combination written in it. I think Barry may have had another locker. . . . Oh, it's too complicated to explain. Georgie cleaned out Barry's regular locker and didn't find anything—"

"But what about the key?" he persisted.

"I told you, the police have the key. Don't you see, it has nothing to do with the case. The key is a hospital key of some sort. Maybe it got in my pocket after the accident when I was with the paramedics or at York Emergency."

"Okay, babe, fine. I get it. What can I do? I want to see you tonight anyway. That's why I called."

The phone rang, rang again, and again. Harold had gone out for lunch and

Smith was still toasting herself in the garden. "Hold on a minute, Rick, I'm sorry to do this to you." She hit the hold button and answered, "Smith and Wetzon."

"Wetzon, m'dear, this is Leon. I must talk to you—"

"Leon, I'm sorry, I'm on the other line and I'm the only one here. I'll call right back."

"But—"

She broke the connection and went back to Rick, as Harold entered carrying their lunch, and she motioned him out to the garden. "Rick, I've been invited to a networking session at the Caravanserie tonight." She saw Harold say something to Smith, and they both looked back toward the office.

"What time?"

"Six. Can you meet me?"

"Not till seven, but if you have the number of the locker and the combination, why don't you give me the numbers now over the phone, and I'll get everything and meet you there."

"Wetzon, come on, you're missing the best sun." Smith stood in the doorway, arms folded, reproving.

"One more sec, Smith," Wetzon said. "I'm talking to Rick."

Smith didn't move.

"Okay, I'll meet you at seven, in the downstairs lounge. Can you get there? You can get in through the club."

"I know. And I know you can't talk," Rick said. "Just tell me, do the cops know about this locker?"

"I don't think so."

"Later, babe."

She hung up the phone and smiled. He sounded like such a thug when he called her babe. A little like Barry, come to think of it. Barry had also called her babe.

"You're too much," Smith said. "Come on, I'm starving."

Funny, Wetzon thought. Normally she would have shared the matchbook with Smith, and they would have worked out the strategy together, but she had not yet figured out how she felt about Smith and the key. Silvestri *could* have set a trap for them.

The sun was mildly tranquilizing. Wetzon tilted her face toward it gratefully. She needed soothing. She felt as if she'd been beaten up, physically and emotionally. But it would be better tonight. Tonight she would get the tapes and turn them over to Silvestri. And he would realize that she was straight and honest, and maybe even smart and terrific. She took off her jacket and put it on the back of the chair.

"Where are you?" Smith demanded. "I've called to you twice. You look like you're a million miles away. That Dr. what's-his-face has really gotten to you."

"No, I'm just beginning to unwind, and Dr. what's-his-face is about to disappear from my life as suddenly as he appeared."

"Oh? What's up?" Smith's voice was guilefully uninterested.

"He's got a job in San Diego heading up emergency medicine at one of the hospitals there."

"Too bad," Smith said, but she didn't sound very sympathetic. "Your cards keep coming up with danger, you know. I'm worried about you." She leaned over and patted Wetzon's hand. "You must take better care of yourself." She was very sincere now. "What are you eating?"

"Egg salad."

Smith grimaced. "Yuk, bird food," she said. "You should be eating red meat. Look how thin you've gotten."

"Oh, please, Smith, I'm the same weight I always am, maybe a couple of pounds off."

"Humpf," Smith said. "Did you set up Howie Minton?"

"Yes, with Shearson, D. L. J., and the Bear."

"He won't move."

"I think he will this time."

"I think he's just jerking us around again, but if he does move, I'll buy you dinner at the Four Seasons. You've certainly put the time into him over these years."

"What do you have in the works today?"

"There's an offer out to Bill Davis, from Pru-Bache, but Oppie wants him."

"Davis'll get a better deal from Bache. What did you tell him?"

"That he has to choose the type of firm he wants to work in, a big impersonal wire house like Bache or an elite boutique, like Oppenheimer. Macy's or Martha's." They both laughed at her analogy.

"We'll do better if he goes to Oppie." There, Smith and Wetzon were paid on the broker's future production, so if the broker did well, they did well. Wetzon never minded doing that because it was betting on the broker. She was rarely surprised when she bet on the broker at OpCo or Lehman or Bear. It was usually a good bet. At firms like those, a well-paid sales assistant relieved the broker from all paperwork, leaving him free to sell and sell and sell.

"Only if he has a good year."

"Right. Which depends on the market. So the hell with it. It's his choice, anyway. Where do you think he'll go? And will he go?"

"Who knows? He's unhappy at Merrill, so he may do it." She turned to Wetzon. "I'm sorry about the doctor."

"It's okay. You were right about him. He's not for me." She paused. "Honest."

Wetzon backed her chair out of the sun. Too much, too soon. She'd get salmony pink. Not her best shade. And the last thing she needed right now was a sunburn. "You're seeing a lot of Leon lately." She didn't know why it had surprised her, but it had. She made a mental note to call Leon back after lunch.

"He wants to get married."

"Are you kidding?" Wetzon sat up, shading her eyes with her hand, and looked at Smith. "He's really serious? But you—"

"I'm thinking about it."

"Well, that's new." Wetzon was surprised all over again. Smith looked away. "Do you want to talk?"

"No. I'm just thinking about it. He would take good care of me—us. He's very successful. Sometimes a woman wants to be taken care of. . . ." She seemed a little defensive.

"How does Mark feel about it?"

"Mark will be happy if I'm happy."

Wetzon didn't think it was that simple. Mark and Xenia had a special relationship, almost husband and wife, in a sense. The boy might resent the intrusion.

"Smith," Harold called, "Bill Davis, line two."

"Oh, great," Smith said, jumping up. "Maybe this is it. Back in a flash with the cash. Cross your fingers."

Cross your fingers. Wetzon had crossed them when she promised Howie Minton she wouldn't tell about the conversation between Barry and Mildred that he'd overheard. Should she tell Silvestri? Did it matter anymore? Mildred and Barry were dead. Wetzon went back to her desk reluctantly. There was still a lot of work to do.

By the end of the day, they had a done deal on Bill Davis and a start date in three weeks. He had chosen Pru-Bache, which would mean a thirty-thousand-dollar commission for Smith and Wetzon.

"Not a bad day," Wetzon said.

"Not bad. I'm dead, if you'll pardon the expression," Smith said with an exaggerated yawn shortly before five. She did look a little tired. "I'm going home to take a nap before dinner. Are you coming?"

"No, go ahead."

"Do you need Harold? Come on, Harold sweetie, it's been a long day, and you've done a super job fielding everything." Harold looked eagerly at Wetzon. He wanted to leave with Smith, have her to himself. He was so obvious.

"Go ahead, Harold," Wetzon told him. "I'll lock up. I'm meeting Rick around seven," she said to Smith.

"Oh, I quite forgot. Good night then, sweetie pie." Smith gave her a hug and a kiss, just like old times.

Wetzon washed her face and redid her makeup. She was wearing her black wool crepe suit and a white silk blouse. The collar of the blouse was ruffled and her mother's cameo looked perfect pinned at her throat. She took the hairpins out of her hair and brushed it, then rerolled it, but not as tightly as before.

"The Good Humor man," Smith had said. She meant Rick, of course, because he was a doctor in a white coat. She had seen him in his white coat the other day. It seemed so long ago, but it wasn't even a week.

Her dream . . . the Good Humor man in her dream . . . who wore a Mickey Mouse watch and sold only rocky road ice cream. The tricks the subconscious played. She hadn't liked the Good Humor man in her dream. There was something mean and manipulative about him. Rocky road. That could be the Pulasky Skyway. No. It was all too silly. It didn't mean anything. It couldn't mean anything.

Roberta was due momentarily. Roberta's phone call had been so baffling. How could *she* save Roberta's life? There it was again. She had not been able to say no to someone she barely knew. But Roberta had said it was a matter of life and death. No, she would refuse to let Roberta draw her in further, and besides, Silvestri would be there.

She'd walk, she decided, to the Caravanserie after the Roberta business was finished. It was still light and it would be a pleasant walk. Her fingers crept to the matchbook in her pocket. Just to be sure.

Maybe she shouldn't be such a hotshot about doing it herself. Maybe she should tell Silvestri when he got here. In the silence of the empty office, she thought about it. She locked the door to the garden and pulled the blinds. Oh, hell, she was being a fool. Yes. She would tell Silvestri and take herself out of the game. After all, he was the pro. She had a sudden, tremendous urge to tell him immediately, even though she knew she would soon see him. That way he would know before he got to her office and had to deal with Roberta.

She searched in her handbag for his card, couldn't find it, and ended up calling information again.

The switchboard answered, "Seventeenth Precinct," and switched her upstairs.

"Metzger."

"Sergeant Silvestri, please."

"He's not here right now. Can I take a message?"

"Just tell him Leslie Wetzon called. I guess he's already on his way over. . . . Never mind. I'll tell him when he gets here."

"Where?"

"Here—in my office—for the meeting Roberta Bancroft set up." There was a peculiar pause. "Detective Metzger?"

He came back on the line. "Sorry," he said curtly, his attention elsewhere. The line went dead.

51

Jittery, she checked the back door to the garden. Of course it was locked. She had just locked it. Checked the front door. Locked it. Harold should have done that when he left. No. She had told him she would do it. Where was her mind?

She was feeling antsy, so she sat down at her desk and went through her messages again to be sure she had called everyone back. One by one, she crumpled them and dropped them into the wastebasket at her feet.

Mike Antonio liked to be called at eight in the morning. He started his day early. She'd call him tomorrow from home before she left for the office.

She looked over the suspect sheets which profiled the brokers she was working with and made a list of people she had to call. Then she added those brokers whose appointments had to be confirmed.

Oh, God, she had forgotten to call Leon back. She could do it now, while she was waiting. She picked up the phone and started to punch out Leon's number. An odd sound came from the front room. She cradled the phone, listening. There it was again. Someone was rattling the doorknob. She froze. *Don't be a jerk,* she told herself. She looked at her watch. It was just five. Could it be Roberta already? And where was Silvestri? No. It was probably a broker who wanted to talk. It had happened before. When a broker made up his mind to move, he invariably wanted to get things going fast.

She went into the front room and slipped the chain lock on. Then she opened the door cautiously, thinking how flimsy and ridiculous the chain lock was. A strong man could shove the door all the way open, easily tearing the lock from the frame.

Through the small opening, she saw a big man in an expensive, dark blue pinstripe suit. There were scratch marks on his face.

"Wetzon." It was not a question.

She felt a cold chill. She had seen him only once before, under unfortunate circumstances, but she recognized him. Jake Donahue.

"Yes. What do you want?" *How stupid, Wetzon. You know exactly what he wants.*

"Let me in, please. I want to talk to you." He spoke in that easy, smooth way of powerful men. The assumption of command.

"I don't have anything to say to you, Mr. Donahue. Please go away." Her voice shook, and she was furious with herself for showing weakness.

"You're frightened," he said, apparently compassionate. "I don't mean to frighten you."

She looked at him. He had Paul Newman blue eyes, set in a coarse, fleshy face, a large nose, dark red hair flecked with white, billowy eyebrows, and a deep bronze tan, as if he'd just gotten back from the islands. Decidedly gross, larger than life, but infinitely better than the last time she had seen him.

"How did you know I'd be here?" she asked. "Wait—don't tell me—I'd rather not know." Now she understood why Smith had left earlier than usual. "Goddammit," Wetzon cursed under her breath. Smith had set her up again.

She slammed the door closed, unhooked the chain, and swung the door open.

"Thank you." Jake Donahue stepped inside, closing the door behind him.

"Make yourself at home," she said flippantly. "I know you've paid for your time with me, so you'll want to get your money's worth."

He eyed her, arching his left brow.

"I do want to warn you," she added, "that I am expected elsewhere very shortly, and if I'm late . . ."

"Okay, fair enough." He became brisk. "I just need a few minutes—" He broke off. "Why are you looking at me like that?" He was such a big man, tall and square, very self-assured. And why not? He was a many-times-over millionaire, he had power, he had celebrity. But he seemed disconcerted by the intensity of her stare.

"I was thinking about the last time I saw you," she said, not knowing why she was standing there calmly talking to him as if they were two ordinary people meeting under ordinary circumstances.

"I hadn't realized we'd met before." He frowned. He obviously didn't like the unexpected.

"We haven't—not officially," she said. "I was in Mildred Gleason's office the other day when you made your grand entrance."

"Christ," he said, with a self-conscious grin, running blunt fingers through his thick hair. "Look, the situation got a little out of hand. Do you mind if I smoke?"

She shook her head. He took a Marlboro out of a box and lit it with a gold Dunhill lighter. "Come into the back office," she said, motioning him through, closing the door after them. The last thing she wanted was to have Roberta see Jake or vice versa.

Jake looked around curiously. "So this is a headhunter's lair." He sounded amused. "And we are alone at last, Wetzon." He turned to her then and saw the look on her face. "I've frightened you again," he said, extending his arm.

She backed away, feeling her face tighten.

"Hell, I'm really not a bad fellow," Jake said, his voice beguiling. "A lot of people like me. I'm not going to hurt you. Why would I?"

"Because you think Barry told me something before he died," she exclaimed, thinking even as she spoke, *You're being stupid again, Wetzon.*

"Sit down, please," he said, motioning her to her own chair. He sat in Smith's chair, which disappeared under his bulk.

The phone rang. They stared at it as it rang again, and Jake Donahue shook his head at her. He saw the answering machine on the worktable and pressed the auto-answer button. The machine clicked on and answered the phone on the fourth ring.

"Hello, Wetzon, this is Scott Fineberg. Please call me. I'll be in my office till seven." The machine clicked off.

Donahue and Wetzon looked at each other. Jake inhaled deeply and breathed smoke out slowly through his nose. "So that little scumbag was two-timing me with you."

She looked at her watch. Almost five-thirty. She was beginning to feel cornered. Where was Roberta? Where was Silvestri? She had to get out in time to meet Rick.

"Yes," Jake said, "I want to know what Barry said to you. He had some things that belong to me."

"You and the late Georgie Travers." She couldn't keep the scorn out of her voice.

"I'm not interested in Georgie Travers. It's Stark I want to know about. That dirtbag was spying on me."

The pieces of the puzzle were shuffling around again in Wetzon's head in a peculiar jumble. She didn't respond.

"Fuck this," Donahue said impatiently. "I didn't kill Stark. I wanted to, but I didn't. I didn't even know he was there that night—it's not exactly his kind of place—and I was long gone by the time you found his body."

Wetzon tried to keep her head clear, but small waves of panic were beginning to wash over her. She tried to shift her weight in the chair, but her arms and legs were numb.

Jake Donahue had just admitted he was at the Four Seasons that night.

"Please try to see my position," Donahue was saying. He pulled his chair over to hers and took her hand. She did not pull away, but stared at her hand, swallowed up in his big one. She felt his voice begin to lull her.

"My wife was a bitter, vindictive woman. She was trying to put me out of business for good. Stark was my employee. He was working for her and taping my phone calls."

"How do you know that?"

"I have one of the tapes."

Her eyes widened. "You stole the attaché case," she accused, pulling her hand away.

"Someone did it for me," he admitted, not moving. "No one was supposed to get hurt. He just got a little carried away." Donahue shrugged. "Stark left the office that day with that big attaché he always carried. Someone at the Four

Seasons tipped me to the murder. I was told you left with a big attaché case. I needed that case. That's it. I'm sorry."

"Sorry?" She was angry. "Is that all you can say? What kind of power trip are you on?"

He stood and she flinched, expecting a blow.

"Ms. Wetzon," Donahue said, meeting her guarded glare, leaning against Smith's desk. "I've done some rotten things in my life, but I am not a murderer, and I'm not going to hurt you. If you gave me some time and got to know me, you might even like me."

"Sure. You may be a crook, but you're not a killer."

His blue eyes reproached her, and she felt a brief twinge of guilt. Was she being too rough on him? *What the hell is wrong with you?* she thought. What a soft touch she was. Maybe Smith was right. She was too naïve for this business.

"What do you want of me, Jake?"

"I want you not to tell the cops about the tapes, the key, the money. I need time to try to find the rest of those tapes."

"And do what with them when you find them?"

He grinned at her, suddenly full of Irish charm. "Do what Nixon didn't have the guts to do."

52

In spite of herself, she laughed. "This is a crazy conversation we're having, Jake Donahue."

"Leslie Wetzon," Jake Donahue said, inclining toward her. "I like you."

The piercing buzz of a doorbell interrupted their dialogue. Although she had been expecting Roberta and Silvestri, Wetzon literally jumped.

"Good God." Donahue froze, alert. "Who the hell—"

"I told you I had an appointment—" She was uncomfortable. Perhaps against her better judgment, she half-believed Jake's claim that he was not a murderer. If he weren't, then which of the cast of characters she had met was? Whenever she had her fingertips on the solution, it would melt away like ice cream. "Jake, look, I don't have what you're looking for. I don't know where it is, and even if I did . . ."

The doorbell rang again. Two impatient rings.

There was no back way out, through the garden, for her to send Jake. What should she do?

As if in response to her silent question, Jake said roughly, "Get rid of whoever it is." He stood up, a meaty mass of a man, dwarfing her.

"Oh, hell. Wait here," Wetzon said. At least she wasn't going to be alone with him. What could he do with Roberta and Silvestri there? Silvestri. God. It would be awful if Silvestri found Jake Donahue with her after she had told him she didn't know the man.

Wetzon went into the outer office, closing the door firmly behind her. The doorbell rang several times more and someone rattled the doorknob impatiently.

"Who is it?" Wetzon called, leaving the chain lock on and peering into the dusky twilight. A tall, slender woman with long hair, wearing a dark, tightly belted coat, stood in the small brick vestibule. It had to be Roberta.

Wetzon slipped off the chain lock. The woman who came through the door into the light of the office was the woman with the extraordinary hair whom Wetzon had seen at the Four Seasons. The woman whose picture Wetzon had picked out for Silvestri, the woman she hadn't been able to name for Silvestri. No wonder he had thought it strange. He knew she'd met Roberta the day before. What he had not known was that Roberta, in a turban that covered her head and under the guise of a headache, had managed not to be recognizable. No wonder Silvestri had concluded Wetzon was either nuts or hiding something. Her first reaction was dismay, swiftly replaced by fear.

"You are—"

"Roberta Bancroft." The woman offered Wetzon a long, thin hand. The beautiful copper hair was full and smooth, in a perfectly rolled pageboy cut. She brought with her the unmistakable floral scent of lily of the valley.

Wetzon took Roberta's hand but found it impossible to pull her eyes away from the woman. She was the ultimate in chic in a black leather trench coat. A Hermès print scarf was tied loosely at her throat, as if she had just slipped it off her head. Wetzon's mind conjured up a fleeting image of a woman in a black leather trench coat and scarf tied under her chin, who got out of the cab on Second Avenue right behind Wetzon the day after Barry was killed and just before Wetzon was pushed into the street.

"Is anything wrong?" Roberta had amazing light green eyes with dark rims—cat eyes, with dark lashes and brows. A blue and yellow bruise stained the pale skin under her right eye.

"Oh, no," Wetzon said, looking away. She had been staring. "You did reach Sergeant Silvestri, didn't you?"

"Yes, of course, but he said he might be delayed." Roberta let her eyes drift around the room, as if she was taking inventory.

Delayed. Not very likely that he would be coming at all. Wetzon's mind roiled. What was she to do? But she said calmly, "Would you like to sit down?" She pointed to one of the two small modern chairs upholstered in a Jack Lenor Larsen black, white, and brown wool. She looked at her watch. Five-forty. Jake was in the other room, listening; she was certain of it. Could he be counted on for help? Of that she wasn't so certain. She glanced at her watch again. Roberta's cat eyes narrowed. "I have another appointment outside the office," Wetzon explained.

"My timing lately is always off," Roberta murmured. She stretched thin, deep red lips over oddly small teeth. Cat eyes, rat teeth.

If Roberta had been at the Four Seasons that day, she could have killed Barry. Panic crept slowly up from the base of Wetzon's spine. *Keep your wits about you, old girl. Stay with it.* "Why do you think your life is in danger?" she asked, sitting on the edge of Harold's desk. "And what does it have to do with me?"

Roberta seemed curiously serene. She opened her black leather bag, searched through it, and took out a long slim cigarette. She lit it ostentatiously with a match from a Four Seasons matchbook. "Oh, my dear, it has everything to do with you," she said, drawing deeply on the cigarette.

Black leather trench coat and floral scarf. The pieces began to click into place. Roberta was the woman Buffie had seen with Barry at the zoo in Central Park. How well had Roberta known Barry? Was she simply Mildred's liaison? "Were you having an affair with Barry?"

Roberta actually snickered. "That slime. Hardly. It was Mildred's idea that I be the go-between. I didn't like it, and I didn't trust him. I warned her not to get involved with him. Why do you ask?"

"Barry's girlfriend saw you with him."

"Ha!" She had an explosive laugh, like a bark. She showed just the tips of those rodentlike teeth. She inhaled again deeply and slowly let the smoke out.

Jake was at the Four Seasons, Leon was there, and Roberta was there. What if they had all been together? What if Barry had seen them— "Oh, my god," Wetzon said out loud, her face crumpling.

"Ah, well," Roberta said, standing. She looked around for an ashtray.

Eyeing her warily, Wetzon emptied a small metal box that Harold used for paper clips and handed it to Roberta, who ground out her cigarette methodically.

"You're the only one, I think, who can put me there."

"I don't understand," Wetzon said, sliding off Harold's desk, pulling clips with her. They scattered on the wooden floor. "I didn't see you at the zoo."

Roberta gave Wetzon a smoldering look. "I'm not talking about the zoo. Do you take me for a fool? Barry saw me at the Four Seasons. After you saw me. I was with Jake." She was rummaging in the black leather purse, looking for something. "There was no deal, you understand. I only agreed to help him to protect Mildred. But Barry was going to tell Mildred, and I couldn't have that." She looked up and smiled reassuringly at Wetzon. "It was no loss, you know. They should give me a medal—" She found what she was looking for in her purse and pulled it out. Wetzon gasped. It was a Swiss hunting knife, the kind she always saw advertized at Hoffritz.

It was not until that moment that Wetzon fully realized the danger. She had the odd sensation of spinning out of her body and standing a little to the side, watching the action. "What about Georgie?" Wetzon said, playing for time, but needing to know.

"He was worse than Barry, if that's possible. That stupid girl called Mildred about his having written an autobiography, so we figured she had the tapes and was going to make us pay to get them. He caught me searching her apartment and cut himself in." Showing the tips of her teeth again, she added serenely, "So I cut him out." She contemplated Wetzon for a moment and then took a small step forward.

"Roberta, I found the tapes. I'll give them to you," Wetzon said, backing toward the door to the inside room.

Roberta opened the knife slowly, in an oddly sensual movement. "You have the tapes?" She stopped. "Where are they?"

"Not here. I have to get them."

"You're the only one who knows about me. I don't need the tapes."

"No, I'm not. Jake Donahue and Leon, his lawyer, know." *And Silvestri knows, but he's not coming.*

"They'll never tell."

"I wouldn't count on it. Leon, after all, is an officer of the court."

"But if I have the tapes, they'll never talk. They'd be afraid to."

"That's right." Wetzon leaned on the door to the back office. Roberta was mad. She was afraid to take her eyes from either Roberta or the knife. Afraid to move. Oh, Silvestri . . .

"He's not coming," Roberta said, as if they were having a conversation over tea. "I never called him." She showed her teeth and moved closer.

Wetzon pressed her body against the door. Her hand touched the knob. She was ready to spring back. Her mind worked at high speed. If she could only get to the bathroom, she could lock the door and wait till she was rescued.

But she had forgotten about Jake Donahue. The door swung open and she was jolted backward into the room. Donahue caught her and roughly pushed her aside. She fell against her desk. Terror hit her like a tidal wave. Jake couldn't save her. He couldn't save himself. They would die.

"Roberta, goddammit, are you nuts? What the hell's wrong with you?" Jake lurched at her as if to grab her.

Roberta's face shifted rapidly from surprise to anger. Her cunning eyes almost disappeared into their sockets. "I wouldn't say that, if I were you." Her voice menaced, but she backed off. "Don't you touch me."

Damn Jake, Wetzon thought suddenly. *He was handling her all wrong.*

"Roberta, calm down," Jake said, standing in place. "Just tell old Jake what this is all about." The insincerity in his tone was offensive and condescending.

You asshole, Wetzon wanted to shout at him. He badly underestimated Roberta. It would anger her more—

"Don't humor me, you bastard." Roberta's thin lips curled. "You were hiding there, listening." She gestured with the knife as if it were part of her hand. The blade found its key light in the fluorescent and hung there, glinting. "You're all alike. First Mildred, then you. Promises. I'll take care of you, Bobbie . . ." she said, doing a fair imitation of Mildred's raspy voice.

Wetzon's hands began to shake. She couldn't swallow. A tight band closed over her chest; the room began to whirl.

Then Roberta screamed—a long, furious scream—and lunged toward Jake, who backed away. Wetzon's head snapped up. No, she wouldn't, she couldn't let herself cave in now. She stepped forward. *Pretend she's just an upset broker,* she thought desperately. *Pretend she's just been dumped by Shearson and . . .*

"Roberta, talk to me, please," Wetzon pleaded. "*I* didn't promise you anything. I don't even know you."

Roberta's eyes darted toward Wetzon, momentarily distracted. "You saw me," she said. "You were always turning up. I couldn't get away from you. You'll tell on me."

"You crazy—" Jake's face changed rapidly from red to purple.

Wetzon interrupted. He was making a mess of it. "I won't tell anybody anything, Roberta." Wetzon was on home ground. She had handled crazies before. If only Jake would shut up and let her do the job she did well.

"That's right." Roberta nodded, smiling rat teeth. The beautiful copper hair rolled forward around her face.

"I don't understand, Roberta," Wetzon said, determined to keep her talking. "What were you doing with Jake if you were working for Mildred?" Her mouth was parched.

Roberta's eyes dismissed Wetzon. "Mildred was going to take care of me, but he—" The knife made a deadly little circle, indicating Jake. "*He* ruined everything. And now I'm going to show him how grateful I am. I'm going to kill him." She smiled at Wetzon. "And then I'm going to kill you."

"You fool," Jake raged, making two potent fists of his hands. "You didn't need Mildred anymore. I would have taken care of you, didn't I promise you that?"

Wetzon shuddered. What had Smith said? *A woman sometimes wants to be taken care of.* And Wetzon, what about Wetzon? Wetzon, who always took care of herself. Right now, Wetzon wished fervently for Silvestri to come riding up on a white horse and save the day. But she knew he wasn't coming.

"Don't worry, you said, I'll take care of you. What a joke. On me. You were going to take care of me, weren't you, Jake? You showed me a copy of Mildred's will, and you were right, it doesn't include me. She lied to me." She brushed her hair away from her face with her free hand. "Isn't it funny? Mildred didn't think you were a killer, Jake. I kept at her that you were, but she began to put it all together after you broke in that day—"

Wetzon looked at Jake and then at Roberta. If she were Roberta, she would probably stick the knife in him right now. The man was a monster. They were both evil, but Roberta was a victim. Wetzon had the feeling that Jake always knew exactly what he was doing.

"You should have trusted me," Jake said, his expression weary.

"You're a lying, cheating son of a bitch," Roberta said, continuing in her tea-party voice.

Jake moved precipitously, going for the knife. Logic told Wetzon that Jake was moving fast, but it seemed as if she were watching a film in slow motion.

Roberta recoiled. She cried, "Stay away from me, you bastard!"

The knife moved lazily through the empty space between Roberta and Jake.

Wetzon, her heart thudding in her ears, moved backward, slammed into the lip of her desk, bruising her tailbone. The jarring shock would have thrown her forward into the fray had she not clutched the desk with her fingers.

Jake's voice was a muffled roar. Roberta was slicing the air between them with the knife, back and forth, back and forth . . . back and forth.

How strange . . . there is no blood, Wetzon thought. *Like in a play. The knife is not real.*

"Stop, stop, please stop." Wetzon heard someone scream and realized it was she.

A brilliant crimson flower began to create itself in time-lapse photography, blooming on the white desk top near Wetzon's hand.

Blood, crimson like the flower, spattered on papers, on the desks, on the telephone answering machine, on the floor. The phone began to ring. Automatically, Wetzon groped for it, and her hand found the heavy marble peach she kept on her desk as a paperweight. Without thinking, her fingers closed on it. She picked it up, spotted, as she had as a dancer, on Roberta's white forehead, and hurled it with all her strength.

Jake shuffled a strange dance and slipped to his knees.

The answering machine clicked on and whoever it was hung up.

There was a soft thump as the marble peach made contact with Roberta's forehead. She stopped, stepped toward Wetzon casually, as if she was about to begin a conversation.

"No, please," Wetzon cried.

Roberta's eyes burned. The marble peach hit the floor and shattered. Roberta took another step, then fell.

"Oh, God, I've killed her." Wetzon's face was wet. She hadn't known she was crying. She swayed. The room was heady with the sickening, sweet smell of blood mixed with lily of the valley. Gasping, she made her way to the bathroom, gathered up all the towels, and brought them back to Jake, who was kneeling on the blood-spattered floor.

He looked up at her, face streaked with blood. She almost didn't hear what he said, his voice was so low. "Lady, you are something else."

His hands were badly cut, bleeding profusely. Docile as a child, he held them out to her and she wrapped them as best she could. His clothing was in streamers of tailor-made blue pinstripe and white shirting. The left lapel was cut away from the jacket and his shirt became various shades of pink to crimson as she worked. The red paisley silk tie was red on red among the tangles of his suit.

Jake's face twisted in pain. She bent over to touch him.

"If you get too close to me," he said harshly, "I'll get you dirty, too." He stood up awkwardly, swaying, and then slumped into Smith's chair. Blood seeped from an ugly gash on his left cheek.

"You need a doctor," she said.

"We'll have to do something about that first," he said, pointing to Roberta's motionless body. "You didn't kill her, worse luck, and the crazy bitch'll come to and—"

"I'll call the police." She was amazed. Jake was taking no responsibility for what had happened, and yet, by buying Roberta, Wetzon knew he was indirectly responsible for the deaths of at least three people. Four, if she counted Sugar Joe. Was it really possible that Roberta had followed her that day from

Mildred's office, then had struck at her on the dark and quiet street as she crossed Amsterdam Avenue? She shivered, thinking of Roberta watching as she met with Laura Lee, with Amanda, and Howie, of her watching as she stood in line at Zabar's. It was not something a sane person did. But Roberta was not sane.

"We can't stop for that now," Jake said. "I'm in no shape to fight her off." Roberta moaned. "And you may not have another—what the hell was that anyway?"

"A marble peach." Wetzon stared at the fragments of the marble peach. She couldn't believe what she had done. She had saved their lives.

"A marble peach," he repeated. "For chrissakes. Does any door here lock from the outside?" He was beginning to assume his old role of command.

"Yes. The supply closet. There."

"Good. I'll help, but you're going to have to do most of the work." He gestured with his clumsily bandaged hands. Blood was already seeping through the towels, staining them pink, then red. Wetzon looked away. The office was a mess. Smith would be furious. "What's with you?" Jake growled. "Get that fucking knife away from her."

She pulled some Kleenex from the box on her desk and picked up the bloody knife by the handle. She placed it squeamishly on her desk.

She leaned over Roberta's body. The air in the room reeked, and she began to gag. She touched Roberta's ankles tentatively. Leather boots, very expensive, high heeled, black leather boots, bloody leather boots . . . red leather boots . . . She swallowed a nervous giggle.

"What are you waiting for?" Jake demanded. "Pull."

She pulled and Jake pushed, until Roberta was propped up in the supply closet like a bag of old clothes. Jake slammed the door with his foot and Wetzon locked it.

They nodded at each other like coconspirators. Crimson dripped into his eyes from a gash on his forehead. "Christ, I think I'm going to pass out," he said, grimacing. He sat back down in Smith's chair, heavily.

Wetzon washed her hands, shrinking from the color of the water in the sink, then wet a paper towel with cold water, taking it back to Jake, gently blotting up some of the blood from his face.

Jake opened his eyes. "I love you, Leslie Wetzon," he said. His eyes closed.

She took a deep breath and dialed 911.

"My name is Leslie Wetzon. I'm at Six-ninety A East Forty-ninth Street. Please send an ambulance right away. Someone's been badly hurt. Yes. There is also a murderer locked in the closet." She paused. "I know, please believe me, and please notify Sergeant Silvestri at the Seventeenth Precinct immediately."

Jake opened his eyes. "You're not going to give me any time."

"I'm sorry, Jake. It's too late."

"Yeah." He closed his eyes, not arguing.

"I hope it doesn't go too badly for you," she said haltingly, not sure she meant it.

"Hey, I'll be okay. I'm a survivor. I came on the Street without a penny, without a contact, and look where I am today."

"Yes, look." *Just like a broker,* she thought.

"Yeah." Derisively.

At that moment there was a loud noise at the front door, and Metzger—tall, melancholic, and pouchy-eyed, but indescribably beautiful—appeared, followed by the detective with the ankle holster Wetzon had seen at the precinct house.

"God, I'm glad to see you," she said, starting to cry again. She clung to Metzger's arm, wanting to hug him, holding tightly to his arm. "She's in the closet, the closet . . . we put her in the c-c-closet. . . ." She couldn't get the words out. Her mouth was too dry. Her heart was pumping with such force, she wasn't able to stand still.

"Are you all right?" Metzger gave her a skeptical once-over.

"Yes, yes, yes. But, but Jake—"

"In here," Jake called weakly from the next room.

Metzger motioned with his head, but the other detective and two uniformed police had already moved into the back room.

Wetzon kept nodding at Metzger that she was all right, but she couldn't speak. She couldn't let go of his arm. Where was Silvestri?

"Here now," Metzger said, patting her awkwardly on the shoulder. "Sit down." Metzger put her in one of the reception chairs, took his arm away gently, and went into the back room. Wetzon could hear Jake and the others talking. Sirens blared and stopped. An ambulance arrived. More police. More noise.

Wetzon dried her eyes with the back of her hands and stood at the door to her and Smith's office, leaning on the door frame. The room was a mess. The smell of blood mixed with antiseptic.

A white-coated medic was cleaning Jake's wounds and had him on an IV. "These are going to need stitching," he said to the other paramedic. "Let's get out of here." The other nodded. He was down on one knee near Roberta, who was slumped on the floor, leaning against Wetzon's desk. The medic was trying to put a white patch on her forehead, but Roberta kept moving her head from side to side, not fully conscious, resisting. One of the uniformed policemen stood over her, handcuffs swinging from his index finger.

Metzger and the other detective were talking to Jake. They both glanced at Wetzon. She backed out and into the reception room and sat down at Harold's desk, face in her hands, eyes closed.

She heard Metzger come back and opened her eyes. He sat uneasy, in one of the small chairs. He looked silly, like a giant, mournful beagle. She started to giggle, then put her hand over her mouth.

"Are you up to talking?"

She nodded, took a deep breath, and ran quickly through Roberta's call, Jake's unexpected arrival, Roberta's entrance. "She never phoned Silvestri, did she?"

Metzger shook his head. "He would have told me. He would have been here."

"Where is he now?" *Why isn't he here when I need him?* is what she wanted to say. She felt an overwhelming desire to have him frown disapprovingly at her.

"He's on another case. Couldn't reach him. I knew something was wrong when you called."

"She murdered Barry and Georgie Travers and Mildred Gleason," Wetzon said, "and she would have killed us—"

"You did a good job on her," Metzger said solemnly. "We're going over to Bellevue now. You look okay, but you should have them give you the once-over. After that, we'll need to talk to you at the precinct."

She shook her head. "If you don't need me right away, I'd rather go home, clean myself up. I promise I'll come over to the precinct later." She knew what she was going to do, if she could summon up the strength. She felt an enormous calm, in control for the first time since seeing Barry's body slide from the phone booth a week ago.

A skeptical Metzger studied her for a moment, then nodded.

The group moved out, Roberta in handcuffs, head down, a policeman on each side, supporting her. Wings of copper hair hid her face. Jake followed, leaning on a paramedic. "Take care, Jake," Wetzon said.

"I'm a hard man to keep down, Leslie Wetzon," he said. "I'll be back."

The outside door closed. The sudden silence was a sedative. Wetzon continued sitting at Harold's desk, losing touch with time.

The phone rang. Rang again. Her hand reached out and picked it up. "Smith and Wetzon," she said.

"Oh, hi, Wetzon. I'm glad you're still there. I have to talk to you."

"Who—" *Why in hell are you talking on the phone, Wetzon?* she thought.

The woman kept chattering. "I had a really good meeting at Alex Brown," she said.

Amanda. "That's wonderful, Amanda." Wetzon was happy for her. "When do you start?"

"Well, that's just the thing I wanted to talk to you about, Wetzon. I told them I'd get back to them. After all, why should I take the first offer? I think I should be looking at other firms, don't you? I'd like to talk to Pru-Bache. I hear they're giving the best deals—"

If you were really smart, you'd hang up on her right now, Wetzon told herself. *She deserves to be hung up on.* But she said, "Can we talk about it in the morning, Amanda?"

"Sure, I'm clear all day. Call me as soon as you set the appointment. 'Bye, Wetzon." She hung up.

Not even a thank-you, Wetzon thought. She replaced the receiver and went into the bathroom and washed her face thoroughly with cold water. Her shoes were stained with blood, and she wiped them passingly with a wet towel. They were ruined. Maybe it would be dark at the Caravanserie and no one would notice. "Get going," she told her pale reflection in the mirror, as she hastily pinned her hair back in place. She looked like a ghost. There was nothing she could do about it.

She pulled her handbag and her briefcase from under her desk.

She took a long last look around the office and forced herself to walk away from it. She didn't have time to think about it now. She was late.

53

On the corner of First Avenue and Forty-ninth Street, a well-dressed woman was sitting on a suitcase heartily singing, "But square shaped or pear shaped, these rocks don't lose their shape . . ." Only a few people paused to stare. It was, after, all New York.

Wetzon took a deep breath to steady herself and hailed a cab. She was desperate to get away from the insanity she had just been part of. It was almost over. She had to do this one more thing, finish it up, hand the tapes over to Silvestri, and write an end to this nightmare. Just a little while longer.

The crowd going into the Caravanserie this early evening wore business suits, even the women. It was a convention of gray pinstripes. It would have to be; it was Wall Street Night.

The world of Wall Street was no different from that of other professions: there was a costume that helped create the conservative aura, which quietly said: "We are taking good care of your money. Trust us."

She remembered Harvey Inman, a stockbroker she had met in her first year as a recruiter. " 'Trust me,' " he had told her facetiously, " 'is really code for 'fuck you.' "

Wetzon felt weak and disconnected. There'd been blood everywhere. She had almost been murdered. Jake Donahue had been badly cut. She didn't know if she could go through with this. Her head began to pound as she presented her invitation and her business card with six dollars at a small table just inside the entrance of the Caravanserie.

She followed the stream of people into the room with the long bar. A good mix of men and women were standing around in small groups drinking and talking, exchanging business cards and gossip. She paid for a Perrier and lime and wished she could get rid of the cloying smell of Roberta's lily of the valley perfume.

"Hi there." A tall, light-skinned black woman with a very short Afro approached her. "I'm Gail Enders." She offered her hand, which Wetzon took, shifting her briefcase to under her left arm. "My card." It said: *Gail Enders, Vice President, R. A. Lane, Licensed Real Estate Brokers, for the sales of condominiums and cooperatives.*

"You're not a stockbroker, then," Wetzon said, reading the card.

"No"—wide smile, an expanse of slightly bucked teeth—"but I sell a lot of apartments to stockbrokers, and other people, of course," she added hastily. "Are you a stockbroker?"

"No, I'm a headhunter. I work with stockbrokers."

Mechanically, Wetzon exchanged cards and conversation with a man from the trust department at Citibank, a woman who did marketing for the New York Stock Exchange, and an ex-stockbroker, whom she had known from Paine Webber, who was now on the staff of *Money* magazine. She kept checking her watch. The ache in her head worsened. Migrainelike, it had settled on the right side of her head, pressing painfully on her eye. She dipped her fingertips in the ice-filled Perrier and touched her right cheekbone: for a moment the pain receded. Someone named Al Comfort tried to sell her insurance, term life, and annuities.

She talked to an attorney with a major corporate law firm, who wanted to cross over into corporate finance with an investment bank. It was almost seven. The pain in her head beat on without respite.

She bought herself a refill of her Perrier and strolled into the Day-Glo–colored lounge, feeling jumpy and apprehensive. She sat down on a shocking pink plastic chair that was molded like a mushroom, one of the sixties' ugliest designs, and tried to think things through. Men and women in business suits, clones of one another, passed in and out of the restrooms, talking gibberish, or so it seemed to Wetzon. On the hem of her skirt she saw a dark red stain of dried blood. She looked away. She couldn't let herself think about it now. She needed all her will to finish this.

There was a powder-blue pay telephone to her right, built into a wall painted the same shade. Gail Enders, of condominiums and cooperatives, strode in, punched out some numbers, left a message for Charley on his machine that she was still at the office, and went back to the bar fluttering her fingers at Wetzon, not even a little embarrassed.

Rick did not appear, and it was almost quarter past seven. She had been foolish to try to do this herself, not to mention headstrong. Maybe Rick wasn't going to be able to come after all. There could have been an emergency, and he would have no way of getting in touch with her. She'd better try to reach Silvestri. By this time Metzger would have located him and told him what had happened with Roberta. She put the Perrier on the powder-blue ledge near the phone, fished a quarter out of her purse, and dialed, gnawing on her lip as she waited for someone to answer.

"Cooperman."

"Is Sergeant Silvestri there?"

"He just left. Wait a minute—who's calling?"

"Wetzon. Leslie Wetzon."

"Hey," Silvestri came on the line, his voice warm in her ear, "I've been trying to find you, lady. Where are you?"

"At the Caravanserie."

"Stay there. I'm on my way."

"Oh—God—" She jumped. The center door that she had been watching so carefully opened a crack, and she saw Rick peering through. What a relief.

"Les? Are you all right?" Silvestri sounded uncharacteristically anxious.

"Sure . . . yes. Have to go. Talk later." She hung up, picked up her briefcase, and went to the door to the health club. A fat woman in a tight white wool dress came out of the bathroom and looked at her curiously. Another woman followed almost immediately and they left together.

"Come on," Rick said urgently and held the door wide. She slipped through, closing it quickly behind her.

He pushed the jacket of her suit away, grasping hands rough around her waist. "Mmmm, you feel good, babe." Her back was pressed against the wall, which she could feel was carpeted, like the floors, with that crisp indoor-outdoor carpeting. Then he was kissing her, passionate, demanding kisses, but his eyes were shiny and hard.

Silvestri had called her Les.

She broke away from Rick, faking dizziness. "Come back to me," he said, catching her. "Whatsa matter?" His speech was slurred. "You look a little pale."

She thought of telling him what had happened, but didn't, not knowing why. He seemed as nervous as she was. More. He was holding her so tightly her ribs ached. His large duffel bag rested on the carpeted floor beside them.

"What's this?" she asked, joking, straining to lighten up. "I hope you weren't expecting to empty a lot of stuff out of the locker."

"Hell, no." Rick laughed, agitated. But he let her go, leaning against the wall over her, an arm on either side of her head, closing her off, making a cage. "You didn't give me a chance to tell you . . . I'm going to the Coast tonight." That's why I called you—to see if we could get it on before I left."

"Oh, Rick, I'm so sorry." She was mortified. How selfish of her. No wonder he was nervous. "I'm so single-minded, this was all I was thinking about."

"It's okay, babe, but now you have to come out to the airport to make it up to me." He smiled, coaxing. Jake had smiled at Roberta that way. . . . She felt herself begin to tense.

"But—" First she had to get the tapes and take them to Silvestri. If Barry really had another locker and it was here, and if the tapes were—

"No buts. Let's get this show on the road. I have a nine o'clock flight from Kennedy. Where are those numbers?"

She checked her watch. "We're cutting it awfully close," she said doubtfully. She took the matchbook out of her jacket pocket, opened it, and showed him the numbers.

"Here, let me have that," he said, grabbing the matchbook from her hand, shocking her, making no apology.

He was in a hurry, and he was doing her a favor, she thought, forgiving him. He glanced at the writing in the matchbook. God, he was hyper. She had never seen him like this. She shook the thought away. Why was she so suspicious? He was in a rush, on his way to California. It was a major career move for him.

But it was something even more than that. She couldn't put her finger on it.

Club members in sweats, shorts, women in gleaming color-coordinated leotards and tights, everyone in the absolute best possible shape, came down the hall, passing them singly and in chattering groups, on the way to and from racquetball, tennis, exercise machines, classes. Every so often someone gave them a searching look, for Wetzon still wore her business suit. Rick, at least, was wearing jeans and a sweat top.

He pointed behind her. "Follow this corridor and make a left, and you'll see the entrance to the health club. Wait for me there. I'll be right back." He slipped the matchbook in his sweatshirt pocket, picked up his big duffel, and moved in the opposite direction.

She hated to part with the matchbook, but there was no other way. Why hadn't she copied the numbers in the matchbook when she was in the office? The pain in her head gripped her and crept down into her neck.

"Rick," she called after him, "why are you taking your bag? I can take it with me."

"It's too heavy for you, little girl," he said. "Besides, where am I going to put—what did you say we're looking for in that locker?"

In the confusion, she had forgotten to tell him. And he had almost forgotten to ask her. They must both be a little crazed.

He swaggered back to her, hips forward, teasing. He was selling seduction in his tight jeans and bulky white cotton sweatshirt. She wasn't buying.

"The tapes Barry made. Anything that looks like cassettes or tapes," she said. "A diary or notebooks—papers, stuff like documents."

"Okay, babe, you know you can rely on old Dr. Rick." He leaned over and kissed her ear, then turned and sprinted up the corridor.

54

What's wrong with you? she asked herself. *He's full of fun, handsome, and he likes you. Why can't you accept that?* What she had just been through—however horrible it was—had nothing to do with Rick, was not his fault. He didn't even know about it. So why was she angry with him for not being sympathetic? Because that's exactly what she was feeling. It didn't make any sense. Nothing about this past week made any sense.

She followed Rick's directions, found the reception area, and settled in to wait. What if she was wrong? What if it wasn't a locker combination? What if the police had already found the locker? What if there were no tapes? These what-ifs were going to drive her crazy. Well, screw it, she would just be wrong again. She should be used to it by now.

She shifted uncomfortably in the chair. What if Rick didn't come back? He could just take the cassettes and leave. Her stomach flipped. What a wild thought. She shook her throbbing head. She would tell him she felt ill, which she did, and couldn't go out to Kennedy with him. He'd said she was pale but hadn't bothered to ask why.

She stretched her legs out in front of her, flexing, and saw uneven red splotches on her hose, spots of blood on her ankles and shins, and her thoughts spiraled back to the office, Jake, blood, Roberta's mad eyes, the knife slashing down—

"May I help you?" An attractive brunette in a Caravanserie T-shirt, very tight iridescent blue leotards cut high up the leg, and matching blue tights with white ankle warmers, approached, beaming.

Wetzon started. "Oh, no, thank you, I'm waiting for someone." She looked at her watch. Seven forty-five. What was taking him so long? She crossed her legs, jiggling her heel. She was shaking with apprehension. She stood up, feeling panic fluttering in her chest, as if she were on a caffeine overdose. It was just a combination of everything: Barry, Georgie, Buffie, Mildred, Jake, Roberta . . . Leon and Smith . . . Barry, who had been so many diverse things to so many different people, and whose greed had started an avalanche . . . but he was not alone in the greed department. And whatever Barry may have been, he didn't deserve to die.

She suddenly felt almost euphoric with relief that it was Roberta who had committed the murders, not someone Wetzon knew well. Smith was—

"Let's go, babe." Rick was suddenly at her side, arm firmly around her, and they were out on the sidewalk, racing. A fine drizzle made the streets shimmer. The rush of passing cars, the reflections of their headlights on the wet pavement, dazzled her. She blinked to clear her eyes, but they didn't clear.

"Yayho!" Rick shouted a cab down. "Kennedy," he said, pulling the door open. "TWA, International, and make it fast." He pushed her into the cab.

"Do you want to put that in the trunk?" the driver asked.

"No, let's just get the hell out of here."

So much for her plans. Without a chance to protest, she found herself sitting in the cab beside Rick, speeding to Kennedy Airport. "Did you find them?" she whispered. Had he said International?

"Uh-huh." He leaned over and unzipped a small section of his duffel. It was a bonanza. She tried to count them in the dark, lost count. How many were there? Twenty? Thirty? "They're marked," he said. "You'll see when there's some light.

Her hands shook as she pushed aside her datebook and her papers and stuffed the cassettes into her briefcase. The distended case would not snap shut. Frantic, she shifted everything around; finally, she heard the click of the catch. *Look,* she'd say to Silvestri, *see what I've done—I've come up with what everyone was looking for.* She'd worked it out herself. Maybe this would make up for the fiasco with the key. Then maybe he'd care, just a little bit. . . . "Thanks so much, Rick, but weren't there letters and papers in the locker?" The briefcase was heavy and she slid it from her lap to the seat.

"I was running out of time. Didn't look after I saw the tapes. Just some sweats, I think, reports, junk. So, do I get high marks?" He leaned back in the seat and put his arm around her. Possessively.

They were plunging along dark roads through what had turned into a hurricane rain. Traffic was thin. The sky was at times midnight blue-black, pierced now and then by an eerie violet light. The lights from the traffic and the Triborough Bridge gave the outside world a nightmarish cast. A loud crack of thunder followed quickly on a flash of lightning. A Transylvanian night.

By the time they were in Queens, the cab had picked up even more speed, and it was as if they were flying through darkness. Rick laughed triumphantly. *Shrieking through the night,* she thought, irrationally.

"Well, high marks or not, what do you say?"

"High marks," she said, her words muffled by his lips.

"You taste sweet," he said. "So sweet." He was holding on to her, even as she shrank away. *Ice cream man,* she thought.

"Too many Perriers while I was waiting for you," she said matter-of-factly, trying to keep her heart steady. What was wrong? Something kept teasing her memory. She was having trouble breathing.

Silvestri had called her Les.

"I wish we could have been together one more time before I left," Rick said.

"We are together."

"You know what I mean, little girl. I want to make love to you, really make love to you. I don't want you to forget me." His hands were on her breasts.

She was frightened. "But not in a cab, Rick," she said with a firmness she hadn't believed herself capable of. Outside, it was dark and violent. The lights were bouncing in the rain. Thunder rumbled. Shadows carved hollows in Rick's face. She had no idea where they were.

"You're so straight," he said, turning her face to him. "I didn't want it to end like this."

What did he mean by that? Did he mean to hurt her? Was he going to try to take her on the plane with him? Against her will? She was cold, freezing cold.

Over Rick's shoulder she saw with relief the signs for the TWA terminal. She was determined not to get out of the cab when Rick did. She would just say goodbye and take it back to New York and Silvestri.

"Come on," Rick said, hurriedly shoving bills at the driver. She was on the side by the sidewalk, so she stepped out of the cab to let him out. Cold rain flew in her face and dampened her hair and clothes in a few seconds. She was eager to get back into the cab and away. Rick came out after her, grasped her elbow, and dragged the duffel with him, slamming the door. The cab took off.

"Wait—" she cried, but it was lost in the noise of the announcement that TWA flight 310, to Mexico City, leaving at nine o'clock, was now being boarded.

"That's my flight," Rick said, pulling her along with him. Around them passengers were rushing about with luggage, children in hand: Skycaps were wheeling loaded carts. "No, I'm taking this on with me," he told the attendant, hanging on to his duffel.

She couldn't go beyond the metal detector, and as they neared it, she felt her sense of dread begin to dispel.

"I'm going to miss you, babe," Rick said, keeping his eyes on his bulging duffel bag as it went through the metal detector. His fingers absently played with her hair, and before she realized what he was doing, he had pulled out the pins that held it up. It tumbled in slow motion down to her shoulders. "This is the way I want to remember you," he said.

She was annoyed and showed it. Above her was a huge sign advertising Disneyland. Mickey Mouse and all the gang. The Mouseketeers, the Three Musketeers, Barry, Georgie, Buffie . . . No, Buffie had said Barry was D'Artagnan. Who, then, was the third Musketeer? The one Buffie had called after Georgie was murdered.

The metal detector went off with a small buzzing noise, and Rick leaped forward. "Wait a minute," he shouted, "I'll get that. Must be my keys." He was wildly agitated. "Here, I'll show you." He opened the duffel and pulled out some keys on a ring, zipped up the duffel, and they sent it through again. No buzzing this time. "See, I told you," he said. He set the duffel down, leaving it, and came back to her. He looked distracted. His eyes were black and they frightened her.

"I want to remember you as you look right now," he said, with an odd laugh. "Pissed as hell at me, and beautiful." He kissed her on the lips. "Right person, bad timing." He touched her cheek for a moment with a peculiar gentleness, then he broke away. She watched him racing down the hallway to his plane.

She shook herself. Something was terribly wrong. He wasn't going to San Diego, he was going to Mexico. She'd enjoyed—no—needed him, but she wouldn't miss him. Hell, she hadn't even liked him in her dreams. But he had helped her get the cassettes.

Smith had never liked him, seemed not to trust him. Smith. Wetzon felt a ripple of guilt run through her. Smith was innocent, only concerned for Wetzon, and Wetzon had doubted her, even suspected she might be involved in the murders. Suddenly it all seemed so absurd.

Sighing, she turned to go and bumped squarely into Silvestri, who had been standing close enough to touch her, perhaps even to read her thoughts.

"Goddammit, Silvestri. What are you doing here?" She was angry and embarrassed.

"Working on a case. Besides, weren't you coming to see me?" He was looking down at her appraisingly. He did not move away. She touched her hair, self-conscious. It was the second time that he had seen her romantically entwined with Rick.

"Yes, but I said I'd get back to you."

"We had a little unfinished business."

"With me?"

"With the good doctor."

"Rick?"

"Yup."

She half-turned, seeking Rick in the streaming crowd. But he was gone. A child began to cry and its mother tried to soothe it, crooning in Spanish. Why did Silvestri want to talk to Rick?

"A little question of unauthorized commerce." Silvestri always seemed to be able to read her thoughts. He was scowling, but it wasn't at her. His attention seemed to be elsewhere.

She was so tired. "I don't know what you're talking about, Silvestri. I have something to give you. The cassettes Barry made of Jake Donahue's conversations. Barry had a secret locker at the Caravanserie. Rick helped me get them."

He looked down at her; his eyes were slate-colored. "Along with a cache of drugs, uppers, downers, painkillers, Quaaludes, you name it. Drugs and money. A hell of a lot of money. Oh, and papers, letters, and a diary."

"What? I don't understand."

"He took the stuff out of Stark's second locker. The one you had the combination for."

"No, it can't be." Her head spun. "Rick said there wasn't anything else there." Something eluded her. "What does the locker, Barry, everything . . . what does it have to do with him?"

"Stark and Pulasky were buddies. They grew up together. Pulasky was his connection. Just coincidence that you and I ended up at York Hospital after being sideswiped, but it made it easy for Pulasky to approach you. He had to find out if Stark had told you anything. York Hospital, for your information, Ms. Wetzon, does not have an emergency outpatient program."

"I can't believe this—" The Three Musketeers, Buffie had said. Georgie, Barry, and Buffie, only Barry was D'Artagnan. Rick was the third Musketeer, the man Buffie had run to when she was alone and frightened, after Georgie died.

"Pulasky went back to the hospital that night because he'd been told by a resident that narcotics was doing a search of the lockers. The serious drugs were kept in a special cabinet."

"Then the key—" she said. "It was *Rick* who put the key in my pocket?"

"Yeah." Silvestri shoved his hands in his pockets. "It was the new key to the drug cabinet. They had just changed the lock. He was being watched. He's been lifting drugs from the hospital for a long time. We had someone undercover there. Pulasky was feeding the stuff to Stark, who sold it on the Street. When the hospital authorized a search, he got worried we were on to him, so he parked the key with you temporarily, figuring he could get it back easily enough."

"I don't understand why he let me have the tapes. He could have used them. . . ."

"Who knows? We'll ask him. Didn't cost him anything; didn't mean anything to him. They weren't what he was after. It was easy enough to let you have them. It made you happy, didn't it?"

"I feel like a fool," she said miserably. "Now I understand why the police were so conspicious that night at the hospital. I thought it was because of you."

The corners of Silvestri's mouth lifted slightly. "It was a little of both. You'd better stand here, out of the way." He stepped back, pulling her with him. "We're going to bring him through."

"You've taken him off the plane—oh, God—"

"We had to catch him with the stuff."

"Will he be handcuffed?"

"What do you think?"

"I don't want to see him. I don't want him to see me, please." She was shivering. He'd think she gave him away. But she hadn't. Why did she care what he thought, damn him. He'd made a fool of her. But there was something horribly humiliating about having people see you in handcuffs, she thought, projecting. What nonsense. He deserved to be treated like that. "You're saying that Barry was the Wall Street connection," she said, her back to the hallway down which Rick had disappeared. "And Rick was his supplier."

"Yup."

Silvestri was not looking at her. He was watching something happening behind her. They were taking Rick away. She knew she had to face him. Turning slowly, she saw three men in street clothes, one carrying the duffel, several airline security guards, and four uniformed policemen walking toward them. Rick was positioned between two of the men in street clothes, his gray head down; his hands were behind him, and she knew, without looking, that they were cuffed.

Unexpectedly, Wetzon felt anger well up. "You bastard," she yelled, "you were running out on Buffie." Rick's head came up. Their eyes locked. Then he dropped his head and the entourage passed from view.

Wetzon turned back to Silvestri, shaken by her rage. Her cheek brushed the rough wool of his jacket. "Oh, shit. How stupid could I get? Rick was hanging around me trying to get the key back, trying to find out if I knew where Barry had stashed the money and drugs. That's why my things weren't where they should have been. . . ." She looked up at Silvestri unhappily.

Silvestri's eyes, turquoise now, met hers. He didn't say anything. He needed a shave. There were dark circles under his eyes.

"How could I have been so dumb?" she said. "Why don't you say something, Silvestri? Don't just stand there."

He looked at her, his face thoughtful, then put his hand on the place where her neck and shoulder met. She felt the same strange, soft electric shock when he touched her now that she had felt before in the lobby of her building after he had barged in on her the first time.

"Come on, kid," he said. "Let's go home."